blessing to me.
God works in mysterious
ways, indeed.
Robin Helm
Phil. 4:13

Forever Yours

Yours by Design, Book 3

ROBIN M. HELM

Scripture quotations taken from the New American Standard Bible®, Copyright© 1960, 1962, 1963, 1968, 1971, 1972, 1973, 1975, 1977, 1995 by The Lockman Foundation. Used by permission.

DEDICATION

I dedicate this book to my teachers and my students, both past and present. There are few joys in life greater than receiving and imparting knowledge.

ACKNOWLEDGMENTS

I offer my gratitude to my beta team: Gayle Mills, Wendi Sotis, M.K. Baxley, and Stephanie Hamm. I also want to thank my cold readers: Terri Davis and Billie Morrison.

I am also indebted to Gayle Mills for doing the final edit of the manuscript and Wendi Sotis who formatted *Forever Yours* for e-books.

CHAPTER 1

The great advantage about telling the truth is that nobody ever believes it.

Dorothy L. Sayers

The Oaks, 2014

Sitting behind Elizabeth in Cielo's saddle, Fitzwilliam gently pulled on the mare's reins to bring her to a halt. The grove of oak trees provided shelter and relative privacy, so he took a few seconds to relish the feeling of having Elizabeth in his arms, dreading the moment when he would tell her the truth about himself. His chest tightened at the thought of it. *This will probably be the last time she ever allows me to hold her close. She will surely think me a liar or a lunatic – or perhaps both.*

He breathed in the scent of her hair one final time, knowing that she would likely reject him rather than believe his story. *I would never believe it myself,* he reflected silently, *if it were not happening to me. How can I expect her to trust me that much? Especially given her past experiences with men.* Even so, he was determined to do what he knew was right, and he quickly

3

dismounted Cielo, leaving Elizabeth astride in the saddle. He looped her horse's reins, as well as those of his stallion, Diablo, who had walked obediently beside them, around a low branch.

Less than a quarter hour had passed since Cielo had been spooked by a dog and raced wildly through the open fields, almost throwing a badly frightened Elizabeth. Fitzwilliam looked carefully at Elizabeth's face to make certain she was all right before he checked again that both horses were securely tied and calmly grazing.

He then turned back to reach up for the young woman he now was certain he loved. *If I had harbored any doubts about my love for her before now, nearly losing her has shown me just how strong my true feelings are.* He lifted his arms to her. *My hands are still shaking. I think the hold she has over me frightens me more than the near-accident did. More than two hundred years ago, another Elizabeth, her ancestor, rejected me. Will this Elizabeth do the same when she knows the truth about me? She has accepted my attentions, but will she think of me in the same way after we talk, or will she think me a perfect candidate for Bedlam? I wish I could remain silent, but that would be unfair to her and dishonest on my part.* He shook his head.

Elizabeth appeared to be in control of herself, though her dark eyes were still large. She allowed him to help her down, and he held her gently against his chest, his chin just touching the top of her head. Fitzwilliam was encouraged when she didn't push him away, and his heart told him the time was right to speak.

"Elizabeth?"

She turned her face up to his, a question lingering in her beautiful eyes.

He groaned silently within himself, struggling against a strong inclination to kiss her. He gently shook his head and sighed. *It would not be honorable to take advantage of her ignorance. She should know the truth before we kiss; otherwise, she might be angry with me, and justifiably so. I shall not risk losing her again by taking what I want without regard to her feelings. To do that would make me no better than Wickham.*

Fitzwilliam dropped his arms from around her and stepped back. He was shocked by the hurt look he saw in her eyes before she quickly lowered her gaze toward the ground. *Can she truly think I do not want her?*

He reached out across the space between them and took her hands in his. "Elizabeth." His voice caressed her name, and she raised her troubled eyes to him again.

"You're confusing me," she said.

He grimaced. "I beg your forgiveness, but we must talk."

"It can't wait?"

"Do you think I would have stopped had it not been absolutely necessary? No, it cannot wait."

She smiled weakly. "I suppose not. Is it that bad?"

He looked down at their hands, clasped together. "You shall have to decide that for yourself. I cannot speak for you, and, unfortunately, I cannot change what has gone before. There are things you must know about me before you allow me any further liberties."

She looked heavenward and sighed. "You've lapsed into eighteenth century syntax again. It must be really terrible." She squared her shoulders. "Just tell me and get it over with. What have you done?"

Fitzwilliam blinked. "I have done nothing." He hesitated. "I suppose that statement is not entirely accurate. I did do something, but I cannot help what happened because of it, and I have no power to change it."

She pulled her hands from his and looked up at him in irritation. "Men!" she exclaimed bitterly. "Nothing is ever your fault, is it?" She narrowed her eyes. "Tell me whatever it is immediately, or I'm walking away. Do you have a child? Did you leave some poor girl pregnant in your earlier years? Guys like you, who look like models and have lots of money, usually get what they want."

5

He stiffened. "That is most unfair."

"Is it?" she asked. "Then what have you done?"

He bit his lower lip. *In actuality, I was rather a rogue, though I do not believe I have fathered a child. Is her question so untoward? After all, what Greg Whitman did to her might have resulted in an infant. Naturally, she would think of that behavior first.*

"Elizabeth, I will not pretend that I was a saint, but if I have any children, I was never made aware of it. Also, to my knowledge I have never molested an innocent, nor have I forced myself upon any woman. I have broken no promises, and no ladies have lost their reputations because of me. What I have to tell you is not so mundane. Had I fathered a child, I would have taken care of the mother and the babe. This is not about my morality or the lack thereof."

She threw up her hands in a sign of exasperation. "Again with the Regency speak. Did you just walk out of a period novel or something?"

He swallowed hard and shut his eyes. "From my brief study of the past 230 years of history, at least as it is recorded on the internet, I believe my time period would be more accurately labeled 'Georgian'."

She stared at him, speechless.

Fitzwilliam opened his eyes and saw the shocked expression on her face. "Elizabeth, say something. Please."

She shook her head. "I am, without a doubt, the worst judge of men in the world. I really know how to pick winners, from abusive to delusional. Do I have a sign on my back that says, 'Clueless Woman'?" She turned abruptly and began to walk back toward the bridge.

He caught her arm. "Please, hear me out. Let me attempt to explain," he pleaded.

Elizabeth glared angrily at his hand on her arm, and he withdrew it. She breathed deeply and faced him again, arms crossed protectively over her chest, as if she could stop him from breaking her heart by holding herself together. "I'm waiting." Her face was hard, her mouth a grim line. "This should be good," she said, tapping her foot.

He bowed his head and rubbed his temples. *Dear Lord above, please help me not to say the wrong thing. I seem to have a gift for that.* After a moment, he stood straight again. "Will you pray for me first?"

She was incredulous. "Are you serious?"

He nodded slowly. "I am. This could be the most important moment in my life up to this point, and I want guidance. You are a Christian, are you not?"

"Aren't you? You go to church, too."

His face was earnest. "I go to the stables, but that doesn't make me a horse, Elizabeth. I have always thought I was a Christian, but now I am not so certain. I want to know that God is hearing the prayer, so will you pray for me?"

She thought for a moment. "Okay. I'll pray for you."

He took a deep breath and released it quickly, reaching for her hands. "Will you join hands while we pray together?"

She looked at him speculatively. "Is this a trick?"

"Do I look as if I'm joking?" His hands were still stretched out to her. *Please, Lord.*

She took his hands and bowed her head, looking up at him from beneath her lashes. He closed his eyes, and she began to pray. "Dear Lord, please help Fitzwilliam to find the words to tell me what he thinks I need to know, and please help me not to judge him harshly. Father, please help me to listen to him and to You. Please guide both of us. Amen."

He raised his head and watched her nervously. "Thank you. Shall we find a place to sit down?"

She looked around and pointed behind him. "Is that fallen log good enough?"

He nodded and pulled her toward the log. They both sat down, slightly facing each other, still holding hands.

"Elizabeth, there is no easy way to say this, so please be patient and hear me out."

She nodded. "I'm really trying, Fitzwilliam. You may as well tell me. We'll both feel better. Or maybe not."

He looked away from her, staring at the bridge they had just crossed, and tried to arrange his thoughts into coherent speech.

"Do you remember when I told you I had a sister?" he asked, turning his face back to hers.

She nodded. "You mentioned her at The Oaks when you were helping me get up on Cielo the first time. You said her name was Georgiana and that she died a long time ago."

"Did you never wonder at the strangeness of a man named Fitzwilliam Darcy having a sister named Georgiana in this time period?"

She chuckled. "Remember you're asking a woman named Elizabeth Bennet who has a sister named Jane Bennet. I figured your mother had an Austen fixation, just like ours did."

She laughed a little. Surely that is a good sign. "Actually, my valet's name was Henry Austen, and he was Jane Austen's uncle. My mother never met him, and I highly doubt that she ever heard of Jane Austen."

She raised both eyebrows. "You had a valet when you were growing up? That's quaint, but surely you mean he was Jane Austen's great-great-great-great nephew. I have no idea how many 'greats' I should put in there."

Fitzwilliam was silent. *How can I say this without sounding absolutely out of my mind?*

When he didn't reply, Elizabeth's eyes grew round. "You mean it the way you said it, don't you? You actually think you had a valet named Henry Austen who was Jane Austen's uncle, and you think you had a sister named Georgiana who's been dead for – let's see – about 200 years."

He looked back at the bridge. *What should I say? Is there*

anything I can tell her that will make this more palatable?

She pulled her hands free and stood to her feet. "Please tell me you don't have some crazy idea that you are the original Fitzwilliam Darcy. In the first place, he is a fictional character in a novel. Secondly, even if he had been a real person, he would be long dead now."

He closed his eyes tightly and bowed his head. *I cannot bear to lose her. This is worse than losing the first Elizabeth. At least that was my own doing. I shall lose this Elizabeth, after spending enough time with her to truly love her, through no fault of my own. I could not control these events. Should I have kept my silence? Could a marriage built upon a lie have been a good one?*

He was miserable, and he began to think of the sermons he had heard since he had awakened in Atlanta. He thought of things that Mrs. Thomas and Lance had said to him, and suddenly he knew how to tell her his fantastic story.

Fitzwilliam reached up and lightly touched her hand. "Will you sit with me, Elizabeth?"

Something in his voice or his expression must have moved her, because she did as he asked. He wisely clasped his hands between his knees, instinctively knowing that she would resist the physical contact even though he so badly needed it.

"Do you believe in miracles?" he asked.

"Sure. There are plenty of miracles in the Bible, and I think they really happened."

"Do you believe that God still works miracles?"

She looked at him skeptically. "You mean like Jonah and the whale, Moses parting the Red Sea, and the walls falling down at Jericho? Jesus being born of a virgin, healing the sick and blind, multiplying the bread and fish for a huge crowd of people, casting out demons, and rising from the dead?"

He nodded his head. "Yes – like that. Miracles that transcended the normal physical laws of time and space. Things which seemed to be impossible, yet they actually happened."

She threw up her hands, exasperated. "How can I respond to that? I'm in the medical profession. I work with absolutes. I was trained in the sciences. Yes, God worked miracles in Biblical times for specific purposes, but you want me to think that He's still doing that? I don't see any healers walking through my clinic healing people. Surely, if anyone could heal children dying with cancer, he would."

"Have you ever known of anyone who recovered from an illness who, by your reasoning, should not have done so? Our pastor has told us of many people who were apparently healed by Divine intervention."

"I can't explain those cases," she replied. "I've seen a few of them myself, but it isn't common."

He smiled a little. "Miracles are, by definition, uncommon."

"True. I'll bite. Tell me your miracle," she said, challenging him.

"Have you ever read Austen's novel, *Pride and Prejudice?*"

She tilted her head and looked into his eyes, holding his gaze. "I have. I have also seen several variations of the book in film. Are you telling me that you are the living, breathing embodiment of Fitzwilliam Darcy?"

He returned her stare with boldness. "Although I know not how, I am more than the embodiment of Fitzwilliam Darcy. I am the actual, real, person – Fitzwilliam Darcy – transported through time and space to change places with Will Darcy, my descendant. Or rather, my ancestor, as things are now."

She looked around, calling, "You can come out now. I know you're in there videoing this, so show yourself."

Silence.

Elizabeth laughed. "This has to be the best punking I've ever seen. You took weeks to set this up, didn't you?" she asked, punching his arm a little.

He stood, looking down at her with hurt in his eyes. "You think this is comical? Like those inane television programs in which people play tricks on other people, using their embarrassment for the amusement of the masses? I assure you that in my estimation, the loss of my family and everything familiar to me is no laughing matter. If God 'punked' me, as you say, it was a cruel trick to play, and He is not the loving God you Christians portray Him to be."

She stood and faced him, disbelieving. "You're serious, aren't you?"

"Do you remember the scene in which Darcy proposes to Elizabeth in which she rejects him due to his insulting manner of offering for her and her mistaken notions of his actions toward Wickham?" He nearly spat the final word. *May God help me, I still despise him. She would be far less suspicious of men had the present day equivalent of Wickham not violated her twice. He plagues me through the ages. Shall I never be rid of him?*

Her eyes were shrewd. "I do. Colin Firth played that perfectly in the 1995 BBC mini-series, but you are not Colin Firth. I hope you don't think you are."

"Colin Firth is but an actor, and my grasp on reality grows stronger by the minute, thanks to you." He frowned. "Be that as it may, though I can see that this probably will not end well, I will still tell you the truth. You deserve to know my past if we are ever to have a chance at building a future together."

"A future together? I hardly know you," she replied, stepping back in her astonishment. "That becomes more obvious with every word you speak."

"Elizabeth," he said firmly, "I know very little about how courtships are conducted in this era, but I am a gentleman of honor. However old-fashioned it may seem to you, I do not toy with the affections of respectable women. Had I not been interested in pursuing a lasting commitment from you, I would never have been so unguarded in my attentions toward you. To be frank, my intentions are to marry you eventually, if you will accept me."

She raised her eyebrows. "Well, that's certainly honest. It's also refreshing and more than a little scary." She chewed her lower lip.

"I'm listening, so tell your story. I'll try not to comment, as long as you don't ask me any questions."

"Thank you," he answered. "To be truthful, I am not totally selfless in wanting to tell you the full account of how I came to be here. I think you deserve to know the truth, but I am also selfish enough to wish for a wife who loves me even though my life has been somewhat strange. We can have no marriage if you do not accept me as I am. We must each respect the other."

She nodded her head.

"Excellent. Then no matter how this ends, we agree that I should tell you of my background. After all, you have entrusted your story to me, not knowing how I would receive it. There are men who would turn from you because a rogue took advantage of your youth and inexperience, yet you trusted me to understand. I can do no less with you, even if you did not desire a future together when you confided in me."

She started to speak, but he held up his hand.

"I did not say that to beg for assurances or explanations from you, Elizabeth. I merely wanted to point out that you have already exhibited a degree of confidence in me, and I should reciprocate." He clasped his hands behind his back and looked at the forest floor.

"I lived that book, though some things were different. We can discuss those things later if you are interested. My final memories of that life center on the evening and morning after I paid my addresses to Elizabeth Bennet. The book and mini-series are fairly accurate in relating the details of that humiliating debacle.

"That night, I returned to Rosings and wrote a letter filled with anger and bitterness." He looked up at her, unsurprised to see that she watched him with great intensity. "It was much worse than what was written by Miss Austen or quoted in the films. I unleashed my full, prideful wrath on Miss Bennet. While I thought I loved her, I cannot think that I would have spoken to a woman I truly loved in such a disgraceful way, no matter how she had acted or what she had said. I now believe that I desired her more than I loved her. I thought of her as an acquisition, and because I felt I could not have her due to her unsuitability, her value in my eyes increased." He looked Elizabeth squarely in the eyes. "There have been very few things that I could not have. My life has always been one of privilege, and I did not learn to appreciate it until I came here."

She smirked a little, and he saw it. "Yes," he said, "I am still quite wealthy, but, even so, this life is very different from the one I led before. Servants hurried to accommodate my every wish. In fact, they anticipated what I would want and made certain that it was readily available to me. No one had ever denied me anything I desired, and when Miss Bennet refused me, I took it very ill."

He looked away. "I can now see that her actions were correct. Because it never occurred to me that she would reject my suit, I did not treat her with respect, and she was right to respond in the way she did. I cannot think of it without abhorrence. My treatment of her would not have improved had we married under those conditions. I thought her beneath me in social standing, wealth, education, and manners. In the eyes of my family, my marriage to her would have been a degradation. I congratulated myself on my liberality in offering for her at all."

Fitzwilliam sighed wearily and turned his gaze to Elizabeth again, only to find her studying the ground. He began to pace as he continued. "The next morning, after a night spent drinking and nursing my wounded pride as I spewed out my vitriol, I rode toward the parsonage on my stallion, Diablo, to deliver the envelope to Miss Bennet myself. You see, back in that time, writing to her was improper, and I still had my dignity – my superiority – to protect." He laughed unpleasantly. "After I found her walking in her usual place in the grove, I handed her the letter and recklessly spurred Diablo to race away, wishing for nothing more than to be out of her presence. I hated her all the more, for when I saw her, I still wanted her as much as I ever did, and I knew that I could never have her. I was in no fit state to ride, but as usual, I did what seemed right in my own eyes. The last thing I remember is praying that I would never have to see her or hear her voice again. Then I was flying over Diablo, head first into a massive oak tree. When I regained consciousness, I was in a hospital in Atlanta, and people were referring to me as Will Darcy."

He stopped before her, awaiting her response.

When the silence became oppressive, he began to speak again. "Elizabeth, what are you thinking?"

She looked up at him sadly. "I don't know what to think or what to say. My first impulse is to encourage you to find a good psychiatrist or a neurologist, but I doubt that anyone can help you. You seem firmly entrenched in your delusional state, and it seems unlikely that any doctor or drug could change that. Destroying the delusion could even prove to be harmful to you. I don't know. Perhaps the head injury you received in the car accident was more traumatic than the doctors thought it was. Since you learned to hide your conviction that you were Fitzwilliam Darcy from *Pride and Prejudice*, they didn't explore a cause for your condition. It's also possible that you have some sort of mental illness or neurological condition which can be treated. People who experience delusions could be suffering from schizophrenia, bipolar disorder, paraphrenia, or psychotic depression; however, you don't exhibit the other indicators of those illnesses. I'm not qualified to diagnose you, but I haven't observed any symptoms of anything unusual until today."

He felt utterly exhausted, spent. His voice was low and quiet. "You do not believe me."

"I'm really sorry, Fitzwilliam. I can't deal with this right now." She turned and walked away.

He watched her cross the bridge and climb the hill, and he knew that she would be gone before he returned to The Oaks.

I could have proven it to her, but I wanted her to believe me without the proof. I wanted her to take the leap of faith, but she is unable to do so. It was important to him, though he didn't understand why until he remembered a verse the pastor had preached on one Sunday morning. *Jesus said to him, 'Because you have seen Me, have you believed? Blessed are they who did not see, and yet believed.' John 20:29.*

Even Jesus had wanted Thomas to believe Him without having to prove that what He said was true.

Fitzwilliam turned and walked deeper into the grove of trees. He did not look back to follow her progress as she walked out of his life.

CHAPTER 2

If you tell the truth, you don't have to remember anything. It's no wonder that truth is stranger than fiction. Fiction has to make sense.

Mark Twain

Pemberley, summer, 1795

Before the sun had risen above the trees on the hills at Pemberley, Will was pacing nervously in the rose garden beneath his balcony. As the first rays of light peeked over the horizon, though he had not yet seen Elizabeth, he felt her presence. He stopped and turned to see her walking quietly towards him, smiling in the early morning mist.

He held out his hand, and she took it, placing her small hand within his much larger one, matching her steps to his as he led her to a wrought iron bench just off the pathway which wound among the flowers.

They sat, and he turned to her. "Thank you for coming, Elizabeth."

She smiled again. "How could I not? The prospect of questions and secrets was too interesting to resist. What information can I give you which you do not already possess? I am even more curious as to what you would wish to tell me."

Suddenly grave, as if her thoughts had taken a different direction, she took a deep breath before she spoke again, looking down at their clasped hands. "Have you changed your mind since I arrived with my family and you spent an exhausting evening confined to their company? Do you no longer wish to be in a courtship with me?" Her voice broke on the final word, and she squeezed her eyes shut from the effort to say it.

He started to speak, but she opened her eyes and cut him off. "If that is your desire, I would never hold you to your previous words. There was no promise involved, and no one except my father knows of our conversations. You are not bound to me in honour. I will release you if that is your wish, with no damage to either of our reputations."

He was shocked. "Elizabeth! How could you think such a thing? I told you yesterday that I love you, and a moment ago I reached for your hand," he replied with agitation. Will took a calming breath and used his fingers to tilt her face up to his as he spoke gently. "Why would you say that?"

She closed her eyes with a pained expression, and then opened them when she began to speak. "You have yet to smile at me this morning, and I well know how my mother, sisters, and father offend your sensibilities. You made that quite clear to me at Hunsford."

He stroked the top of her hand with his thumb, gazing at her, unsmiling, speaking slowly. "Elizabeth, you quite misunderstand me. I love you with my whole heart, and nothing you or your family could do will ever change that. However, I need to ask you several questions before I relate to you what I must say." He cleared his throat. "You may not wish to speak to me or continue our courtship after you know all there is to know about me."

"Will, I will hear whatever you think you must tell me, but I daresay my feelings for you are as strong as are yours for me. Do

17

you really think I would refuse to speak with you because you are honest? I believe I know you very well, and there is nothing in your past which could change my present opinion."

She thinks I've had a mistress or some such thing. She has no idea of what I'm going to tell her. How could she? It's all too strange. She'll never understand it – I don't myself. But I've prayed about it, and I still think this is the right thing to do. She must know the truth.

He smiled weakly. "You truly care for me? At least I shall have the memory of your declaration after you walk away."

"I am disheartened that you think my resolve so feeble, Will."

He dropped her hand and stood before her. After taking a deep breath, he asked, "How old is your brother?"

Elizabeth was obviously puzzled by the question and the abrupt change in subject. "John is eighteen."

"And how many sisters do you have?"

She raised her eyebrows. "I know you cared little for my family, but I did think you at least took note of how many of us there were and our names."

I have insulted her. "As I told you earlier, my accident resulted in memory impairment, and I am quite different now from the way I was before. I remember very little of what happened prior to my injury, but we shall address that later. For now, please answer my questions."

She nodded her assent, looking up at him. "Very well. Jane, the eldest, is one-and-twenty; I am twenty; Mary is nineteen; and Lydia is sixteen. I have already told you that John is eighteen. I have three sisters and a brother."

"And is John to inherit, or is the estate entailed on your cousin?"

"Of course John will inherit Longbourn. Why should there be an entailment when there is a male heir? Are you concerned that you might have to care for my mother and sisters in the event of my father's death?"

"Not at all. To be quite honest, I like your family, and I would protect them as my own. If you marry me, they will be my family, and the prospect pleases me immensely. Will you hear me out, Elizabeth, without trying to guess the reasons for my questions? I will explain all in due course."

She nodded again.

He sat beside her on the bench. "What do you know of George Wickham?"

Elizabeth frowned and sighed. "I know that you were right about him, and I was sorely deceived by his appearance of goodness. He said that you withheld a living which was left for him in your father's will. You explained in a letter to me that Mr. Wickham refused the living and was paid its value."

So, he was to have a living after all, though not the one at Kympton. Richard didn't know that, but I'm sure he was correct about the farm. If my father wanted to do something for Wickham, yet felt that Wickham would likely reject the church, it makes sense that he would have made further provision for him. "There is even more to the story. Not only did he refuse the living, he also refused the farm and land my father provided for him in the event that he did not take orders. My father hoped that Wickham would enter the clergy, but he did not really expect for him to do so. It appears that Wickham had no taste for either the church or the honest life of a farmer. At any rate, he was well compensated, and in return for the solicitude of the Darcy family, he attempted to elope with Georgiana in order to gain her fortune."

Elizabeth lowered her eyes. "I can understand how Georgiana believed him ... and even loved him. Mr. Wickham can be most persuasive, and he cuts a fine figure, even though he is despicable. Georgiana was but fifteen, a quite impressionable age, so he took advantage of her youth, her lack of experience with men, and her trusting nature. Since she had known him all her life, she thought there would be no objection to the match. After all, your father treated Mr. Wickham almost as a son."

Will smiled. "Yes, my father's kindness was well known, but it nearly led to heartbreak in this case. However, I am more interested in the present than in the past at this time." He hesitated. "Have you noticed any young ladies who are particularly favoured by Mr. Wickham? Does he pay more attention to one than to the others?"

She looked up at him, her eyes gleaming with sudden realization. "He flatters all the young women of my acquaintance, but he favours my sister Lydia and her friend Catherine Lucas above the others. To my profound mortification, they allow his attentions and even encourage them." She paused. "Lydia is careful in front of Mama and Papa. She knows that they would never permit her to engage in such folly if they saw it."

He placed his hand on her arm. "Perhaps Lydia and Catherine are indulging in a harmless, though unwise, flirtation with an unsuitable young man. Now that they are here, I intend to make certain that they are parted from George Wickham." He paused, and then asked, "Has Mary ever seemed interested in Wickham?"

Elizabeth laughed softly. "Mary's beauty and talent certainly attracted him, but she is wiser than anyone gives her credit for being. My sister spoke with him only a few times. She soon tired of his vanity and shallow conversation. Mary would remain unwed before she would marry a person she could not respect."

"Admirable," he answered. "Are you acquainted with Phoebe Barlow?"

She raised an eyebrow. "Colonel Barlow's young sister? Why, yes. Phoebe visits at Longbourn nearly every day. She has no taste for being the lone female in a camp full of soldiers."

"Is she particular friends with Lydia or Catherine?"

"All of us enjoy her company, but she, Lydia, and Catherine are inseparable. In fact, she had invited both of them to go to Brighton with her for the summer, but when my father refused his permission, Sir William Lucas did the same. Neither girl was permitted to go."

He could be after either or both of them. His eyes narrowed. "Does Miss Barlow enjoy Mr. Wickham's company?"

Elizabeth blushed. "I fear that she does. I often hear her giggling with Lydia and Catherine. But Phoebe is not as silly as the two of them. Surely she would not be ensnared by the charms of such a man." She gasped. "You think he may be planning to take advantage of her as he did Georgiana? Oh, I should have warned them all! I felt I could not without betraying what you told me in confidence, and now, one of them may be ruined."

Richard must talk further with Colonel Barlow. He stroked her arm to comfort her. "Colonel Fitzwilliam and I will handle the matter. Do not distress yourself. Richard has already written to Colonel Barlow with a full account of Wickham's activities. By this time, Wickham has probably been dismissed from the militia. Perhaps we shall invite Phoebe to spend the summer with us here at Pemberley as her closest friends are all here. She should not be the lone young woman in a military encampment."

She smiled brightly and put her hand over his. "You would do that?"

"I would," he answered. "Georgiana will write to her this very day, and I shall offer to send a carriage for her."

"You are too good. I think you were always a man of honour, but your pride in your family and fortune stood between us. How is it that you have changed so?"

She goes right to the heart of the matter. Well, this is my opening. Please help me, Lord. Please guide my words and open her heart and mind. He took both of her hands in his. "Elizabeth, what I am about to tell you is fantastical and nearly beyond belief. Had it not happened to me, I would not believe it to be possible, so I cannot fault you for doubting the truth of the story."

This is an eighteenth century woman who has never seen television, cell phones, electricity, computers, the internet, or airplanes. The people of this age have no indoor plumbing, heat their homes with fireplaces and draw water from wells or streams.

21

Their servants wash clothes by hand and boil water in kettles. There are no fantasy movies or paranormal books in this age to stretch their imaginations. Jules Verne and Bram Stoker haven't been born yet, and Mary Shelley won't publish Frankenstein for more than twenty years into the future. The works of Anne Radcliffe are Gothic, but nothing like what I'm about to tell her. After all, I don't want to terrify her or awaken a sense of horror. He sighed out a breath of dejection. *I have no hope that she will believe me.*

As Will thought through the situation and his loss of Elizabeth, his emotions played across his countenance. He was unaware of how closely she was watching him.

A light touch on his cheek brought him from his reverie, and he saw her beautiful face close to his, green eyes troubled. "What saddens you so? Whatever you have done, I will forgive you," she said in commiseration. "I cannot bear to see you so distraught. Know that I do not require you to tell me anything you would wish to remain private. Can we not begin our courtship with the first time we met after your accident, when I saw you riding Guinevere at Rosings? After all, you are a different man now. Whatever happened before that time is unimportant, for it was not you."

The combination of her beauty, her compassion, and his love for her was too much for him to withstand, and he drew her to him, kissing her gently. When she did not push him away, he realized the enormity of the sacrifice she was willing to make, and he was ashamed of his selfishness.

He broke their kiss, drawing back slightly from her and looking into her eyes. "Elizabeth, my cousin should not be privy to information about me that I would withhold from my wife. I cannot begin a life with you knowing that you might choose differently if you knew everything about me. To do so would be duplicitous. It would be building our house on a foundation of sand."

She recognized the Biblical allusion. "And a wise man builds his house upon a rock?"

He smiled wanly. "Yes, my love, he does. If I am not forthright now, I may never tell you, and my past would always be between us, separating us. I would fear that you would find out and feel betrayed, and later you would wonder what else I did not tell you. You would never trust me again. You must be in possession of all the facts before I ask you to enter into an engagement with me. My confession will either break us apart or make our union stronger."

She moved down the bench, withdrawing her hands from his and folding them in her lap. "Then I shall do whatever I can to make the telling easier for you."

He blushed. *She isn't withdrawing from me,* he thought. *She knows that her nearness distracts me, and she's trying to help me get through this.*

"You are the best of women," he said.

"Yes, I am wonderful," she teased as she tilted her head and batted her eye lashes before once again returning to a serious demeanor. "Proceed."

"You have remarked on several occasions that I am a different man since my accident."

She smiled in encouragement. "I have indeed."

"Your observation was astute. You are correct. I am a different man." He watched her face.

She was silent a moment. "Is that all?"

"That is the home point, but you do not understand me fully. I am not the same man. I am not Fitzwilliam Darcy. I am Will Darcy, an entirely different man, born in London and reared by my grandmother in Georgia."

Her eyes grew round. "Georgia? The state in America named after King George? But you look like Fitzwilliam Darcy. If you are not Fitzwilliam Darcy, where is he? How is it that you have taken his place?"

"Have you ever heard of Jane Austen?" he asked.

"No, but I know that your man's name is Austen. Is she a

relative of his?"

My Elizabeth is quick. Trust her to notice the servants. No other lady would. "Miss Austen is Henry Austen's niece, and she is a writer, though none of her works have yet been published. Before my grandmother died, she and I spent many pleasant evenings reading Miss Austen's novels. Two of the main characters in her book, *Pride and Prejudice*, were Fitzwilliam Darcy and Elizabeth Bennet." He sat quietly, waiting for her to think over the information.

She did not speak for several minutes. "You read about me in a book? Which has yet to be published?"

"The book will be published in 1813, and I first read it nearly two hundred years after that. I thought it was a complete fiction, but obviously, some of the events in the book were real. For instance, the proud Fitzwilliam Darcy did propose to you, and you refused his offer. He wrote you a scathing letter in response and hand-delivered it. After that, and even before the proposal at Hunsford, the true story and book are different in many particulars."

She bit her lower lip, brows furrowed. "If you read a book which has not yet been written two hundred years into the future, how do you come to stand before me now? How did you travel back in time?"

Will's voice was earnest. "Elizabeth, I was never truly happy in that time, especially after my parents and my grandmother died. I always felt like a man who had been born in the wrong era. The women were very different from the way they are here, and I was lonely. I wanted to find someone like you, and although I searched, I could find no one in my time who came close to capturing the essence of Miss Austen's heroine. One day when I was particularly miserable, I prayed to God that He would let me meet the 'real Elizabeth.' I told Him I would be willing to suffer anything to meet you. Understand that I thought you were a fictional character. I wanted to meet someone just like you, but I never believed that you truly existed."

"You prayed to meet me," she said, releasing a long breath. Again there was silence. When she spoke again, her voice was even. "It appears that God answered your prayer, but I am fairly certain that Fitzwilliam Darcy was not a praying man. Where is he? What happened to him?"

His expression was grim. "I cannot be certain, but I think that he took my place at the same moment when I took his. Just after I prayed to meet you, I was hit by a car – the modern equivalent of a carriage – and rendered unconscious. He must have prayed just before his horse riding accident, and God answered both of our prayers. He was my ancestor, but now he will be my descendant."

She smiled sadly. "He probably told God that he never wanted to see me again. I was quite vicious in my refusal to him. It was not my finest moment."

Will moved quickly from the bench, dropping to his knees before her and grasping her hands in his. "Do you believe me then?"

She tilted her head and gazed at him. "I need to think upon it, but I cannot imagine that you are lying. You, at least, believe that what you are saying is the truth."

"I can provide proof if that will convince you that my words are true."

"I do not need – " she began.

At that moment, the French doors were flung open, and Mr. Bennet strode into the garden. He walked to the bench with purpose and surveyed the couple sardonically. "Have I interrupted a tender moment? Mr. Darcy, you do know that it is entirely improper for you to be alone with my daughter at this early hour. To more suspicious minds, it might even appear that this was an arranged meeting between the two of you. You are in full view of the servants, and there will be gossip."

Will instantly rose to his feet, dropping her hands, but before he could speak, Elizabeth stood and faced her father. "Then let us not delay in making the announcement, Papa. We shall forestall the rumour mongers by telling the truth as quickly as is possible. I am sure that you will share our joy this morning. Will Darcy and I are engaged."

Will took her hand, his face radiant with hope and the love that shone for her, and she turned to him with a smile. "Are you quite sure, Elizabeth?" he asked in amazement. "I would not rush you into accepting my offer."

"I have never been more certain of anything in my life," she declared, smiling at him.

Mr. Bennet cleared his throat and spoke sternly. "Then, Mr. Darcy, I shall have to beg you for a private audience in your study, as mine is located at too great a distance from here for my use."

As he turned and walked away, Will heard him mutter, "Nothing good ever comes from leaving home."

CHAPTER 3

I'd rather be hated for who I am, rather than loved for who I am not.

Kurt Cobain

Fitzwilliam returned to the log and sat, holding his head in his hands, trying to think: however, all thought was eclipsed by the constant droning in his mind. *I have lost her again. Dear God, will no one ever truly love me? Am I destined to lose everyone I ever care for? How shall I bear it? What is wrong with me? Is honesty no better than arrogance if they have the same result? Am I to be left to navigate this path alone?*

He wiped his eyes with the back of his hand and breathed deeply, filling his lungs with fresh air and clearing his mind as he slowly exhaled. *Enough self-pity!* he scolded himself.

Fitzwilliam stood and began to walk aimlessly through the woods. Eventually, he picked up a large stick and began to swing it at the trees. A squirrel jumped from branch to branch, catching his attention. As he watched it, he thought, *The animals are better off than humans. They do not feel such pain. They are happy living their small lives in one place, gathering food for the day, escaping from predators, mating in season.* He laughed bitterly. *Am I now wishing I were a squirrel or a bird? Perhaps a stag or a stallion?* He shook his head. *Fitzwilliam, be careful what you wish for,* he reminded himself. *A foolish prayer spoken in anger brought you here, after all.*

Distraught, he wandered until he came across a path. *I have nothing better to do and nowhere I need to go.* He began to follow it, and before long, he walked out of the woods and saw the lodge. *Caleb lives there, and I have no wish to see anyone.* He turned to walk back into the trees, but a familiar voice beckoned to him; he stood motionless at the edge of the forest.

"Fitz! Wait!" Lance called as he hurried toward Fitzwilliam.

Though he wanted to be alone, Fitzwilliam squeezed his eyes shut and was still, pinching the bridge of his nose between his fingers.

Lance, out of breath, was soon beside him. "Where have you been? We've been looking everywhere for you. Mrs. Thomas is worried sick."

Fitzwilliam looked at the ground. "Why were you worried? I'm a grown man walking his property. I can take care of myself," he said, his voice expressionless.

"Obviously," replied Lance, looking pointedly Fitzwilliam's rumpled clothing and disheveled hair. "I told her that, but she insisted that I find you and tell you that supper's waiting. You know how women are."

Fitzwilliam clenched his jaw and broke the stick against a tree. After a moment he said in a low voice, "Yes, I know how women are. I suppose you saw Elizabeth, stalking away from me? Did she talk to you about my delusional state?"

Lance shook his head. "No. Should she have? I saw her walk around the house. I supposed she wanted to get to her car without going in, though I had no idea why. She loves Mrs. Thomas, and she didn't even tell her goodbye. Jane and I followed her, because she looked upset, but she wouldn't talk while I was there. I went back in the house to get their things for them, and, when I came out with their stuff, they were already in the car. I put everything in the backseat, kissed Jane, and they left without a word. Jane was driving. Liz wouldn't even look at me. She didn't speak when I told her goodbye."

"She was angry, I suppose. I wasn't what she thought I should be."

"I didn't get that impression. She was sort of hunched over, like she was sad or hurt. She turned her head away from me, so I couldn't see her face. You guys were getting along so well. What happened? Did you have a fight?"

Fitzwilliam began to walk back down the path, and Lance fell into step beside him.

"No," answered Fitzwilliam tersely.

Several moments passed with only the sounds of their footsteps echoing through the silence.

"I'm guessing you don't want to talk about it," said Lance, "but you probably need to. Maybe I can help you."

Fitzwilliam glanced at him and shook his head. *By abandoning me like everyone else has?* He frowned and turned back to the path. *That isn't quite accurate. Mrs. Thomas knows the truth, and she loves me still.*

"There is no help for me, but I'll tell you what happened," he said solemnly, his eyes focused straight ahead. Turning to Lance, he continued with cheerless laugh. "Perhaps it will amuse you, and you will be able to show me the humor in my situation. God knows I could use a laugh." Fitzwilliam's voice held a note of challenge. *And you can run away, too, just like Elizabeth did. I can lose two people in one day. Quite an accomplishment. A very good day.*

Lance pointed to the left. "Let's go that way. It leads to the bridge, and we'll be headed back toward The Oaks."

"Fine."

"So, what happened?" asked Lance.

Fitzwilliam sighed. "I told her the truth about me, and she didn't believe my story."

Lance's eyes betrayed his curiosity. "The truth? What truth is that?"

Fitzwilliam stopped walking and looked at Lance. "The truth that I'm not Will Darcy; I'm Fitzwilliam Darcy."

"Meaning, you told her that when the car hit you, you lost all memories of your life before that time?"

"No, I mean precisely what I said. I have a lifetime of memories, but no memories of this place." He continued stubbornly. "I am Fitzwilliam Darcy of Pemberley in Derbyshire, England. I remember my childhood, my parents, my sister, my cousins, my family, my home – my life. I had a horse riding accident in 1795, and I woke up here in the year of 2013." *Now despise me, if you dare. I've grown weary of living a life of lies and secrets. In truth, deceit is becoming my abhorrence. I said it before, but I mean it now.*

Lance sat down hard on a tree stump.

Fitzwilliam crossed his arms and glared at him stonily. "Do you believe me, or do you also think I'm suffering from delusions and have need of a physician for the mind? Are you ready to have me put into a lunatic asylum?"

"Just give me a minute to digest this," answered Lance. He thought for a few minutes, and then said, "Tell me what you remember just before your accident."

"My life was similar to the book *Pride and Prejudice*. Are you familiar with the story?"

"Yes, but mainly from the movie with Keira Knightley. Jane and I went to see it before we grew apart. Are your memories like that? Jane told me at the time that that movie wasn't much like the book."

"Jane was correct. My recollections are more similar to the Colin Firth and Jennifer Ehle version, although not exactly the same. Mrs. Thomas told me that the director of the movie you saw changed the time period on purpose, and he made Mr. Darcy less proud and disagreeable. He was shy. I was never like that. I am reserved but not timid."

Lance chuckled. "You certainly weren't shy or timid in the hospital. You terrorized the entire female nursing staff."

Fitzwilliam dropped his arms and clasped his hands behind his back. "In 1795, women did not dress in trousers or touch men to whom they were not married." He paused. "Everything was quite strange to me, and thus I behaved badly. In actuality, I was frightened and confused." He looked away. "Try to put yourself in my place. I had never watched television or used electricity. I had no knowledge of computers, the internet, or telephones. Everyone I had ever known had disappeared from my life. The food, clothing, and manner of speaking were all quite different." Fitzwilliam turned his face back to Lance, letting his hands fall with his palms open, fingers spread. "Not only was I in a different time period, I was in a different country than that of my birth. If you believe me at all, you must see that my actions weren't quite so unusual as they seemed at the time."

Lance nodded slowly. "I can accept that, but I don't understand how you got here in the first place. What happened to Will? If you're here, where is he?"

Fitzwilliam gazed at him, unfocused. "He went to live my life in 1795. It seems that I prayed I would never have to see Elizabeth Bennet again, and he prayed that God would lead him to her." He looked at Lance and smiled wryly. "Ironic, isn't it? It appears that God answered both our prayers and switched us in time when we both had simultaneous accidents. We both wanted the *Pride and Prejudice* Elizabeth. The Elizabeth here is very different from the Elizabeth of 1795." He sighed. "I heard from him yesterday. They are engaged – or they were engaged," he said, shaking his head. "This time traveling is a complicated business."

"How is it possible that you've heard from him?" asked Lance.

Because he is clever and thoughtful, and I am stupid and

selfish. He found a way. "He wrote letters to me and to Mrs. Thomas and left them with Mr. Philips, an attorney in Meryton, a town near Elizabeth's home. Mr. Philips, her uncle, founded a law firm which became Philips & Associates, now my lawyers, and they deliver the letters on the dates Will specified. Will even took care to provide money for the Philips descendants to attend law school if they wished to so that there would always be someone to keep the firm going. There has been at least one lawyer in that family on a continuous basis for more than two hundred years."

"That's brilliant," said Lance in wonder. "Just like what Will would do. He would find a way to contact you and Mrs. Thomas, and he was well known for his philanthropy, especially in the form of scholarships. He was a champion of education." He thought a moment. "Did you tell Elizabeth that? If you showed her the letters, surely she would believe proof she could see with her own eyes."

Fitzwilliam looked at the ground. "No, I withheld that information when she gave her opinion of my mental state. I have no wish to pursue a relationship with a woman who will not believe me without incontrovertible evidence. I want her to trust me – to love me – and I want her to do so without seeing or knowing of the letters. Had she done that, I would have shown them to her."

Lance stood. "So you would hold on to your pride – the same pride that separated you from the woman you loved in 1795. You would give up Elizabeth without giving her a chance to know the truth?"

"Our points of view differ," answered Fitzwilliam. "I gave her an opportunity to show that she trusts me, and she could not. I told her what I had not told even you, and you have been my best friend for these past months."

"But you offered to show me proof," replied Lance, reasonably.

Fitzwilliam's voice was decisive. "No, I did not. You asked if I had proof, and I told you about the letters. There is a difference.

She immediately leapt to the conclusion that I am mentally disturbed. She didn't ask for proof, because she obviously thought there was none. Had she requested it, I would have told her, just as I told you."

They began to walk slowly back toward The Oaks. After a moment, Lance said, "Liz and I both were trained in the medical field – the sciences. Our professors drilled into us that we shouldn't believe what we couldn't quantify, and though I saw many contradictions in what we were taught, she didn't."

"Interesting. Such as?"

"We can't prove macro evolution, yet we were taught that it was a fact. She believed it, but I didn't."

Fitzwilliam was puzzled. "Evolution?"

Lance looked at him sharply and stopped walking. Fitzwilliam halted beside him.

"You've never heard of evolution?" Lance chuckled. "Of course you haven't. Darwin published *Origin of Species* in the mid-1800s. Your knowledge of history between 1795 and 2013 must be somewhat limited."

Fitzwilliam rolled his eyes. "I have spent some time on the internet, but my knowledge of the 1800s and 1900s is scanty. I've tried to watch The History Channel, but those people seem to be obsessed with war. They are interested in little else."

Lance laughed. "My mom used to say that The History Channel was invented so that men could watch World War II over and over. Dad likes it, but she doesn't."

"I have to agree with your mother."

"She would like that," he said, chuckling.

"Why did you not believe in something you were taught as truth, yet Elizabeth did?"

Lance started walking again, and Fitzwilliam fell in beside him. "Elizabeth claims to believe the Bible, but she limits anything supernatural to Biblical time periods."

Fitzwilliam was thoughtful. "She doesn't believe miracles can happen now – such as time travel. Do you?"

Lance smiled. "I believe that God can do whatever He wants to do. He isn't limited by time, space, or anything else. He is the same yesterday, today, and forever. If He switched the two of you, He had a purpose and a plan for both of you that required what He did. I don't believe in ghosts or other paranormal activity, but I believe in God. Nothing is impossible for Him."

"I suppose before this happened to me, I would have said she is right and you are wrong."

"So, are you ready to show her the proof?" asked Lance.

Fitzwilliam shook his head slowly. "I think not. She rejected my story outright, and I cannot suppose that the letters would change her mind. She might think I somehow managed to forge them and paid people to say what I wanted them to say. She could even think that I somehow tricked Mrs. Thomas into thinking her letters came from Will when they did not. I do not want a marriage with Elizabeth when she insists on believing the worst of me."

"You're assuming that she won't accept the evidence. Shouldn't you give her the chance to see it and decide for herself?"

"I haven't shown you the letters, or any other sort of proof, and you believe me. Why can she not do the same?"

Lance grimaced. "I haven't wanted to speculate, but I think some experiences Liz had in high school probably damaged her. It's very hard for her to trust people, and, while she goes to church, I think she might resent God. Perhaps to her way of thinking, He could have protected her, and He didn't."

"She told me about Greg Whitman that day we saw him at the restaurant."

"She told you what he did to her?" asked Lance in astonishment.

"Yes. There is more to it than either you or Jane knows, but I'm not at liberty to talk about it."

"Then, Fitz, she really does trust you. Liz never talks about Greg."

They walked in silence for a few moments before Fitzwilliam spoke again. "Just like another man I knew in 1795, Greg destroys lives and leaves others to clean up the wreckage he leaves in his wake. George Wickham had a hand in separating me from Elizabeth in 1795, and it appears that Greg Whitman will accomplish the same in this time period."

"George Wickham? I remember him from the movie. He told lies about you, but he didn't seem to have much to do with keeping you and Elizabeth apart. She resented that you had stepped between her sister and your friend."

Fitzwilliam's laugh was unpleasant. "Yes, I parted Jane from Charles, but because I thought Jane didn't love him. I thought Jane was being forced into a marriage by her mother. You really should read the book or watch the Firth adaptation. It's quite a bit longer than the later version and goes into more detail. Wickham tried to elope with my sister, and, from the film, it appears that he may actually have succeeded in convincing Elizabeth's younger sister to run away with him, unless Will is able to prevent it. Wickham nearly ruined the Bennet family. However, that has little to do with what has happened today."

"Wickham and Whitman may be even more alike than you realize, and from the way Greg talked to Liz at Canoe, I don't think he's finished with her."

Fitzwilliam nearly stumbled over a fallen tree branch. "What? You think the fiend may try to hurt her again?"

Lance raised an eyebrow. "Why should you care? Aren't you done with her?"

Raising his chin, Fitzwilliam replied, "I am. If she wishes to speak with me, she has my number." *Although I shall certainly see that she has a bodyguard after this.*

Lance smiled. "I don't doubt that. Liz probably does have your number."

"What does that mean?"

"It's an idiom. Google it."

They crossed the bridge without speaking further and climbed the hill. As the back porch of The Oaks became visible, Fitzwilliam could see Mrs. Thomas looking out the door. She had something in her hand, and she was waving it. She came out the door and nearly ran down the steps, still holding it up.

The men jogged to meet the older lady, but Fitzwilliam couldn't tell what was in her hand until he and Lance were nearly face-to-face with her.

It was his cell phone.

CHAPTER 4

Time is God's way of keeping everything from happening at once.

Anonymous

Will opened the door of his study and stood aside, allowing Mr. Bennet to enter the room before him. The elder gentleman chose a seat in front of the desk, so Will sat in his customary chair behind it. After opening a drawer, Will drew out a packet of papers which he handed to Mr. Bennet.

Mr. Bennet received the small tied stack of documents with a raised eyebrow. "Marriage settlement, I suppose?"

"Yes, sir."

"Certain of being accepted, were you?"

Will's smile was small. "I think 'hopeful' would be the better word. If Miss Elizabeth ever decided to agree to wed me, I wished to be ready."

"No doubt you sought to forestall a change of heart on her part. So you had these drawn up whilst you were in London, I suppose?" asked Mr. Bennet drily.

Will nodded. "I had them drawn up in London, yes, but I would not want a marriage in which my wife was unhappy. I had no plans to convince her to accept me and then rush her into signing a settlement. There is an identical set of papers in my study in London. I brought these papers with me in the event that your daughter and your family should learn to like me before your visit ended."

Mr. Bennet's face conveyed hardness, but his eyes were sad. "The question is not whether my family will like *you*, Mr. Darcy, but whether or not *you* will accept my family. She seems determined to have you, but are we all to be separated from Elizabeth when you marry? Are there any of us who are not offensive to you in our vulgarity?"

Will raised an eyebrow. *How does he know that Fitzwilliam called them vulgar?*

Mr. Bennet smiled wryly. "Surprised you, did I, Mr. Darcy?"

"Sir, I have never said anything untoward about your family."

Mr. Bennet glared at him. "Do not think me a simpleton, young man. Meryton is a very small village, and people love to talk. Servants especially. The servants at Netherfield are quite friendly with our Longbourn servants. Though we may not have nearly so many as that grand estate, they are exceptionally loyal. Most of our people have been with the Bennets for generations, and they were most unhappy with your characterization of us, and by extension, them. Even the maidservant, Martha, who went with Charlotte Collins when she moved to Hunsford is from Meryton. The walls of the parsonage parlour are thin, and she overheard every word of your ill-fated proposal to my daughter. Martha's sister, Ruth, is lady's maid to my girls, and she wrote quite a long letter to her. Mrs. Hill brought me that letter before we left for Pemberley. She was most affronted, and she thought I should know what you truly thought of us before I consented to a union between you and my daughter."

This is a catastrophe! Will closed his eyes. *Father, give me the words.* He opened his eyes and looked at Mr. Bennet. "Sir, why do you think Elizabeth has agreed to marry me? Do you suppose that she would ever accept my offer if she thought I would separate her from the people she loves most in this world?"

Mr. Bennet snorted. "She has some ridiculous idea that you have changed. She says you are a different man, and that you no longer feel such animosity towards us. Her lack of experience in the world makes her an innocent. You have lied to her, and she has believed you because of some nonsensical notion of romantic love."

And that was before I told her the whole truth. She is indeed a Proverbs 31 woman. Priceless. "Mr. Bennet, why do you think I was kneeling before your daughter when you entered the rose garden?"

"Were you not offering for her hand again?" he asked in anger. "After you expressly promised me that you would not press her? We have been here for only one night, and you have already convinced her to abandon us and marry you."

"You are mistaken, sir," said Will gravely. "I was not proposing. I was on my knees before her in humility, for she had believed the truth about me without requiring any evidence which would prove my story to be factual. Your manner of entrance into the conversation propelled her declaration. I have kept my word to you, though I am quite happy to be engaged, and I will not disappoint her. Should she wish to take back what she said, I will accept it, but I will not break the engagement myself."

Mr. Bennet narrowed his eyes as his face suffused with colour. "What truth is that? Pray, enlighten me as well."

"She has already told you. I am a different man now. I am not the man who proposed to her at Hunsford."

"Forgive my confusion. Do you mean that your actions and words prove that you have changed? You can act very well, I grant you. Perhaps you should make your living onstage," he answered with vitriol.

Will was calm. "It is more than that." *Shall I take a chance and tell him the truth? Can I trust him? Do I have a choice? I want him to accept me and love me as a son. If he does, the rest of Elizabeth's family will follow his example.* He sighed and straightened his back. "No, I meant exactly what I said. I am a completely different man. I am not Fitzwilliam Darcy; I am Will Darcy." *There. It's done.*

Mr. Bennet's expression hardened further. "What nonsense is this? If you are not Fitzwilliam Darcy, where is he? What have you done with him? And how is it that you look exactly like him, though you seem to have gained more bulk in your shoulders and arms." Mr. Bennet tilted his head and crossed his arms over his chest. His curiosity was marked as he looked the younger man over carefully. "When I think on it, your facial features are the same, but your countenance is altogether different. Your clothes have changed as well. You wore trousers instead of breeches last night, and you no longer wear hats. Your jackets have a less confining cut, as well."

He is intelligent. He can't resist the puzzle. Will smiled. "Do you believe in prayer, Mr. Bennet?"

The elder man appraised the younger in silence. Finally, he spoke. "I do."

"Do you believe in miracles?"

Mr. Bennet's eyes were shrewd. "I have no idea what game you are playing, Mr. Darcy, but if I am to keep my respectability as a church-going man, I must answer in the affirmative to that question as well."

Will leaned forward and put his clasped hands in front of him. "If I tell you what you wish to know, can I trust you to keep my secret?"

"I dislike secrecy," Mr. Bennet replied abruptly.

"Then I shall not burden you with it."

The quiet was unbroken for several moments.

Mr. Bennet huffed. "Did you not say that you have already told Elizabeth whatever must remain so closely guarded?"

Will nodded solemnly. "I did. I would never ask her to be my lifetime companion without knowing such an important revelation concerning me. Colonel Fitzwilliam also knows."

Mr. Bennet swallowed visibly. "Then I shall vow to protect your secret, as long as I can discuss it with Elizabeth and the colonel."

"Agreed. Fitzwilliam Darcy proposed to your daughter at Hunsford, as you already know. What you may not realize is that he found her walking in the grove the next morning and gave her a letter. He rode away in anger and, in his distraction, had a horse riding accident. He was thrown into a tree and suffered a head injury."

Mr. Bennet nodded impatiently. "Yes, yes. It seems that Mr. Darcy, whoever he might be, has no qualms about corresponding with my daughter, however unsuitable it might be. How does that affect the present situation?"

"Quite simply, I was not that man. I am Will Darcy, born in London and reared in Atlanta, Georgia. In the year 2013, I prayed that God would lead me to a woman like your Elizabeth. Immediately after the thought left my mind, I was also in a serious collision and sustained a blow to my head. I think we must have switched places in time, each waking in the time period of the other. Fitzwilliam was my ancestor, but now he will be my descendant."

Mr. Bennet eyed him coldly as he rubbed his chin, obviously thinking through Will's story.

After a few long minutes, he sat up straighter in his chair. "That is quite the outlandish tale. So my Elizabeth believed it, did she?"

Will thought back through her words carefully. He hesitated before he spoke. "She said she did not think I was lying and that I believed that what I told her was true."

Mr. Bennet tilted his head and smiled. "You do realize that she did not say she thought it was the truth herself?"

Will shook his head slowly, with the dawning awareness that

she had not, in fact, accepted his story as reality. "She said she needed time to think upon it. However, at the same time, she emphasized that she did not require proof."

The older man leaned forward in his chair, eyes sharp. "That is more like what my daughter would say. Because she loves you, she will try to trust that what you tell her is the truth as it appears to you. She is so honest herself that it is difficult for her to believe anyone whom she loves and admires would invent such a story. She wants your narrative to be true, and she will marry you even if she thinks your mind was unbalanced by your accident. In fact, you may have secured her hand by awakening her sympathies. Quite ingenious, I must say."

What if he's right? What if Elizabeth is accepting me because she thinks I'm damaged? Does she love me, or is it pity?

Will stood and walked to the fireplace in agitation, turning his back to Mr. Bennet. After pacing the room a few times, Will stopped and looked at Mr. Bennet. "I must insist that you allow me to prove myself."

Mr. Bennet leaned back and crossed his legs, folding his hands in his lap. He was clearly enjoying the discomfort of his daughter's betrothed. "And how do you propose to do that?"

Will took a deep breath and exhaled slowly. "I have already written letters to my grandmother and our housekeeper, Mrs. Thomas. I have left several with your brother, Mr. Philips. I will leave many others in his protection to be delivered on certain dates by his descendants during my childhood, as well as after I leave that time period. Mrs. Thomas will not begin to receive her letters until after my grandmother passes away. Shortly after that event, I experienced the accident and time-switch. However, my Nana Rose will know what is in my future from the time I am a child, living with her after the deaths of my parents. They will not survive an accident while travelling when I am eight, and she will receive her first letter from me shortly after that. I will not burden her with knowing what will happen to them before it actually occurs. She might try to prevent their deaths, and she would be upset if she failed. Conversely, if she did not try to intervene, thinking that she should not change history, she might live the rest of her life regretting that she had not acted. While I will not burden her with knowledge she should not possess, I need for her to prepare me for this without telling me exactly what will happen. After all, I would not have my early years to be those of a fearful child, and I would not wish to plant any doubt in my younger mind about the mental stability of my grandmother."

He saw the interest in Mr. Bennet's eyes as the older man asked, "Exactly how did your grandmother prepare you without your knowledge of what would happen to you in your future?"

"She encouraged me to learn all that I could about this time period and the history leading up to 2013. We played games, read books, looked at pictures." *There's no need to talk about movies or any other modern inventions. He wouldn't understand any of it, and introducing those things would only confuse the more important issue.* "I was so enthralled with the study of the past that I spent several years at a university and became something of an expert."

"So, you have knowledge of what will happen?"

Will cleared his throat. "Yes, to some extent I do. I know quite a bit about major historical events around the world during these years, but I cannot be certain of what will occur in my own life. I have no idea when or how I shall die, for instance, though I do know that I shall father children. Whether or not Elizabeth will be their mother is unknown."

Mr. Bennet nodded. "Otherwise, there would be no Will Darcy in the future. Fascinating."

"My background in history is our surety that our financial ventures will be prosperous. I must be careful, though, not to change events by interference."

"You would use your insight to make money? Is that not rather selfish?" asked Mr. Bennet.

Will crossed the room back to his desk and sat again, placing his clasped hands before him. "You misunderstand me. Money to me is only a means to an end. I have no desire to amass a large fortune just for the sake of having wealth and privilege. I do like to be comfortable, but I am not materialistic. I greatly desire to do good deeds with money – to help Wilberforce fight the slave trade, to fund struggling inventors and medical researchers who can improve the lives of millions of people, to bring Pemberley into the new century as a model of a successful, classless, capitalistic enterprise."

Mr. Bennet smiled. "How very revolutionary of you, Mr. Darcy. You will give up your land?"

Will looked directly into his eyes. "No, sir. I intend to keep the estate intact, though I shall end the master and tenant relationship. I can tell you that estate owners who cling to the old system will lose their homes and lands by not instituting such reforms. Pemberley shall not suffer that fate, and neither shall the Darcy family. I will secure the future of my family, and I will help as many people as I can while I accomplish that goal."

"Very admirable," said Mr. Bennet, warming a little to the subject. "Now to the question of your evidence. Clearly, while you may have letters delivered after your death, there is no way for letters to come to you from the future. I am having some difficulty wrapping my mind around the idea that God performed this miracle. Is the past not unchangeable? Is it not complete?"

Will templed his fingers, barely touching his chin with his fingertips. "I have spent much time contemplating that very thing, and I have a rather unusual idea."

"Pray, share your thoughts."

Will pulled his pocket watch from his waistcoat and placed it before him on the desk. "I think God has no need of one of these. He does not see time as the past, the present, or the future as we do. It is a continuous loop to Him, all happening simultaneously until He returns and a new age begins. Switching me with

Fitzwilliam suited His purpose, evidently, and, as nothing is too difficult for Him, it was as easy for Him as it would be for me to turn this watch back an hour. God did it for Joshua in Joshua 10:13 when He caused the sun and moon to stand still so that the Israelites could finish their battle with the Amorites. He also healed King Hezekiah in Isaiah 38 and II Kings 20 as the king lay on his deathbed, and He turned the sundial back ten degrees as a sign to Hezekiah that he could defeat the Assyrians. If you believe the Scriptures, why then would you doubt that God would do this for me?"

"Interesting. I never took you for such a deep thinker, Mr. Darcy," he said, nodding at the younger man in a show of respect. "You are quite the philosopher and Biblical scholar, but that is not evidence of the truth of what you say. I am intrigued, but not convinced."

"I proved it to Colonel Fitzwilliam by telling him in advance the date that Warren Hastings would be acquitted."

Mr. Bennet pursed his lips. "Many people thought he would be acquitted. You may have had contacts who could have told you the upcoming date. You must do better than that."

"Very well," answered Will, his mind delving back into what he had learned of history. "On the fifth of June through the seventh of June, a fire will devastate Copenhagen. It will likely begin in a naval warehouse."

"You have the means to make that happen, though I would hope you would not do such a thing only to vindicate yourself," said Mr. Bennet.

"I would never do such a thing. I can also tell you that it may start in a family apartment rather than a naval warehouse, destroy over 900 homes, and kill thousands of people. Accounts differ widely, and I cannot be positive of either location. Some think a young boy accidentally knocked over a candle and began the blaze. Accounts differ as to the exact numbers, but about twenty percent of the population was rendered homeless by the devastation."

Mr. Bennet frowned. "You could cause all that. You could hire people to set fires yourself."

"But the fire will be finally put out by rain, according to many historical accounts. That's an act of God, Mr. Bennet." Will was calm. "Surely you cannot think that I can make it rain. I have no control over the weather."

Mr. Bennet bowed his head. "This is an awful thing to contemplate. Can you not prevent it from happening?"

Will sighed. "That is the burdensome part of the gift which God gave me. I cannot change the defining moments of history, or I may cause something much worse in its place. I will not play God. What I am willing to do is send someone to watch the warehouse and the surrounding area in the evening hours, though they may not have time to travel there and locate the proper area at this late date. The fire will start after everyone goes home for the day, and since the structure and the surrounding buildings are all made of wood, the blaze will be out of control before it can be contained. The fire department will respond rapidly, but their equipment is primitive and they will not be able to get it through the narrow streets. They will fail in their attempt to put the fire out. They will try blowing up houses with gunpowder in their desperation to contain the damage, but that will also fail. In fact, more people will die because of it."

"You sound as if it is hopeless."

Will's face clouded with his sorrow. "I believe that it is. I am nearly positive that I cannot stop it. It will happen no matter what I do. If I send someone to guard the warehouse, the boy will knock the candle over. If I somehow manage to locate the correct family, it will start in the warehouse. If the boy can be prevented from knocking over the candle, it may be started by a person casting candles. This event impacted human history too much for me to be able to undo it without possibly causing ripples in the time line which could be even more catastrophic. If I sent a hundred men, who's to say that I have changed anything except to condemn more people to death?"

"What on earth could be worse than the fire? What good could it accomplish not to interfere?" asked Mr. Bennet.

"After the fire, the city planner will decide that future structures should be built of masonry instead of wood. Street corners will be designed diagonally, and the roads will be widened. Doing those things will probably save far more lives in the long run than the fire will take," replied Will sadly. "The fire will also be a main contributing factor to the establishment of Denmark's first credit institution. Would you have me play with the economic security of an entire country to prevent a calamity in one city? What of the other countries and cities who adopt the safety measures which will be instituted in Copenhagen after the fire? How many more people might die if those ideas are not implemented? There are very few tragedies which produce no benefit at all."

Mr. Bennet looked at Will somberly. "I am inclined to believe you. You feel the burden of it keenly, and I doubt that you would invent such a story. I suppose I shall know of a surety in a few days as to whether or not you are telling the truth, but I would prefer to keep this conversation between the two of us. No one else should have to know the grief of having this information with no way to prevent the destruction from occurring."

Will smiled wanly. "I think you begin to understand me very well, Mr. Bennet, and I heartily agree with your idea. I am sorry to have shared this sorrow with you, but perhaps we can help each other to bear the knowledge. I hope you will forgive me, but it was the only way I could think of to convince you of my sincerity and honesty."

Mr. Bennet's eyes were bright with unshed tears. "You will, of course, not tell Elizabeth of your knowledge of such horrible things. It would crush her that she could not prevent the pain and death. If you must relieve yourself of such things from time to time, confide in me. Together we can withstand the great weight."

Will looked at the older gentleman and nodded with new found respect and admiration. *Maybe ... he will truly be a father to me.*

CHAPTER 5

Learning to trust is one of life's most difficult tasks.

Isaac Watts

Fitzwilliam took the phone from Mrs. Thomas's outstretched hand, noting that while her lips smiled, her eyes did not.

"I think Elizabeth has texted you," she said a little too eagerly.

"Thank you." Fitzwilliam nodded as he slipped it into his pocket without checking it.

Mrs. Thomas watched him closely. "She left without saying goodbye. That isn't like her."

Fitzwilliam smiled crookedly. "She certainly told *me* goodbye."

"Is supper ready?" asked Lance, smiling and filling the awkward silence. "I'm so hungry I could eat a horse."

Fitzwilliam looked at him in surprise. *I had heard that it is acceptable to eat horseflesh in uncivilized places such as Australia, but surely Lance would do nothing so horrible.*

Mrs. Thomas's voice was a little strained. "Sorry. We're fresh out of horse here in the house, and Caleb took your four to the stables long ago." She turned to go back into the house through the hall by the kitchen, saying over her shoulder, "I do have a lovely beef stew with potatoes and carrots, though, and I even have hot tea for you, Fitzwilliam."

Fitzwilliam attempted a smile and gently shook his head. *The 'eat a horse' thing was a joke, I suppose. They're both trying so hard to make me feel better. Maybe I should think of someone else besides myself for a change. Have I always been this selfish?* "That sounds wonderful," he said in a forced, cheery voice, following her. *Mrs. Thomas must be very concerned if she made hot tea for me. She's never done that before.*

He heard the noise of a motor and saw an odd contraption in the sink. "What's that?" he asked, pointing at it.

She bustled over to unplug it. "It's an electric ice cream churn making our dessert – homemade peach ice cream. I hope both of you like it. I stopped at a farmer's market yesterday for fresh produce, and I just couldn't resist the lovely fruit. Georgia is known for its peaches. We're called 'The Peach State,' you know."

Lance added, "Even our beautiful girls are called Georgia peaches."

What does fruit have to do with a woman, beautiful or otherwise? I don't think I'll ever completely understand what they're talking about around here. Elizabeth doesn't remind me of peaches or any other kind of fruit or vegetable. An hour ago, I might have said she reminds me of a sunflower, but now ... "Do you need any assistance, Mrs. T.? Shall Lance and I help you take the food to the table?" Fitzwilliam asked.

Her eyes crinkled with her smile. "I thought we would serve ourselves in here, buffet style," she answered, leading them into the kitchen. "The stew's in the crock pot, and the ice cream needs to harden a bit. We can take our dishes to the dining room after we get our food. By the time we finish the main course, the ice cream should be the perfect consistency." She covered the electric churn with a towel.

Lance went to the counter and picked up a large soup bowl. "Yum. It smells wonderful!" He removed the lid from the crock pot and placed it on the counter. "There's enough here for an army. I'm hungry, but I don't think we'll put a dent in that."

Fitzwilliam tried to suppress a frown. *She must have thought that Elizabeth and Jane would stay to eat. I guess I ruined that for her, too, and after she worked so hard on it.*

Mrs. Thomas looked at his expression and spoke quickly. "Mrs. Jenkins, our neighbor, lives alone, and she's been sick. I thought I'd take some stew to her. Caleb's coming back to eat, too, once he finishes with the horses and the rest of his work. Don't worry, boys. It won't go to waste." She fixed her eyes on Lance and said sternly, "You go wash your hands, young man. The food can wait while you two clean up a bit."

She shooed them from the kitchen, and they headed up the stairs to do as they were told. Fitzwilliam took the additional time to change his clothes and comb his hair. By the time he had finished dressing and washing his face and hands, Lance had already gone back to the kitchen. As Fitzwilliam walked back down the stairs, he heard Mrs. Thomas and Lance talking quietly. He went through the hallway and stood in the dining room near the kitchen door, listening.

"What in the world happened?" asked Mrs. Thomas in a muted voice. "I thought they were getting along so well."

"Fitz decided he needed to be honest with her. He told me that you've already heard his history, so you know what he said to her," answered Lance, just above a whisper.

"She didn't believe him? But I have letters that prove he's telling the truth."

"She intimated that he needed psychiatric help," said Lance.

"I love Elizabeth," replied Mrs. Thomas, "but she shouldn't have run off like that. Why didn't she come talk to me or you? Anyone who knew Will before the accident knows that he and Fitzwilliam are two very different men. It's not at all difficult to see that."

There was a pause. "Maybe that's the problem," said Lance.

"We knew Will, but she didn't. We could see the complete change, but Elizabeth can't."

Lance's comment sparked Fitzwilliam's interest. *That's true, I suppose.*

"Well, I'm going to show her something that will prove my dear boy is telling her the truth."

He smiled in the shadows of the late afternoon sun coming through the curtains. *I'm still her 'dear boy.'*

Lance shook his head. "I suggested that already, and he said not to. He thinks Elizabeth might even think that he forged the letters or paid to have someone else do it. He also wants her to believe in him because she loves him – not because he can prove what he says."

Fitzwilliam stifled a chuckle when he heard her, "Humph!" Her voice was strident when she spoke again. "He was unconscious when I got my first letter, so he had no time to set anything up, unless she thinks he stepped in front of a car on purpose and had the letters arranged ahead of time. Why would he do that? What possible reason could he have? He was very nearly killed. Only an idiot would go that far to set up some time-switch story. And, I know Will's writing and manner of speaking as well as my own. Will wrote those letters. Fitzwilliam has had a hard enough time without having to go through this. I really do like Elizabeth – she's a wonderful person – but maybe she doesn't deserve him."

Lance chuckled. "It would cheer him up considerably to hear you fussing in his defense."

I can no longer listen to their conversation without their knowledge. It isn't honorable. Even so, I'm glad that I did. My own relations would never have defended me so vehemently.

Fitzwilliam stepped into the doorway and cleared his throat. "That stew smells wonderful, and suddenly I have discovered my appetite. Shall we eat now?"

Lance looked at him sharply. "How long have you been standing there?"

"Long enough." He walked to Mrs. Thomas, surprising both her and himself by leaning down and softly kissing her cheek. Quickly continuing to the counter, he picked up a bowl, and began filling it with the stew. Glancing to his right, he noticed a new appliance. "What's this?"

Mrs. Thomas smiled broadly and hurried to his side. "It's a Kuerig, used for making hot beverages. Let me show you how to operate it." She pulled up the lever and put in a container of Earl Grey tea. Since she already had a cup in place, she had closed it again and pushed the blinking light for medium. Before long, he had a steaming cup of tea.

"Brilliant!" he said. "Thank you, Mrs. T."

"I bought the machine yesterday," she replied, beaming. Pointing to a circular, metal object, she said, "This little stand is filled with all sorts of goodies – coffee, tea, cider, hot chocolate. You men can have whatever you want to drink in a few minutes, whether or not I'm here. There's liquid creamer and lemon juice in the refrigerator and powdered creamer in the cabinet here." She opened the cabinet door as she spoke, pointing to the container. "The sugar bowl is on the table."

Fitzwilliam leaned toward her, putting his arm around her and catching her in a side hug. *She's the nearest thing I'll ever have to a mother, and she's my family now. We avoided public displays of affection during my era, but I notice people embrace here routinely. She won't take it amiss.*

Mrs. Thomas gasped a little, but recovered quickly and put her arm behind him, patting his back. "I'm going to take good care of you, Fitzwilliam. You're such a good, strong man; I'm very proud of you."

He dropped his arm from her shoulder and looked down at her, smiling. "You've already taken excellent care of me, Mrs. T. I really haven't done anything yet to make you proud of me, but I hope to become a man who will deserve your confidence and high opinion. I've been thinking about it, and now that I'm recovering so well, I feel I should start going back to my business a few days a week. I need to learn more about Darcy Enterprises and the philanthropic foundation which was so important to Nana Rose and Will. I understand it is the Darcy legacy."

"That's wonderful, dear, and yes, it is. Now," she said with delight, "let's take our food to the dining room and talk about it." Mrs. Thomas smiled at him, filled a bowl for herself, and then turned to leave the kitchen. "Come on, Fitzwilliam," she said, looking over her shoulder at him.

Once they were seated, Lance said grace, and they all began to eat.

After both men had offered their compliments to Mrs. Thomas, Lance put down his spoon. "If you're ready to go back to work, Fitz, I think it's time for me to move back to my apartment."

Though Fitzwilliam had known all along that Lance was living at The Oaks temporarily, he hadn't considered that his return to Darcy Enterprises would signal his friend's departure.

"I'm not going to work every day, Lance. I hope to adjust gradually – maybe two days a week. I still need your help in adjusting to this life."

Lance shook his head. "You've learned to do things for yourself, and you're a smart guy. You'll figure it all out. You can continue the therapy on your own or go to a physical therapy rehabilitation center. There are several really good ones in Atlanta. I can even refer you, if you want me to."

Two in one day. I've lost Elizabeth, and now I've lost Lance. He's the only male friend I have here. Actually, I have no female friends my age anymore either. Fitzwilliam decided to change his tactics. "How am I supposed to get to work or a therapy center? I can't drive."

"You can hire a chauffeur, or you can learn to drive. It's your choice," answered Lance.

Mrs. Thomas had been quiet, looking at her stew. She looked up. "If you really want to leave, Lance, I can handle those details for him, or Mrs. Gray can do so. I'm sure she'd be happy to help him any way she could. After all, you've been here far longer than we originally agreed upon. You've helped Fitzwilliam so much, and we both appreciate it. Don't we?" she asked, looking pointedly at Fitzwilliam.

"Yes, of course," he answered. "I will certainly miss your company, Lance, but I'll manage. I'll have Mrs. T. and – Mrs. Gray? Is that her name? I have yet to meet her, but I'm sure that she's a very nice lady."

Lance rolled his eyes. "It's not that I want to leave; it's that I should leave before I become even more of a crutch for you. I want to finish my degree in physical therapy, too. We'll still be friends. We can work out together, and I can introduce you to some of my friends. We get together to watch football and other sports. You might like it."

Fitzwilliam nodded. "I'm certain I will. Perhaps you can drop by here and visit, if you're ever in the area. I suppose now that Elizabeth and I are no longer talking, it would be awkward for you to stay here and date Jane."

Lance's face was earnest. "Maybe you and Liz can work this out, Fitz. Don't give up so easily."

Fitzwilliam knew that he was playing on Lance's heartstrings, but he continued anyway. *I am truly shameless.* "I doubt I'll see her any more, once you move back to Atlanta. It was easy to be included on dates with you and Jane; however, when you're no longer here, I shall have no connection with her. I suppose it's just as well, since she thinks I'm a lunatic."

Lance sighed. "That's hitting below the belt." He held up his hands in surrender. "I know when I'm beaten. I'll stay another couple of weeks, and I'll teach you how to drive before I leave, if you promise to really work at it. You may still need to hire a driver to take you into Atlanta until you get enough experience to handle city driving. Meanwhile, I'll drive you to Darcy Enterprises two or three days a week and go to my apartment while you're at work."

Mrs. Thomas smiled. "That's very kind of you, Lance. Are you boys finished with your stew? I can go get the ice cream. It should be well set by now." They passed her their bowls, and she took them into the kitchen.

"I'm really curious," said Lance.

"About what?"

Lance made a face. "About the text message."

Fitzwilliam frowned and sighed. "I'm sure it's nothing. She was very clear that she was done with me."

"Well, check it anyway."

"If you insist," answered Fitzwilliam, retrieving the phone from his pocket. He typed in his pass code and touched the message icon. After he read it, he turned it toward Lance.

The message was short: "I'm sorry."

Lance's voice sounded impatient. "See. She's already sorry that she left like that."

"I think not," replied Fitzwilliam. "She's sorry she hurt me by telling me I need psychiatric help, but she doesn't regret leaving me." He paused and thought a moment before he said, "Or perhaps she's merely sorry that, in her opinion, I'm a lunatic. Either way, she's not sorry she left. She's glad of that."

"I think you're wrong, and I probably know her better than you do."

Fitzwilliam's smile was tight. "You have known her longer than I have, true, but you didn't see her face or hear her tone of voice. She may be sorry she injured me, but she still thinks I've lost my mind."

"There's only one way to know for sure," said Lance.

Fitzwilliam raised an eyebrow. "And what is that?"

"Call her."

He held his mouth in a stubborn line. "She left. She should call me."

"She did call," said Lance. "Well, technically, she didn't call you, but she left you a message."

"She left a very cryptic, short text which could be understood to mean a multitude of things. If she wants to talk further, she obviously has my number. I will not subject myself to further rejection at her hands. And before you take this further, remember how many years you waited before you talked to Jane again."

Lance's eyes lit up. "Exactly. I wasted all that time when I could've been with her. Don't do what I did. Talk this out now."

Fitzwilliam tilted his head. "I'm willing to talk to her – whenever she decides to call me. Until then, I shall leave her to her own devices."

"So you and Liz are at an impasse."

"It would seem so." His voice held a note of finality.

"You know, in her mind, she's reached out to you. If you don't reply, she'll take it as a rejection of her," said Lance.

"Lance, if I called her now, she would be most unhappy at what I would say. I think it much better to wait until I am no longer upset. It's not as if either of us is going to meet a potential mate in the near future."

Lance nodded thoughtfully. "You may be right. In your present mood, talking to Liz could make it all worse. She'd probably get defensive, and you two might have a real fight. Your chances with her could get even slimmer."

Mrs. Thomas walked back in with a tray holding three bowls of peach ice cream. "Maybe Elizabeth should meditate on the pleasure to be obtained by gazing at a pair of fine eyes in the face of a handsome man. Maybe she should think about her chances with Fitzwilliam diminishing. There are plenty of women at Darcy Enterprises and in the greater Atlanta area who would love to go out with him."

Fitzwilliam smiled, remembering what he had said to Caroline Bingley at Lucas Lodge. He had been remarking on the beauty of Elizabeth Bennet's eyes then. *I love Mrs. T. I wonder if there are any younger versions of her in Atlanta.*

CHAPTER 6

When I host a party, I hope my guests get along. But if not, how interesting!

Andy Cohen

Will had found it quite difficult to restrain his joy during the morning's activities on the beautiful grounds of Pemberley, enjoying the events meticulously planned and organized by Georgiana, but if any of the guests thought the normally rather sober young man was uncharacteristically happy, they kept their thoughts to themselves.

He watched Elizabeth closely after nuncheon, and as the afternoon progressed, he began to wonder if she was as content in her situation as he was. He casually studied her facial expressions when he thought no one was looking, and because she was always cheerful, he could detect no elevation in her mood. He could see no change. Her eyes sparkled in their usual way, and she laughed as she did routinely. He began to suspect that she was not as deliriously happy as he himself was, and he thought of reasons why that might be so. As he pondered their marriage, it seemed more and more to him that every advantage of the match was on his side, and his anxiety grew.

After all, he thought, *she will come to live at Pemberley, leaving her home and family. She will have to leave a jolly, lively group of people she loves dearly for my smaller, more subdued circle. Her behaviour as my wife will be scrutinized and criticized, and, furthermore, she'll have to contend with my difficult relations.*

Then there was the matter of his most unusual history. *She might come to regret an alliance with a man who has such a strange past as mine.* The more he dwelt upon the matter, the more pensive he became. *She may regret her choice, even now. I love her too much to risk making her unhappy.*

In order to put his mind at rest, while Georgiana, his cousin, and the Bennet siblings were entertaining themselves with games of battledore and shuttlecock, horseshoes, and a modified form of cricket, he accomplished the great feat of isolating Elizabeth for a full twenty minutes. Will had seen and seized his opportunity when Mr. Bennet had settled himself on a bench under a tree with a book in his hand, and Mrs. Bennet had taken up her embroidery in a chair placed in such a way that she could keep an eye on her offspring. Will tried to look nonchalant as he strolled over to Elizabeth's side.

"Have you changed your mind, dearest?" he asked quietly as they walked a little distance away from the group, trying unsuccessfully to keep the note of concern from his voice.

She smiled impishly. "Not at all. You shall not be rid of me that easily. I meant what I said, Will. If you wish, you may announce our engagement whenever you think it suitable to do so."

"Are you not fearful of marrying a madman?" His voice was strained. "You have not yet said that you believe my story."

She gazed at him levelly, her face serious. "You exhibit more sanity than anyone else of my acquaintance, and I trust you implicitly. Whether or not you actually switched places with Fitzwilliam is unimportant, for I certainly prefer you to him, however that came to be. I view it as a blessing, for I now love you with all my heart. I could never have loved Fitzwilliam."

She loves me! His face lit up as his eyes began to twinkle.

His relief was enormous, and he wished to tease her a bit.

"What of my relatives? Surely you cannot wish to be the niece of the extremely interfering Lady Catherine de Bourgh."

"Will, I can abide your intimidating aunt once or twice a year in exchange for a lifetime with you. Just as you have accepted my family, I will accept yours. In any case, Lady Catherine will not affect my happiness in marriage with you. As you know, my courage always rises with every attempt to intimidate me."

He smiled broadly. "You are all that a young woman should be, and I am the most fortunate of men. However, perhaps after fifty years with me, you may not continue to feel that way about me. You may think me truly insane, for my ideas may seem more and more foreign to you when you know me better."

"Then you shall never bore me," she answered, laughing. Her green eyes were brilliant and lively. Her mood changed to one of sympathy, and her voice was low as she asked, "Was my father very rude to you? Did you suffer greatly at his hands? He can be a bit of a curmudgeon."

Will answered somberly. "I told him the truth, and he bore it very well, though he required the evidence which you did not."

She drew her brows together. "What proof did you offer?"

He hesitated a moment. *I will always tell her the truth, and I will always answer whatever she asks me.* "I know of many historical events which will happen, because I studied this era intensively when I was in university. I actually hold an advanced degree in history." He looked away for a moment, and then turned his face back to hers. "I told him of something which will occur in a few days. There is no other way for me to know this will take place unless I come from a time in the future."

She studied his face. "And you have not wished to share this information with me?"

"I have not, and your father agrees with me. He asked me not to tell you these sorts of things."

Realization dawned in her eyes. "Then you and Papa are protecting me." Her lovely eyes were full of sadness. "It must be something truly terrible."

He reached for her hand, shifting to protect them from the view of the rest of the party. "Yes, there will be many lives lost, and I can do nothing to stop it from happening. I do not wish to take your peace from you, my love. You need not know about horrific things which we cannot change."

"I would share your grief, Will, and take some of your burden," she answered, covering his hand with hers. "I shall be your wife, and I would not like secrets to stand between us."

He nodded. "Perhaps after we marry then, but for now, I would respect your father's wishes. Do you understand?" he asked. "Let this be a happy day, for we have joyous news to announce."

She nodded slowly. "Very well then; I suppose I shall know of the catastrophe soon enough, but you must not seek to shield me from everything unpleasant, Will. I am stronger than either you or Papa think I am."

He brought her hand to his lips and kissed it, looking at her from under his lashes. "I do not doubt it, my love."

~~oo~~

After a day filled with contests and laughter, the party adjourned to their rooms to dress for the evening. Afterwards, they assembled in the parlour, chatting quietly, reliving the day through conversation, as they awaited the summons to sup.

As soon as he received word from the butler, Mr. Carlson, Will offered his arm to Elizabeth and led her into the dining room. Mr. and Mrs. Bennet fell in behind them, and Colonel Fitzwilliam followed with Georgiana holding one arm and Jane the other. The rest of the group walked in order behind them, and upon entering the large room, they sat in the seats which they had occupied during the previous evening. Will sat at the head of the table with Mrs. Bennet to his left and Elizabeth to his right. Georgiana sat at the other end of the table, flanked by Mr. Bennet and Colonel

Fitzwilliam. Jane was beside the colonel, and John sat between Elizabeth and Jane. Mary, Lydia, and Catherine were across from them. Lydia took her seat by Mr. Bennet and Catherine sat by Mrs. Bennet. Mary was between the two younger girls.

Before the servants began to serve the first course, Will stood and cleared his throat. Everyone looked towards him expectantly.

His smile quite shocked several of the ladies, for they had never before seen such a display of dimples from Mr. Darcy. "It is with great joy that I share with you some wonderful news. Today, Miss Elizabeth Bennet agreed to be my wife. I am blessed beyond measure. I would like to give her a lasting token of my affection while we are assembled with all of you, our closest family." He knelt beside her and said, "I give her my grandmother's – Rose Darcy's – ring and my heart." *Nana Rose, I'm so glad that you and Fitzwilliam's grandmother had the same name.* He looked up at her, smiling, as his sister, cousin, and future relations erupted into applause and congratulations. While Will slipped the delicate ring on her finger, Colonel Fitzwilliam raised his glass and proposed a toast to the couple.

Will thought everyone was quite pleased with his announcement, until he heard a faint sniffle from his left.

Had Mrs. Bennet not been so close to him, he would not have heard the noise. He returned to his seat, turning his head towards the sound, and was amazed to see Elizabeth's mother discretely dabbing at her eyes with her napkin, apparently trying to avoid attracting attention to herself.

He sat down and motioned for the butler to have the footmen start serving the soup. *Perhaps no one will notice Mrs. Bennet's tears if they are all distracted with the food, and she may stop crying if she has something else to occupy her mind.*

Will leaned toward the woman who would become, for all practical purposes, his mother. His voice was kind and concerned. "Madam, are you indisposed? What can I give you for your present relief?"

His action drew Elizabeth's attention. "Mama," she whispered across the table. "Whatever is the matter? I thought you would be happy for us."

Mrs. Bennet sniffled a little and attempted a rather watery smile. "It is the shock, I suppose. I had hoped to have you with me for another year or two at least. I do love you so, Elizabeth. I love all my children, and I cannot think of your leaving Longbourn without some degree of sadness."

Elizabeth's face was earnest. "But, Mama, we shall see each other fairly often."

Mrs. Bennet raised her reddened eyes to Will's. "Shall we? I fear not."

She must have read the letter Charlotte's maid, Martha, wrote to the Bennets' maid, her sister Ruth. I guess Mr. Bennet wasn't the only one to whom Mrs. Hancock, the housekeeper at Longbourn, showed the letter. The entire household must have been upset about it. They all know what was said in that failed proposal at Hunsford, and Fitzwilliam was very clear in expressing his low opinion of all of them.

Will gently placed his hand on the lady's shoulder. "Mrs. Bennet, let me assure you that you and all your family are always welcome to come to both Pemberley and our home in London. I hope that you will consider our homes as second homes for your family, and that you will consent to allow us to visit often at Longbourn."

Mr. Bennet saw the gesture from the other end of the table. He pushed his chair back, stood, and walked to his wife. He stepped to her right, between her and Will, and his voice was quiet as he leaned over to speak into her ear. "Marianne, my dear, are you unwell? Has anything distressed you? Shall I escort you to your chamber?"

Will dropped his hand back into his lap as Mrs. Bennet looked up at her husband, saying in a trembling voice, "Quite well, Mr. Bennet. I think I was simply overcome with astonishment at Mr.

Darcy's announcement, since I was not expecting it so soon. Are you not surprised?" She shook her head and looked at her plate. "Of course not. You have always been so clever. You have probably known of this for quite some time, and they must have talked to you about it. Mr. Darcy would not have given Elizabeth a ring without your consent, after all."

Mr. Bennet bent even closer to her and whispered, "I was not at liberty to share the news with you, Marianne, for, while I knew they were engaged this morning, I had no idea Mr. Darcy would announce it tonight." He glanced up at Will, frowning. "I suppose he was so elated at the prospect of marrying our daughter that he did not consider allowing me, her father, to proclaim the happy news to the assembly." His voice softened. "Had I known this was an engagement dinner, I would have told you." He patted her shoulder to comfort her.

As silence fell over the assembly, Elizabeth glanced at Jane in desperation, and she began to talk with Colonel Fitzwilliam. Together, they garnered the attention of the rest of the table.

Mrs. Bennet's voice was so low that Will could barely hear her next question. "Mr. Bennet, will they be happy? Are they well suited to one another?"

Mr. Bennet glanced at Will briefly, and then replied quietly to his wife, "Yes, I believe they are very well matched, and they shall do very nicely together. Rest assured that our daughter and her husband will be quite happy. I would never have consented had I not been confident on that point."

She attempted a smile, touching her hand to his. "Then I am content, and I am indeed pleased for them both. My little fit of nerves has passed, Frederick. I appreciate your concern, but you should return to your seat now. I have raised the curiosity of the other guests and likely made them uncomfortable. I shall try to make it up to Miss Darcy by not causing such scenes in future gatherings. She must have worked very hard to design such a wonderful day for us."

"Very well," Mr. Bennet answered. He patted his wife's shoulder again before he turned to fulfill her request and resume his place across from the colonel and to Georgiana's right. Soon, Will heard the older man's voice join in the conversation, though he noticed the gentleman kept a close watch on his wife for the rest of the meal.

Will was puzzled. *Why did Fitzwilliam not like this woman? She isn't mercenary at all. She loves her daughters and evidently is in no hurry to marry them off. She's certainly a little high-strung, but I would never call her vulgar. Perhaps he sensed that she didn't want to be excluded from her daughter's life, and therefore, would oppose the match. I suppose that if he was used to getting everything he wanted, he may have seen Elizabeth's family as an obstacle to his happiness. He could have called them unflattering names to avoid telling the truth. They didn't like him, and he must have known it.*

~~oo~~

After the remainder of the meal had passed with no further upset and everyone in congenial spirits, they adjourned to the large drawing room for the evening's entertainments. Will took his position beside Elizabeth on the settee as Colonel Fitzwilliam claimed his place by Jane. The younger ladies gathered around the piano, discussing which music would be diverting for the evening while Mr. Bennet selected a book from a side table and Mrs. Bennet sipped a cup of tea. John settled himself near enough to the colonel to talk of political affairs.

Thus, everyone was pleasantly occupied in pleasing conversation when a carriage drove up to the main entrance, crunching the gravel under its wheels. Georgiana went to the window and peered out. "Whoever could that be at this time of the evening? Were you expecting anyone, Brother?"

"Only Mr. Wentworth-Fitzwilliam next week." He stood and

walked to join her. "Perhaps he decided that he could no longer bear to be away from you, and he came impulsively without taking the time to write."

She frowned. "It would be unlike him to act so rashly, and he would think it discourteous to inconvenience us this late in the evening. Surely he would have stayed in Lambton and visited us here on the morrow in order to ascertain whether or not we were prepared to receive him."

Will smiled at her. "Men in love often behave strangely and out of character, Georgiana. If it is your suitor, he will be welcomed. There is plenty of room."

It was too dark for them to see who stepped out of the carriage, but the lantern light revealed that more than one person was being helped from the conveyance. Georgiana stepped back from the window.

Will remained a moment longer. *Is that a shadow, or is someone moving in the gardens beyond the carriage?* When he could not make it out, he followed his sister. *I must be imagining things.*

Georgiana spoke to the assembly. "Let us return to our activities rather than gawking out the window. Carlson will soon solve the mystery for us," she said with decorum. "Perhaps a physician was called for one of the servants, though I cannot think why I was not notified or he did not go in the entrance to the servants' quarters, if that is the case."

Will heard voices in the hallway and turned to face the sound. As Carlson opened the door, he was stunned into total silence.

Carlson's expression was perfectly correct as he announced, "Mr. Charles Wentworth-Fitzwilliam, Mr. Charles Bingley, and Miss Caroline Bingley." The butler stood by the door, awaiting instructions, as the party advanced into the silence of the room full of curious faces.

The master quickly gathered his wits about him and arranged his features into a smile, walking towards the group with his hand outstretched and Georgiana by his side. "Mr. Wentworth-Fitzwilliam, it is wonderful to meet you at last. I have heard so much about you from my sister, and all of it good."

Mr. Wentworth-Fitzwilliam bowed and had the grace to look embarrassed before he shook his host's hand. "I am sorry for disturbing you so late in the evening, Mr. Darcy, but Bingley and I happened across each other in London two days ago early in the morning, and when he heard I was to come to Pemberley next week, he insisted upon accompanying me and travelling immediately. When he relayed our plans to his sister, she expressed her wish to come as well. I wanted to stop in Lambton for the night, but they both assured me that you were all intimate friends, and you would take it amiss if we did not come directly to your home rather than staying in an inn. We left within four hours of our meeting and have barely stopped to eat and change the horses. Miss Bingley assured me that she would write to you and your sister, apprising you of my changed plans, so there was no need for me to do so. Did you not receive her letter? Before we left London, she said that the letter had already been sent express."

Well, this is awkward. Will nodded and smiled at Charles and Caroline. "The letter must have gone amiss. I shall send someone immediately to ask after the rider. He may have had some sort of accident, and I would not wish to leave it to chance that another traveller will discover him. However, we are all the best of friends, and even though I was not expecting to see you at Pemberley this summer, Bingley, you know that you are always welcome here."

Charles smiled coolly and raised an eyebrow. "Were you not? You yourself invited me before Easter to come and bring my sister. Today was to be the day of our arrival for a long summer visit." His look of concern was not convincing. "Your mind has deteriorated most shockingly, Darcy."

I have no foolproof way of knowing whether or not he's telling the truth. They did visit Pemberley in the book, but everything is so different. It seems to me that if I had invited the Bingleys earlier, they would have already been on the road and couldn't have met Charles Wentworth-Fitzwilliam in London. At any rate, even if he is lying, it makes no difference.

Will fought to keep his facial expression pleasant and his voice friendly. "Charles, you know that I suffered a riding accident in Kent. When we saw you in London, I told you that the injury to my head had affected my memories. I have no recollection of inviting you for a summer visit, but that is of no significance. We are all happy to see you arrived safely." *Forgive me, Lord, for most of us aren't excited at the prospect of a house party with Charles and Caroline. However, I am glad that they all made it here with no mishaps, and I can say the same of everyone in the room. No one would have wished for them to be injured. I've been as honest as common courtesy allows.*

Georgiana stepped forward to welcome them. After she had introduced the new arrivals to the room, and all the conventions had been satisfied, she said, "You must all be quite fatigued after such a journey." She turned to the butler, saying, "Carlson, please ask Mrs. Reynolds to order rooms prepared right away for our guests, and have Mrs. Adams to send a meal to their rooms."

He bowed and left without a word.

Charles and Caroline smiled. "Thank you, Georgiana," he said, glancing past her around the room. "This seems to be such a jolly party. I'm quite glad that we decided to come along with Mr. Wentworth-Fitzwilliam, for town had grown unbelievably dull."

Caroline nodded in agreement. "All of our close friends had left for their country estates, and with all of you here, as Mr. Wentworth-Fitzwilliam told us you would be, Netherfield would have been such a desolate place. Neither I nor my brother wished to go there for the summer. Coming to Pemberley was certainly the most attractive of all of our limited options."

Will raised an eyebrow. *Was that supposed to sound snide, or is she just naturally unpleasant?*

Caroline looked directly at Elizabeth and Jane. "My dear friends," she cooed. "It has been too long since I last saw you. We shall have to visit in the morning and exchange news. I am most eager to know everything that has happened to you both in these past weeks."

Jane smiled at her placidly. "Then allow me to share the most joyous news I have had in quite some time, Caroline." She looked at Elizabeth. "My sister and Mr. Darcy have just announced their betrothal. I expect they shall wed by the end of the summer. Perhaps you shall even be here for their nuptials."

Caroline's mouth dropped open most unbecomingly, and Colonel Fitzwilliam burst into a fit of coughing so severe that Jane began to pat his back in an effort to relieve him.

Mr. Bennet's eyes showed his enjoyment in the scene as he looked around the room.

Awkward doesn't begin to cover it, thought Will. As he looked at Mr. Bennet's expression, he remembered what the older man had said in *Pride and Prejudice*. *'For what do we live, but to make sport for our neighbours, and laugh at them in our turn?'*

Will smiled. *He's actually enjoying this. It is funny.* "Yes, just this morning Miss Elizabeth did me the great honour of accepting my proposal of marriage, and I am the happiest man alive. I shall marry her as soon as she will agree to it. I do hope all of you will stay for the wedding."

Fortunately, Mrs. Reynolds arrived at that moment to show the unexpected guests to their rooms, for only Mr. Wentworth-Fitzwilliam had had the presence of mind to wish the couple joy.

The Bingley siblings seemed grateful to have an excuse to leave the room, following behind the housekeeper, speaking of their extreme fatigue and wishes to wash the stain of travel from their persons.

Will truly hoped that the Bingleys had not heard the titters from Catherine and Lydia as the door closed. The rest of the party appeared to be determined to continue as if they had never been interrupted, and he was of the same mind.

He sighed a little. *This will be an interesting summer, I suspect. Bingley and my cousin will compete for Jane's attentions, and Caroline will try to separate me from Elizabeth. I had sworn to myself that I would not take sides between Charles and Richard, but this little escapade has shown me a different side of Bingley. Every time I've seen him since the accident, he has been rather rude and not at all similar to the happy, friendly man of Austen's book. I have to stop assuming that the book characters are like the actual people. Maybe the Charles Bingley of Pride and Prejudice isn't like the real life version and that's why he got along so well with Fitzwilliam Darcy. Jane must make her own decision, but she may not be happy if she chooses Charles. Caroline definitely will not succeed in her endeavours, and I'm beginning to hope that her brother will fail, too.*

The corners of his lips turned upward as he glanced from Jane and the colonel to Elizabeth. His movement caught her attention, and she returned his smile.

His chest expanded with happiness. *It will all work out for the best.*

CHAPTER 7

Some people are worth melting for.

Olaff in Frozen

Fitzwilliam leaned back in the comfortable chair behind his desk at Darcy Enterprises. His first week had gone very well; everyone had been extremely helpful and eager to ease him back into the office routine. His administrative assistant, Mrs. Gray, had made certain that fresh flowers were in his office, along with his favorite beverages and snacks, and she had gone over his schedule with him in meticulous detail. Her help had been invaluable to him as he learned to navigate the corporate waters. There was very little that went on at Darcy Enterprises to which Mrs. Gray was not a party.

He looked around his large, corner office with a smile. *Mrs. Gray must have talked to Mrs. Thomas,* he thought. *I doubt that my tastes are the same as Will Darcy's.*

On a table by the couch, there were a couple of pictures of a smiling couple and a little dark-haired boy. *Those must have been Will's parents. Ummm ... Very handsome couple.* He recognized a picture of Will with his Nana Rose. *That's exactly like the picture which was on my nightstand at The Oaks when I first arrived home.* He had put it in a drawer. *I think I'll leave the pictures out on display here. I need to learn more about my family in this era anyway.*

He heard a light knock on his office door. *That's unusual. Mrs. Gray usually buzzes me over the intercom.* "Come in," he said.

Mrs. Gray stepped into the room and closed the door behind her. "Mr. Darcy," she said quietly, "you have a visitor. She wishes to surprise you, so she declined to give me her name, though she is oddly familiar to me. It's possible that I met her several years ago, but I can't be sure. I did tell her about your two o'clock meeting, but she insists that you would want to see her. Shall I send her in?" He could hear a faint tone of disapproval in his secretary's voice, and he chuckled.

Mrs. Gray, like Mrs. Thomas, seeks to protect me from those who would take advantage of my position and wealth. I think I can look after myself sufficiently well against a woman who is a little more aggressive than is strictly proper. "It's fine, Mrs. Gray. Please allow her to enter."

Frowning slightly, she turned and left the room, leaving the door open behind her. Fitzwilliam heard her tell the visitor she could go in.

He stood as a perfectly proportioned woman with long, honey-blond hair glided into the room. He gestured to a chair, intending to ask her how he could be of assistance, but she cut him off by walking around his desk with her manicured hand outstretched in a position to be kissed, nails painted a glossy red.

Her black dress, while covering her body, was so form-fitting that little was left to the imagination, and his mind needed very little encouragement to fill in the details. All the faceless women he had bedded before he had switched places with Will Darcy raced through his mind, and he knew instinctively that she would have no qualms about joining that group, though she would be affronted at any mention of payment for services. *This woman wants something besides money. Power? Social position? Pictures on the society page? Surely not marriage. She cannot think I would marry her.*

Fitzwilliam took her hand and kissed it, and her green eyes glittered. After dropping her hand, he gestured to a chair in the conversation area, and she walked with feline grace in the direction he indicated. He followed her, watching her hips sway, recognizing the seductive nature of her actions and accepting it for the invitation it was. *I have acted honorably during these months, and what have I gained? I've kept my passions under control in my attempt to be more like Will, but I have nothing to show for my efforts. I've told the truth, and it has cost me dearly. If Elizabeth doesn't want me, perhaps I'll find companionship elsewhere.*

The woman draped herself across a chair, legs crossed provocatively. Her red high heels caught his notice as she swung her foot slightly. "I don't suppose you know who I am. I left here years ago, and I don't think I've seen you since I watched you play football in college. I went to a few games with my brother, but after hearing him natter on and on about how saintly you were, I left without meeting you."

As he took a seat across from her, his mind reached back to earlier conversations with his best friend. "Are you Lance's sister? He mentioned that he has a sister who lives in New York."

She smiled, revealing straight, white teeth.

"My brother actually told you he has a sister?" She laughed lightly. "I thought he'd disowned me. I've never been as good as he has, though his first year in college, I wondered if he might be more like me than he would care to admit. He was fun to be around then, once he got away from the angelic Jane Bennet." She sighed dramatically. "Ah, well. Now they're back together, and the two of them are as tiresome and boring as ever. I think they were made for each other. I could barely hold my lunch down yesterday, watching them make goo-goo eyes at each other."

He raised an eyebrow. "What brings you here, Miss Bingley?"

She leaned forward, placing an elbow over her arm on her knee and resting her chin lightly on her cupped hand. "Miss Bingley? My, my, aren't we formal? Call me Karlyn, and I'll call you whatever you want." Her voice was musical and low, with only a slight hint of her Southern drawl remaining. "I saw my brother yesterday and asked him about you. He told me to leave you alone." She laughed. "But I never was good at taking orders."

Fitzwilliam smiled in appreciation of the view she provided as his eyes slowly traced down the front of her low cut dress. "Neither am I. I've always preferred to be in charge." He paused, considering whether or not he wanted to encourage her. Finally he shrugged. *What can it hurt?* "You may call me Fitzwilliam, though your brother persists in calling me Fitz."

"How interesting." She sat up and stretched languidly, like a cat basking in the morning sun. He fully expected her to purr, and he suspected she had claws.

"Why did you leave Atlanta?" he asked.

"I moved to New York to model, and I was quite successful. I strolled all the exclusive runways and was on all the big covers." She yawned, and then smiled apologetically. "Jet lag and late nights, darling. Sorry." She pursed her lips. "Even though I established a name in the business, nothing stops the march of time. Everyone wants sweet young things now, and I passed sixteen a few years ago, so I started my own modeling agency. I'm back in Atlanta scouting out the Southern beauties for a fashion photo shoot. I'm looking for the most photogenic girls in all the major regions of the U.S."

She looked at him with lazy hunger, as if he were something to eat.

Did she just lick her lips? He raised an eyebrow. "So, you're in Atlanta on business. Splendid, but you must have misunderstood my question. I suppose I was rather vague. Let's try this again, and I shall be more specific. Why are you here – in my office?"

Her gaze intensified as she looked slowly up his body, from his feet to his face. She took her cell phone from her clutch and took a picture of him. "You're quite handsome, you know," she said, returning the phone to her purse. "Yummy, actually. All those lovely muscles, dimples, and that chiseled profile. I have no doubt there's a killer bod under that stiff suit. The camera would love you. I could include you in the Atlanta shoot." Her eyes lit up. "We could do something here, on location at Darcy Enterprises. This place just oozes macho power. I'd make it worth your while, and I guarantee that you'd enjoy it. Let me show you a good time. If you've spent all your time with Lance, you probably have no idea how much fun you can have in this stuffy old city. I know all the best clubs."

I have never before been looked at with such open lust, and I'm a man of the world. He very nearly blushed. *Somehow, it just isn't as satisfying being stalked and bagged like game as it is to win a woman by pursuing her.* He thought of how much he had enjoyed his time with Elizabeth, and the way she had let him know he was attractive without ever throwing herself at him in such an unbecoming fashion. He remembered all the days he had spent with Lance as they worked out, rode horses, and went to church. Lance was his dearest friend, and Karlyn was his sister. *What would Lance think if I entered into a carnal liaison with his sister, even if they aren't close?* He knew that Lance, as well as Mrs. Thomas, would be disappointed in him, and he made a decision. *How could a brother and sister be so different from each other? I thought I had finally avoided the advances of Caroline Bingley, but she's even more forward and bold in this century. No, it will not do.*

He stood, speaking in a detached, professional voice. "Why would I agree to have myself photographed to further your career? You surely don't think I need money, and while I don't doubt that there are other ways you could 'make it worth my while,' I think I would prefer to maintain a lower profile. I probably would enjoy myself greatly in your company, but I have so many other things on my mind right now. This is my first week back at work since my accident, and I have a meeting at two." He looked pointedly at his watch. "I really must prepare for it. Thanks for stopping by, Karlyn." He walked to the door and opened it, standing to the side.

She looked up at him in astonishment as it dawned on her that she was being dismissed, but she recovered quickly. She rose gracefully to her feet, walked over to his desk, retrieved a card from her clutch, and placed it atop on his calendar. "Here's all my contact information, just in case you change your mind. Maybe you're more like my brother than I thought." She shook her head and gave him another scorching, head-to-toe look. "What a waste."

Karlyn picked up one of his cards and put it in her purse. On her way out, she stopped to reach up and kiss him on the cheek. "Call me," she whispered. "I promise you won't regret it. Forget about the pictures. I suspect you're the type of man who doesn't like to sit still that long, anyway."

He closed the door as soon as she exited, and all that was left was the smell of her perfume.

"Don't hold your breath," he said into the empty room.

Fitzwilliam had been studying his notes for a quarter hour when his telephone rang. Seeing that the line his assistant used for private conversation with him was lit, he picked up. She used that line when she wanted to avoid having him on speaker phone in front of anyone else.

"Yes, Mrs. Gray?"

"You have a visitor, Mr. Darcy."

"I have a meeting in just over half an hour. Who is it?"

"The visitor wants to surprise you, Mr. Darcy."

Her voice sounds cheerful, so it must not be someone I wish to avoid. Maybe it's Lance or Mrs. Thomas. I can think of no one else who would come here. He straightened the papers on his desk. "Very well. I suppose I can spare a few moments."

He looked up as the door opened. Elizabeth stood in the doorway, dressed in a simple yellow sundress, brown curls cascading down her back. She was holding a bag in one hand and a covered drink cup in the other. The contrast between her and Karlyn was stark. *She is lovely. No tight, provocative clothes or heavy makeup. She is naturally beautiful.* His heart softened toward her. He wanted to touch her. *I miss her.*

"Am I interrupting you?" she asked.

He stood and walked quickly around his desk to meet her. "Not at all."

She swallowed visibly. "I thought you may not have had lunch yet, so I brought you what you usually order from Murphy's. If you don't have time, I understand. I should've called first. I was driving by the restaurant and thought of you, so I took a chance and stopped in."

As she looked at him, examining his face, her expression changed.

What in blazes is wrong with her? What have I done now?

She walked past him, placed the food on his desk, and turned to leave. He caught her arm as she tried to pass him.

"Wait, Elizabeth." He tried to think of the right words – the ones which would make her stay. "I appreciate the food. Will you not sit and eat it with me?"

She looked at the floor. "No, I can see that you're busy. You've probably already eaten anyway."

"I haven't eaten with you. Please don't go. I've missed you."

She turned her face up to his with resignation.

"Your face says otherwise, Fitzwilliam."

"What? I have no idea what you mean."

"Then look in a mirror," she replied sharply. "I recognize the color, because I just talked to the underdressed woman wearing that shade in your lobby. I didn't want to believe her when she said you two were dating and she had stopped by for a little 'afternoon delight,' but I guess she was telling the truth." Her expression was pained. "It hasn't even been a week, and you've already moved on."

He dropped his hand from her arm.

Afternoon delight? What does that mean, and what do you think I did with that woman? I shouldn't have to defend myself. I did nothing wrong. Fitzwilliam, annoyed by her lack of confidence in him, replied angrily, "You were the one who walked away from me. How has this become my fault?"

She stood very still, as if willing herself not to run away. "I know that I should have stayed and talked further with you, Fitzwilliam, but I was too upset to think straight. I thought that I should leave before I said something we would both regret, but I did text you, and you never replied."

"You texted, 'I'm sorry.' What did that mean? Were you sorry that you left? Were you sorry that you couldn't bring yourself to believe me? Exactly what were you sorry for, Elizabeth?"

She crossed her arms. "It doesn't matter now, anyway. I refuse to compete with Karlyn Bingley for your attention. If that's the sort of woman you want, we don't belong together." Her voice held a note of finality.

And again, she does not trust me. "If that is your opinion of me, perhaps we are not suited for one another."

She let her arms fall by her sides as she started to leave, but then she turned back to face him. "I'm not walking away again with unanswered questions in my mind, though I know I have no right to ask them."

He nearly smiled. "Excellent idea. Ask your questions. I would relish an opportunity to answer them rather than seeing your back as you walk away from me for the second time in a week."

"Why was Karlyn Bingley here?'

"She wanted me to model with women for some sort of photographs."

"What did you tell her?"

"I told her no. No to the photographs and no to anything else she had in mind."

Elizabeth's expression softened. "You didn't – *do* – anything with her?"

He released an exasperated sigh. "You really do think I'm a lunatic, don't you? Of course, I didn't *do* anything with that woman. That was the first time I ever met her, and I will be a happy man if it's the last."

"Then why did she say that you two were a couple?"

He rolled his eyes. "To borrow a modern expression from Lance, 'duh.' She lied. People like her are continually dishonest. She wanted to make herself seem important, or she saw you as competition – just as you saw her, by the way – or she's merely a habitual liar. She probably enjoys the drama and problems she leaves in her wake. I told her no, so she got back at me by planting doubt in your mind about me. She said she has talked to Lance. He may have told her we were dating. She probably wanted to cause trouble for us, and she did."

"She had your card."

"She took it from my desk."

"Her card is on your desk."

"She put it there."

"Did you kiss her?"

"No. I never touched her at all voluntarily. She reached her hand out to me, placing it practically under my nose, so I kissed it. To do otherwise would have been rude." He grimaced. *Tell her the whole truth.* "To be perfectly honest, I thought I had lost you, and I did briefly entertain thoughts of amusing myself with her. However, after a few moments in her presence, I reached the conclusion that I would rather be alone than with her. There was a time in my life when I could have indulged in such a dalliance with no guilt, but I fear that time has passed. You, Lance, Mrs. Thomas, and Pastor Franks have worked a change in me."

She was silent for a few moments, and then she looked up again, watching his face. "Did *she* kiss *you*?"

Fitzwilliam knew that her question was a test of some sort, so he thought back through the time he had spent with Karlyn in detail before he answered. "Ah! I had forgotten that. Just before she left, she kissed me on the cheek and told me to call her."

Elizabeth smiled for the first time since she had arrived. "She kissed you, and you forgot it?"

He returned her smile. "It was not memorable, unlike the moments I've spent with you."

"You've never kissed me."

"Exactly. Holding you close to me meant more to me than her kiss." He reached for her, and she walked into his arms. *This is so natural and right. It's as if she belongs here.* He bent his head to kiss her hair, enjoying the enticing scent of her, wondering if she would accept a kiss from him. *Not now. Not a hurried kiss in my office before I must rush away to a meeting.*

After a few moments, his intercom buzzed.

"Mr. Darcy," said Mrs. Gray apologetically. "Don't forget your meeting. You have ten minutes."

They broke apart. He walked to his desk and pushed the button. "I'll be right there, Mrs. Gray. Thank you."

He turned around, surprised to see Elizabeth standing not a foot away, holding a tissue. She began to dab at his face.

"What are you doing?" he asked.

She laughed. "I can't send you to a meeting with a big, red lipstick kiss on your cheek. They'll all wonder what you've been doing … and with whom you've been doing it."

He took her hands in his. "So you knew all along that she'd kissed me. Why did you ask?"

"You obviously didn't know that when a person wearing lipstick kisses you, it leaves a mark. I wanted to see if you'd tell me the truth."

"And I did."

"You told me more than that. You told me you don't know things that modern men know. Even young teen males know that lipstick leaves an imprint. Little boys know it, too. You didn't grow up in this era. You've been telling the truth all along. I'm sorry."

"You're sorry? What does that mean?" He thought he knew what she meant, but he wanted to be certain.

"It means the same thing it meant when I texted it to you. It means that I'm sorry I ever doubted you. I'm sorry I walked away. I'll never walk away from you again without finishing a conversation. That said, you have a meeting, so I have to go."

She began to pull her hands from his, but he held on.

"I am the 'Darcy' in Darcy Enterprises. They work for me, and they can wait a moment. Can I see you tonight?"

"Just the two of us?"

He smiled. "Just the two of us."

"Then I'll pick you up here," she answered.

His facial expression was comical. "*You'll* pick *me* up? Why?"

She laughed. "You have taken two or three driving lessons from Lance. I think I'm more qualified to drive than you are at this point."

So she has asked Lance about me? I wonder if he talked to her about the time-switch thing, too. She certainly changed her mind quickly. "Lance dropped me off at work today. I've hired a driving instructor, but I don't drive in Atlanta yet. However, I can hire a car and driver for tonight if you wish."

She chuckled. "You hired a driving instructor? I haven't heard anyone say that since I was fifteen. What time shall I come by for you?"

He bit the inside of his lip, trying not to smile. *She is adorable.* "Would six fit into your schedule?"

"Perfectly."

"Then six is good. Dress up. I want to take you to a special place."

She stood on her tiptoes and kissed his cheek. "Any place with you is special."

She kissed me! He touched his cheek. "Why did you do that?"

Her eyes sparkled with humor. "Well, duh, Fitzwilliam. I was marking my territory. You didn't really think I'd leave you with the memory of Karlyn's kiss being the last you'd received, did you? I want you to remember me for the rest of the day."

She turned and made a show of flouncing from the room, leaving him laughing.

He went to his desk to retrieve his papers for his meeting, and he saw Karlyn's card. He ripped it into tiny pieces and threw them into his trashcan.

I could never forget you, Elizabeth, and Lord knows, I've tried.

CHAPTER 8

Once exposed, a secret loses all its power.

Ann Aguirre, Grimspace

As Will and Elizabeth were breaking their fasts the following morning, Carlson approached the young master and spoke quietly into his ear. "Mr. James Wright is here to see you, sir."

Will spoke at a normal volume. *I will have no secrets from Elizabeth.* "Do I know him, Carlson? I have no recollection of the name."

"Yes, sir. He has often been here at Pemberley, and I think you meet him in London as well. He is an employee of yours. Since you usually meet with him privately, shall I show him to your study?"

"Yes, that will do," replied Will quietly. "Have coffee and tea sent in for us and tell the gentleman I shall join him shortly."

After Carlson nodded and left the room, Will looked at Elizabeth. "It appears that I have a guest, dearest. I'm confident that someone will soon join you, or I would tell the man he could wait until a more decent hour. I dislike leaving you alone, and I am unhappy at losing my few moments with you without a houseful of people surrounding us. However, he may be here on an important matter, and since he is here so early, I fear that it may be urgent."

She placed her hand on his arm. "It is of little significance, Will. We shall be together all day, and if you finish your business now, you will not be distracted later. I shall not be alone for long, though the other ladies do not rise as early as I. In fact, I am amazed that my father and Colonel Fitzwilliam are not already here."

As if by design, the two men walked into the room.

Will stood. "Good morning, gentlemen. I have a visitor waiting for me in my study. If you will keep Miss Elizabeth company in my absence, I would be most obliged to you."

Mr. Bennet nodded and walked to the sideboard to select his food. Colonel Fitzwilliam, however, raised an eyebrow at Will.

"Who is calling at this ungodly hour?"

"A gentleman by the name of James Wright," answered Will. "Are you acquainted with him?"

"I have been privy to several meetings between you and the gentleman," he answered.

Richard's expression changed when I said the man's name. "Would you join us, then? I may need your help, especially since I have no memory of him at all."

The colonel nodded. "Perhaps Mr. Bennet will entertain Miss Elizabeth until we return?"

"Certainly," the older man replied. "I welcome any time to visit with my daughter."

Elizabeth smiled brightly at her father.

"Shall I have Carlson bring in your meal, Colonel?" she asked, glancing up at the gentleman. "I am not yet lady of the house, but I do not think Georgiana would take it amiss."

"Thank you, yes," said the colonel. "Mr. Wright may appreciate a meal as well, and I see that Will has not finished his food."

"I shall send plenty for all of you," she said.

Will smiled at her. "Thank you, my dear. I hope our business may be concluded promptly so that we are able to rejoin the party before long." He leaned over and spoke softly into her ear. "We shall discuss this later. Whatever he tells me, you will know."

She nodded as he stood. After Will had bestowed one last smile on her, he and Colonel Fitzwilliam bowed and left the room.

~~oo~~

Will opened his study door to find a man an inch or two shy of his own height. He was wearing a plain, shabby coat and standing with his back to him, facing the fireplace, holding a dusty hat in his hand. He turned at the sound of hinges, nodding and bowing.

Will strode across the room and extended his hand to the visitor. After a moment, an obviously puzzled Mr. Wright shook his employer's hand. He then used both of his hands to grip the edge of his well-worn hat.

Two maids carrying trays laden with coffee, tea, and assorted breakfast foods followed closely behind their master. They placed the trays on the table between the couches, curtseyed, and left the room.

"Have you eaten yet this morning, Mr. Wright?" asked Will.

Mr. Wright shook his head slightly, a surprised look on his face.

Will continued, gesturing toward the table. "Colonel Fitzwilliam has not yet broken his fast either. Please help yourself to food and drink."

Wright's jaw dropped open before he managed to recover and nod. "Thank you, sir. 'Tis early to be sure, and I came away from the inn at Lambton without so much as a morsel. You always wanted my reports before the rest of the house stirred, and I try to make certain that you are pleased with my work."

So Fitzwilliam actually wanted the poor man to be here at the break of dawn. His curiosity was piqued. *What in the world was he trying to hide from Georgiana and the servants?*

Will looked pointedly at the colonel, eyebrows raised.

Colonel Fitzwilliam smiled as he walked to the couch and sat down. He then busied himself with filling his plate. Mr. Wright followed the colonel's lead, electing to sit on the couch across the table from him, placing his hat beside him on the cushion and selecting his food quickly. Will watched both of them as he took the seat beside his cousin.

The colonel glanced up at the man. "What have you to tell us of Wickham's movements, Wright?"

Will leaned forward. *Wickham! This man must be a private investigator hired by Fitzwilliam whom Richard mentioned in the carriage.* He poured himself a cup of coffee to mask his agitation. *If the investigator is here to give an update, Wickham must have done something worthy of reporting.*

"Wickham has been a very busy man since he left Meryton in disgrace," said Wright. "He went straight to Hunsford and skulked about. I even saw him go into the servants' entrance of Rosings once or twice."

Rosings? Why would Wickham go to Rosings? "Has he been often at Rosings in the past?" asked Will.

Wright nodded. "He goes there two or three times a year, Mr. Darcy, as I've told you before. None of the servants appear to know why, though I saw him with the former steward, Stevens, a few times, and they seemed very chummy. A scullery maid once told me he meets with Lady Catherine herself, but I have no way of knowing whether or not that is true. She could have been repeating gossip. The above stairs servants at Rosings can be uppity, and they tend to protect the family. If I dig around too much there, they'll be suspicious."

Why would Wickham meet with Stevens or Lady Catherine? "So you have no idea of his business there?"

"No, sir," answered Wright. "But he appeared to be flush with money when he left. He stayed at the inn in the village a couple of nights before he left for London, and he was mighty free at the gaming tables and with the drinks and women. He didn't leave no bills unpaid neither."

Colonel Fitzwilliam uncrossed his legs and leaned forward. "Where did he go in London?"

"He made straight for the Bank of England. I followed him in and saw that he cashed a cheque. He left there with a bag of money and went to a hotel to put up for a few nights. The next day he visited a tailor and several gentlemen's clubs." He took a sip of coffee. "I saw him sneaking around your house, too, Mr. Darcy. One of your maids let him in the back door. The girl was friendlier with him than your housekeeper, Mrs. Evans, would like."

Darcy narrowed his eyes. "What was the maid's name?"

"Abigail, sir. I did some footwork and found out that she's sisters with Martha, Mrs. Collins's maid, and Ruth, a maid at Longbourn. She found her way to London to work as an above stairs maid for Madeline Gardiner, sister to Mrs. Bennet, but took a position in your kitchen when Mrs. Gardiner asked her to leave. The girl took quite a step down in pay to do it, too, so she must have really wanted to be in your house. She certainly didn't do it for more money or a promotion, as she took a lower job with less money and little chance of moving up."

Something stinks about all this. "Why was she let go by the Gardiners, and how did she get the position in my home?"

Mr. Wright grimaced. "The rumours are that she was seen in the company of a young man when she was supposed to be attending the Gardiner children on a walk in the park. Fortunately, Mr. Gardiner went looking for his children when they were late returning home, and he found them alone but recovered them safely. When he got home, he went to his wife straightaway, and as soon as the maid came in the back door, Mrs. Gardiner had her called directly to her sitting room and let her go. As far as how the girl came to be in your employ, Mr. Darcy, your Mrs. Evans is a fine lady, but it seems she's always had a soft spot for Mr. Wickham. I heard that he asked Mrs. Evans to take her on, and she did it as a personal favour to him."

"Why would Wickham intervene for her?" asked Colonel

Fitzwilliam.

Wright chuckled. "I believe he was the man the maid was with when she neglected the children. Though nobody at the Gardiner house saw him, and he must have somehow sneaked passed me to go there, the smallest Gardiner girl was rattling on about 'Wicky man.' I heard her myself as I was walking by Mr. Gardiner and his brood. I suppose since Wickham got her sacked, he thought he should get her another job."

The image of little Sarah Gardiner's innocent face came into Darcy's mind, and he remembered carrying her while she slept. He was angered at the thought that a careless maid had put her in danger and exposed her to such a man as Wickham. "I will contact Mrs. Evans posthaste. If Wickham is the one who procured the position for Abigail, the maid will need to seek other employment immediately. I shall not have his mole in my household." *What if the girl agreed to let Wickham in the house when Georgiana is there?* He blanched. *What if he took it into his head to hurt Elizabeth or her sisters right in my own home? There is no end to the mischief he could do. I shall have to tell Mrs. Evans that he is not allowed on the grounds at all. I'll speak to Harrison and Mrs. Watson as well. The senior staff should all be made aware of my feelings concerning Wickham.*

Colonel Fitzwilliam frowned. "Perhaps Wickham set all of it up. He may have arranged an assignation with the maid in order to make her lose her position. That way, he could use his friendship with Mrs. Evans to have her installed in your house, Will. Rather than realize that he caused her to lose her position, she might even feel indebted to him for getting her another."

He would be that devious. "Is he still in London, Mr. Wright?"

He shook his head. "No, Mr. Darcy. I followed him here to Derbyshire. He met Stevens in the inn at Lambton a couple of days ago, and they were like long-lost brothers, drinking and talking about how you'd mistreated both of them. Stevens said you're a thief and that you lied to Lady Catherine about him. He said he lost the stewardship position at Rosings because of you. Wickham said you cheated him out of a living, and he has a plan to get even with you. Stevens was eager to help him. They're up to no good for sure, Mr. Darcy."

He's here? Bent on revenge? "Is he still at the inn?"

Wright nodded. "He's been creeping around the grounds here at Pemberley, too, Mr. Darcy. I followed him here and saw him last night, just as that carriage pulled in. He was caught in the light of the lantern."

The shadow I saw. It was Wickham! "Where are you staying?"

"I have a room in the inn, but I could sleep in your barn if you want."

The barn? Has he often had to sleep in barns? Will looked closely at the man. He took in the shabbiness of his dress and the tired lines around his eyes. He noticed how much he had eaten and drunk. *This man was hungry, and it's my fault.* "Have I paid you recently?" he asked kindly.

Wright looked at his feet, and Will's eyes were drawn to his worn shoes. "Well, no, sir," said Wright, "but I heard you were in an accident that caused you to forget things. I knew you'd set things to rights sooner or later. We have a long history together, and you've always paid your debts."

So he didn't ask for his money. He patiently waited, still doing his job while he went hungry. Will spoke with authority. "Mrs. Reynolds will find you a room in the servants' quarters, and you can eat with them. I shall talk with Mr. Miller concerning your back pay, and we shall clear up this matter today. If you have need of a fresh horse, the head groomsman – " He looked towards his cousin.

"Mr. Hill," interjected Colonel Fitzwilliam.

"Mr. Hill will provide one for you. Do you have any clothes other than those you're wearing?" asked Will.

Mr. Wright's face flushed red. "I have a nicer set for church."

Will was quiet for a moment. "I shall instruct Austen to see if any of my older clothing can be altered for you. Much of what I wore before the accident is too small for me now, but there is nothing wrong with it. I have closets full of perfectly good clothes which should be put to better use. After all, you may need to be inconspicuous by dressing up instead of down in some instances, though the clothing you're wearing now insures that you will be unnoticed in other situations."

The man's expression was so grateful that Will felt guilty he had not thought of his condition sooner.

Wright inclined his head. "Thank you, sir. I'm not too proud to accept your generous offer of food, clothing, and shelter. I've always thought you were the best of men. Now, begging your leave, sir, I'll go to the inn and collect my bits. I'll be back very soon, but first I shall ask around about Wickham and Stevens." He stood to his feet and retrieved his hat from the cushion beside him.

Will and Colonel Fitzwilliam also arose. After Wright had bowed to both men, he left the study.

The colonel smiled at Will. "That was well done, Cousin. You do remember that you owe him a tremendous debt, do you not?"

Will nodded. "Yes, Richard. You told me not so long ago that Mr. Wright had followed Wickham to Bath and reported seeing him with Georgiana. Had he not done that, Fitzwilliam would never have gone there, thus preventing the scoundrel from eloping with Georgiana. In light of how much we owe the man, I cannot understand why Fitzwilliam did not take better care of him." He exhaled with force. "Our stable boys and scullery maids are better dressed and fed than that poor soul. For heaven's sake, he was starving. Did you note how much he ate? The tray is practically empty. There is no excuse for that when he worked so faithfully for the Darcy family." He raked his hand through his hair. "I am thoroughly ashamed."

"Do not chastise yourself for something that was not your fault. Fitzwilliam paid him the going rate for men in his profession. He thought he was being generous and fair; he had not your kindness of heart," the colonel said gently. "To his mind, Wright was beneath him and fortunate to be working for such an august personage as himself," he continued, shaking his head a little. "Fitzwilliam actually thought, along with Aunt Catherine, that the distinction of rank should be preserved in that way. To his way of thinking, Wright's clothes were good enough for him. Our family thought he deserved no better."

"Because of an accident of birth?" Will's voice was incredulous. "Wright was not born into the landed gentry, and for that he deserves to be cold in the winter and hungry most of the time? If he were a ne'er-do-well, I might understand, but he does his job with pride, and he appears to be quite good at it. I was ashamed to offer him my discarded clothing, but I feared that offering to buy him new clothes would be offensive to him and possibly raise too many eyebrows. A private investigator surely must not attract too much attention."

Colonel Fitzwilliam patted Will's shoulder. "You are making it right, so let it go. Do not be so hard upon yourself."

Will swallowed hard. "I wonder how many more people there are who work for me and are treated the way he was. Things shall not continue in this fashion."

The colonel smiled. "Then perhaps we should begin to ride this estate for a couple of hours each morning before the ladies arise and are dressed for the day's pleasures. There is much work to be done at Pemberley. I have long been distressed at the state of the tenants' houses, but Fitzwilliam would not be bothered."

Will nodded slightly. "I will have to give up my only private minutes with Elizabeth, but she would agree that this is important. I shall talk to her about it today."

"Perhaps she could ride with us?"

"I thought she did not enjoy riding horseback," answered Will.

"While it is true that she prefers her morning walks, she may agree to ride if you offer to teach her. We shall go at her speed and make certain of her safety."

Will smiled. "Do you think Mr. Bennet would ride with us?"

Colonel Fitzwilliam laughed. "I would imagine it would be difficult to stop him. He obviously thinks he is the best chaperone for the two of you."

"Then I could grow to know him better while doing something worthwhile and necessary."

"Exactly so, and Miss Elizabeth may have some good suggestions as to the best methods of improving the lives of your tenants. Mr. Bennet may learn more about estate management while he rides with us. Before your accident in Kent, you told me about your stay in Hertfordshire and said that Longbourn could do with some improvements."

Will was silent for a moment. "I shall ask Mr. Justice Miller to ride with us. I feel certain that he has more knowledge of the estate than I do, and I value his opinions."

"Perhaps now is a good time to share this plan with Miss Elizabeth and Mr. Bennet, before everyone else comes downstairs."

All of them might want to go with us – Charles and Caroline! "I think you have the right of it, Cousin. Let us go back to the breakfast parlour and see if Elizabeth and her father are still there."

"Excellent plan. You are not the only one who knows the Scriptures, you know. According to Ecclesiastes, 'Whatever your hand finds to do, do it with all your might, for in the realm of the dead, where you are going, there is neither working nor planning nor knowledge nor wisdom.'"

Will gave a low laugh. "The first part of the verse is more encouraging and applicable than the last. I believe it refers to Sheol – the grave, or, as we call it, hell."

The colonel snorted. "Truly? Aunt Catherine used that verse many, many times as we grew up. I never knew she was saying that we were on our way to hell."

"Do not feel foolish, Cousin. I doubt that she understood what it meant, for she would never think a Darcy or a Fitzwilliam could ever inhabit hell. That place would surely be reserved for less exalted personages."

Colonel Fitzwilliam pursed his lips. "Though in her case . . ."

"Do not think it," answered Will. "I have to hope that redemption is possible for anyone – even our Aunt Catherine."

They both chuckled as they left the room, intent upon their conversation with Mr. Bennet and his daughter.

CHAPTER 9

I think most of the time when people have big disagreements and big misunderstandings, when time lessens that blow it creates a deeper understanding for both people.

Amos Lee

Just before six o'clock, Fitzwilliam was waiting for the elevator at Darcy Enterprises, anticipating a romantic evening with Elizabeth. Seeing his reflection in the metal doors, he adjusted his tie with one hand and checked his watch, fidgeting. *I'll be with her in a few minutes. Finally, she knows the truth and accepts me as I am. I don't have to keep secrets from her any longer. I can be myself and not worry about losing her. Maybe she can learn to love me now that she truly understands me.*

His plan to meet her in the lobby was forgotten when the doors opened and she stood before him. She had always been beautiful to him, but he could tell that she had taken special care with her appearance, and he appreciated that the extra effort was for him alone. Normally, she wore very little make-up and let her hair wander down her back in layered waves, but she had curled it for their date, and the effect was so soft and inviting that he wanted to touch it. He wanted to hold her hair and feel its weight, to watch it

93

slide through his fingers like silk, to smell her shampoo.

He had rarely seen her in anything except casual clothing, and he had always loved her natural beauty; however, this evening she had actually dressed to impress, and he was speechless with admiration. *Words would spoil this moment.*

She had chosen to wear flowing chiffon pants in a beige and black chevron pattern with a black fitted blouse of the same material which came just below her waist, emphasizing how slender and shapely she was. The sleeveless top featured a man's tie knotted loosely, and the masculine touch accentuated her femininity. Her cosmetics, while not heavy, made her brown eyes seem huge and her skin luminous, her lashes long and thick. He couldn't stop looking at her.

Fitzwilliam stepped into the elevator with her and mutely handed her the rose he had bought from the downstairs gift shop. She smiled and smelled the flower before she pushed the parking lot button. His gift seemed puny in comparison to her loveliness, but, to his regret, he hadn't had time to shop for anything else.

He was fortunate that he always dressed in a suit and tie for work, and that Mrs. Gray had insisted he keep several fresh dress shirts and ties in his office closet in case he spilled anything on himself at lunch. There hadn't been enough time to shave again, but he had noticed that some men wore a little stubble intentionally, so he hadn't worried about his five o'clock shadow.

She cleared her throat delicately, and he realized that he hadn't yet spoken to her. Before he could think of anything to say, she said, "Thank you for the rose, Fitzwilliam. I know you were busy. It was very sweet of you to think of me."

I have had considerable trouble thinking of anything else. He smiled. "I am never too busy for you, though I admit freely that having you with me at the office would prevent me from accomplishing very much."

Her eyes sparkled with mischief. "Well, I guess I shouldn't drop by with lunch again. I'd hate to keep you from your work with my endless chatter."

"No," he said, taking her hand. "You know that's not what I meant. You distract me in a good way. When you're with me, I just want to be close to you. I don't want to think about numbers and spreadsheets. I don't wish to read scholarship applications or grant requests and decide which person or cause is more worthy than another to receive funding. The work is important, of course, but there's an endless stream of it."

"So I should stay away?" she asked, looking up at him with laughter in her eyes.

"No," he insisted. "Perhaps if you were with me more I would adjust to having you close by." He rubbed his thumb over the top of her hand. *I want to kiss that little smirk from her lips.*

Her expression encouraged his mind to continue to wander forbidden paths, and her next words did nothing to help his mind settle into acceptable conversational patterns. "Oh, so you'll get used to me, and you'll be better able to ignore me."

She plans to be with me enough that I will tire of her? The thought is ridiculous, but I like that she is looking toward a future with me in it.

He shook his head slightly. "Your beauty will always secure my attentions, but I'll learn to manage it better if you're around me more often." He smiled. "I think I've made a very good argument for seeing more of you, not less."

She laughed. "You *would* think so."

He touched her shiny dark hair softly with his free hand. "You look especially beautiful tonight, Elizabeth." His voice caressed the words.

"I tried a little harder than I usually do. You said to dress up, and I didn't want you to be embarrassed to be seen with me."

"Elizabeth, you really should stop teasing me before I kiss you right here in the elevator," he warned, his voice a low growl.

She opened her eyes wide in astonishment. "But the elevator could stop at any floor, and someone might see us."

"Hardly anyone else is here, and I truly don't care if we are seen." His eyes gleamed. *Dare me if you will.*

"You're well known." She looked down at the floor. "I used to see you in the society pages and on the news before you had your accident, though it was common knowledge that you were a very private person. There was never any hint of scandal attached to your name. People would love to get a picture of you in an unguarded moment and try to make something of it."

"I've always been mystified at the curiosity people display concerning the business of others. It seems that the ease of communication in this era encourages such familiarity. Celebrities actually use the social media to promote themselves constantly in ways which do not portray them in a positive light. I don't understand it."

She looked up at him. "So, I take it you wouldn't want anyone to get a picture of us kissing and splash it across Twitter, Facebook, and Instagram."

He shook his head. "You completely misunderstand me, Elizabeth. I'm merely expressing my astonishment at the way people put their most private moments on public media for others to see and discuss. However, I am not concerned about photographers taking pictures of us. I probably wouldn't post photographs myself, but I truly am not worried about our relationship becoming public knowledge."

"We have a relationship?" she asked, smiling.

His gaze was serious and intense. "Do you want a relationship?"

She tilted her head. "What kind of relationship are we talking about?"

He raised an eyebrow. "What kind do you wish for?"

She looked at their hands, still linked together. "This is a heavy conversation for a short ride."

What does that mean? How can words be heavy? Perhaps she means the subject matter is too weighty to discuss in so little time. If so, I shall wait and come back to the subject at dinner.

The car came to a stop, and the doors retracted, revealing the parking lot beneath the building. He stood aside and gestured for her to leave the elevator before him. She retrieved her keys from her small shoulder bag as she walked.

Her car was parked in his spot. "Lance told me where to leave my car and gave me a card that would open the gate." She pointed her key at the car to unlock the doors.

Fitzwilliam opened her car door for her. After she was settled, he walked around the car to slide into the passenger seat.

"You talked to Lance today? He failed to mention that when I called him."

"He called me after the two of you talked." She fastened her seatbelt and started the car. "Since he wasn't going to drive you home after work, he and Jane made plans. We're supposed to meet them back at the townhouse after our dates. He's going to drive you back to The Oaks."

I should have thought of that. "That's a good idea. I hadn't realized until just now that you would've had to drive to The Oaks and then back into Atlanta late at night. I should have made arrangements myself to prevent that from happening. I am a selfish being."

She reached across the console and covered his hand with hers. "Fitzwilliam, we just planned this a few hours ago, and you've been in meetings since then. You didn't really have time to think of everything. You bought me this rose, and I hope you made reservations for dinner. That's enough. Don't be so hard on yourself."

"I bought the rose from the gift shop, but Mrs. Gray handled the reservations for me. We're going to Kevin Rathbun's, if that's to your liking. She wrote down the address for me in case you need to use your GPS." He took a slip of paper from his jacket pocket and handed it to her.

She took the paper, removing her hand from his, and looked at the location. "I think I know where this is. I've wanted to go there for a long time. Everyone raves about how great their steaks are."

"Mrs. Gray said that it was highly recommended. She also said that I've been there many times before, so I had to tell her about my 'memory loss.' Mrs. Thomas had already warned her that the injury to my head had caused me to forget my previous life, so she readily understood." He watched Elizabeth as she backed out of the parking space and maneuvered her way to the gate.

"What shall I do if I see people who knew Will? I will have no recollection of them." His voice betrayed his anxiety.

"You've met the people on the board of Darcy Enterprises." She glanced at him. "You also know church members, and the doctors and nurses from the hospital. You told me your lawyers came to visit you, too. I'll bet you know more people than you think you do."

She used her card to open the gate. After it lifted, she pulled out into traffic.

"You may be right, but, all the same, I wish to sit in a secluded area. I would like for us to have a chance to talk privately. Besides, it would be embarrassing to have old friends come up to me and see my blank expression." He sighed. "I've grown used to having Lance help me with those situations, I fear."

She glanced at him and then back at the road. "I've lived here all of my life, Fitzwilliam. I probably know as many people as Lance does, even though his blood is quite a bit bluer than mine. I can probably help you more than you realize."

"Lance's blood is blue?"

Elizabeth laughed. "The term 'blue blooded' refers to the nobility or higher classes. Lance comes from a very old, extremely wealthy family."

"And you don't?"

She pursed her lips. "The Bennet family can be traced back as far as the Bingleys, but we are not really rich. My family is quite comfortable, but we don't run with the country club set."

He watched the traffic around them. "The Bennet family I knew were landowners, while the Bingleys were one generation removed from trade. The Bennets had the higher social standing, though the Bingleys had more money."

"You're talking about *Pride and Prejudice*, aren't you?" She frowned a little.

He nodded. "Much of that really happened, you know."

"You can't be certain of that. According to what I understand, you switched places with Will just after you delivered the letter to my counterpart in Hunsford."

"I hadn't thought of that! You're absolutely correct. I can be certain only of what happened while I was there, and there was still at least half the story to be told when I came here. I have no idea what took place after I left. The letters I've received from Will have been mostly letters of encouragement with no real details."

She hit the brakes so hard that he was thrown against his seatbelt. Fortunately, they were approaching a stop light, and the cars behind them had already begun to slow down. A moment later, she had pulled up a safe distance from the car in front of them.

She looked over at him with a stony expression.

What have I done now?

"Why are you staring at me like that?" he asked.

"You just said you have letters from Will. Is that some sort of a joke?"

She sounds almost angry.

"Well, I do. I got my first one when I was in the hospital, and I've received several since that time. He left them with his lawyers to be delivered to me at specific times. Why are you upset with me?" He was truly puzzled and felt the stirrings of aggravation himself.

Her voice held a note of exasperation. "Why didn't you tell me you had those letters when you told me your time-switch story? If you had proof, real hard evidence, that what you were telling me was true, why didn't you say so?"

He looked at her, and the pain of her rejection came back with a vengeance. He saw her walking away again in his mind, and he lived it over and over. "I wished for you to believe me on my own merits. I thought if you truly cared for me, I shouldn't have to prove that I was telling you the truth, but it seems I was wrong. Mrs. Thomas and Lance wanted me to show you my letters, and Mrs. Thomas was willing to show you hers, as well, but I refused."

"Mrs. Thomas has letters, too?"

"Yes, as well as Will's grandmother. I understand that you can have the paper and ink analyzed and dated. I feel certain that specialists can prove that the letters are over two hundred years old."

During the oppressive silence which followed, the light changed, and traffic began to move again. Neither Elizabeth nor Fitzwilliam spoke a word, brooding over the situation until they were parked to the side of the restaurant, choosing to be alone rather than use the valet parking.

She turned off the car, pulled the keys from the ignition, and put them in her purse. She took a deep breath and looked at him, tears filling her eyes. "I can't believe you let me suffer for nearly a week when you could have prevented it by simply showing me the letters. How could you do that if you cared about me at all?"

He stared at her. "*You* suffered? You didn't watch me walk away from you. And had you asked for proof instead of choosing to believe that I was truly a lunatic, I would have given it to you. Do you remember what you said to me? Think about it. You said that I was delusional and beyond help." He swallowed hard, forcing the liquid past the knot in his throat. "I would have shown you everything if you had exhibited the tiniest spark of faith in me. I wanted you to trust me, to believe me, just the smallest bit, but you would not. You walked away, Elizabeth, not I."

She clasped her hands in her lap so tightly that her knuckles were white. The tears spilled from her eyes and fell on her hands. "I'm good at that," she said quietly. "I'm the damaged one,

Fitzwilliam. Do you really want to be with me?"

He pulled his handkerchief from his coat pocket and reached across the console to dab her cheeks. "Neither of us is perfect, and, may God help me, I think I love you. So, yes, I want to be with you."

She looked up at him, trying to smile through her tears. "No one apart from my family and a few friends has ever loved me before."

"I think the same can be said of me, apart from a few family servants. I was not very lovable, it seems. And what is worse is that everyone loved Will, and I have taken his place. I'm not Will, and I never will be."

"Then maybe we're perfect for each other. Following Jane was not easy either. I think Will must have been the male version of her."

He grinned at her crookedly. "Is that so? You've never felt good enough?"

"No, I haven't. I could never be like Jane. That ship sailed long ago."

He touched her hair, running his fingers through it. *It really is like silk. Just as I imagined it would be.* "You know, I like Jane, but she's too sweet for me. I always feel inferior to her somehow, though that isn't her fault."

Elizabeth laughed quietly. "I live with that every day, but I love her too much to move away, so I try to listen when she enumerates my good points. She's always trying to make me feel better. I could never be like her. Jane doesn't see the faults in other people very often. When she does, you can write that person off as hopeless."

Like Greg Whitman? "I hope I have avoided that category," he said drily.

"You?" She chuckled. "Jane thinks you're wonderful. She pushed me to send you the text, and when she heard from Lance that you didn't know how to take it, she practically drove me to your office herself. She was quite adamant about it. I don't know that I've ever seen her so determined about anything before."

"Jane knows my story?"

She looked down. "I hope you don't mind. I was such a mess when I got to the car that day that I told her everything. I know it was wrong, because it was your secret, but I couldn't handle it by myself. I'm sorry."

"You say that quite a bit. However, since Jane helped you to see reason, I suppose it was for the best." He smiled.

She lifted her face to his. "Why are you smiling? We've probably lost our reservation."

Fitzwilliam shook his head. "I doubt it, but even if we have, I don't care."

Her stomach rumbled. "But I'm hungry."

"So am I." He pulled her close to him. "And I don't care if one hundred cell phones take pictures."

He kissed her gently, framing her face with his hands and using his thumbs to stroke her cheeks. After a few moments, he pulled back a few inches. "Elizabeth?"

"Hmmm?" Her eyes were still closed.

She is adorable. "Are we in a relationship?"

Elizabeth opened her eyes. "I don't know. What do you think?"

"Well, I think we're dating, or going out, or committed to each other, or whatever you call a courtship in the twenty-first century."

"Courtship? As in the stage before an engagement?"

"Yes … I suppose so," he answered, pulling her face toward his again.

"Mmmmm … I think I like that."

"One more kiss, and I promise we'll go inside the restaurant and eat."

"You drive a hard bargain, Mr. Darcy, but I suppose a good steak is worth it."

"I hate this console," he whispered.

"The console is evil," she replied against his cheek.

He stopped her from talking in the best possible way, and he didn't forget to wipe the lipstick from his face before they walked into the restaurant ten minutes later.

CHAPTER 10

Be thankful for all those difficult people in your life and learn from them. They have shown you exactly who you don't want to be.

Unknown

During the early afternoon, Will and Elizabeth mounted their horses and waited at the head of the party as they made ready for their excursion into Lambton. Georgiana had planned a tour of the village and surrounding countryside, and most of her guests were happy with her arrangements.

After his meeting with Mr. Wright that morning, Will had confided to Elizabeth and her father his plan to ride out on the estate early each day and asked that they join him. Consequently, she had consented to ride Guinevere as he rode Diablo to the village in order to improve her horsemanship in preparation for the more strenuous tours of Pemberley. He had been most pleased when she had told him that, though she preferred walking, she had grown up riding about the grounds of Longbourn, and she considered herself to be a tolerable rider. Her father had been adamant that all his children learn to handle a horse, for he considered it to be an important part of country living. Mr. Bennet had further insisted that they be well trained in the art, for he was much concerned with their safety.

Colonel Fitzwilliam and the other gentlemen had taken their places a little distance behind them on horses from the Darcy stables, while Adam Hawkins, Will's customary driver, took charge of Mrs. Bennet, Jane, Mary, and Georgiana in an open carriage.

Lydia, Catherine, and Caroline were crowded into a phaeton driven by Mr. Bingley. Though he was openly displeased with the assignment, arguing that he wanted to ride with the other men or stay behind at Pemberley, Caroline had insisted that they go to Lambton with the others, and she would have no other driver, regardless of how much her brother protested or how sincerely Will offered the services of Robert Hawkins, the son of Adam Hawkins. Upon hearing the siblings quarrel, Mr. Bennet had said that he would drive the ladies and allow Mr. Bingley to use the horse selected for him, but Caroline refused to capitulate. Will had noticed the smile on the older man's face as he rejoined them.

At least Mr. Bennet finds some amusement in their incessant bickering. Will sighed. *I hope Caroline and Bingley don't spoil the day for the rest of us. Georgiana has worked so hard to make the days pleasurable for everyone.*

Elizabeth turned her head at the sound and smiled at him. She glanced behind them, and then looked at him and spoke quietly as they began to ride toward Lambton. "Is the day not perfect for riding, Will? The weather is beautiful and temperate – most congenial – even if all the company is not."

He quickly glanced behind them and noted that even though everyone was now following them, they were a good distance ahead of the rest of the party. "Yes, the weather is cooperating admirably, although there does seem to be a perpetual thundercloud over the phaeton." He pulled Diablo closer to her and lowered his voice. "I really do not know the Bingleys as well as you do. I thought Charles was a happy-go-lucky fellow, but all three times I've met him, he has been in ill humour. Is that customary behaviour for him?"

"Happy-go-lucky?" she asked, puzzled. "I am not familiar with the phrase."

"Cheerful, carefree, never seeing a fault in anyone."

She laughed quietly. "When he is getting what he wants, he is quite amiable, but when he is not – as you can now see – he can display an ill temper as well as anyone of my acquaintance."

"How is it that such a person won your sister's heart? Jane is all that is lovely and sweet."

Elizabeth peeked quickly over her shoulder again and returned her gaze to Will. "He was quite careful to be all that was pleasing around Jane and the rest of my family. They never saw this unpleasant side of him. However, I did, but only in unguarded moments when I came upon him with Caroline while Jane was ill at Netherfield." She paused, chuckling to herself. "It appears that his sister does not bring out the best in him. I endeavoured to enlighten Jane concerning his true nature, but she could not believe it. She always seeks to see only the best in people, especially those whom she loves. Caroline showed her true colours by snubbing Jane in London before we arrived there, so Jane is wary of her. Mr. Bingley made a grave mistake in leaving Jane without offering for her hand, and now he is unwise enough to allow her to observe how he behaves when he is thwarted. If the Bingleys continue to behave in this manner, she will soon feel the same way about the brother as she does the sister."

"Would you be sorry to see your sister married to my cousin? He is not as wealthy as are the Bingleys."

"I want only for my sister to be happy. If Colonel Fitzwilliam is the man for the job and he is so fortunate as to secure her affections, there will be no objections from me. I think he would treat her well. Mr. Bingley has always been a close friend of yours. Would it not be awkward for you if my sister chose the colonel?"

Will shook his head slightly. "Not at all. Remember that I, in reality, have no history with Charles Bingley, though I know his descendants to be very good people. In fact, one of them was my best friend at university, and his father and I worked together closely for several years. Our families will remain business associates for many generations. However, my friend's sister was similar to Caroline. I avoided her when it was at all possible."

Elizabeth shuddered slightly. "Two Carolines."

"Yet there were not two Elizabeths."

She was silent, apparently considering what he had said. "Perhaps there was another, but you never met her."

"Perhaps, though I doubt she would have been much like you are."

"Why would you say that?"

"The era in which I lived likely would have changed you in fundamental ways. People's ideas and lives were so different there."

"Are you not the same as you were?" she asked.

"You have a point: I am basically the same man. However, remember that I was not born here. I came here after living there for twenty-eight years. Had I been born in this era, I have no idea how it would have affected me. Had you been born in modern times, I think you would have been somewhat different."

Her eyes twinkled. "It appears that your switch was fortunate indeed. While a modern man suited me more than one born in this time, it seems that you prefer a woman from the late 1700s over the ladies you knew in the future. It is as if we were designed for each other."

He smiled broadly. "We are in complete agreement. Though I loved my grandmother, mother, and Mrs. Thomas, my housekeeper, and I respected the women with whom I worked, no one before you ever excited my interest in a romantic way. I never found a woman there who suited me so well as you do. Had I not come here, I doubt that I would have ever married."

"And I would have remained a spinster had you not replaced

Fitzwilliam." They rode in companionable silence for a few moments before she said, "Twice now you have referred to working. Were you in," she gasped dramatically, "trade?"

Will looked behind him and noted that the men were talking to each other. Colonel Fitzwilliam appeared to be relating some of his adventures as a soldier, stories which were filled with humour and colour, for the men laughed loudly at regular intervals. *My cousin is certainly enjoying himself.* He returned his attention to Elizabeth.

"My family owned a large corporation, and I always assumed that Nana Rose was grooming me to take my place at the head of it. Now, I am not certain of that, for Nana Rose knew when I was a boy that I would move back in time. To answer your question, I worked, but with my mind, not my hands. Tradesmen would be considered 'blue collar' labourers. They worked in factories which made things like clothing or vehicles. Executives were called 'white collar' workers. We worked in the offices that ran the factories. I know you cannot understand all that I am saying, but I know not how I can better express it. There was no true class system. People were divided along the lines of wealth, though I never considered myself to be better than anyone else. I was born to wealth and privilege through no effort of my own."

"Nana Rose was your grandmother?"

He nodded. "Yes, and I loved her with my whole heart. She reared me after my parents died."

"How did she know that you would move back in time?"

"As I told your father, I have already written letters to her, Mrs. Thomas, and Fitzwilliam. I particularly needed for Nana Rose to know that I would require an extensive knowledge of the history of this time period. I have arranged with Mr. Philips, your uncle, to keep the letters and pass them on to his progeny to be delivered on certain dates to the people I mentioned. Your uncle's family will become wealthy as my attorneys, and I will set up a scholarship fund to make certain that there will always be a lawyer among his descendants. Obviously, the scheme worked. Nana Rose honoured my requests. You already know that I have an extensive knowledge of the history of the next two centuries."

"Yes," she replied sadly.

She's thinking of the fire in Copenhagen. We should hear of that this week. So far, my contacts have not replied. They are watching the area, but I know in my heart they can't stop the fire. It will happen, one way or another.

When she did not speak for several minutes, Will became concerned. "Elizabeth, are you tired? I think we are fairly close to Lambton now. We shall stop at the inn for tea. I believe Georgiana has reserved a private room for us, as well as a room for you ladies, should you require it."

She smiled sadly. "No, I do not become fatigued so easily, though I will be glad to walk again. It has been quite a while since I have ridden horseback."

"Shall we walk now? We could follow the carriages rather than ride in front."

She lifted an eyebrow. "You truly do not know much of the practicalities of life in this era. If we followed the carriages, we would breathe dust, and our clothes would become filthy. Though the early morning rain has kept the dust to a minimum so far today, I think I still prefer to ride the remainder of the way to the village. It cannot be much farther, and the horses are still fairly fresh. Shall we pick up our pace?"

Will had been careful to hold Diablo back until he was certain that Elizabeth was capable of controlling her mount. However, to his amusement, she now pushed ahead, calling playfully to him to keep up with her.

He prodded his stallion into a canter, and the rest of the group followed suit. Within a quarter of an hour, they saw the celebrated horse chestnut tree on the green by the smithy.

~~oo~~

By previous arrangement, several stable boys met the group at the inn. After the men had dismounted and Will had helped Elizabeth from her sidesaddle, the boys took the horses to the trough for watering. The rest of the men handed the ladies down from the carriage and phaeton, and Adam Hawkins took charge of the horses and equipages, instructing one of the young men to relieve Mr. Bingley of his driving duties. Stable hands fetched wooden buckets of water for the beasts, thus eliminating the need for removing their harnesses.

Will noticed that Elizabeth was discreetly attempting to stretch. *She must be stiff from riding so far. I should have ordered a larger carriage or a pony cart. If she rides for the rest of the afternoon, she may be too sore to go with us tomorrow, and I want her to be with me as we make decisions. She probably knows much more than I do about living standards among the tenants and the best way to go about improving their conditions.* He turned and walked back to Mr. Hawkins, speaking quietly with him for a few moments. Mr. Hawkins nodded his understanding.

Soon he was back by Elizabeth's side. "I feel certain that Georgiana ordered a room in which the ladies could refresh themselves before tea. Are you very uncomfortable, my love?"

"Once I walk a bit, I shall be myself again." She placed her hand in the crook of his arm.

Georgiana walked up and took her place on the other side of Elizabeth. "I thought you were over exerting yourself. You must be exhausted. If need be, you may rest before tea. Our room should be in readiness."

"My goodness!" exclaimed Elizabeth, laughing. "I am not some hothouse flower. Have you both forgotten that I grew up in the country, roaming the wilds of Hertfordshire? While I do appreciate the offer of a room, I believe I am as hardy as any lady of our party."

They heard a most unladylike snort behind them.

Elizabeth turned, eyes bright with mischief, though her face feigned concern. "Caroline, are you unwell? Georgiana has a room reserved for your relief, if need be."

"I would rather fall over from fatigue than lie on a bed in this establishment," she replied with rancour.

"Really?" Georgiana looked over her shoulder with her eyes narrowed. "My brother and I have stayed in this inn before, and we suffered no ill effects. Several years ago, there was a fire in the family wing of Pemberley. We spent a fortnight here before we went to London to stay while our rooms were being refurbished." She glanced at Elizabeth. "Though the guest rooms were not burned as badly as those of the family, the entire house smelled of smoke, and it was difficult to breathe." She stopped and faced Caroline boldly, with icy courtesy. "We preferred to stay close by so that we could give specific directions concerning the new furnishings, but perhaps we are not as fastidious as you."

Charles Bingley took his sister's arm, saying firmly, "Caroline will be fine with whatever accommodations were made for the ladies. Thank you, Georgiana. I shall escort her to the room if you will lead the way."

"But, Charles – " she began.

"Caroline," he said in a low, sharp voice. "You well know that no one is going to sleep here. Georgiana has been most thoughtful to provide all of you with a private room for you to use. Be quiet, or I will direct one of the stable hands to see you back to Pemberley."

She stiffened. "That will not be necessary."

"I thought as much," he replied curtly. "Georgiana, please proceed."

Georgiana did as Mr. Bingley requested, entering the large room after her brother had opened the door for her. The gentlemen stood outside as the ladies filed in after their hostess. A maid awaited them and led the quiet group up the staircase.

"I will not hold my tongue!" yelled a drunken voice. "He ain't no better'n me, for all his money and high birth. He's a liar and a cheat, and you can't make me stop talkin' 'bout 'im! He stole money from his own aunt."

Will looked towards the sound and recognized the man immediately. *Stevens! Can this day get any worse?* He strode over to the man, followed closely by the men of his party. "Do we have a problem, Mr. Stevens? What are you going on about?"

The innkeeper bowed nervously. "I'm that sorry, Mr. Darcy. This 'un comes in here ev'ry day and bellows from mornin' 'til night. He's run up a fair tab, and he says that you'll pay it."

"Do not concern yourself about him. I will settle his account directly. Go about your business and leave him to me," said Will.

Colonel Fitzwilliam patted the man's shoulder. "This is no fault of yours, Samuel. Return to your duties and let us handle Stevens."

As Samuel hurried away, Will turned to Stevens. "Why are you not working at the farm which I provided for you?"

Stevens tried to stand, but fell back into his chair. "Mr. High-and-Mighty. That farm ain't worth nothin'. Won't nothin' grow there. You knew it was worthless when you foisted it on me to shut me up about you stealin' from your aunt."

Colonel Fitzwilliam took a step forward. "You lying – "

Will shook his head, and his cousin stopped behind him, red-faced with his fists clenched.

Will folded his arms across his chest and spoke in a voice which brooked no argument. "I have already heard reports that you spend your days in this establishment, drinking and running up a bill under my name while you spread malicious gossip and lies about me." He paused and looked around the room before he continued, "My steward, Mr. Justice Miller, assured me that the farm was profitable. In point of fact, he thought it much better than you deserved." Will fixed his eyes on Stevens. "Now I find that you have not been farming the land, for you are here when you should be working. You have broken the terms of our agreement with your blather, and I will give the farm meant for you to someone more worthy and appreciative. Clear out your belongings today, for the house and land will be assigned to another tomorrow. The ale which you have in your hand is the last thing of yours which shall be charged to me. From this moment, you pay your own way." *The innkeeper heard me, I'm sure, because everyone is listening. This place is quiet as a tomb.*

True fear shown in Stevens's eyes. "Who told you about my comings and goings? Wickham?"

Mr. Bennet and Colonel Fitzwilliam moved to either side of Will.

"Wickham is here?" asked Mr. Bennet.

"I found that out this morning. I was going to tell you and Elizabeth later today," answered Will. "Precautions have been put in place. He can do none of us any harm."

"I'd dearly love for him to try," said Colonel Fitzwilliam. "Tell us what you know of Wickham's plans, Stevens."

The man set his jaw. "Nothin'. I don't know nothin'. I'm well out o' this mess. There's some people you don't cross, and Wickham's in cahoots with 'em."

Wickham has a partner? "I would pay well for the name of Wickham's cohort."

"Money ain't no good to a dead man." Stevens staggered to his feet.

Colonel Fitzwilliam stepped up to Stevens and looked him directly in the eyes. "Before you leave, tell these people that Mr. Darcy has not stolen money from our aunt. We visited the bank in London and talked personally to Mr. Daniel Giles, Governor of the Bank of England. He has papers proving that Mr. Darcy did not take that money, and we know who did."

Stevens blanched. "Well, then, you don't need me. I'll just be goin' on my way. It don't pay to get on the wrong side o' some people." He stumbled through the staring crowd and out the door, cursing under his breath.

"Good riddance to bad rubbish," declared Colonel Fitzwilliam.

"We shall see no more of him." The other men nodded as they followed him to a table.

I wish I could be sure of that, thought Will. *He gave up too easily, and I don't trust him. Maybe I should have let him stay in here drinking all day. At least I knew where he was. Now, I have to watch out for him, Wickham, and his mysterious partner.*

CHAPTER 11

When people talk, listen completely. Most people never listen.

Ernest Hemingway

Fitzwilliam and Elizabeth followed the hostess to a private room in the restaurant. Though the space was large enough to accommodate at least forty people, they had the room to themselves. After showing them to their table, the young woman left them alone with their menus, promising to send their waiter in a few moments.

"I've heard so much about this place," said Elizabeth, looking around with interest. "This room is used for private parties. One of my friends had her rehearsal dinner here. You didn't have to rent a whole room for us, you know."

Fitzwilliam pulled out Elizabeth's chair for her and waited for her to be seated. "As I said in the car, I wanted to have the privacy to talk without fear of being overheard or interrupted, so I asked Mrs. Gray to secure an area in which we could be alone." He opened his menu, laying it on the table as he looked at her. "Would you prefer to be in the crowded room?"

"No, but this must have been quite expensive."

"I don't think it was. Mrs. Gray said that Darcy Enterprises does a great deal of business here, and they were happy to have the opportunity to return the favor. She said that they aren't as busy on week nights as they are on the weekends."

She laughed softly. "I'm all wide-eyed, but you don't seem to be very impressed."

"I like it well enough in here," he said diplomatically, "though I confess that when we first arrived, I thought it looked more like a warehouse than a restaurant. In several places the exterior plaster had fallen completely away to expose the brick underneath. It is in dire need of repair."

"A group of highly skilled and well paid architects and designers worked very hard to give it that appearance."

He raised his eyebrows. "The owners want it to look run-down?"

"It's shabby chic, Fitzwilliam. The look makes an artistic statement," she said, smiling.

"Do *you* like it?"

She nodded. "I think it's beautiful. Things that look too new and shiny don't appeal to me much. I appreciate the antique look. The patina of age makes it feel solid, as if it's been here for a long time. It makes me wonder about the history of the building, though it probably isn't very old in actuality."

His eyes twinkled. "Well, now I know why you like me. And I thought it was my devastating charm, impeccable manners, and noble visage." He turned his face and lifted his chin to show her his profile.

She smirked at him. "Yep, you got it. Charm, manners, and good looks are plusses, but they have nothing to do with it for me. I like that feeling of stability you give me because you're over two hundred years old."

Conversation stopped, and Fitzwilliam glanced furtively at Elizabeth when the waiter appeared, introduced himself, and took their drink orders. *I'm not really two hundred years old. I am twenty-eight. At least, I think I'm twenty-eight. Heavens above! I'm not certain of my own birthday. While my mind is twenty-eight, I have no idea how old this body is. I should ask Mrs. Thomas about that.*

Once the waiter was gone, Elizabeth leaned toward Fitzwilliam. "You wanted to talk privately? Is it a serious topic?"

"Not particularly, though it's nobody else's concern." He reached across the table and took her hand. "We've spent many hours together, and I've learned a great deal about you, but I don't know you as well as I wish to. I know that you're a physical therapist, but where do you work? Do you have any siblings other than Jane? I want to know all about you."

"Why?"

"I wish to be a part of your life. I want to send you flowers at work and meet your family. You know all that is important about me, but I know very little of that sort about you."

She nodded. "Fair enough, though I warn you I'm not very interesting. Prepare to be bored."

"I think I can endure a little boredom on your behalf."

The waiter returned with their drinks and asked for their dinner order.

Fitzwilliam looked at Elizabeth. "You know much more about this place than I do. Order whatever you want for both of us."

She glanced up from her menu, smiling with enthusiasm. "There *are* several items my friends have raved about and I've wanted to try. Would you mind if I ordered different dishes for us and we shared them? I'm having a hard time making up my mind."

He closed his menu. "I'm sure everything will be delicious, and, of course, we can share." He glanced at the waiter. *I'm glad I was listening when he told us his name.* "John, please bring us extra plates."

Elizabeth continued to scan the menu. "My friends have recommended some dishes which are on your catering menu, but I don't see them listed on the dinner menu. Is it all right if I order them?"

"We are catering several events tonight, so choose whatever you want, and I'll ask if we have it," John answered.

"If the items aren't available, that's fine. Just tell me, and I'll order something else." Elizabeth smiled up at him.

The young man nodded, and Elizabeth wasted no time ordering several appetizers, salads and steaks with sides to share, and two different desserts.

Fitzwilliam watched her, listening to her voice as she talked. *I really do love her. I love her excitement and joie de vivre. The people I knew before I came here seemed to be bored with life, but she is excited about everything. She makes me feel more alive than I have since before my parents died. She talks with her hands and laughs in a way that ladies wouldn't have done in my time. They were taught to hide their true feelings and thoughts behind a veneer of manners. She's intelligent and witty, and she isn't afraid to show it.* He smiled to himself. *I don't intimidate her, nor do I want to do so.*

"Fitzwilliam?"

Her voice jolted him back to the present. He refocused on her face and noticed that the waiter was gone. She was watching him with a glimmer of amusement.

"Where were you?"

His face showed his confusion. *Am I to be cursed with invisibility now?* "I never left my seat."

"You were thinking about something, and it wasn't our dinner order. What was going through your mind to cause that far-away look on your face?"

Do I dare to tell her? I don't want to frighten her away. He clenched his fists in his lap and then relaxed them. *I think it's time for more honesty – with the hope that she receives this better than she did my history last week.* "I was thinking of you and how much you differ from the women I knew long ago."

She tilted her head, eyes sparkling. "And did I suffer in

comparison?"

He chuckled. "Not at all. Why would you think such a thing?"

The expression on her face held a challenge. "You must have known many beautiful, very accomplished women. The idea of being compared to them is a little scary."

He instinctively knew that she would be able to tell if he held back the complete truth, so he reached across the table and took her hands in his, hoping that she would understand. "Scores of lovely young women were paraded before me for several years – each one of them looking, thinking, and sounding much like the others who preceded her. The mothers of my circle sought to push their daughters forward to make a conquest of me, for I was a desirable match due to my money and social standing. The ladies were all quite skilled at dancing, idle conversation, painting screens, embroidery, playing at least one instrument, singing, writing poetry, arranging flowers, planning social events, and managing a cadre of servants. None of them were reared to work; they would have been properly horrified by the idea. Not one would have dared to profess an opinion which would have displeased me, so they avoided any conversation of substance. Politics and religion were forbidden topics because of their controversial natures. Those women were unable to hold my interest as you do."

She looked at him with open skepticism. "Not one? I have watched *Pride and Prejudice*, you know." She paused. "Honestly, I re-read the book and watched the miniseries again this past week, since I had plenty of free time. Lance laughed through the entire program."

"Lance?"

Elizabeth sighed. "He came over to watch the 1995 version with Jane and me. He said that when you first arrived in Atlanta, you were more like Colin Firth than Matthew Macfadyen in the 2005 movie."

"Why would he find that amusing?"

"That's not really why he was laughing. He thought *I* was funny."

That makes no sense. "I don't understand."

She looked away. "I kept making remarks about Jennifer Ehle, trying to find fault with her, and I couldn't." She glanced back at him. "When she was jumping to conclusions, she seemed to be like me, but when she was charming and witty, I was jealous. Lance thought it was hilarious. She used to be my favorite character, but now I don't like her. In other words, I have her character flaws but not the good things about her. I'm not much like the woman who caught your attention more than two hundred years ago."

"Ah," he answered. "The Elizabeth Bennet of 1795 interests you. You were comparing yourself to her."

She stared at him knowingly. "You can't say that she was as vacuous as the rest. After all, you wanted to marry her."

And she refused me. He looked at their hands, hiding his eyes from hers. The memory still hurt, though he knew she was right to decline his offer; nevertheless, he wished to conceal the pain.

"Elizabeth was very different from the other women I knew. Like you, she was intelligent and unafraid to disagree with me. I was intrigued by her; however, I can now see that she and I would not have been happy together. I, particularly, needed to change, and I would never have done so but for coming to this time period and meeting you."

"So, she and I are alike?"

He raised his eyes to hers in surprise. *Do you worry that I still have feelings for her, and you are merely a substitute, or do you think I'll love you more if you're like her?* "Elizabeth, you are unlike any other woman I've ever known. Though you and the other Elizabeth have being outspoken and knowledgeable in common, you are not at all the same in other ways. I had never truly loved a woman who was not of my own family before I met you. Try to understand. I didn't know her as I know you. I thought I loved her, but we had no serious conversations. We spent very little time together, and most of that was in large groups. We walked together a few times in the early morning, but we bantered more than anything else. She argued with me constantly, and in my foolishness, I did not see that as a problem. People in that era were not encouraged to become well acquainted before they married. Obviously, I never really knew her well, or I would not have proposed to her in that manner. I could tell you a few of her personal preferences, such as which books she read, but I know more about you than I ever knew about her, and I want to know you better still. You have confided your deepest concerns and secrets to me. While it's true that I don't know every detail of your life, I believe I know how you think and feel – and why you think and feel in the way that you do."

Her expression softened. "I wondered if you were just transferring the affection you had for her to me. I don't want to be a poor reflection of her." She hesitated before she asked, "Do we look alike?"

He organized his thoughts before he spoke. "To be candid, she *was* beautiful, but no more so than you. You do *not* remind me of her, if that is truly what you wish to know. She did have dark hair, but yours is darker and thicker, and, of course, your hairstyles are nothing alike. I never saw her wear her hair down around her shoulders, as you do, and I must say, I like looking at your hair and touching it. Her eyes were green; yours are brown. You are taller than she was, and more fit. Remember, people did not view health in the same way two hundred years ago. We were not as careful about what we ate or how much we exercised, and we didn't have access to modern dentistry," he added ruefully, remembering how Will had lectured him in his first letter concerning dental hygiene. "We had only the most rudimentary medical care, and much of it would be as likely to kill us as to heal us."

He smiled broadly, remembering his outrage when he had first awakened in the Atlanta hospital. "All the ladies of my acquaintance wore dresses that were not nearly as flattering as is your attire. Though I thought it was shocking to see women in trousers when I first arrived, I have since come to appreciate how attractive the clothing of this century can be when a woman is careful with her choices, as you are. In many instances, ladies' pants are more modest than are the dresses now." The image of Karlyn Bingley came to his mind, and he shuddered slightly.

Her eyes sparkled. "So I don't have to run out and buy sprigged muslin to please you? Must I buy a bonnet to protect my face from freckling?"

He assumed a haughty, aristocratic demeanor. "I have developed quite a horror of sprigged muslin, and should you have the misfortune to display any freckles, I would most certainly object to anything which hides your face from me, preferring the sight of the freckles to the loss of being privileged to readily behold your loveliness."

She chuckled. "You just love to drop back into a British accent and eighteenth century syntax, don't you?"

He sighed. "With you, I no longer have to pretend, and, frankly, I am relieved. I don't think you can fully appreciate how difficult it is to speak with a Southern American accent. Contractions are easy and natural by comparison."

The waiter arrived with the appetizers and extra plates on a tray. He set the tray on a nearby, empty table and transferred the items, efficiently arranging the food and plates on the table between Elizabeth and Fitzwilliam. Since the waiter had told the head chef that the two of them were going to share, the chef had decided to serve them family style.

Fitzwilliam thanked the waiter. "This is a much better arrangement than taking food from each other's plates. Please relay my compliments to the chef."

"Yes, Mr. Darcy." The young man nodded, picking up the tray and walking briskly from the room.

Elizabeth watched the door close, and then she turned to Fitzwilliam. "Actually, I do know how hard it is." She nibbled on an eggplant fry.

He drew his brows together. "I confess you've lost me."

"I know how hard it is for you to speak with a Southern accent."

Fitzwilliam raised an eyebrow. "Really? How so?" He selected a lobster fritter.

She snickered. "Because you're really bad at it. People who aren't born Southern rarely get the accent right. True Southerners always cringe when they hear an actor butcher the way we speak. They are uniformly terrible."

He pursed his lips. "Then what shall I do? Lance told me to drop my natural accent."

Elizabeth laughed. "He was right. You couldn't go around with the name Fitzwilliam Darcy and speak with a British accent. That's just too bizarre. Can't you go for American but not Southern? Try for neutral, like a newscaster, radio announcer, or favorite actor."

Fitzwilliam was quiet for a moment. He tried to sound like Henry Cavill in *Man of Steel. Cavill was British playing an alien who was trying to pass for American. People thought he did it well.* "Like this?"

"Very good. That was more like the Brit, John Mahoney, playing Martin Crane on *Frasier* than Nicholas Cage botching a Southern accent in *Con Air.* I couldn't believe Mahoney was British until I read it online."

"I've watched every episode of *Frasier,* and I never suspected that Martin Crane was British," replied Fitzwilliam with surprise.

"I know. Right? I do have to say that Jean Smart in *Sweet Home Alabama* is an exception to the rule. My family watches that a couple of times a year, and we all agree she nailed the accent. She got it right in *Designing Women,* too. It's hard to believe she grew up in Seattle, Washington."

"I wasn't really trying to sound like Martin Crane."

She smiled. "I didn't mean that you sounded exactly like him. I meant that you didn't sound like a British man trying to fake a Southern accent. Who were you imitating?"

He grinned. "Your favorite – Henry Cavill in *Man of Steel*."

She chuckled. "I heartily approve of your choice. Keep practicing. Maybe we should watch that movie a few hundred times to help you."

His look was innocent. "You would do that for me?"

"It would be a great sacrifice," she intoned, "but I would suffer through it to help you."

"You are, indeed, an angel."

She shook her head. "No, you have me confused with Jane. I can assure you that no one in my family makes that mistake."

They both laughed.

The time had passed so pleasantly while they were eating and talking that they hardly noticed when the waiter quietly returned to replace the empty appetizer platter with a selection of soups and salads.

Fitzwilliam chose a bowl with English pea puree. "And we return to the reason for having this private room. I want to know more about your family and your life. So far, I know that your mother loves Jane Austen, you have a sister named Jane, and you enjoy watching *Sweet Home Alabama* together. This entire conversation has been about me. I'm beginning to think you are using underhanded tactics in order to avoid talking about yourself."

Elizabeth grimaced. After serving herself a portion of spinach salad, she began to speak. "You have found me out. I thought I was boring before I met you, and now, I seem even worse. Your life has been so interesting. Mine has been like everyone else's I know."

"I'll try to stay awake. Proceed," he said. "If my head falls into my soup, and I appear to be drowning, call for help. You look too pretty tonight to spoil your outfit with this pea soup."

She blushed and held up her hands in surrender. "Okay. I'll talk. My mom and dad are named Anne and George Bennet, and I have a younger sister named Mary." She made a face. "I know, I know – Jane, Elizabeth, and Mary. We're just lucky that Mom stopped at three, or we would have had Kitty and Lydia, too."

"How old is Mary?" *Is she anything like the Mary in the book, or is she more similar to the real Mary Bennet? I remember a Kitty from the film, but I don't recall a Bennet sister with the name. Could she be referring to the Lucas girl? Lydia, I do recall – a rather silly girl with a fondness for soldiers, but harmless enough. I remember thinking she was vulgar, but my opinions appear to have changed.*

"She's eighteen, and she'll be a freshman in college in the fall. Unlike Austen's Mary, my sister is beautiful. She isn't a great scholar either. In fact, she doesn't apply herself like she should to her studies. She would rather be popular and have an active social life." Elizabeth sighed. "Jane and I concentrated on our academics, but Mary was a cheerleader in high school and is going to be one at the university, too, so she'll be very busy. I doubt she'll spend much time in the library."

She shook her head. "Jane and I worry about her. She's rather naïve for her age, and we're afraid that she'll get in with the wrong crowd in college. At least she'll still live at home. Dad insisted that she go to Georgia State University so that she could commute. He doesn't think she's mature enough to live on a college campus, and he's right. It's also a lot cheaper that way. She didn't win any academic scholarships like Jane and I did, so Dad and Mom will have to pay for her, or she'll have to take out loans. Since, Dad didn't want any of us to owe money when we graduated, I guess he'll pay. She hasn't chosen a major yet, so she's going to take general freshman courses."

"Does your dad work?"

"Yes, he's a professor at GSU, so that's another reason Mary's going there. She'll get a huge break on her tuition as a faculty member's child. My mother works there, too. She's a librarian."

"Your parents must be quite educated and intelligent."

She nodded. "My dad has a doctorate, and he's very involved in research – cellular molecular biology and physiology. Mom has her master's degree in library science. She has always loved books, and she's an avid reader."

His eyes held a thoughtful expression. "So they are quite different from Austen's characters – as are you."

She nodded. "My father teases my mother about her nerves, but it's all a family joke. My mom has actually written and published several books herself. She plays the piano, too."

"You speak very highly of them. You must love them a great deal."

"I do. Even though I joke about getting away from Atlanta, this is my home, because they're here."

"And you work as a physical therapist?" he asked, gently prodding her to talk about herself.

"Well, sort of." She reached for a small bowl of the English pea puree and tasted it. "This is delicious," she said appreciatively.

Fitzwilliam tried the chopped salad and immediately downed the contents of his water glass. "Those flavors are too strong for me." He pushed the bowl away. "How does one 'sort of' work as a physical therapist?"

"I am a trained, licensed physical therapist, and that was my sole means of support while I worked on another degree in business through night school. Right now, I work part time for the Emory University athletic department as a PT while I'm finishing my MBA there. Being a grad assistant pays my tuition and living expenses."

She tasted the chopped salad. "This is really good, but I've noticed that you aren't a very adventurous eater. I hope you'll like the main course. Everyone recommends the dry aged steak for two. I didn't get fancy with the vegetables either. I'm beginning to think I shouldn't have ordered dessert for me. I'm going to be too full to eat mine."

His smile was crooked. "We can have the desserts boxed and take them back to your apartment to eat together later. You're trying to change the subject again. What's an MBA?"

She made a face at him, wrinkling up her nose. "It's a master's degree in business administration; I'm specializing in finance. I want to run my own business some day."

She's learning how to run a business? His attention was fully engaged. "When will you finish your degree?"

"I'll graduate in December. I'm working on my dissertation now." She looked at him with curiosity. "Why?"

"We'll talk further about it after you graduate. I may have a proposition for you," he answered, eyes gleaming.

John chose that opportune moment to arrive with their main course, and all conversation was temporarily suspended.

Before the waiter left again, Fitzwilliam asked him to box their desserts for them. He wanted to leave as soon as they finished eating, and he disliked waiting.

For the rest of the evening, he steered the conversation to less weighty topics, but his mind kept working out the details of the plans which had taken root there.

CHAPTER 12

We live at home, quiet, confined, and our feelings prey upon us.
You always have business of some sort or other to take you back
into the world.

Anne Elliot, Persuasion, Jane Austen

Will and Colonel Fitzwilliam waited at the foot of the stairs, talking quietly about the morning's events until Elizabeth and Georgiana descended, followed by Mrs. Bennet, Caroline Bingley, and the other ladies. Will took Elizabeth on one arm and Georgiana on the other, and they laughed and chatted as he led them to the room in which their party would assemble for tea. The colonel escorted Jane, earning glowers from Charles Bingley, which he ignored with good humour. Mr. Bennet stepped forward to claim his wife, leaving Mr. Bingley to escort his sister, while John Bennet took charge of his younger sisters and Catherine Lucas.

Several tables had been set for them, and the innkeeper's daughter, Meg, who had been previously pointed out to Will by the colonel, stood by to replenish the trays of meats, salads, breads, cheese, cakes, coffee, and tea as needed.

Mr. Wentworth-Fitzwilliam approached Will and the ladies.

"Mr. Darcy, with Miss Georgiana's permission, I beg the honour of sitting with her while we take refreshments."

"Please, call me Will; 'Mr. Darcy' is so formal, and I would very much like for us to be friends." He turned to Georgiana. "My dear, shall I give you up to Mr. Wentworth-Fitzwilliam?"

She smiled prettily. "Brother, I shan't go far, as I have arranged for several tables to be placed together. We will be quite close to you and Elizabeth."

"And, if you please, address me as Wentworth," added the young man with a smile. "We seem to have an abundance of Charleses and Fitzwilliams, and my hyphenated name is too formal. I find myself looking around every time I hear Charles, Fitzwilliam, or any combination of the two. After careful reflection regarding the problem, I think Wentworth is the proper solution. Unless another Wentworth shall join us?"

Laughter met his pronouncement. Georgiana took his arm and guided him to their seats. "I believe I can assure you that our party is complete, unless Phoebe Barlow should choose to accept our invitation. So far, we have received no answer from her or Colonel Barlow, and I begin to fear that my letter has gone amiss."

"Colonel and Phoebe Barlow? I have not had the pleasure of meeting them. Did you meet the couple in London during the season?"

Georgiana smiled. "They are not married, and I have never before met Miss Barlow. She is a friend of the Bennet ladies as well as Catherine Lucas. They became acquainted when she and the colonel were in Meryton over the winter. Colonel Barlow is her brother, and the militia is now encamped at Bath for the summer. My brother is so thoughtful that he asked me to write to her, informing her that we would be pleased if she would join us at Pemberley for the next two months. She could then be with her friends instead of a camp full of soldiers."

Will, privy to their exchange, had heard Mr. Wentworth's questions and noticed his puzzled look. He glanced at Elizabeth and noticed that she was watching the young man with a speculative expression. *Does Elizabeth wonder, as I do, whether Wentworth approves of our choice of company? Are his opinions concerning proper companionship more similar to Caroline Bingley's than they are to ours? Well, I have the next couple of months to get to know him, and I intend to use that time to the fullest. My sweet sister won't be tied to someone too proud to acknowledge our family and friends.* He smiled as he realized what he'd thought. *I know she's not really my sister, but I'm beginning to love her as if she were, and I'm getting very protective.*

"Why do you smile so?" asked Elizabeth.

"You are observant." Will glanced back at Elizabeth. He had not realized she had turned her attention from Wentworth to him.

"And you are quite skilled in avoiding answering questions."

He chuckled. "Is it so unusual for me to smile that it draws attention when I do so? I smile because I'm happy. I am surrounded by people I love, and the day is full of promise."

Will held her chair for her, careful to ascertain that Elizabeth and Georgiana would be to his right and left, and then he sat at the head of the table. He leaned forward and whispered so that only Elizabeth and his sister would hear him, knowing his words were covered by the noise of the rest of the group, talking and moving chairs while they took their seats.

"I am determined to adjust our travelling arrangements when we leave here," he said in a low voice. "Just follow my lead and agree with me as if we had already planned this."

"Brother, what are you about?" asked Georgiana.

He scanned the table to discover whether or not he had attracted any attention before he continued. "I will solve several problems with one move; however, I cannot fully explain myself now. The others are starting to eat, and it is becoming quieter. They will hear me. Trust me."

Both Elizabeth and Georgiana nodded.

Colonel Fitzwilliam caught Will's eye and winked. He was

sitting between Elizabeth and Jane and had caught the last few sentences of Will's instructions. His eyes gleamed merrily as he picked up a platter of ham and offered it to Jane before selecting several pieces for himself.

Wentworth was to Georgiana's left. Caroline Bingley, who had taken an opportunity to seize the seat beside him, had engaged him in conversation as soon as they sat down, thus ensuring that neither of them heard any of the whispers. Beside her, Charles Bingley's attention was firmly fixed on Jane, who sat across the table from him.

Mr. Bennet, who faced Will from the other end of the long table, smiled enigmatically, as if he enjoyed some secret the others had no way of knowing.

~~oo~~

Will stood as soon as everyone had finished their repast. "My sister has planned a treat for us. If you have never walked the paths at Dovedale Ravine, prepare to be awed and amazed. There are stepping stones on which to cross the River Dove; two caves, known as the Dove Holes, to explore; rock pillars to view: Ilam Rock, Viator's Bridge; and limestone features: Lover's Leap and Reynard's Cave. Along the river we could see Charles Cotton's Fishing House, which was the inspiration for Izaak Walton's *The Compleat Angler*. Our explorations will be limited only by our endurance and the length of the day."

Most of the guests were quite pleased by his speech and the itinerary, the notable exception being Caroline Bingley. "I fear my shoes will not be suitable. I see that the other ladies wore stout boots, and I have none." She sniffed.

Will's expression was suitably sympathetic. "I thought as much, and I have arranged with Mr. Hawkins that he shall return to Pemberley with any of you who do not feel up to the rigours of The Peaks. If several of you wish to return, he will drive you back in the phaeton. If Miss Bingley alone chooses to forego the trip, he can easily rent a pony cart from Sam, the innkeeper. What say you?"

Miss Bingley looked imploringly at Jane, but Miss Bennet smiled at Elizabeth before she turned back to Caroline with a serene expression and a gentle voice. "While I do not pretend I am the excellent walker my sister has been acclaimed to be, I profess that I am excessively intrigued by our excursion. I would not give up a chance to see such scenery for all the pretty shoes in the world. My sisters and I have not had the wonderful travelling experiences enjoyed by many of you, and we have been most excited about touring the area ever since Georgiana told us all that we would be walking today. I came prepared, though I am sorry you did not, Caroline."

Georgiana looked at Caroline with kindness. "Perhaps you could borrow a pair of boots from Meg or buy them from the cobbler. He keeps several ready-made pairs for travellers."

Caroline looked properly shocked at the idea of wearing another person's shoes. "Meg?"

Georgiana nodded towards the girl who inclined her head. "The innkeeper's daughter. We often played together as girls when I came with my father into the village. She is about your height, so it is possible that your feet are of a similar size."

Caroline shuddered and glanced around the table. "Mrs. Bennet, surely you would rather return to Pemberley with me."

Will felt a bit sorry for her. *She really is desperate.*

The lady shook her head calmly. "Whether or not I walk so far as Elizabeth and my other children, I still enjoy the outdoors. Mr. Bennet and I will explore the area which is close to the carriage. We can sit in the conveyance when we are tired. My shoes are thick, you see, and if the sun is too bright, I am certain we can find a shady tree. I must go with my daughters, but you are welcomed to stay close by Mr. Bennet and me."

Charles spoke rather sharply. "There are several choices before

132

you, Caroline. Please make up your mind quickly so that we can be off. Let us not delay the rest of the party."

She bit her lower lip. "I would hate to miss the drive and the company, therefore, I suppose I will accept Mrs. Bennet's kind offer." Her eyes brightened. "However, since I am not properly attired to walk with the rest of the group, I request that I be allowed to ride in the carriage. I have already visited with Lydia and Catherine. I am certain that all of us would be happy to change our travelling arrangements and spend time with others in the party. Perhaps Mary would like to trade places with me."

I thought she would try to put herself in the carriage with Jane and Georgiana. I'm ready for her. "I agree that a different plan is in order, and I have thought it out myself. I fear that Elizabeth has ridden too far today, so she will move to the phaeton with Mary, leaving a place in the carriage for you, Caroline. I will drive them. Charles, do you think you can handle Diablo?"

Charles nodded vigorously, smiling broadly. "I would certainly relish the opportunity to try. You have always kept him to yourself."

"Well, now is your opportunity to prove yourself. Would any of you ladies like to ride Guinevere as she has a side saddle? I can borrow a gentleman's saddle from the inn's stables if need be."

Jane spoke up immediately. "That is unnecessary. I will ride the first leg of the journey, and perhaps one of my sisters would take my place on the return trip. All of us learned to ride at an early age."

Will smiled. "Excellent. That leaves Caroline, Lydia, Catherine, and Mrs. Bennet in the carriage. Mr. Hawkins will continue to drive."

"What of Georgiana?" Caroline asked. "Surely five can ride in the carriage. It is quite spacious."

Georgiana grinned at Elizabeth. "I think I can fit into the phaeton with Elizabeth and Mary. None of us are very large, and that will give me a chance to talk with them. I have not spoken a word to Mary all day, and I really should discuss the evening's music with her."

Elizabeth's eyes were merry. "If you are too crowded, I can sit on the driver's seat with Will. It is as wide as the phaeton."

Mr. Bennet raised an eyebrow. "Well, that was very nicely done."

Mrs. Bennet nodded sagely. "It is most pleasant for everyone to be so well accommodated and so well pleased. Mr. and Miss Darcy have arranged everything perfectly. I have already noted what a superior hostess Miss Darcy is. Everything is always so comfortable and in perfect order."

Caroline was seized by a fit of coughing so severe that her brother patted her back several times, the picture of concern. If he used a little more force than was absolutely necessary, no one seemed to notice.

~~oo~~

Mr. Hawkins insisted that Will drive the phaeton just behind the horses, ahead of the carriage, for, as he explained, "The carriage can be closed, protecting the occupants from the stains of travel; however, the phaeton is open. The morning rain before we left kept the dust somewhat at bay during the drive from Pemberley to Lambton, but the sun has now dried the roads. Both you and the ladies would be covered in dirt after such a long drive." He then proceeded to raise the top of the carriage, with the help of the stable hands, giving emphasis to what he had said.

Because he had no wish to exhaust his guests or return during the night, after conferring with Mr. Hawkins and Colonel Fitzwilliam, Will had decided to limit the day's journey to a spot on the River Dove near Hartington, as most of the gentlemen wished to see Charles Cotton's Fishing House. They could examine the cottage and the section of the river made famous for trout fishing by *The Compleat Angler*. The walk along the banks of the river would have to suffice for the day.

Once everyone was comfortably placed, the caravan set out.

From her place beside Will on the driver's seat of the phaeton, Elizabeth's discontent showed in her expression, though Will could see that she struggled to conceal it, using her bonnet to hide her face. *If only I had a car. England is about the size of Louisiana, and we could drive it easily.*

He knew her very well, having made it a point to study her whenever he was in her presence, and it pierced his heart to know that he was causing her unhappiness. He could not be happy while she was not. "I know that you desire to see the caves and limestone formations, dearest, and it pains me to disappoint you, but they are farther away than the cottage. In our eagerness to surprise everyone, Georgiana and I neglected to confer with those who know the area better than either of us. I am certain that I knew the area well before my accident, but I have forgotten the geography of the county. We shall come again and make arrangements to stay overnight at an inn. If we leave Pemberley early enough on the morning of our next excursion, we shall have the better part of two days to explore. Perhaps we shall make another journey to visit Chatsworth. After we marry, we shall travel as much as you wish."

From behind them, Georgiana clapped her hands and leaned forward between them, eyes sparkling. "Though I live on a large estate, Elizabeth, I am more like you and your sisters than you imagine. While I have travelled on occasion to see our family at their homes, I have toured neither my own county nor anything beyond it. We are a very quiet set of people when we are here in Derbyshire. It is only in London that I have company and entertainment, so I have been looking forward to your visit with great anticipation. To have such friends as you and your family with us for the entire summer will be a treat indeed." She was quiet for a moment. "We women are not so free as men, you know. They are always going from place to place with their business to occupy them. We stay at home, and our feelings prey upon us."

She still thinks about the business with Wickham.

Elizabeth looked back at her. "You have a sister now, and you will not be alone at home anymore. In fact, my sisters will be yours as well." Mary nodded in agreement.

I love this woman more with every passing day.

Elizabeth put her hand on Will's arm. "Please do not think me so selfish as to pout because our plans for the day were changed. I have rarely been outside Hertfordshire, and any new place is a wonder to me. I am certain that I will find riverbanks and rocks enough to amuse me at Mr. Cotton's cottage."

She turned her head to look back at Georgiana and Mary. "Would it be a great inconvenience to plan a ball? Would you not enjoy the company? My mother, sisters, and I would enjoy helping you, Georgiana, and I believe Miss Bingley would be more enthusiastic about a ball than she has been about outdoor amusements."

Mary's agreement was most enthusiastic. "Oh, yes, Georgiana. Please do. We will all promise to perform. The entertainment for the evening would not be an imposition in the least. I feel sure that Miss Bingley will also agree to exhibit. She plays prodigiously well, for I heard her at the Netherfield Ball, and I was impressed with the degree of her accomplishment."

Georgiana was thoughtful. "She does indeed, and a ball is more to her liking than climbing the peaks or playing at battledore and shuttlecock. If we were to give a ball, I would be happy to know that I have considered the preferences of all our guests." She smiled. "What an excellent proposal, Elizabeth! Do you not agree, Brother?"

He smiled at her over his shoulder. *They're very sweet and considerate. Caroline has made life difficult for all of us, yet they want to do something she'll enjoy.* "I do, indeed. In all likelihood, Mrs. Reynolds has a list of guests who have been invited in the past. I fear I will be of little assistance in that regard. Colonel Fitzwilliam will no doubt be happy to help in any way he can."

Georgiana's tone was serious. "There have been no balls at Pemberley for many years – since before our father died. The beautiful ballroom has been shut up since I was a young girl. There are several families – friends of the Darcys for generations – who live close enough to come. If we give them sufficient time to arrange everything, perhaps they will invite their younger relations to visit them and bring them to our ball." She glanced from Mary to Elizabeth. "Our Aunt Margaret, Colonel Fitzwilliam's mother, will be in raptures. She and my uncle will come from Matlock to make certain that everything is done properly." She smiled broadly. "This is a perfect excuse for her and Uncle Edward to come meet Jane, your parents, and the rest of your family."

Will glanced at Elizabeth. "If all could be arranged in a month's time, could it not be our engagement ball? Would you agree to marry a month after that?"

She smiled. "I think it a lovely idea to use the ball to celebrate our engagement, and I am certain that my parents would approve of that idea; however, my mother may be saddened if we do not marry from Longbourn. Our friends in Meryton cannot afford to travel this far for the wedding, and I would prefer to respect her wishes. I would like to consult her on the subject before anything is decided. However, if you want to marry in two months, Mama may feel that we need to leave within a month's time in order to prepare for the wedding."

His answer was quick. "If that is what your mother wishes, we shall marry a month after you arrive back at Longbourn, but you need not leave early. Georgiana and I will come to Hertfordshire. Richard will certainly come as well."

Georgiana's delight was boundless. "I could return with you to Longbourn, if that is agreeable to your family. We could break the trip in London and stay at Darcy House for several days whilst we visit the dressmakers. I am certain that Aunt Margaret would agree to meet us there and take us to the best shops. It would be such fun."

Georgiana, Elizabeth, and the other Bennet sisters can't be left unguarded while Wickham is on the loose. Richard and I will be with them. Will's tone was decisive. "If that plan becomes reality, Richard and I will also go to London. Perhaps we could go to the opera or the theatre while we are there. At any rate, we have business we must attend with our lawyer and our banker."

Elizabeth laughed. "I suppose I began this speculation with the suggestion of a ball. Shall we be satisfied with planning the ball instead of our wedding until we talk to my mother? She will be your mother, too, Will. You should join me. We should talk to her and my father together."

He nodded. "I agree. Let us not start our life together by offending your parents – my future parents."

She put her arm through the crook of his elbow and leaned into him a bit. "Thank you."

He wanted to kiss her, but her bonnet would have prevented such an intimacy in any case. *God bless the bonnet. It'll help keep me on the straight and narrow.*

CHAPTER 13

Who has words at the right moment?

Charlotte Brontë

When Fitzwilliam and Elizabeth were back in her car after dinner, he took his cell phone out of his pocket.

She sat in the driver's seat. "Where to?"

He was busily retrieving the information Mrs. Gray had texted him. "I'm going to pull it up on my GPS."

"I may know how to get there without your GPS if you'll tell me where we're going. As slow as you are at typing, we won't leave the parking lot until morning, and one of us has to work tomorrow."

He drew his brows together and looked at her. "I wanted it to be a surprise."

She smiled. "When you tell me, I promise to be surprised."

He sighed and returned his phone to his inside jacket pocket. "The Georgia Aquarium."

She widened her eyes. "You do know that it's closed this late at night?"

"Most of it is closed tonight, but Mrs. Gray managed to secure us entrance to a place called …" He paused to read what she had sent him. "… Ocean Voyager."

"How did she do that? I hope you didn't spend a fortune." Elizabeth's expression was faintly disapproving.

He returned her look, his voice defensive. "Some of the Aquarium employees are being well-paid to give us a private viewing of that one exhibit, not the entire park. Mrs. Gray showed me pictures of it on the internet, and I want to see it when it isn't crowded. I've never seen anything like those pictures before. No doubt you've been there already, but I was quite excited about our trip. Besides, there's an adult sleepover there tonight, so they aren't opening only for us, though the sleepover doesn't include Ocean Voyager."

"Oh…" Her tone was apologetic. "I have to remind myself that your life has been very different from mine. Even so, I feel bad that you've spent so much on a date."

"This was not just a date for me. I wanted to share the experience with you. If it makes you feel better, Darcy Enterprises bought one hundred Champion Memberships to the Aquarium as part of our entry fee tonight. That accounts for six hundred season passes which will be given to inner city children and their parents or guardians who would be unable to visit the Aquarium otherwise. The Darcy Foundation is presently taking applications from families in the Atlanta schools for the passes. In addition, the fees for the Champion Memberships aid the Aquarium's efforts in aquatic animal research and conservation. The Georgia Aquarium is a 501; they rely on corporate supporters, such as Darcy Enterprises and the Darcy Foundation, in order to continue to operate. We make substantial, annual contributions to them, for entry fees are not enough to keep the Aquarium open to the public. They were very happy to allow me to see Ocean Voyager. Even had they refused the request, we would still have supported them, and they knew that. This was one of Will's favorite bequests, and I wish to see the results of his work with them."

She was quiet for a moment, her cheeks tinged with pink. "I'm sorry. I didn't fully understand your company's involvement as a contributor, and I should think before I speak. My dad's research is funded in much the same way, and he spends time showing donors and potential supporters his labs and presentations. I don't view it as giving them special treatment when he does it. I think of it as the donors giving him an opportunity to convince them that his work is worthy of their investment. That's what the Aquarium is doing, too, with you."

He smiled and reached out his hand for hers. "There is no need to apologize, Elizabeth. You gave me a chance to explain without walking away from me or shutting me out. You're embarrassed, but I think of this as progress. Shall we go? We mustn't keep the Aquarium employees waiting, for they have to work tomorrow, too. Do you need my GPS?"

"No. I've been to the Aquarium before. I love it; Jane and I go every year."

His eyes sparkled, and he gave a low chuckle as she released his hand and started the car.

She looked over at him. "You knew that, didn't you? Jane must've told Lance that I've always wanted to come to this restaurant and that we make an annual trip to the Aquarium."

"You know I can't reveal my sources. We have a confidentiality agreement. Would you have me break my word?" He laughed.

She smiled. "No, because I want you to have the same agreement with me. What's between us stays between us. If we have a problem, we should talk to each other first from now on – not Jane and Lance like I did this past week."

He nodded. "Agreed."

They continued to talk as Elizabeth drove. Fitzwilliam was interested in everything he saw around him. He had never been in downtown Atlanta at such a late hour, and he peppered her with questions.

When they arrived at the Aquarium, Elizabeth turned into the parking garage. "I've never seen it this empty before. We can have a prime spot."

He reached into his pocket and produced a parking pass which Mrs. Gray had downloaded for him.

Elizabeth smirked when she saw it. "She thinks of everything, doesn't she? I'll bet she was the one who actually thought of our meeting Lance back at the apartment so he could drive you back to The Oaks. She probably suggested it to him."

"She?"

"Mrs. Gray, silly. I know you didn't think of purchasing a parking pass in advance. You'd better treat her well, because she makes your life easy."

He grinned. "Yes, she does at that. I'm fortunate to be surrounded by lovely women who are also intelligent and thoughtful. Mrs. Thomas and Mrs. Gray are jewels, and so are you."

She smiled. "Though you probably wouldn't say that I make your life easy."

"I would say instead that you make my life interesting and happy. Perhaps one day, I'll add 'easy' to that list."

She laughed at him.

~~oo~~

Fitzwilliam and Elizabeth stood before the park entrance.

"This is beautiful." His eyes lit with wonder.

"Yes, it is. The façade is designed to look like a ship breaking through a wave."

They were met by a representative as they walked through the doors. He introduced himself as Dan, although his name was on his badge, and then led them to the Ocean Voyager pavilion, through the entrance to the exhibit.

Elizabeth was surprised to see Lance and Jane waiting for them, each of them holding a small backpack.

She looked at Fitzwilliam. "You're sneaky. I'm going to have to keep an eye on you every minute."

He rubbed his hands together, mimicking fiendish glee. "You've discovered my evil plan to keep your attention focused on me."

"Seriously, I'm impressed that you got all this together in a couple of hours. Your minions are brilliant."

"I have minions? Lance, are you a Darcy minion?" His blue eyes twinkled with good humor.

Lance grimaced. "Nope, but I know a good deal when I see one. A free swim with the fishes is too good to pass up, even if I did have to loan you a swimsuit."

Elizabeth's mouth formed an O. "We're going to swim with the whale sharks? I've always wanted to do that!"

Jane held up her backpack. "I brought your one-piece."

Dan glanced at Fitzwilliam. "Would you like to walk through the tunnel first?"

Elizabeth put her hand in Fitzwilliam's, entwining her fingers with his. "I think it would be a good idea, Dan. Fitzwilliam has probably never seen whale sharks or mantas before, and it might be better for him to look at them through an acrylic wall before he gets into the water with them."

Fitzwilliam noted that Dan's expression never changed. *If he has previously met Will or showed him the exhibit, he gave no indication of it. Maybe Mrs. Gray warned them that my memory is impaired.* He then thought about what Elizabeth had said, and he began to feel a slight stirring of nervousness. *What have I gotten myself into now? Mantas? Whale sharks? Is this safe? What if Elizabeth or the others are hurt?* He struggled to keep the apprehension from showing in his expression.

Lance looked at him, green eyes sparkling. "You'll love the tunnel, Fitz. It'll seem like the animals are swimming all around you. Lead the way, Dan." He took Jane's hand as they followed the guide. Fitzwilliam and Elizabeth fell in behind them.

Their guide talked as they walked slowly through the tunnel. "The Ocean Voyager exhibit is home to many gentle giants of the sea, including four whale sharks and four manta rays. They're the only manta rays ever to be in a U.S. aquarium. This exhibit was specially designed to house whale sharks, the largest fish species in the world. We also have trevally jacks, small and large stingrays, a huge goliath grouper, and several other types of sharks sharing this ocean habitat. It contains more than six million gallons of saltwater. There are 4,574 square feet of viewing windows, a 100-foot-long underwater tunnel, 185 tons of acrylic windows and the second largest viewing window in the world; it's 23 feet tall by 61 feet wide and 2 feet thick. No other aquarium in the world has ever attempted to manage the variety and size of fish as are found in this major exhibit."

He seems to be very proud of what they've accomplished here, and rightly so. Fitzwilliam tilted his head to look up, mesmerized by the beauty of the fish, swimming serenely all around and above him.

Dan continued, "The Aquarium is the only institution, outside of Asia, housing whale sharks – the park as a whole was designed around this whale shark exhibit. We were the first to attempt to import them from Taiwan using airplanes, trucks, and boats, and we did it to save them from being slaughtered. They were deducted from Taiwan's annual fishing kill quota, under which they would have been eaten had they not been purchased by the Aquarium. There's now a ban on the capture of whale sharks." He pointed to one of the manta rays. "Nandi there had been caught by accident in nets protecting the South African coast from sharks. We rescued her in 2008, and she was the first manta ray to be on display in this country; the Aquarium is one of only four sites in the world displaying one. We actually have four, as you can see."

Fitzwilliam then remembered a story he had heard before he

had switched places with Will. *There was a family attacked in Boston around 1730. I read about it in a book of their family memorials. Mr. Sampson was said to have been a reputable gentleman from London who had visited Boston for the benefit of his health, with every intention of a speedy return; however, he met a lady and fell in love, so he stayed and married her. While they were upon a pleasure excursion in Boston harbor, his boat was attacked by a shark, and he was tipped overboard and devoured.*

Fitzwilliam shivered as he watched the huge beasts, wondering if their appearance of serenity was deceptive. *Surely the people who run the Aquarium would not put us in danger. I assume they have done this many, many times.*

Lance and Jane pointed out different animals to each other, exclaiming over their beauty, but Elizabeth watched Fitzwilliam.

She released his hand, slid her arm under his, and put it around his waist, drawing him closer with her fingers. Her voice was low. "Can you swim?"

He nodded as he put his arm on top of hers, feeling her slender body against his as he drew her to his side. "I swam often as I was growing up. There were lakes and streams in many places on the Pemberley estate."

"They offer two types of excursions here: one is snorkeling and the other is SCUBA diving. Jane, Lance, and I are all certified divers, but I would imagine you aren't."

"No, I'm not."

She nodded. "You have to take a course for that. We can do it later if you think you want to after tonight. For now, I'll snorkel with you. We'll just swim across the top of the water, breathing through a snorkel tube. They'll give us wetsuits and a cylinder of air if you'd rather not use the snorkel. Flotation devices are included in the package, too. I've read up on it, because I've always wanted to do it."

He lowered his voice so that it was barely audible. "Is this safe? Am I putting us all in danger?"

She shook her head. "No one has ever been attacked in this Aquarium, though there have been a few accounts of workers having close encounters in other places. If a person is going to be bitten by a shark, it will almost always happen in the ocean, and even then, it's rare. Besides, whale sharks, unlike other sharks, eat mainly plankton and small fish. They're filter feeders."

His face showed his confusion, so she explained. "They don't eat people; they couldn't if they tried. As for the other sharks, remember we're going to be in that tank with people who are trained to keep us safe, and since we're going to snorkel, we won't be surrounded by the fish. We'll be watching more than anything else."

His eyes betrayed sadness. "But you would rather dive, I know. You want to be in the middle of the animals. This is supposed to be for you, yet you won't be doing what you want to do because of me. I should just stand on the side and watch the three of you dive. I could go to the big observation window while you're down there. I would enjoy that – seeing you swimming and enjoying yourself."

She stopped walking and looked up at him, determination in her eyes. "I won't get in the tank if you don't. We do this together, or we don't do it at all."

Lance and Jane caught up to the couple, eyeing them curiously. Dan stopped to wait for the party.

Embarrassed, Fitzwilliam motioned for the others to go ahead of them. When he and Elizabeth were alone again, he faced her and took her hands in his.

"Very well. We can use the cylinders and stay near the surface. I was always a strong swimmer. Perhaps we can go a little deeper than you think. I'll talk to Mrs. Gray about arranging SCUBA classes so that I can dive with you next time." His smile was a little self-satisfied.

"I'm glad you're going to be sensible." She looked at his face and tilted her head. "Why are you smiling like that?"

His smile grew broader, showing his dimples. "You said that

you wouldn't get in the tank if I didn't."

She raised an eyebrow. "I did. And?"

"You think you got your way, don't you?"

She raised both eyebrows. "Yes? Didn't I? Am I missing something?" She dropped his hands.

He smirked. "You said if we didn't do it together, we wouldn't do it at all."

"Is that so revolutionary?"

He wrapped his arms around her, pulling her to him as he lowered his head and kissed her softly. "Not for people who truly care for one another." His voice was a low whisper.

Her answer was to put her hands on either side of his face and hold him there while she stood on her tiptoes for another kiss.

She released him, looking up into his eyes.

His expression was serious. "I told you I love you, but you haven't said it to me. I think you return my feelings. Is it so hard for you to say?"

She nodded. "I've said it to only one man, and it was a mistake."

"You were much younger, then. Little more than a child." He kissed her forehead, and she looked down, hiding her face.

"I was stupid."

"Perhaps a bit. He was older, and he took advantage of you. No one could blame you."

Her voice was low. "Maybe so, but I do."

He pushed her away gently and tilted her chin up with his fingers so that he could see her eyes. "Remember that we're together now. You won't ever be alone again. We'll face everything that comes our way, side-by-side. And if you never can say you love me, I can accept that. I will still love you."

Lance's exasperated voice echoed down the tunnel. "Are you two coming? We need to get in the water."

Fitzwilliam chuckled. "We'll be there in a moment. You two go ahead. Just tell Dan to wait for us."

He kissed her quickly, and then took her hand. She smiled up at him as they walked quickly to join the others.

~~oo~~

Fitzwilliam was so excited as Elizabeth drove them back to her apartment that he could hardly stop talking. They had opted to use the air cylinders rather than the snorkels, and as a result, they had been able to descend a little lower in the tank. To his delight, a whale shark had swum beside him. He had actually reached out and touched the creature.

Elizabeth smiled as she listened to him, eyes glistening.

"Are you free to take diving lessons next week?" His enthusiasm was contagious. "I know you're already certified, but I would still like to have you with me while I learn. Jane and Lance seemed to be having such fun."

She laughed. "I have a couple of weeks before my classes start back, so I'm free in the afternoons and evenings after work."

"Dan said there are beautiful places to dive in the ocean, near reefs. Have you ever done that?"

"Not yet, but I want to." She glanced at him. "It's wonderful to see you so animated. I don't think I've ever seen you like this before."

"Because I've never been this happy until now." He reached for her hand and squeezed it. "My life was never as good in the past."

"Everything won't always be easy, you know, but I really enjoyed tonight. Thank you."

Fitzwilliam felt a chill. "That almost sounds like good bye."

"No, no. I'm just trying to be realistic. If I build this up too much, it will hurt more when I'm disappointed."

He was silent for several minutes. "You expect me to leave you."

"No."

He thought for a few moments. "You think that I'll hurt you."

She looked at him quickly, and then turned her attention back to the road. "I don't think you'll mean to hurt me. But you will, all the same. We all hurt each other. That's the way life is."

"That's true." He sighed. "But perhaps it would be better not to expect it. That may lead to finding pain where there was none. Don't look for the injury that isn't there."

Her voice was even. "That's good advice. I'll try to remember it."

He rubbed the top of her hand with his thumb. "If I ever hurt you, please tell yourself that it isn't intentional. I'll never hurt you on purpose, Elizabeth. I love you."

She nodded. "I know."

They were quiet as they drove up to her townhouse.

She turned off the ignition and stared through the windshield. He waited, giving her time to do or say whatever she wished.

After a few seconds, she turned her head and looked at him. "I'm sorry I'm moody sometimes. Forgive me?"

He smiled. "Always."

She reached for him. "I love you."

He knew a moment of perfect happiness as he kissed her.

~~oo~~

The first thing they saw when they opened the townhouse door was Jane and Lance sitting on the couch. She had her cell phone in her hand, staring at it, while he held her close with his arm around her shoulder. She was crying softly.

Elizabeth ran to her and dropped to her knees, looking up into her sister's face.

"What's wrong, Jane?"

"It's Mary," she said between sobs. "Dad just called to say she's missing. She's run away from home, and they can't find her... All her clothes and her car are gone... Her friends don't know where she is... She left while they were at work."

Elizabeth grabbed her phone from her purse. Fitzwilliam looked over her shoulder as she pulled up her log. There were several missed calls from Dr. Bennet. She went to her messages and opened a text from him, confirming what Jane had just told her.

She turned her head and looked up at Fitzwilliam, misery in her eyes, tears spilling down her cheeks. "I silenced my phone on our date so that nothing would spoil it."

He pulled her to her feet, turning her to face him. "You couldn't have stopped it. It's not your fault. Let's go."

"Where?"

"To your parents' house. Lance, are you coming?" He started toward the door.

Lance stood to his feet. "Right behind you. I'll drive the four of us in your car. Liz and Jane shouldn't drive while they're upset."

Fitzwilliam nodded his agreement.

Elizabeth followed him. "But you've never even met them or Mary."

"This certainly isn't how I planned it, but I'll meet them now. The circumstances aren't the best, I know, but I hope they'll accept my help."

They went out on the porch, waiting for Jane to wash her face and get her purse.

"Why are you so eager to help people you don't know? This could turn out very badly, and you'd be in the middle of it."

He stared at her. "Did you think I'd run at the first sign of trouble? I love you, Elizabeth. Together, remember? Your problems are my problems. Your hurts are my hurts. I hope that one day, your family will be my family."

Lance and Jane hurried out, closed the door and locked it, and headed for the car.

"It's going to be all right, isn't it?" Elizabeth asked as they walked down the steps.

He took her hand in his, glad that she couldn't see the steel in his blue eyes, keeping his voice calm and deliberate. "Yes, it will be fine. We'll find her." *If money and connections can accomplish it, we'll find her. I just hope she's all in one piece when we do. Whatever rock Greg Whitman is hiding under is the first place to look. If he's hurt her, he will pay dearly.*

CHAPTER 14

Deceiving others. That is what the world calls a romance.

Oscar Wilde

The next week flew by pleasantly for Will, his family, and his guests. Every day brought some new activity, and much time was spent in preparation for his and Elizabeth's engagement ball. Mrs. Reynolds and Mrs. Adams were often conferring with the ladies concerning the menu, guest list, and decorations, and once the date had been firmly set, Georgiana and Elizabeth, with the assistance of Mrs. Bennet, Caroline, and Mary, began to write the invitations. Caroline had been quite pleased when Mrs. Bennet pronounced her handwriting to be "very elegant, indeed."

To the relief of the entire party, the amusement of Mr. Bennet, and the chagrin of the staff, Miss Bingley had thrown herself wholeheartedly into the planning of the grand event and had been elated to spend many hours dispensing her wisdom and knowledge of the correct manner in which to celebrate such an august occasion as the formal announcement of a Darcy betrothal.

Will also spent many mornings riding the Pemberley estate with Elizabeth, Mr. Bennet, John Bennet, and Mr. Justice Miller. Three gentlemen in residence chose to remain behind at the great house most of those mornings, though they did ride with the group on occasion. Colonel Fitzwilliam admitted privately to Will that he was loath to spend too much time away from Pemberley while Charles Bingley was present and determined to court Jane. Will assumed that Mr. Wentworth-Fitzwilliam likewise wished to further his suit with Georgiana, though Wentworth did not say that when he made his excuses to stay behind.

Since Charles had shown little inclination to ride on the early morning excursions, Colonel Fitzwilliam had begun to manifest an unusual interest in the preparations for the ball. He spent many hours helping the ladies with the guest list as he was a great repository of knowledge concerning the Darcy and Fitzwilliam relatives and close acquaintances. He also knew their preferences in food and entertainment, which he related with delightful anecdotes and embellishments. The ladies accepted his presence and suggestions gladly, for wherever the colonel chose to be, he was always genial and amusing, as well as exceedingly charming.

After breakfast one morning, before their morning ride, Will was in his study, conferring with his steward when Carlson came in bearing the recently delivered post on a silver salver. He stood before Will's desk and cleared his throat.

Glancing up at the butler, Will began to tell him to put the mail on his desk, but something in Carlson's expression stopped him. "Is there a problem, Carlson?"

The man stood up very straight, his back stiff. "I am not entirely certain, Mr. Darcy; however, I have noticed an *irregularity* ..." He said the word as if it tasted foul in his mouth. "... and I thought it best to bring it to your attention."

"Thank you, Carlson." Will looked up at Mr. Miller. "I believe our business is concluded for today. Please see to the roof of the cottage Smith and his family inhabited, as well as the broken windows and the damage to the walls of the dwelling in which Stevens lived. The new tenants can move in as soon as the repairs are finished. I hope to have them comfortably installed before the late growing season is completely passed."

Mr. Miller nodded, and Will continued, "When we ride today, I wish to discuss ideas concerning the latest farming methods. We may also look at a piece of land near the river which I think would be a good location for a business producing pottery and glass. Mr. Josiah Wedgwood, who has just this year given his son the proprietorship of his business, has agreed to advise me as to the particulars.

Noting the astonished faces of both Mr. Miller and Carlson, Will smiled and continued. "We have tenants which could work in the mill during the winters to supplement their incomes. In addition, I plan to introduce farm equipment to Pemberley which will mean that fewer of our people will need to work the land. For instance, Thomas Jefferson has just invented a moldboard plow of least resistance which will greatly refine and speed up the planting process. We will improve upon his idea by casting it in iron rather than using wood. Those tenants who are displaced by the machinery would have employment and regular pay. I also wish to discuss updating the toilet facilities here in the house. After all, Queen Elizabeth had fairly modern plumbing two hundred years ago. I see no need to wait to use the same invention she had installed in her Richmond palace."

Carlson wrinkled his nose. "But, sir – the odor."

Will smiled. "Alexander Cumming of Bond Street in London invented a flush toilet twenty years ago which addressed that very problem. I have thought of several changes which could be made to his design that would improve it, and I shall contact him directly. The kitchens would also benefit from modernization. Centrifugal hand pumps were invented one hundred years ago. There is no good reason why we should not have them at Pemberley. People are so averse to trying anything new that they deny themselves the conveniences of doing so. I shall not do that."

I even made a hand pump for a science fair in elementary school, and I won. Nana Rose suggested it. Now I know why.

Both the steward and the butler raised their eyebrows, and Will smiled. "Change is coming, and we will embrace it here. Pemberley will not suffer the fate of so many other estates. We will adjust, and we will prosper."

After a rather awkward moment of silence in which both men looked quite shocked, the steward recovered and nodded again. "Of course, sir, and we are all fortunate to have such a forward thinking master."

Will smiled and Mr. Miller left the room, closing the door behind him.

Will then looked up at the butler with interest. "Well, Carlson. What have you noticed that is out of the ordinary?"

Carlson placed the salver on the desk and, frowning, handed Will a letter from the top of the stack. "Miss Georgiana has received a letter from a Miss Phoebe Barlow."

Will drew his brows together, examining the letter before he spoke. "My sister and I invited Miss Barlow to join us for the remainder of the summer and attend the ball. She is obviously replying to the invitation. How is that unusual?"

Carlson cleared his throat. "My apologies, sir. I had no intention of implying that there was anything amiss in your sister's receipt of a letter from the lady."

"Then I fail to understand your concern."

"It has to do with the handwriting, sir."

Will examined the missive closely. "Very lovely and feminine. Again, I fail to see the problem."

Carlson shifted from one foot to the other, clearly uncomfortable. "Miss Barlow's handwriting has changed, sir."

"Do not distress yourself, Carlson." Will's voice was kind. "How do you know of Miss Barlow's handwriting? Where have you seen it before? I know that Georgiana has never met the young lady, and this is the first letter my sister has received from her."

Carlson drew his brows together. "Very true, sir, but Miss

Lydia Bennet and Miss Catherine Lucas have received numerous letters from Miss Barlow. Nearly every day, one or the other of those young ladies has a letter from her. Not only is the handwriting dissimilar, but also the directions are different."

He took another letter from the stack and handed it to his master. "See for yourself, sir, for Miss Lydia has another this morning. Could the young ladies be friends with two Miss Phoebe Barlows?"

That's highly unlikely. Will took the offered missives and placed both of them on his desk, studying them intently. After a few minutes, he looked up at his butler. "Carlson, please ask Miss Elizabeth and Mr. Bennet to join me here as soon as possible. And, Carlson, I appreciate your attention to detail and ask for your complete discretion in this matter." *Something smells fishy here, and I'm going to get to the bottom of it immediately.*

Carlson bowed deeply. "Thank you, sir. You may depend upon my silence." He turned and left the room.

After a few minutes, Carlson opened the study door for Elizabeth and her father.

Will looked up, unsmiling. "Carlson, we are not to be disturbed."

"Very good, sir. I will remain just outside the door."

As Elizabeth and Mr. Bennet approached Will's desk, the butler quietly left the room and closed the door.

Will stood to receive them. "Shall we sit in the more comfortable chairs?" he asked, gesturing to the seating area before the fireplace.

"As you wish." Mr. Bennet led Elizabeth to the settee, and Will followed, holding the letters in his hand and seating himself across from them.

"This is a most delicate matter," he began.

Mr. Bennet eyed him shrewdly. "I have already come to that conclusion. Please relieve my anxiety and simply say whatever it is you have to tell us."

Will nodded solemnly. "Georgiana received a letter from Phoebe Barlow this morning."

Elizabeth's expression showed her relief. "From your demeanour, I thought that someone had died, or that you planned to call off our wedding. Whatever you have to say cannot be as bad as that."

Will smiled faintly. "Surely you know that I would never give you up, Elizabeth. However, what I have to tell you may be very serious. I need your help to get to the bottom of it as quickly as possible."

Mr. Bennet leaned forward and spoke forcefully. "Out with it, man! I think we are fully prepared for news which may be unpleasant."

"As you wish." Will took a deep breath. "Since you have arrived at Pemberley, Miss Lydia and Miss Catherine have been receiving letters on a daily basis from Miss Barlow. My butler, Mr. Carlson, told me this morning that the handwriting on the letters they received is quite different from the handwriting on this letter from the young lady to Georgiana. In addition, their letters were sent from an address different from the one to my sister. Do they know another Phoebe Barlow besides Colonel Barlow's sister?"

Mr. Bennet raised an eyebrow. "No, they do not. It seems we have a mystery here."

Elizabeth nodded. "It does indeed, Papa. How shall we solve it?"

The older man's voice was determined. "Will, what do you propose? Should we search their rooms for letters to compare to the one your sister received?"

Will shook his head. "Fortunately, that will not yet be necessary, for Miss Lydia received a letter, supposedly from Miss Phoebe Barlow, this morning. Examine them for yourself before taking any further action." Will handed him both letters.

Both Mr. Bennet and Elizabeth looked closely at the letters, comparing the handwriting and directions.

Mr. Bennet nodded. "They are, indeed, quite different. It appears that Lydia's letter was sent from Nottingham. That is in this county, not all that far from here."

Elizabeth turned Lydia's letter over in her hands. "The paper is not the same either. However, Lydia's letter looks exactly like the ones she received at Longbourn, though they were first sent from Meryton and then from Brighton once the regiment departed."

Her father looked at her with surprise. "How long has Lydia been corresponding with Miss. Barlow?"

Elizabeth thought a moment. "Since she met Phoebe in Meryton. I thought it rather odd that Miss Barlow would write to Lydia when they saw each other nearly every day, but I concluded that it was a silly affectation. I remembered how much I enjoyed receiving letters from anyone when I was her age. Lydia always replied promptly, as well, which further astonished me. She is not usually so responsible about her social obligations."

Mr. Bennet's face hardened. "Will, do you mind opening your sister's letter?"

Will frowned slightly. "I would rather not, but as the alternative is to involve Georgiana in this by having her open it, I suppose I will. After all, there can be nothing of a personal nature in it, for they have never met. I think it would be better if this remained among the three of us for now."

"I have no such compunction concerning opening my daughter's correspondence, as you well know."

Elizabeth put her hand on her father's. "Gently, Papa. We may need to reseal it so that Lydia does not know we have read it."

He handed Georgiana's letter back to Will and Lydia's to Elizabeth. His voice was gruff. "As I do not feel particularly gentle towards your sister at this time, Elizabeth, perhaps you should open it."

Will and Elizabeth opened the letters and read silently.

He was through reading before she was, and he looked up at her only to see her expression change to one of horror. He broke the silence. "As I suspected, Georgiana's letter is a very short one. Miss Barlow accepts our invitation and will arrive tomorrow."

As tears began to roll down Elizabeth's cheeks, Will stood and walked quickly to her, kneeling by her, placing his hand on her arm. "Whatever it is, we can take care of it, my love. Can you tell me what is in Lydia's letter?"

She lifted her face, looking from Will to her father. "It is far worse than I ever expected. Lydia has been corresponding regularly with George Wickham, and he pretends to have a *tendre* for her. The letters to Catherine seem to have been written to Lydia as well, sent to Catherine only to divert suspicion from Lydia, for he asks if Catherine has given her his letters. Had Lydia received a letter every day, we would have been more likely to notice and question her."

Mr. Bennet stood. "I shall put a stop to this at once." He strode briskly towards the door.

"Please, wait!" Will called out to stop him. "At the present moment, Wickham has no idea we are on to him. Perhaps we can use this to our advantage." He turned his attention to Elizabeth, wiping a tear from her cheek and retrieving his handkerchief from his pocket for her. "What else does he say?"

She sobbed aloud, crumpling the handkerchief and holding it to her forehead. "They are planning to elope in two days' time. All the particulars are in this letter. He intends to come to Pemberley in the night and sneak her away. Stupid, stupid girl! She is silly enough for anything, but this? I cannot believe that he loves her. He will not marry her, and her life will be ruined."

Will smiled at her tenderly. "Elizabeth, it shall be well. Wickham has made it easier for me to catch him. We will be ready for him, and he will never touch your sister." *Beyond what he already has done. I'm sure he hasn't been writing her this long without their having secret meetings. Those details would be in the other letters. Would it be better if Mr. Bennet and Elizabeth never know?*

Mr. Bennet walked slowly back to the settee and sat down heavily. "Does he write in detail of their previous relationship?"

Elizabeth's expression was unutterably sad. "He refers to kisses and touching, but nothing more. They were certainly indiscrete, but perhaps not truly intimate. Do you want to read it, Papa?"

"No, and neither do I want to read her other letters, though I shall find them and make a blazing fire of them. She shall not keep them to moon over as she pines for the man who would destroy both our family's reputation and her life."

Will rose to his feet. "Lydia must not have any suspicion that we know about her elopement. She might find a way to alert Wickham, and then she could leave with him later. After all, you cannot lock her in a room with barred windows."

Mr. Bennet nodded. "I am very tempted to do just that; however, I do see the wisdom in what you said. I shall wait until we deal with him before I search her belongings for the other letters." He looked up at Will. "Why would he settle on Lydia? He well knows that her dowry is very small, and I can give him nothing else. To be candid, of all of my daughters, Lydia is the one with the least to offer in marriage. She is silly and vain, without an ounce of common sense."

Will's voice was quiet and low. "Elizabeth and I will marry soon, and Lydia will be my sister. Her material value will increase substantially. Wickham knows that I would not allow my sister to live in poverty. In addition, he hates me and seeks to revenge himself upon me and my family. We were great friends as boys, but he always resented that I was the master's son and he was merely the son of a steward. In his mind, I inherited everything for which his father worked." He paused to collect himself. "I feel certain that you have heard the lies he spread about me. What you do not know is that he tried to elope with Georgiana when she was but fifteen years old. Fortunately, I found out about his plan in time to stop him."

Mr. Bennet looked at him aghast. "He has tried this once

before? And with your sweet sister?'"

"He has, but he did not succeed. He shall fail this time as well."

Elizabeth folded the letter in half and held it in her hand. "What shall we do with this? Lydia must receive it, for Wickham expects a reply. He may not come if she does not answer, and I would prefer to catch him here than to wait, always expecting to hear the worst – that she is gone and beyond our help."

Will smiled. "My thoughts exactly, my love. Do you think you can refold it exactly as it was? There was no seal to speak of – merely a blob of wax. We can remove the old wax and affix a larger one to cover the mark. It is an easy matter to slip it back into the mail and put the salver in its usual place. Lydia will be none the wiser. I shall do the same with the letter to Georgiana."

She raised an eyebrow as she carefully folded the letter as it was before. "I had no idea you were so devious, Mr. Darcy. I see I shall have to pay close attention to you and watch you vigilantly."

Will's eyes brightened, and his smiled widened, showing his dimples. "I shall depend upon it."

Mr. Bennet stood wearily to his feet, looking older than his years. "Come, you two. Fold the blasted letter and seal it. Let us have an end to the matter." He sighed. "How I shall act normally for the next two days is beyond me. Perhaps I shall put on my cap and nightshirt and take to my bed, feigning illness, for if I see Lydia now, I might strangle her. Even should I manage to avoid that, your mother would certainly know all is not well with me, and she would worry until I told her everything."

Elizabeth looked at him with compassion. "You may do that if you wish, Papa. It would be no trouble to supply you with books and deliver your meals to your chambers. I will distract Mama with plans for the ball. We can even plan the wedding. We must set a date very soon."

He attempted to smile. "You will find me in my room, then. If I begin to talk to myself, I shall send for you, my dear, so that we may take a long walk to clear my head." He walked slowly from the room, sadly lacking his usual jauntiness.

As the door closed behind Mr. Bennet, Will tenderly pulled Elizabeth to her feet and held her in his arms. "I am happy to hear you speak of wedding plans, my love. Do not fret about Wickham. We will be well prepared for him."

She tilted her face up to kiss his cheek. "I will not worry, for I am as ready to be wed as you are. Besides, nothing will command my mother's attention like arranging a wedding. The ball will pale in comparison."

"Then, as your father said, let us put an end to the matter of Wickham and Lydia. Would you help me reseal the letters?"

"I can better accomplish that goal if you release me."

He made a sound of regret and dropped his arms to his sides. "There ... I have let you go, but only temporarily."

Elizabeth smiled as she walked past him to his desk. "Come help me."

He joined her. "We shall do this together."

Her voice was gentle. "Always."

CHAPTER 15

We cannot change our past. We cannot change the fact that people act in a certain way. We cannot change the inevitable. The only thing we can do is play on the one string we have, and that is our attitude.

Charles R. Swindoll

Fitzwilliam and Lance followed Elizabeth and Jane up the steps to the Bennet house. Before they reached the door, Anne Bennet had opened it and stepped out on the porch to meet them, gathering her daughters into her arms.

Fitzwilliam and Lance paused on the steps, allowing the mother and daughters a few moments to comfort each other. *She puts on a brave face, but her eyes are red and swollen. This must be terrible for her and Mr. Bennet.*

After a moment, Mrs. Bennet released Jane and Elizabeth, extending her hand to Fitzwilliam. "Hello, I'm Anne Bennet."

He stepped up and took her hand, shaking it as he lowered his eyes. *What can I say? Conventional greetings would seem to border on rudeness in this awkward situation.*

Elizabeth spoke up quickly. "Mom, this is Fitzwilliam Darcy."

Anne's voice trembled slightly as she spoke. "Very nice to meet you, though I'm sorry it's under these conditions. Please call me Anne."

He looked up and nodded his agreement. *I, too, am sorry.*

She looked at Lance, attempting a smile. "Hello, Lance. It's always good to see you. Why don't we all go in the house?"

Mrs. Bennet turned, leading the group through the door and into the foyer where Mr. Bennet waited to greet them.

He looks so tired. Fitzwilliam's anger mounted as he set his mouth into a grim line. *Whoever caused these good people all this pain will pay dearly for it.*

Anne Bennet went to stand beside her husband, moving aside so that Jane and Elizabeth could embrace him. After a moment, the girls stepped back. Anne took a breath and turned to face the two young men. "George, this is Fitzwilliam Darcy. You already know Lance, of course."

Mr. Bennet reached out his hand, nodding in acknowledgement of both young men, as he shook Fitzwilliam's hand firmly.

I know how you feel. I remember how dark it seemed when I found Georgiana ready to elope with George Wickham. "I wish we were meeting under happier circumstances, but I hope to be able to assist you, if you'll allow me to do so."

The older man smiled sadly. "I've never been a particularly proud man, Fitzwilliam. My daughter's life may be at stake, so I'll gladly accept help from anyone who offers it. The police won't get involved until tomorrow night at the earliest. They say she has to be missing for forty-eight hours before they can begin an investigation. Since we didn't see her this morning before we left for work, they'll start their countdown from when we saw her late last night. She could've sneaked out in the night without our knowledge, though I doubt it. Her car was still here this morning."

He ran his fingers through his already disheveled gray hair. "Since she's eighteen, they don't consider her to be a runaway, and there's no evidence that she was taken against her will. In their eyes, no crime has been committed. She won't be classified as a missing person until tomorrow night at the earliest. I have a feeling they don't consider Mary's disappearance to be a serious matter, but they don't know her like we do."

Anne patted his arm. "Let's go sit down, dear. Maybe Lance and Fitzwilliam have some ideas."

He nodded his agreement. The two of them then turned and walked into the den, followed by their daughters and guests.

After they were all seated, Lance leaned forward. "Has Mary been hanging out with a new crowd? Has she been dating anyone?"

Mr. Bennet shrugged. "When we called her high school friends, they said they haven't seen much of her since graduation. She used to be with them all the time. At first, I thought it was because she had a summer job, but now I'm not so sure. As far as her social life, I don't think she's dated anyone since she and her boyfriend broke up just before graduation, though she's still gone nearly every evening. She said she was at work, but who knows? She may not have told us that she was meeting someone. It's possible she outright lied to us, telling us she was at work while she was really with a man."

Elizabeth's eyes narrowed at the information. "I didn't know she was working this summer. What was she doing?"

Anne frowned slightly. "I was sure I told you about that. I guess not. She was waitressing at Canoe. Didn't you say it was a nice place? We've been there before. We saw nothing out of the ordinary, so we thought she'd be fine there."

Surely she couldn't be with him. Fitzwilliam was careful to keep his agitation out of his voice. "Has she mentioned any new friends from the restaurant?"

Anne shook her head. "She really doesn't tell us much anymore, and she hasn't invited anyone over in the last month or so. But now that I think of it, that's not like her. Her friends have always hung out here. I guess I've been too busy with work. This is my fault."

Elizabeth's voice was strident. "It's not your fault, Mom, any more than it's Dad's, Jane's, or mine. Mary is eighteen. None of us should have to babysit her 24/7. We all work. At some point, she has to become responsible for herself and her own actions."

Fitzwilliam put his hand over hers. "Would you mind if we looked at her room?"

Mr. Bennet sighed. "We've already combed it thoroughly. There's nothing there, but you're more than welcome to try." He threw his hands up. "Maybe we missed something that you'll notice since we were upset at the time."

Fitzwilliam stood. "Thank you. Elizabeth, would you come with me?"

"Sure." She looked up at him and then rose to her feet, taking his hand as she led him to the staircase.

Jane and Lance followed them. Jane paused and looked over her shoulder at her parents. Lance stopped beside her. "Are you coming?"

Mr. Bennet shook his head slowly. "No. I'll just stay down here and wait for you."

Anne quickly wiped a tear from her cheek. "You two go on. I'll keep George company."

~~oo~~

Fitzwilliam looked around the rather messy room, unsure of where to start. Elizabeth began to pull out drawers one at a time. She looked over her shoulder. "Fitzwilliam, you're tall. Check the top shelves of her closet."

Lance went to one of the bedside tables. "What are we looking for?"

Jane turned on the lamp on the other bedside table. "She used to keep a diary. Look for a journal of some sort."

Elizabeth was methodical, dumping and refilling each drawer

before she moved to another, spreading the contents on the carpet, searching through the clothing piece by piece. "Look for notes or letters, too – scraps of paper with doodling on them."

Lance emptied the drawer of the small table on the bed, and Jane followed his example. They went through the items thoroughly, putting everything neatly back in the drawers as they finished.

Fitzwilliam sighed. "There's nothing up here but shoes and handbags." He scanned the room. *Maybe she dropped something.* He got on all fours and lowered his head to the floor, tilting his head downward, looking under the chest-of-drawers and dresser. *Just some dust.* After crawling the few feet to the bed, he peered under it and saw a crumpled up piece of something. *What's this?* He flattened out on the floor and maneuvered himself to make the best use of his long arms. *It must have fallen though the space between the headboard and the mattress.*

Elizabeth came to kneel on the floor beside him with her phone lit up, shining the light under the bed, trying to see what he had found.

Once Fitzwilliam had grasped his target in his hand, he backed out from under the bed and handed the small piece of paper to Elizabeth.

Dropping her phone, she took the paper eagerly, and then sat back with her knees tucked under her and flattened it out. As she looked at it, her face fell. "It's a phone number, but there's no name."

Jane turned to look over Elizabeth's shoulder. "Should we call it and see whose number it is?"

Lance shook his head. "No, I don't think that's the best way to handle this."

Fitzwilliam smiled. "Tell me your idea."

"The number may belong to one of her high school buddies, or it may be someone she just met at Canoe. You have the connections to find out whose number this is without alerting the owner of the number. We may need the element of surprise to recover Mary, so it's probably best not to tip our hand too soon."

"So you think I should call in the investigative team we use at Darcy Enterprises?"

Lance nodded. "Definitely. This number is the only clue we have right now."

Jane's expression showed her surprise. "You employ a team of investigators?"

"Of course." Fitzwilliam's voice was matter-of-fact. "They research everyone who applies for a job at Darcy Enterprises or a scholarship through the Foundation."

Jane swallowed visibly. "Do you have files on all of us?"

Fitzwilliam shrugged. "I have no idea. In all likelihood, someone probably did do a cursory background check on you and your family once we became friends. I think they do that with anyone who has a connection to me or the company."

Lance put his arm around her shoulders. "My dad works for Darcy Enterprises, so they certainly keep an eye on me. It's not a big deal."

Ignoring them, Elizabeth was busy on her cell phone. "Canoe is open until 10 PM Thursdays through Saturdays. Maybe someone is still there cleaning and getting ready to lock up." She punched in a number. "Hello. This is Elizabeth Bennet. My sister Mary works there as a waitress. Are you a manager? Great. Would you mind answering a few questions for me, Mr. Tyler?"

Fitzwilliam reached for her phone. She raised an eyebrow and frowned, but handed it to him.

"Hello, Mr. Tyler. I'm a close friend of the Bennet family. Mary is a little late getting home tonight, and her parents are worried. Can you tell me what time she left work?" He paused. "Oh, she wasn't scheduled to work tonight? Thank you so much. We're sorry to have bothered you."

Elizabeth stood and put her hands on her hips, eyes flashing. "Why did you do that? Maybe he could have told us if she's made new friends who work there or was ever picked up after work by a guy."

Fitzwilliam sat on the edge of the bed and pulled her down beside him. "Elizabeth, Tyler may be the guy who has her. We don't want to raise suspicions at the restaurant until we know whose cell phone number this is. She may have told someone there that she was leaving. We have to be very careful."

She bit her lower lip, eyebrows drawn together.

Lance nodded. "He's right, Liz. We don't want the employees to start talking to each other about it. It would be better to get the name connected with this number, and then visit Canoe in person. Looking at someone's face while they talk can help you know if they're being truthful or not."

After returning Elizabeth's phone to her, Fitzwilliam stood to pull his own from his pocket. He held his hand out to her for the paper. After she placed it in his palm, he walked away from the bed and stopped by the door with his back to the group, pulling up a number on his phone. "Hello, Steve. This is Fitzwilliam. Can you check this number for me and get back to me with the name as soon as possible? It's a bit of an emergency." After a pause, he read the number aloud. "After you do that, please pull a background report on a man by the last name of Tyler who works at Canoe restaurant." He was silent for a few moments. "Thanks. I'll wait here for your call."

Fitzwilliam turned around to see three expectant faces. "He's on it. Now we just wait a few minutes." He had just walked across the room and sat down by Elizabeth on the bed again when his phone signaled an incoming call. He swiped the screen with his finger and put the phone to his ear.

His voice was low. "Yes … I see … How about Tyler? … Hmmm … I have an idea. Hold on a minute." He looked up at Elizabeth. "Do you have Mary's number?"

Nodding, she pulled it up on her phone and then showed it to him.

He smiled at her. "My girlfriend's sister is missing. I want you to trace this number and tell me the last number called, where it was used, whatever you can. The number is local." He read it to the investigator as he looked at Elizabeth's phone. "Her name is Mary Bennet; her parents' names are George and Anne Bennet of Atlanta. See if any of their credit cards have been used in the last thirty-six hours or so. And if you can think of any other way to find her, I'm authorizing you to do it. Thanks. Let me know what you find out."

Fitzwilliam ended the call and glanced at Elizabeth.

Her eyes were wide. "What did he say about the number and Tyler?"

He took her hand in his. "I'm sorry, but it belongs to a pre-paid cell phone bought with a phony name and address over a month ago. He couldn't trace it. Tyler has a couple of parking tickets, but otherwise, he's an upstanding citizen."

Lance whistled. "Good idea to check the credit cards. Mary may have taken them."

Jane's voice was quiet. "She wouldn't have had to. Mom added her as an authorized user on several of her own cards. I know because she had them a couple of months ago when we went shopping together." She looked at Fitzwilliam. "How did you know to check them?"

Fitzwilliam's smile was crooked. "Lance and I watch 'Law and Order,' 'Person of Interest,' and 'Criminal Intent' all the time at The Oaks. I've also had to use the investigators a time or two at work already. I'm becoming more familiar with the technology of this day."

Lance started walking back and forth while Jane sat on the bed on the other side of Elizabeth.

Finally, he stopped in front of Fitzwilliam. "There was a reason that cell phone was bought with a fake name and address."

Fitzwilliam nodded gravely. "I've already thought of that."

Elizabeth raised an eyebrow. "This was planned in advance.

Whoever did this has been setting it up for several weeks. He made himself untraceable."

"Who would do that? Mary isn't important enough for all this." Jane began to cry softly. Lance moved to pull her into his arms, whispering to her that everything would be fine.

Elizabeth looked at Fitzwilliam shrewdly. "Mary may not be the real target."

"I've thought of that, too."

Her voice dropped several pitches. "You called me your girlfriend."

"That's how I think of you." He tucked a strand of hair behind her ear. "My people at work know it. I have ensured your protection."

"Then taking Mary could be a way to hurt you. They can't get to me directly, but what hurts me hurts you. Remember?"

"I do, and you may be right." He sighed. "But there's another possibility."

She was puzzled. "Who else here is as important as you are? None of the Bennets are wealthy. We don't run a corporation or have huge amounts of money at our disposal."

Fitzwilliam kept his voice calm as he stroked her cheek. "True, but you have access to me, and I would pay any amount to get your sister safely back in order to make your family whole again. Maybe someone wants to kill two birds with one stone, as you say. Maybe they have a grudge against you, and they want to make you suffer while extorting money from me at the same time."

Fear showed in her eyes, and she made a choking sound. "He wouldn't do it. Surely Mary couldn't be that stupid."

He put his arm around her. "Did Mary ever know what he did to you? She's several years younger than you."

Elizabeth shook her head; her voice was bitter. "No, only you, Jane, and Lance know what he's really like. He paid attention to her when he came here, and Mary thought he was wonderful – the big, handsome, popular football star taking time to play video games with her. We even took her with us to movies and to play putt-putt. She went to games with us to watch him and Lance play. Oh, dear God!" Her words were brittle and cold as ice. "He could be doing to her what he did to me. I should have told her to stay away from him. I could've stopped this. It's him. I know it is." She clenched her hands tightly in her lap as tears ran down her cheeks. "He'll rape her just like he did me."

Fitzwilliam pulled her to him tightly. "Don't jump to conclusions just yet, love. It may not be Greg's doing, and even if it is, he'll probably ask for money before he hurts her. He would want to hold that threat over us to make us pay."

He noticed that Jane and Lance had stopped talking and were staring at them, listening to every word with horror.

Lance hit the wall with his fist; words exploding from him. "I should've killed him when I had the chance. I should've beaten him to death when I caught him with Liz."

"Stop it!" Fitzwilliam thundered. "Stop blaming yourselves. That won't help us get her back. Steve will call back in a few minutes, and I'll handle it." *If he's touched her, I'll take care of him myself in my own way. I won't kill him. He should have to live a long, miserable life.*

They all stopped talking as an agitated voice came from just outside the door.

"Would anyone like to tell us who did what to Liz, and who Lance is going to kill – and who Steve is?" Mr. Bennet and Mrs. Bennet moved to stand framed in the doorway. "And would it be possible to do that without punching a hole through the wall?"

Fitzwilliam was the first to speak. "Mr. Bennet, I –" His ringtone sounded, and he held up his index finger. "I have to take this." He swiped the face of his phone. "Yes? … Okay. I'll meet you there."

He stood up and pocketed his phone. "Steve is one of the private investigators employed by Darcy Enterprises. He just told me that Mrs. Bennet's Mastercard was used this morning at the airport and again a few hours ago at a hotel in Los Angeles. I'm going to meet him at the airport now. We don't have time to buy tickets to fly commercial, so we'll have to take one of the company jets. Steve is calling our pilot while I drive there."

"You shouldn't drive anywhere yet, because you don't really know how to drive." Elizabeth's tone was firm. "I'm coming with you. She's my sister, so don't argue with me."

"I know you well enough to realize that I would be unsuccessful if I tried." He looked at Lance. "Will you stay here with the Bennets in case we have more information to give them or need help on this end?"

He nodded.

As Elizabeth and Fitzwilliam headed toward the bedroom door, Mr. Bennet blocked their way. "Mary is my daughter and my responsibility. I'm coming with the two of you. You can't do anything legally concerning her without me."

Fitzwilliam nodded. "Fine. We'll buy whatever we need when we get there."

Mr. Bennet quickly hugged his wife, and then hurried down the steps with Fitzwilliam and Elizabeth to the car.

As she slipped behind the wheel, her father's voice came from behind her. "It was Greg Whitman, wasn't it? You were never the same after the two of you broke up. What did he do to you? You should have told me, Elizabeth."

After checking to see that both men were in the car with the doors closed, she looked in the rearview mirror at her father. "I can't do this right now. I have to drive, and I can't let myself get upset. We can talk on the plane, Dad, though it won't do any good and certainly won't make you feel any better. I'd rather just drop it. I'm over it now; it won't do any good to dredge it all up again."

She started the car and backed out of the driveway.

The voice from the backseat was quiet and sad. "My strong, sweet girl. He really hurt you, didn't he, my Lizzy?"

Fitzwilliam heard her words catch in her throat. He looked back at Mr. Bennet. "He did, but if he's the one who has Mary, we'll make sure that he doesn't have a chance to do to her what he did to Elizabeth. Lance is nicer than I am."

Mr. Bennet spoke again, but with confidence rather than grief. "You know, I researched you on the internet when my wife told me you were dating my Lizzy, and I think you might be right. Lance may be a little nicer, but you're a good man, Fitzwilliam. He has devoted his life to helping others by his profession, while you, because of your birth, have followed the corporate path. However, you have used your money to do good things, and you have the reputation of always finishing what you start. I like Lance well enough, but given the choice, I'd rather have you in the car with us now for this particular job."

Fitzwilliam glanced back at him. "Thank you. I'll do my best to live up to my reputation."

Mr. Bennet nodded.

And if he's raped Mary, I'll make certain that he will never be able to do that to anyone else. I may have left George Wickham free to prey on other innocents when I left 1795, but I refuse to make that mistake again. He looked over at Elizabeth. *I'm ready to do whatever it takes.*

CHAPTER 16

There are no secrets that time does not reveal.

Jean Racine

Late in the following afternoon, Will sat by Elizabeth, enjoying the excitement of his betrothed and the other ladies as they eagerly anticipated the arrival of Miss Phoebe Barlow. Before Lydia and Catherine could hurry yet the twentieth time to the parlour windows, they recognized the sound of the gravel crunching beneath an arriving carriage, assuring them all that their guest had come at last.

Lydia raced from the room, into the hallway, and down the front steps. Before Miss Barlow had exited the equipage, Lydia was chattering away to her, exulting in all the pleasures of being at Pemberley.

The rest of the party of ladies, minus Miss Bingley and Mrs. Bennet but with the addition of Will, made their way outside to welcome her at a more sedate pace.

Will watched with interest from a little distance as Elizabeth introduced Miss Barlow to the other girls. *It seems to me that*

Lydia keeps trying to pull Phoebe Barlow to the side, away from everyone else. Ummm ... I wonder.

In due time, Elizabeth drew Miss Barlow's arm through her own with a determined expression and led her to Will. *Elizabeth must have noticed the same thing I did. She may suspect, as I do, that Lydia will try to warn her about the letters. Could it be possible that Miss Barlow actually knew Lydia and Wickham were using her in such a way? Surely not.* He smiled and bowed as his fiancée presented their new arrival to him.

Miss Barlow removed her arm from Elizabeth's to curtsey before him. Her auburn curls peeked from beneath her bonnet as she raised her sparkling eyes to his. "It is such a pleasure to meet you at last, Mr. Darcy. I have heard so much about you, your family, and your beautiful home."

He bowed to her with an amused expression. "In truth? I hope you shall find the good things to be true and the bad not as dire as they may have been portrayed to be. And, Miss Barlow, please call me Will. We do not stand upon ceremony with our guests."

She raised one delicate brow, and her brown eyes twinkled in merriment. "Now that is unexpected. I had heard just the opposite."

Will laughed aloud at her impudence. "I know not who has provided you with such poor knowledge of my character, but I hope you will soon learn not to believe everything you have heard about me." Will smiled as he and Elizabeth turned towards the front door. He possessively tucked her hand into the crook of his elbow, and the two of them led the others into the house.

He heard Phoebe whisper to Georgiana as they walked behind him and Elizabeth.

"I was told he was an extremely serious man, but he smiles and seems quite cheerful."

Georgiana chuckled quietly. "I daresay he has changed a good bit since he met Miss Elizabeth. Perhaps your source does not see him often enough to know him as he really is."

"You may be right, but she is a close relative of his. She would have no reason to misrepresent him to me."

"A relative of his?" Georgiana paused. "Then she would also be a relative of mine."

Will was surprised at the revelation. *Could Phoebe Barlow know Lady Catherine? I don't see how, and even if she does, I doubt that my aunt would talk about me in that way to anyone not closely related to us. She would prefer that I be more conscious of my rank and position in society, but she would not expose a family member to gossip. It's more likely that she would seek to hide my faults so that they don't reflect badly upon her.*

Before the newly arrived young lady had time to identify the personage from whom she had received the information, she was interrupted by Lydia who tapped on her shoulder to ask a question concerning the officers of the regiment.

Mrs. Reynolds met the party just inside the door, and she, along with Elizabeth and Georgiana, climbed the stairs to show Phoebe to her rooms. Will adjourned with the rest of the party to the parlour to join Miss Bingley, Mrs. Bennet, and the men. He walked across the room to stand with the other four gentlemen, as Mr. Bennet had elected to remain in his rooms, and they chatted amiably until the three ladies returned.

As soon as Georgiana, Elizabeth, and Miss Barlow walked into the drawing room, Georgiana introduced her to the members of the party she had not as yet met. When she called Colonel Fitzwilliam's name, he stood and bowed.

Miss Barlow's surprise was evident. "You are Colonel Richard Fitzwilliam? How extraordinary. I had no idea that you were here at Pemberley. Your mother did not mention it in her last letter to me. I thought that you would be away in the performance of your duties."

He smiled and tilted his head a little. "Are we acquainted, Miss Barlow? I have no memory of a prior meeting."

She blushed becomingly. "We have never met before, sir. Your mother and mine were school friends – really best friends – as girls, and they kept up the acquaintance through letters over the years. Lady Matlock is my godmother, and we have corresponded regularly for quite some time now."

The attention of the entire room turned to them.

The pieces came together in Will's mind. *Lady Matlock is my aunt, though I've never met her. She must have described the Darcy family to Miss Barlow.*

Colonel Fitzwilliam walked over to her. "I still find it odd that we have never seen one another. My mother is extremely attentive to all the social niceties."

Miss Barlow hesitated slightly. "My father was a military man, not unlike yourself, so I grew up abroad. My family travelled wherever my father was stationed, except when my brother and I were sent to school. As soon as my brother was of age, he followed Father's example, joining the regiment and serving his country. When my father retired five years ago, we returned to our family home in London, but tragedy soon struck." She lowered her eyes. "After all those decades of following war and death, my father and mother were denied the happy, peaceful years of retirement. They both contracted typhus in the epidemic of 1790 and succumbed to it in a very short time, leaving me to join my brother wherever he was stationed. He is my only family now."

Murmurs of sympathy were heard from around the parlour.

Georgiana took her hand briefly. "I am so sorry for your loss, but I hope that you will enjoy your time with us this summer, Miss Barlow."

The lady, with obvious effort, smiled brightly, looking at the gathered assembly. "Please do not pity me, for my brother and I are quite happy. Oh! And you must all call me Phoebe. As Will said, we will not stand upon ceremony. I hope that we shall become fast friends. I am so looking forward to the engagement ball, and I expect a promise from each of you that you will attend my coming out ball in London." She glanced at Colonel

Fitzwilliam. "Lady Matlock is so kind to me and has insisted upon planning it all herself, so I fear that it will be a grand event. I would be so much more comfortable if my friends were there."

Elizabeth chuckled. "My sisters and I love to dance. If it is at all possible, and my parents and future husband have no objections, we would love to attend. You can give us the particulars as we have our tea. Come now! You must be famished after your journey."

Georgiana smiled. "I have instructed Mrs. Reynolds to serve afternoon tea directly. As this is later than our normal time for refreshments, I requested the menu to be a bit more substantial than our usual and to be served in the dining room so that we may all be comfortable."

Colonel Fitzwilliam's stomach rumbled as if by design. "Pardon me. How dreadfully embarrassing." His low laugh belied his words. "I have been on no journeys today, but it seems I, too, am hungry."

Will snorted. "You are always hungry." He took Elizabeth's arm. "Shall we continue our conversation at the table?"

They led the orderly procession from the room. Will glanced back and noticed his cousin wore a look of chagrin. His eyes searched further and found the reason for the colonel's discontent. *Hmm ... Richard was standing close to Phoebe and had to take her arm or appear extremely rude. I see that Charles did not miss the opportunity to escort Jane.* He sighed. *This is going to get even more interesting.*

~~oo~~

During the course of the meal, Phoebe turned to Elizabeth. "Lady Matlock would like to help you plan your engagement ball, should you need her to do so, that is. In her last letter to me, she said that she would greatly enjoy joining the party here if you wish it. I expect that you will soon receive a letter from her yourself."

Elizabeth smiled. "I look forward to meeting Lady Matlock, and I feel certain she is always welcome here."

"Phoebe!" called Lydia, giggling. "Do you remember the card party at my Aunt Philip's house? We had ever so much fun playing whist, and I won every hand. Perhaps we should organize a card party for tomorrow evening."

After looking back at Elizabeth apologetically, Phoebe turned her attention to Lydia.

Elizabeth tapped on Will's arm, speaking quietly. "I received a letter from my Aunt Gardiner today. She wrote to say that she and her family will be here within the week. I know that my family's arrival here has occasioned many extra duties for Mrs. Reynolds and her household staff. I am certain you would want to welcome your aunt in the way to which she is accustomed. If there are too few rooms at Pemberley which are in a state to be used immediately, the Gardiners truly would not mind lodging at the inn in Lambton. My aunt grew up there, you know, and she loves the little village. When all is ready, they could come here."

Will shook his head. "As you saw when we toured the house the day after you arrived, there are many rooms which have yet to be opened. They have stood empty for years, waiting to receive company. Mrs. Reynolds has already prepared rooms for the Gardiners, and I shall notify her of Lady Matlock's impending arrival so that she and her staff can begin to ready her customary apartments at once. She shall attend to whatever needs to be refurbished. Mrs. Reynolds knows there will be more guests arriving for the ball, so the dear lady has likely already inventoried the guest rooms and begun preparing them. I am certain she has employed additional staff suitable for the task at hand, so you need not concern yourself with her increased burden, although it speaks well of your tender heart, my love."

Georgiana leaned forward and caught Will's attention, at the same time garnering the notice of the rest of the party. "Brother,

Mrs. Reynolds and I discussed this very thing at length before the Bennet family arrived. I instructed her to have the maids clean all the rooms in the guest wing. From time to time, she has approached Elizabeth and me concerning new furnishings, and together we chose what we felt to be appropriate and pleasing. The addition of the Gardiner family and Lady Matlock will be no burden at all, even should Lord Matlock and others decide to come now. Most of the rooms stand ready, and the others are near completion."

He smiled broadly. "I should have known that you and Elizabeth would have it well in hand. Why have you not told me?"

Elizabeth turned to him. "You have been so busy that Georgiana and I thought we could manage this and spare you the concern. There is no good reason for you to be choosing fabric and deciding which chairs must be reupholstered or curtains replaced when the two of us enjoy working together on the project. I knew the work was being done, but I have not checked with Mrs. Reynolds in a day or two, and I was not aware that so much had been accomplished. Your sister must have slipped away from planning the ball yesterday and this morning to see the progress." She smiled at Georgiana. "I did note your absence; however, I thought that you had closeted yourself away with the dressmaker or joined Mary with the music master. Now I have found you out."

Georgiana dimpled prettily. "You have, indeed. I wished to surprise you, and it seems that I have."

Mrs. Bennet listened with interest. "I would greatly enjoy a tour of those rooms, Elizabeth. Would that be too much of an inconvenience?"

"Not at all, Mama. We shall look at the rooms after tea, if Georgiana agrees with the scheme."

Georgiana nodded. "I would be delighted to show you the guest suites, Mrs. Bennet. Anyone else who wishes to join us is welcome to come along."

Lydia sniffed. "Phoebe and I have much catching up to do, and

I am certain that Catherine would prefer to remain with us."

Phoebe turned to look at her. "On the contrary, Lydia. You and I must talk later, for I am eager to know Georgiana better, as well as to improve my acquaintance with your sister Elizabeth."

Will raised a brow. *Phoebe must not be in league with Wickham and Lydia after all. She would have welcomed the opportunity to help her plan the elopement if she had been.*

Elizabeth glanced at Caroline. "Shall you come with us?"

The lady shook her head slightly. "Mary and I had already planned to practice several duets together for this evening's entertainment."

Mary drew her brows together. "Caroline, we need not do that again. We practiced this morning, and I feel confident that we are ready. I would rather tour the guest wing before the other guests arrive."

"My dear," Caroline replied, "I hoped to convince you to sing while I accompany you. You have such a lovely voice, and I do so love to hear you."

Mary inclined her head in acquiescence, though her mouth formed a stubborn line

Will's eyes were hooded as he observed. *Interesting indeed. If I'm not mistaken, Caroline has some scheme afoot. I'll have to watch her closely.*

Caroline turned to Jane. "Will you stay with us, my dear?" She took a sip of her tea.

Jane smiled placidly. "I think not. I have so few days left to spend with Elizabeth before she marries that I plan to take every opportunity to enjoy her company. Besides, I neither sing nor play, so I would be of little use to you or Mary. You will do very well without me, as you have before."

Caroline coughed and reached quickly for her napkin, trying in vain to cover her mouth or swallow before the tea could escape in a most unbecoming manner.

Charles patted his sister's back, rather harder than was

necessary, and smiled at Georgiana. "You know, I have never seen those rooms myself, as they have been closed every time I have visited Pemberley. I think I would walk with you ladies and see what you have accomplished, if I am welcomed."

"Of course you are, Charles. Would any other of you gentlemen care to join us?"

Will nodded. "I must see what you and my betrothed have been up to, I think." He looked at the other men. "Richard? Wentworth? John?"

Richard smiled lazily. "Oh, yes. I have never missed a chance to see redecorated suites, and as Miss Bennet so aptly said, you will soon be wed. I must spend what time with you I can."

Will lifted his napkin to cover his smile at his cousin's thinly veiled sarcasm.

Wentworth and John both spoke their agreement, and the conversation turned to other matters.

Will contributed his opinions and knowledge from time to time, but his mind was occupied with more interesting questions. *I understand completely why Charles, Richard, and Wentworth are going with us to see rooms which are of no interest to them; they wish to spend time with Jane and Georgiana. What I don't know is why John Bennet would want to go with us. This is such a boring occupation for a young man.* He smiled to himself. *I am more like Mr. Bennet and Elizabeth than I thought. I must agree that observing people is a very interesting pastime.*

~~oo~~

Later that evening as they sat in the parlour listening to the ladies exhibit, Will leaned close to Elizabeth, speaking in a low voice. "I have waited in great anticipation for your sister's solo. Did she and Caroline not remain behind to practice for this evening?"

Elizabeth tilted her head and raised an eyebrow. She then stood and walked to Mary who stood to the side of the piano, turning pages for Georgiana. Elizabeth spoke quietly to Mary, and then returned to her seat by Will on the settee.

Turning to Will, she replied to his curiosity in a soft voice. "Mary said that she and Caroline practiced one song, but Caroline was displeased with it and quit the room directly. Mary is quite put out about it, for she would rather have gone with us to see the guest wing."

He chewed his lower lip a moment. "So, why did Caroline devise a plan to avoid being with us, and where did she go? Was she with Lydia and Catherine?"

Elizabeth shook her head slightly. Her voice was barely a whisper. "I think not. Mary specifically said that she was with the two of them for the remainder of the time. Her mood was further darkened by having to listen to their silly talk and speculation concerning Phoebe's coming out ball. It seems they are all a-twitter to meet your aunt and rich relations. I am mortified. Does Lydia truly think that she would be received if she carries through with her plan for tomorrow night?"

He patted her hand which was between them. "Do not distress yourself, my love. All will be well. No amount of Lydia's silliness will ever affect my feelings for you, and remember – her plan will not succeed. She will very soon be my sister, and I will care for her as if she were Georgiana."

"You are too good." She looked at his hand and briefly placed hers over it before withdrawing her own.

"No. I know myself very well, and whatever goodness is in me, I owe to others." For propriety's sake, he clasped his hands in his lap.

I almost look forward to tomorrow. At last, I will deal with Wickham once and for all, and he will no longer plague our families.

CHAPTER 17

*Good judgment comes from experience, and a lot of that comes
from bad judgment.*

Will Rogers

After Elizabeth and Fitzwilliam had finished dives among the
beautiful sea creatures earlier in the evening at the Aquarium,
Elizabeth had wasted little time with make-up and toiletries. Her
hair had dried naturally. She hadn't attempted to style it, simply
running her fingers through her curls to give them some semblance
of order.

Now, from his seat across from her, Fitzwilliam observed
Elizabeth unconsciously twisting the loose strands, letting them
drop, then repeating the action, and he marveled at her beauty
under such stressful conditions. *She has never been lovelier to me.*
He set his mouth into a tight line. *I will not see her hurt again.*

Elizabeth had entered the small jet first and sat on the couch
lining one wall, so Fitzwilliam and Mr. Bennet had seated
themselves in the recliners facing her. Steve joined them, and after
Fitzwilliam introduced him to Elizabeth and her father, he took a

seat in the rear of the cabin with his back to them.

Once the jet rose into the night sky, Mr. Bennet leaned forward, elbows on his knees, and looked directly into Elizabeth's eyes. "Tell me what he did to you."

Fitzwilliam left his chair and went to sit beside her, placing his arm around her shoulders and drawing her to his side. His voice was a whisper. "You don't have to do this the hard way, Elizabeth. Just tell him the bare minimum. Leave out the details."

She glanced toward Steve's back.

Fitzwilliam turned her face back to him with his fingers. "Don't worry about him. He needs to know all this anyway. Trust me."

She kissed his cheek and drew her legs up onto the couch, leaning into him. "I do trust you, more than I've trusted any man since I was a teenager, except my father. I should have told Dad and Mom about this long ago. If I had, maybe we wouldn't be in this situation now. They should have known what Greg is capable of."

Fitzwilliam took her hand in his and hugged her, pulling her closer with his arm. *I want her to feel safe and loved while she relives this.*

She turned to face her father. "You know that Greg, Jane, Lance, and I were all close friends in high school. We went everywhere together until Lance and Jane started dating; then Greg and I started going out by ourselves. He asked me to be his girlfriend when I was only fifteen. I was a freshman, and he was a junior, like Lance and Jane."

Mr. Bennet nodded, wearing a pained expression. "I thought you were too young at the time, but I trusted him. He was Lance's best friend, and they're both from good families. They went to church and came over to our house. They both were always polite and courteous."

Elizabeth shook her head. "It wasn't your fault, Dad. He could put on a great act." She glanced out at the night sky. After a moment, she returned her attention to her father. "That first year, I was at every football game to watch him play. We went to movies, or he took me to dinner. We'd play games at the house. Remember? We'd watch TV with you and Mom, shoot pool, bake cookies, pop popcorn. Both of us were active in the church youth group, and we went through 'True Love Waits' together."

Mr. Bennet looked down, twisting his wedding band. "I gave you a promise ring at the service. You stopped wearing it, and I always wondered why, but I didn't want to pry. I should have, I guess, but I didn't know what to say."

She sighed at looked back at him. "Don't worry about it, Dad. I probably wouldn't have told you anyway."

Fitzwilliam kissed the top of her head and stroked her arm.

Elizabeth smiled sadly at him and then turned back to her father. "The next year, he pushed me for a more physical relationship, though it never went past kissing and touching. I thought I was smart enough, strong enough, to handle him."

Mr. Bennet jerked his head up.

Elizabeth continued quietly, her voice flat. "He asked me to the prom that spring." A few silent tears tracked down her face and dropped onto her blouse.

"We went to a party afterward, and I didn't know the punch was spiked. I didn't like it, but Greg certainly did. He got drunk, but I didn't understand how drunk he was. I'd never seen him like that before. He pulled me up the stairs and into a bedroom. Then he pushed me down on the bed and started unzipping my dress. I told him to stop, but he didn't listen."

Mr. Bennet covered his face with his hands. "Dear God!"

She put out her hand to him, moving forward to touch his knee. "It wasn't your fault, Dad. I was stupid in my innocence. I should have known better."

He shook his head, his hands on either side of his face. "Your mom and I should have talked to you. We should have warned you what boys could be like." He put his hands on his knees, patting her hand with his. "This isn't all, is it?"

Her eyes were big, trying to hold back the tears, and she moved back to Fitzwilliam's side. "No. He passed out when he was finished. I dressed and called Jane. She and Lance came to pick me up. I told them Greg was drunk and couldn't drive, but I didn't tell them he had raped me. I thought it was my fault, and I was afraid of what Lance might do to him. I certainly didn't want to tell you and mom. I was too humiliated. What could you have done anyway? It was over and talking about it was pointless. I messed up, and everyone else would have felt that they had failed in some way."

Fitzwilliam clenched his jaws until it hurt. He concentrated on loosening his hold on Elizabeth so that he wouldn't hurt her. After a few moments, he broke the silence. "It wasn't your fault or your parents' fault. Greg Whitman was the one who did it. Stop blaming yourselves."

Mr. Bennet shook his head and swallowed visibly. "I remember that you two seemed to break up for a couple of weeks and then got back together. What happened? What finally separated you two?"

She looked at her hands covered by Fitzwilliam's large hand. "He started drinking all the time. He acted like he was so sorry for forcing me, and I thought I loved him, so I never totally broke up with him. He was able to talk me into taking him back. He kept saying if he hadn't been drunk, he would never have done it, and he promised it would never happen again. A few months later, he started pushing me again for a more intimate relationship, but I held him off. He started calling me names, but I still held on. Afterwards, he would always say he loved me, and that he was sorry. He'd bring me flowers or small presents. In my teenaged mind, since we'd had sex, I should marry him. How could I marry anyone else after he and I had been together? I was damaged goods, and I thought no other man would ever love me. After all, I had nothing to give them; I had already given it to Greg." She laughed bitterly. "I was such a little fool with my romantic ideas.

I've since learned that most abused women act the same way I did, but it doesn't make me feel any better about it."

Both Fitzwilliam and her father began to protest, but she stopped them by beginning to talk again.

"Anyway, when you and mom were gone that summer, he came over. I let him talk me into going with me to my room. We'd been in there before to watch movies or TV on my bed, and nothing had happened. However, that time he'd been drinking again, but he wasn't drunk. While we were kissing, he started unzipping my pants. I tried to fight him off, but he was too strong for me." She shut her eyes tightly. "He held me down with one hand while he slapped me with the other, yelling ugly names at me, saying I was going to pay for the way I'd teased him."

Fitzwilliam had been angry the first time he'd heard her story, but now that he knew she loved him, he struggled to keep himself from displaying his fury. It consumed him. He had to squash the impulse to clench his fists, knowing that she would feel his reaction. *She needs for me to be calm and rational. If she knew how much I want to kill that monster, it would frighten her.*

Mr. Bennet's eyes welled with his tears, and they streamed down the creases of his face. He tried unsuccessfully to wipe them away with his hands, but they kept falling.

Elizabeth put one of her hands on top of Fitzwilliam's, rubbing her thumb across the top of his knuckles. "Lance and Jane came home earlier than we expected. They heard me screaming and ran up to my room. Lance pulled him off the bed while Jane took care of me. She cleaned me up and brought me clean clothes. Lance punched his face over and over until Jane stopped him. She begged Lance to quit hitting him because she thought Lance would go to jail for killing him.

"Lance drove Greg home and left him bleeding there in his own front yard, badly beaten. No charges were filed against Lance, so I guess Greg didn't tell his mom who did it." Her voice was tinged with anger and some regret. "Smart on his part because, to defend

Lance, I would have testified that he had raped me twice. Even then, I knew I was still a minor, and he wasn't. He would have been tried as an adult."

Mr. Bennet looked at her, grief-stricken. "Why didn't you tell us? We would have reported it. He would've gone to jail."

She shook her head. "Jane tried to get me to call the police, but I wouldn't. She said that Lance had a friend on the police force, and he would make it easy for me. But I knew Greg would deny it. He would have said that it was consensual, and I couldn't bear for anyone to think that. I would rather have killed myself first. I couldn't get past the thought that it was all my own fault, especially the second time, because I had stayed with him. How would that have looked in court? It would have been all over the papers and the news. You and mom would have suffered for my stupidity. As it was, everything was made as comfortable for me as was possible. I never even saw the sheets or bedclothes again. Jane took me to her room and gave me one of mom's sleeping pills. She stayed with me until I fell asleep. The next time I went into my own room, several hours later, I saw that she had cleaned everything up and put clean sheets and a different comforter on my bed. I never saw the clothes I had been wearing again. She was so strong for me; I had no choice but to be strong myself for the rest of you."

That's why she and Jane are so close and Lance is so protective of Elizabeth. They were there for her when she needed them the most. Fitzwilliam whispered to her. "Let me hold you."

She nodded. "I'm so tired."

He lifted her across his lap and cradled her head between his jaw and his shoulder.

Mr. Bennet muttered under his breath. "I should have taken better care of you all. I was so buried in my work that I neglected my own children."

Elizabeth glanced at him. "Dad, stop. You've been a wonderful father. Fitzwilliam is right. This isn't really your fault, or Mom's fault, or my fault. Greg is a master manipulator, and he fooled all of us. I only regret that I didn't tell both of you and Mary. I had no idea he would ever be interested in her."

Fitzwilliam rubbed her back. "Maybe she isn't with Greg." *I hate to think of what could be happening to her now.*

He rang for the attendant who appeared in a few seconds. She looked at the three of them, her concern evident. "Is there anything I can get you? Do you need something to drink or eat?"

Fitzwilliam shook his head impatiently, but when he spoke, his voice was all business. "Is there any way we could go faster?"

"I'll check with the captain." She quickly returned with tissues and bottled water which she placed on the table between the chairs and the couch, and a blanket which she laid by Fitzwilliam. "He said that he is flying at the top speed now, and we should be there in about three and a half hours."

Fitzwilliam thanked her, and she left the cabin. He wrapped the blanket around Elizabeth before looking toward the rear of the plane. "Steve, would you join us?"

As the investigator approached them, Fitzwilliam gestured to the seat beside Mr. Bennet. Steve sat down and leaned back, his expression grim.

Mr. Bennet glanced at him before looking down at the floor. "You've been listening, I presume. What do you think?"

Steve's eyes showed his sympathy. "I was listening, yes. I thought it would be easier for Miss Bennet if I wasn't watching her while she talked." His expression hardened. "I already had a file on Greg Whitman because of the altercation between him and Mr. Darcy at Canoe. A bodyguard follows Mr. Darcy constantly, though he has orders to stay in the background, and he relayed the details to me. We also have a man on Miss Bennet at all times because of her association with Mr. Darcy. No question that Whitman's a real piece of work, and he seems to be involved in some extremely unsavory activities. He has many friends and contacts in the criminal underworld, but so far, he's been slippery enough to stay out of trouble himself, for the most part. He's done some jail time, but nothing too serious yet. I kept a tail on him for a few weeks after your run-in at the restaurant, but he stayed away from the two of you, so we dropped it."

All eyes turned to the investigator as Fitzwilliam spoke. "In your opinion, does this seem to be something Whitman would do?"

Steve narrowed his eyes. "Do I think he's behind Mary's disappearance? Probably. There's a very good chance of it. He hates you and Miss Bennet, and there's no other way to get at you because you're both protected 24/7. I contacted the L. A. P. D., and they sent detectives to the hotel for me. Even though it isn't a criminal investigation yet, they're eager for a charge that will stick on Whitman, so they're watching the room Mary checked into. The front desk clerk saw a man matching Whitman's description with her, but the police haven't positively identified him yet. They want to wait until we get there to make a move, but if they see or hear anything suspicious before we arrive, they will do what they can. Right now, they've asked a judge for a subpoena for the hotel security footage. By the time we get there, they should be able to tell us something."

Fitzwilliam could feel the tension radiating from Elizabeth, and he began to rub her back. "It's late there already, so maybe he'll wait until morning to make a move. We may get there in time to stop whatever plans he's made, if it is Whitman."

Steve looked uncomfortable. "Not necessarily. His activities don't usually take place during the daytime. The good thing is the room is on the fifth floor – there's only one exit, and it's too far to jump from the balcony. The door opens into a hallway, so it's much easier to guard."

Elizabeth lifted her head to look at him. "Exactly what do you suspect him of? Do you think he's abusing my sister?"

The investigator shook his head and glanced away. "No. If we're right, he won't touch her himself."

Her eyes widened. "If he didn't take her for himself, why would he want her?"

Mr. Bennet moaned. "You think he means to sell my daughter, don't you?"

Steve was silent.

Fitzwilliam ground his teeth together.

"Dear God!" cried Elizabeth, her voice disbelieving and horrified. "He's involved in trafficking girls for sexual slavery?"

He held her tightly. "Believe this. If he wants money, I can outbid anyone who would pay for her. I will not allow him to do that to your sister."

Steve leaned forward. "Mr. Darcy, let us handle it. The police know more about this than you do, and they want him just as badly. They hope that this case will lead them to girls who have been missing from all over the United States. You'll get Mary back, but let them try to find these other girls, too. If you step in, Whitman will have no reason to talk. We need leverage, and if he's holding Mary against her will, he'll talk to get a reduced sentence."

Mr. Bennet broke his silence with vehemence. "I do care about the other girls, and I feel for their families, but those girls are probably beyond help now. My first priority is my own daughter, and if that sounds selfish, I'm sorry. I failed Elizabeth, and I've failed Mary, but I won't do it again. If it comes down to choosing between Mary and the others, I'll choose Mary. I won't allow anyone to let her suffer so that she can be used as bait in some sort of sting."

"Calm down, Mr. Bennet." Steve's voice was low and soothing. "We won't do that. I promise you that Mary's safety is everyone's first concern. The police will step in at the first sign that your daughter is being hurt. Please understand that, right now, there's no indication that Mary didn't go willingly. She may actually refuse to leave him if it doesn't become clear to her that Whitman isn't really her friend. She's eighteen, and she used a credit card that her mother authorized. He hasn't broken any laws. He didn't kidnap her, and she's not a minor."

No one spoke for several minutes.

Finally, Fitzwilliam voiced his thoughts. His voice held menace. "So we have to wait until he actually hurts her or sells her? No! I refuse to agree to that plan. There must be another way to make him talk, and if there is, I'll find it."

Steve sighed tiredly. "When you think of a better plan, will you share it with me *before* you act? Beating him to a pulp isn't an option, as much as I would enjoy it, and you can't take Mary if she doesn't want to go with you."

Fitzwilliam scratched his chin as his eyes brightened. "I do have an idea, and I think it will work. Listen to this ..."

CHAPTER 18

There comes a time when deceit and defiance must be seen for what they are. At that point, a gathering danger must be directly confronted. At that point, we must show that beyond our resolutions is actual resolve.

Dick Cheney

The following day dawned cloudy and gray. Will stood looking out the window over the front lawn as he sipped his coffee before breakfast. He glanced back when he heard a noise behind him and was surprised by the entrance of Mr. Bennet.

Mr. Bennet walked up beside him, somberly handing him a newspaper. "You were correct." The newspaper from London was dated several days earlier. The front page held the story of the Copenhagen fire which Will had foretold weeks before.

Will set his cup on the table, took the paper from him, and read the article silently. *I tried, but I couldn't stop it. I haven't heard from my men. I hope they survived the fire.* He shook his head. "So many deaths. How they must have suffered. I would much rather have been wrong."

Mr. Bennet placed a hand on his back. "I know that, Will."

"My men have yet to return or contact me." His eyes brimmed with unshed tears. *Dear Lord, let them be all right. I sent them there, knowing what was going to happen, nearly certain that I couldn't prevent it. I may have ordered them to their deaths – for nothing.*

Mr. Bennet dropped his hand to his side and looked at the floor. "You would never have sent those men had I not persuaded you to do so. I should not have interfered, and I will not do so ever again. I fear that your knowledge of future events is a burden you must bear alone. You are wiser than I concerning how to manage it."

Will rubbed his forehead with one hand. "Why have I not heard something from them? I realize that they have not had time to travel back from Copenhagen, but surely they could have sent word of their safety. They must know that I would worry."

He heard the door close, followed by the sound of light footsteps, and turned to see Elizabeth walking towards him, her pleasure evident in her expression. Her smile faded. "Whatever is the matter?"

He handed her the paper and waited for her to read of the tragedy. She looked up at him. "You knew of this before it happened?"

Will nodded. "Even worse, I dispatched men to try to prevent it. I have had no word from them. What if they perished in the fire? They would not have been there had I not required it of them."

Elizabeth embraced him, laying her head on his shoulder. "My love, you did what you thought was right, as you always do." She lifted her face to look at him. "You did not cause the fire, though you act as if you did. As for the men, perhaps there is such confusion that they have been unable to contact you. I doubt that the post is running from Copenhagen, and it is such a far distance that even an express would take days. It is also possible that they are helping in the rescue effort. They may be too occupied to write."

She backed away, pulling his hand, and placed the paper on the table. "Come, dear. You and Father must eat something." They sat around the table after serving themselves from the sideboard. "Shall we ride today?"

Will shook his head. "I think not. I prefer to stay close to Pemberley all day, just in case Wickham decides to make an early appearance."

Elizabeth nodded. "I shall keep Lydia by my side today." She turned to her father. "I must say how much I missed you yesterday, Papa. Will you remain downstairs for the remainder of the day, or shall you keep to your rooms again?"

Mr. Bennet smiled slightly. "How pleasant it is to be missed. I would be less than a good father if I left you alone to watch Lydia, my dear. That would be cruel indeed. No, she shall share company with me today as well. I have decided that hiding in my rooms was cowardly and weak. I must be a better father to you all, and I cannot do that if I closet myself away. My books will wait for me."

A familiar, booming voice coming from the doorway attracted their notice. "What have we here?" The door opened wide to reveal Colonel Fitzwilliam firmly holding Caroline Bingley's arm.

Caroline's face was bright red as she struggled against his iron grip. "Unhand me, you brute!" she screeched.

The colonel advanced into the room, fairly dragging her along beside him.

Mr. Bennet and Elizabeth wore expressions of astonishment, but Will watched the proceedings with narrowed eyes. *She must be in on the elopement. I wonder if she met with Wickham yesterday when she disappeared. I've never trusted her.*

His voice was cool when he spoke to his cousin. "What has she done, Richard?"

Colonel Fitzwilliam released her arm, and she stood rubbing it, letting go a stream of complaints regarding his ill-treatment of her.

He snickered. "I was coming downstairs when I saw her with her ear to the door, so I stopped on the steps to watch her. She cracked the door slightly, obviously to eavesdrop on your conversation. After a few moments, I rushed down the steps and asked her what in the name of all that is holy she thought she was doing. She, of course, denied everything, but I saw her myself. I hope you were not discussing anything private."

Will thought back through their conversation. *Caroline couldn't have been there when Elizabeth came in. Since then, we haven't said anything too damning. No mention was made of my foreknowledge or time switch, and Elizabeth and her father spoke only of staying with Lydia today. Neither spoke of the elopement, though I mentioned that I would watch for Wickham. They said only that they were going to stay close by Lydia. This may be a narrow escape.*

Will shook his head at Colonel Fitzwilliam and then turned his attention to Caroline. "No, I have no idea what Miss Bingley thought she would gain by listening in on our conversation, but unless she has an interest in world affairs or familial obligations, I have my doubts that she gained any information which anyone in the house could not know."

Her voice was loud and shrill. "I was not eavesdropping! I do not listen at doors!" She began to sob, covering her face, but no tears escaped her eyes. "No one in this house likes me. I would leave today were it not for my pathetic brother and his ridiculous infatuation."

A deadly soft, familiar voice sounded from the doorway behind her. "Caroline, I have no idea why you are behaving in such an unseemly fashion, but I am weary of your histrionics. Were it not for you, I would likely be already wed to the woman I loved. You will no longer interfere in the lives of others while I pay for your upkeep. Return to your room and pack your trunks this instant. You will leave Pemberley within two hours."

"But, Charles!" she cried, running to him. "You cannot mean it. Where will I go? Will you go with me? None of this is my doing!"

He laughed quietly. "I am merely your 'pathetic brother,' Caroline, and I no longer am responsible for you. You are certainly of age, and you have £30,000 left to you by our father. I suggest that you spend it wisely, for I will not give you another farthing. I have listened to your grandiose plans and excuses for years, but I am finished." He scratched his chin and smiled. "Perhaps our Aunt Amelia or our sister, Louisa, will take you in, though I advise you not to vex them as you have me. Hurst has no love for you, and he would send you packing much more quickly than I have done. However, Aunt Amelia needs a companion, so she would have more patience with you than would our brother. Perhaps you will inherit her fortune in ten or twenty years – if you are helpful to her."

She looked up into his face, beseeching him. "You cannot send me away in this manner, Charles. You are too much of a gentleman to send a woman unescorted, alone in a carriage. You must come with me."

Charles turned his head to look at Will. "I think not. If Will does not mind, I will stay the rest of the summer here at Pemberley. Your maid can travel with you. I have no need of her here."

Will nodded. "You are, of course, welcome to remain here, Charles, but I must agree that your sister leave Pemberley. I must have the guarantee of privacy in my own house. Had she opened the door and entered the room, I would not have felt that she was trying to glean information without our knowledge. The breakfast room is not a private area, after all."

Caroline kept her eyes on Charles and spoke softly. "But where will I go, Brother? I must have time to make arrangements."

He looked down at her indifferently. "I am not a cruel man, Caroline. Though you have caused me nothing but trouble, you may stay in my London house for the rest of the summer. By the time I get back to town, I expect you and your things to be gone. You have two months. If I leave Pemberley before that time is up, I will go elsewhere. Be out of my house by mid-September, or expect to be further embarrassed by the butler escorting you to the street while the servants pile your belongings around you."

Tears began to run down her cheeks. "Where has my kind brother gone? I cannot believe you would treat me in such a way. Our father would never approve."

"I was weak, and I allowed you to direct my life. That weakness caused me to lose my chance for happiness in this life, perhaps forever. I refuse to be led around by the nose anymore. As for our father, he sent you to live with me before his death. Do you not remember, Caroline? You were continually causing uproar in his household and the village. You tried to run his life as you have tried to run mine. I should have sent you back to Father. You were his responsibility at the time. I have always been too soft."

Elizabeth went to Caroline's side, holding out her handkerchief. "Come, Caroline. I will take you to your rooms and help you pack. You need not be humiliated before the servants or the other guests. We will not speak of this to the rest of the party."

Caroline rounded on her, eyes flashing, striking the handkerchief from Elizabeth's hand to the floor. "I need neither your help nor your pity, upstart. My maid will handle what needs to be done. Had it not been for you and your family, I would not be in this situation."

Elizabeth stepped back. "What do you mean?"

"Do you really think Lydia is clever enough to arrange any sort of intrigue or elopement?" Caroline laughed, and the sound was brittle and unpleasant. "She will ruin you all, and you, Mr. Darcy, shall share in the humiliation."

Colonel Fitzwilliam glared at her. "What have you to do with Miss Lydia?"

Caroline smiled maliciously. "I take pride in helping young ladies with their romantic dilemmas, Colonel. However, you and Mr. Darcy should look to your own houses. There is more to this than you know, and I shan't be the only one to suffer when all is said and done."

With that, she flounced from the room, slamming the door

behind her.

Charles sighed. "I am so sorry for the trouble my sister has caused. How can I ever make amends?"

Colonel Fitzwilliam moved to stand beside the young man. "I cannot see what she thought to gain by helping Miss Lydia to elope with George Wickham. Is she that bent on some sort of revenge against our family? Why?"

Charles raised an eyebrow. "Is that what this was all about? She was doing something underhanded to help George Wickham run away with Miss Elizabeth's sister?"

Will nodded. "It appears that Caroline was a go-between. She may have met with Wickham yesterday when she disappeared." *Should I trust him? I suppose I'll have to. He knows too much now to try to hide it from him.* "I think she carried messages between them. We have knowledge that Wickham and Lydia plan to leave together tonight from Pemberley."

Charles was quiet for a few minutes. "It seems that my sister had not given up her ridiculous designs on you, Will. She told me that she had, and I believed her."

Elizabeth looked puzzled. "I fail to see how becoming embroiled in such a plot would further her suit with Will, particularly now that he and I are engaged."

Charles shook his head slowly. "You have no way of knowing Caroline like I do, Miss Elizabeth. Caroline thought she would never be found out. In her mind, your sister's elopement would cause Will to break off the engagement, particularly if Wickham never married your sister. In the first case, the Darcys would not suffer the degradation of such an alliance. In the second, the scandal would ruin your family, making you an unfit partner for Will. Remember that Caroline sees things as she wishes them to be, not as they really are. Once your engagement was broken, Caroline would think that Will would turn to her for solace. She has done everything in her power for the past ten years to bring about a marriage between herself and your fiancé. I am loath to portray a member of my family in such a light, but there it is."

Will smiled. "I am impressed with your powers of deduction, Charles. I do believe that you may be of some assistance to us."

"I would be glad to do anything which could in some measure restore our friendship. What would you ask of me?"

Will stepped to the wall and pulled the bell. Mrs. Reynolds appeared nearly immediately.

He smiled at her and spoke pleasantly. "Mrs. Reynolds, please make your way to Miss Bingley's rooms as quickly as you can. Do not leave her alone under any circumstances. She is quite angry, and she may be packing. Do not interfere, but if she leaves the room, you must go with her. She must not be out of your sight. I will send further instructions to you very soon."

She nodded her assent before she turned and left.

Mr. Bennet raised an eyebrow. "That was well-done, Will. I had not thought of the possibility that she might still try to work between Lydia and Wickham. She may not have gone to her rooms when she left here."

Charles shook his head, his brows drawn together. "I confess it never occurred to me that she would do anything besides what I told her to do. I am sorry."

Colonel Fitzwilliam started walking towards the door. "I shall check on Miss Bingley's whereabouts now. If she is not in her rooms, rest assured that I shall find her. I know every inch of this property and everyone associated with it."

"Thank you, Cousin." Will looked at the others as the colonel left the room and closed the door behind him. "Now that Caroline knows we are aware of the scheme, we must not let her alert Lydia or Wickham. I want to catch him in the act of trespassing on this land. After his episode with Georgiana, I banned him from the property, so I can have him arrested as soon as he steps a foot on Pemberley soil. If he has broken other laws as well, I may be able to have him transported to Australia. However, I still need your cooperation in one thing, Charles."

The young man smiled. "I will happily do whatever you ask if it is within my power."

Will moved to stand beside him. "It will involve taking back some portion of what you said to your sister and delaying your orders by at least a day."

Elizabeth spoke as if she had followed the train of Will's thoughts. "Caroline cannot be allowed to leave Pemberley today. She must wait until tomorrow."

My Elizabeth is intelligent. "Exactly, my love." Will turned to Charles. "I hate to interfere with your authority over your sister, particularly when I agree with you wholeheartedly, but after further reflection, I must ask that you delay her departure until tomorrow."

Mr. Bennet sat down at the table, head in his hands. "This is all too much intrigue for me. Between the escapades of my daughter and the trickery of Miss Bingley, I find myself exhausted."

Elizabeth went to the sideboard and poured two cups of tea which she took to the table. She placed one cup in front of her father and sat beside him with the other, kissing him gently on the cheek. "All will be well, Papa. Do not distress yourself. Perhaps you should spend the day in your rooms again. Resting and reading may be the tonic you require."

He took a sip of tea. "I am done with that. I will do my duty to my family, tired or not."

Charles looked towards them sympathetically and then returned his attention to Will. "You fear that she may contact Wickham if she leaves here?"

Will nodded. "I have no doubt of it. Furthermore, I do not trust her maid. She may be in league with your sister."

Charles's voice was firm. "I had not thought of that. Lily has been with her these fifteen years at least." He stood taller and spoke with resolve. "I shall make certain that both she and her maid remain in her chambers today. Tell the others that Caroline is unwell, and I am attending her. I fear it is the truth." He turned and left the room.

Will strode across the room and sat down across from Elizabeth and her father.

She rose. "Let me refresh your coffee."

He shook his head. "I will get it myself in a moment." All was silent for a moment. "There are two things which bother me greatly."

Mr. Bennet raised his head to look at him. "Only two? I have ten worries at the very least."

Will smiled slightly. "Two are of greatest concern. First, who else in the Darcy family is in league with Wickham?"

Elizabeth's eyes showed her understanding. "Caroline said that you and the colonel should look to your own houses. Do you suspect Lady Matlock?"

He shrugged. "I have no idea, but anything is possible. Remember I have never met the lady. However, her coming at just this time is suspicious. My first thought, though, was of Aunt Catherine. I *have* met her, and she was formidable. There is also some question of the money she withdrew from her own accounts and placed in one which would be hidden from Fitzwilliam. She is not to be trusted."

Elizabeth's mouth dropped open. "She did that? Why?"

He shook his head. "I cannot say with certainty. All I can fathom is that she wanted Fitzwilliam to marry her daughter, and she was willing to coerce him into the marriage by making it appear that he had stolen the money. Then she planned to blackmail him by telling him she knew of his thievery. The woman would stop at nothing to get what she wants."

Mr. Bennet put down his teacup with a clatter. "Despicable, though it is some small comfort to know that your family as well as mine may also harbour some undesirable traits."

Will chuckled without humour. "I think money and privilege breed undesirable traits."

Elizabeth sipped her tea with a thoughtful expression. "What is the second concern?"

He smiled at her. "I should perhaps have said that the second thing is of interest, but not necessarily a bad thing."

She smiled in return. "Something good?"

"Possibly." He hesitated a moment. "Did you notice Charles's remark regarding his attachment to Jane?"

Both Mr. Bennet and Elizabeth were quiet as they thought through the conversation.

Mr. Bennet spoke first. "I confess I was so amazed at the scene playing out before me that I did not pay such close attention to his exact words. I have never seen Charles Bingley in such a temper. The way that he stood up to his sister was admirable. For the first time, I felt that I would not be sorry to have him for a son-in-law."

Elizabeth's eyes lit up. "He spoke of his love for Jane in the past tense. He called her 'the woman I loved.' I thought that was odd when he said it."

She is quick, my Elizabeth. "So did I, my dear. I think it possible that Charles has finally accepted he may no longer have the opportunity to marry Jane. The time for that may have passed, and, if that is so, I hope he will learn not to regret her."

She nodded and rose to her feet. "Charles is a good man, and I would like to see him settled happily. Now I must see to Lydia. She normally sleeps well beyond this time, but I would be careful with her today."

Will stood as Elizabeth left the room. Then he went to the sideboard, filling a plate and pouring a fresh cup of coffee for himself. When he was finished, he returned to the table with his breakfast, resuming his seat across from Mr. Bennet. "Please have something to eat, Mr. Bennet. We have a long day ahead of us."

Mr. Bennet nodded and followed his example. They ate quietly, each lost in his thoughts until Elizabeth burst through the door.

"Lydia is missing! She is not in her room, and her maid has no idea where she is. Her bed has been slept in, but no one saw her leave her chambers."

Mr. Bennet rose from the table and threw his napkin down. "Job was right: 'Man is born to trouble as the sparks fly upward'."

Will was already out of his seat, headed towards the open door, calling for Carlson. When the butler appeared, Will spoke with urgency. "Find Colonel Fitzwilliam and bring him to me. I must speak with him immediately."

He took Elizabeth into his arms. "Do not be so alarmed, my love. We shall find her. Perhaps she is walking the grounds or in the rooms of one of the other girls. She may have gone to Catherine's room in the night to sleep with her. Please do not assume the worst."

Elizabeth began to cry. "If she has run away with Wickham, what shall we do? Caroline had the right of it. My family will be ruined."

He pulled back from her a few inches to look into her face. "Remember who I am and where I grew up. I do not view this in the same way that Fitzwilliam would, for I was reared in a different time. Whether or not Lydia elopes or marries Wickham, I will still love you, and I will never give you up."

Mr. Bennet walked over to them and put his hand on Elizabeth's shoulder. "Be that as it may, we live in these times. I do not wish for my family to be disgraced, nor do I desire a union between my daughter and that blackguard."

Colonel Fitzwilliam strode into the room. "Carlson told me you wished to see me?" He stopped short when he saw the scene before him. "What has happened?"

Will turned his face towards his cousin. "Lydia is missing. Elizabeth went to her chambers, and no one knows where she is or how long she has been gone."

He smiled. "Calm yourselves. After I assured myself that Miss Bingley was in her chambers under the watchful eye of Mrs. Reynolds, I left to bring you the good news myself. I saw Jane – er, Miss Bennet – in the hallway as I was on my way here just now. Miss Lydia is with her. I saw her myself. It seems that Miss

Bennet heard something outside last night and thought it prudent to fetch her youngest sister to prevent her from rousing the household. She feared that Miss Lydia might be frightened and in need of comfort, though she knew there was no real danger as it was probably a stray dog or cat. Miss Lydia spent most of the night in Miss Bennet's room."

Will raised his brows in surprise. *Hmm ... There seems to be more to Miss Jane Bennet than I thought. Maybe she is more than just a beautiful, sweet lady. She may be sharper than I've given her credit to be.*

CHAPTER 19

Trust is the glue of life. It's the most essential ingredient in effective communication. It's the foundational principle that holds all relationships.

Stephen Covey

A car and driver hired and cleared by the investigative team at Darcy Enterprises met Fitzwilliam, Elizabeth, Mr. Bennet, and Steve at the Los Angeles airport as soon as they arrived, and they immediately left for the hotel. While they were pulling away from the curb, Fitzwilliam heard the driver use the hands-free phone in the car to tell someone they were on their way.

Fitzwilliam turned to Steve. "Have you heard anything new?"

Steve nodded. "While you slept, I used the phone in the forward cabin to contact both the L. A. P. D. and the hotel. They helped me to reserve rooms for all of us on the same floor as Mary's room. One of the detectives told me that as guests had checked out of the surrounding rooms, they had been occupied by police personnel or left empty. Other guests accepted room upgrades to move to different floors of the hotel. No one is on that floor now except us, Mary and Greg, the police, and the FBI. All hotel employees on the fifth floor have been replaced with special agents dressed in hotel uniforms."

Elizabeth lifted her head from Fitzwilliam's shoulder. "So, they have positively identified the man with Mary as Greg?"

Steve's face was deadly serious as he looked at her. "Yes, that's why the FBI has become involved. They've been watching Greg for over a year, and they hope to finally catch him in something that will stick in court. They take human trafficking very seriously. Victims are often beaten and forced to work as prostitutes. But not all trafficking is sexual, and not all victims are sold. Some are made to take jobs as migrant, domestic, restaurant, or factory workers with little or no pay. Some are starved, too.

"The FBI is working hard to stop it, not only because of the personal and psychological toll it takes on the victims and American society as a whole, but also because trafficking involves the illegal transportation of immigrants across international borders. Another concern is that it provides an easy source of income for organized crime and terrorists."

Mr. Bennet glanced out of the window. It was well into the middle of the night, but the bright lights of Los Angeles made it seem almost like daytime. His face was streaked with tears when he turned to look at Steve. "Why do they think Greg has planned to sell Mary into sexual slavery rather than menial labor?"

Steve sighed. "The sex trade is Greg's specialty. Several times he has been the last one seen with young girls who have later disappeared, but, unfortunately, there wasn't enough evidence to hold him. The girls are all middle-class, blonde, and pretty. If he sold them to anyone who kept them in the United States, eventually at least one of them would have found a way to contact their families. None of them have, so they must have been sent out of the country. Another red flag is that he brought Mary here to California. Many people are sold into the U.S., but most of the people who are sold out of this country leave through California and Texas. There's an international airport in Los Angeles, and this is where he usually works. The girls Greg tricks and sells probably aren't common prostitutes in places like China. Those would more likely be poor girls from other countries lured into prostitution with the promises of money, an education, or a high paying job. Their passports and documentation are taken from them when they arrive at their destinations so they have no way to get back out of the country. Average middle class American girls already have access to money and good educations, so those things don't tempt them. The poor girls are controlled through physical and psychological means which wouldn't be as effective on girls like Mary. Most likely, the girls from middle class U.S. families have been sold at high prices to extremely rich men in the Middle East. Of course, not all of them are from families like the Bennets. Some of them are teenaged runaways, or they're children too young to defend themselves. Nearly half of the victims are under the age of 18."

Fitzwilliam reached for Elizabeth's hand and rubbed his thumb over the top of it. "I confess I don't know much about this. Why would men in the Middle East be more likely to buy girls like Mary? Can't they just marry girls from their own countries?"

Steve nodded and clasped his hands in his lap. "They do marry women who are considered to be suitable for them. Prostitution, along with all sexual activity, is illegal outside of lawful marriage in those countries. It has to do with their religion. The women they marry aren't the ones they want sexually, and they can't be with the women they want without violating their laws and belief system. They also want a variety of women, though they prefer young blondes like Mary. They can force them to do things their wives refuse to do. Harems have been in existence since the Ottoman Empire; it's accepted there. There is virtually no legislative action taken by those countries to eliminate prostitution and trafficking, so it flourishes. Extremely rich Arab men from the Persian Gulf area have been known to rent apartments 'furnished with housemaids' for anywhere from a few hours to several months. Very few Middle Eastern countries are completely devoid of commercial sexual trafficking.

"This problem is worldwide. Most of the trafficking victims are from Ethiopia, Nigeria, and Pakistan, though Europe has seen an influx of illegal immigrants smuggled in from Iraq, China, Pakistan, India, and Africa. Those are the women who end up as prostitutes or in grueling, unpaid jobs. Women from extremely poor places like Ethiopia voluntarily migrate to the Middle East and accept working conditions that are more like slavery because they see it as a better alternative than starvation."

Fitzwilliam bit the inside of his cheek with fury. *How can this be in the modern world? I had no idea such horrible things were happening. What is wrong with people? I have to do something to help put a stop to this insanity.*

After taking a moment while his mind worked, mulling over everything he had heard, Fitzwilliam spoke again. "You said that he hasn't broken any laws with Mary. How can the police and FBI become involved when he's remained within the law?"

Steve smiled with grim satisfaction. "The official definition of trafficking includes the words 'recruitment of persons by means of fraud for the purpose of exploitation.' I'm sure that Greg hasn't told Mary what he intends to do with her. I have no doubt that he's told her an entirely different tale, and deceiving her is fraud. If the FBI can somehow get to Mary and find out what he promised her, and then establish what he's actually set up for her, they'll have him. I think your plan will help with that, Fitzwilliam. I've already talked to my contacts, and they're onboard with the idea. We'll just have to be very careful not to alert either of them to the presence of law enforcement. They've placed remote cameras in our rooms which we can activate with the press of a button on a device which looks like a cell phone. The cameras also record sound, like a video."

They pulled up to the service entrance of the hotel where they were met by two FBI agents. The men flashed their badges as soon as the group had exited the car.

One of them extended his hand to each of them in turn as he introduced himself and his partner. "My name is Agent Hal Blackwell, and this is Agent Jason Fry. We're sorry to have to meet you under these conditions, but thank you for coming."

Steve nodded and indentified himself, Fitzwilliam, Elizabeth, and Mr. Bennet to the agents.

Agent Fry shook their hands. "Let's get you to your rooms by the back entrance. We've already picked up keycards for you, and we'd prefer you not go through the lobby area. Since there are still a few hours until morning, you should try to get some sleep. Don't leave your rooms without letting us know. Here's my number. I've also written Agent Blackwell's number on the back of each card." He handed them each a business card. "Tomorrow may be a long day. If there is any movement from the suspect's room, we'll let you know immediately."

Agent Blackwell gestured to them as he turned. "Follow us, please, and be as quiet as you can."

They made their way around the building, entered the docking bay by way of a second service entrance, and took the hotel employees' elevator. When they arrived at the fifth floor, Agent Blackwell motioned for them to stay on the elevator while he spoke into his cell phone. After he had exchanged a few words with another agent, he quietly gave them instructions. "Miss Bennet and Whitman are in room 506, apparently asleep. Agents are in the rooms on either side of them as well as across from them. We've put Miss Bennet in 510 and Mr. Darcy in 512. Mr. Bennet, you're across from your daughter in 511, and Mr. Walker is in 513, the room adjoining yours. If you need anything, call one of us."

They nodded their agreement, and he led them from the elevator and down the hallway, stopping at each of their rooms and giving them their key cards. The agent entered their rooms with them and showed them where the cameras were located, demonstrating how to use the remote to turn the cameras on and off, and then leaving the remotes on their bedside tables.

After Agent Blackwell left, Fitzwilliam looked around his room. It wasn't as large as his bedroom at The Oaks, but he was satisfied with the king-sized bed and kitchenette. *I wish I had another set of clothes. I could use a shower and some clean pajamas, but I suppose I'll just have to make do with a shower.* He was pleased to see the shampoo and other toiletries in the bathroom. *This is certainly more comfortable than the inns I lodged in along the roads during my previous life.* Fitzwilliam brushed his teeth with the complimentary toothbrush and toothpaste but decided to wait until the morning to shower.

He heard a light rap and turned toward the sound to see a metal door. He crossed the room and put his ear against it. His cell phone vibrated in his pocket, so he pulled it. *Elizabeth is calling me? Why?*

He quickly swiped the phone with his thumb and put it to his ear. "Hello, Elizabeth. Is everything all right?"

Her voice was soft. "I'm in the room next to yours, and I can't sleep. I hoped you were still awake. Open the metal door."

Our rooms have a door which opens between them? I suppose that's what 'adjoining' means. I thought it meant side-by-side. He opened the door to see her slip her phone into her pocket and was surprised when she walked straight into his arms. She spoke against his chest. "I don't want to be by myself. Can I watch TV with you? I'll turn it down low so you can sleep."

This is probably not a good idea, but I cannot tell her 'no.' I also doubt that I'll be able to sleep as long as she's in my room alone with me. He smiled. *If Mr. Bennet says that I've compromised Elizabeth and demands that I marry her, I will not mind complying with his request. Somehow, I think that will not happen in this era.*

He kissed the top of her head. "Of course. We'll just leave the doors between the rooms open so that we can hear if anyone knocks on your door or calls your room."

She lifted her face and stood on her tiptoes to kiss his cheek. "Thank you."

Fitzwilliam wanted to kiss her senseless, but he restrained himself. *She trusts me, and trust is difficult for her. If I take advantage of her, I may lose all the ground I've gained.*

He didn't try to stop Elizabeth when she pulled away and went to the television. She picked up the remote and took a blanket from a drawer, carrying both of them with her as she climbed up onto his bed and arranged some pillows behind her back. He stood, shocked, as she casually pointed the remote and flipped through the channels. *She's on my bed. Do I sit in a chair? I have no idea what I'm supposed to do. She said that she and Greg used to watch movies on her bed, so I assume it must be acceptable behavior.*

She stopped on a movie and looked over at him, patting the bed beside her. "I suppose this wouldn't be proper behavior in your time period, but I'm not going to take advantage of you, Fitzwilliam. We're both fully dressed, and we're responsible adults. You can get inside the covers and go to sleep. I'll just cover up with a blanket. If anyone comes to the door, I'll go back to my room. No one will ever know." Her smile was contagious.

She truly thinks I care what people think of her being in here with me? What would she say if she knew that I really wouldn't mind? I would marry her tomorrow and be happy.

He walked over to the bed, placed his phone on the bedside table, and, after propping a couple of pillows next to hers, he sat close beside her, sliding his arm behind her neck. "Elizabeth, I'm not concerned with what people say or think about us. I love you, and I'm very pleased that you trust me enough to come to me."

She turned her face and kissed his cheek again. "I love you, too. I don't want to be alone."

He tried unsuccessfully to stifle his groan. *I hope she didn't hear that.*

She did not move away. "You can kiss me, you know. I won't bite. I promise."

Apparently, she did. He shook his head. *Perhaps one kiss would be all right.*

Elizabeth put her hand on his cheek and moved it into his hair, pulling him toward her. "I'm not afraid of you. You won't scare me away. I trust you." She closed her eyes, his face almost touching hers.

Her lashes lay dark along her cheek bones; her hair tumbled about her shoulders in unruly waves. *She is so beautiful.*

Fitzwilliam lowered his lips to hers and kissed her, losing himself in the sensation of her hand playing in his hair and her warm breath caressing his skin. He deepened the kiss, connecting with her in a way which he had yearned for since she had appeared at his office that warm afternoon following the week they had spent apart. He knew he never wanted to be away from her again. He heard her breath quicken, and he knew he had to stop. *I will not lose her by moving too quickly.*

He broke the kiss but kept his forehead against hers. "Elizabeth, we must rest now, though I do not wish to do so. However ..." His voice was soft.

She opened her dark eyes and smiled. "You're stressed. I can tell, because you lapse into eighteenth century speech patterns when you feel a loss of control."

He rubbed his nose lightly against hers. "You need to sleep, my love. Morning will come all too quickly."

She yawned and rested her head on his chest, snuggling up to him. "Umm ..."

Fitzwilliam watched her until he heard her breathing slip into the deep, regular rhythms of sleep. Then he powered off the television, placed the remote on the bedside table, and turned off the lamp. Slipping his free arm gently around her in a tender embrace, he turned his body slightly toward her, careful not to awaken her.

His exhaustion overtook him, and he slept.

CHAPTER 20

The senses deceive from time to time, and it is prudent never to trust wholly those who have deceived us even once.

Rene Descartes

Following the rather unsettling morning at Pemberley, the weather turned rainy and unseasonably chilly for summer. Seeing the opportunity to keep the party together, Will suggested that they spend the day quietly indoors. His idea was met with enthusiasm on the part of nearly everyone, though a few young ladies rolled their eyes before they acquiesced. After a few moments of indecision, the inhabitants of that great estate found ways to occupy their time with reading, sewing for the poor, practicing at their instruments, playing cards, or conversing among themselves. The upcoming ball was a favourite topic among the younger people.

Caroline Bingley remained in her chambers with her brother, but the rest were together in the main rooms of the house under the watchful eyes of Will and Colonel Fitzwilliam.

In the early afternoon, the two men stood together, apart from the group at a window overlooking the front lawn.

Will glanced around the parlour and, confident that the noise from the multiple conversations, games, and music would cover his words, he turned to his cousin, speaking quietly. "Have you noticed that Wentworth rarely makes any effort to be with Georgiana?"

Colonel Fitzwilliam nodded. "I have. The first week he was at Pemberley, he rarely left her side, and she seemed very pleased to receive his addresses. However, since that time, I have observed that it is unusual for them to be in the same room, much less conversing."

"As he does not seem to play the part of the ardent suitor, I wonder why he remains. Does he feel honour bound to my sister? He has yet to speak to me if he wishes to offer for her hand. If he does not love her, I would not wish for a marriage between them, no matter how grand his family or position in society."

The colonel shook his head. "I have no idea whether or not he cares for my cousin, though he certainly does not act as if he does. In fact, Wentworth spends a great deal of time enjoying the company of the other guests, particularly Miss Mary Bennet. I have also often observed him in conversation with John Bennet and his father."

Will looked at Georgiana, laughing and chatting with Elizabeth. "My sister seems cheerful enough without his attentions. She does not appear to be distressed by his apparent lack of interest in her. She is full young for marriage in any case, in my opinion. I would rather she would wait another year or two at least."

Georgiana turned her head and saw the men looking at her. She rose from her seat and walked sedately towards them, followed closely by Elizabeth. "Of what are you gentlemen speaking so solemnly, and what interests you so that you closely watch Elizabeth and me?"

Will kissed her cheek. "I am merely glad to see you happy, my dear, and I hope that you will always remain so."

She tilted her head and raised an eyebrow playfully. "Serious, indeed. Of course I am happy. I shall soon have the sister I have always wanted. I wish for nothing more."

Will's gaze drifted to Mary Bennet and Wentworth, singing together at the piano. Georgiana turned in the direction of his gaze. She then returned her attention to her brother. "Ah, I understand now."

Georgiana placed her hand on his arm, patting it gently before dropping her hand. She then clasped her hands at her waist. "Do not be distressed, Will. I am perfectly content. Observing you and Elizabeth these past few weeks has shown me what love is supposed to be, and I want what the two of you have before I marry. He and I are not suited to each other – we do not agree on what is important – and I am quite pleased that we realized that before we married. We talked at length and mutually agreed that we should not pursue a deeper connection between us. It would have been a terrible mistake. He is a good man, and I wish him well. He will be right for another lady, but not for me."

Colonel Fitzwilliam touched her shoulder lightly. "So, you are not displeased that he openly pays court to another woman in your own home?"

She smiled. "Not at all. We invited him here for the summer, and I shall not rescind the invitation. He is quite excited about the ball, and as long as he is pleasant, he is welcome to be our guest for the remaining weeks. After all, an extra gentleman is always appreciated at a ball. He may leave whenever he likes, and I shall not miss his company overmuch. He is a friend, and that is an end to it. We shall be courteous to one another and act as good friends if we should meet in company in the future. There is no sense of awkwardness when we are in the same party. I am, in fact, relieved that we have agreed that a chance of any understanding between the two of us is over."

Elizabeth caught Will's attention and smiled brightly. "Georgiana received a letter from Lady Matlock this morning."

Thank you for changing the subject, my love. He turned to his sister. "What did our aunt have to say? When is she coming?"

Georgiana glanced gratefully at Elizabeth before returning her attention to her brother. "This very afternoon. Her rooms are in readiness, and I look forward to seeing her again. She shall be a great help in completing the plans for the ball, and she may even have some ideas for the wedding, should you and Elizabeth wish to accept her suggestions."

Colonel Fitzwilliam frowned, clearing his throat, and Georgiana looked up at him. "Is anything amiss, Cousin?"

He shook his head. "I only wondered why she did not write me."

Georgiana laughed. "When did you last write her? I send her a letter every week. Do you?"

He grinned sheepishly. "I cannot remember when I last wrote her. My mother has never complained to me that I am lax in my duties towards her."

Her eyes sparkled. "She has not complained to me concerning you either. Your mother knew that I would tell you when she is coming. In fact, she instructed me to do so. She was in a hurry to leave and saw no need to write two letters. You know how very practical she is."

The colonel nodded, chuckling. "That is one of my favourite things about my mother – her extreme practicality. She goes right to the heart of a matter, and she wastes nothing. Some might think her abrupt, but I have always admired her economy of words and lack of airs. She simply despises false dignity where there is no real superiority of mind."

Will listened to their exchange with interest. *I think that I shall like my Aunt Matlock, especially since she seems to be the polar opposite of Aunt Catherine. It's difficult to believe they were brought up in the same circles.*

Elizabeth whispered, "Will," and he turned to see what she was observing.

Catherine and Lydia are leaving the room by a side door.

Before Will could speak, Mr. Bennet stood and blocked the girls' way. "Where are you two going? I thought we might play at cards. You always enjoy that, Lydia, and we have not challenged each other today. You have been occupied with others, but I must have my share in the amusements."

Catherine stopped and glanced at him in confusion. "Lydia said that we must visit our friend, Miss Bingley, as she is ill and cannot come to us. We have missed her most terribly, and we worry that her brother cannot care for her sufficiently. Men are not at all good at being nurses, you know."

Mrs. Bennet placidly looked up from her sewing basket. "But, my dear, Miss Bingley is much too indisposed for visitors. We all heard it from Mr. Darcy this morning. Her brother is with her because he has already been exposed to her malady; they do not wish any of the rest of us to contract the disease. Should she need a physician, I am certain that Mr. Bingley will let Mr. Darcy know, and all will be done with great haste. She is being well taken care of. Mrs. Reynolds goes to her rooms regularly to make certain of it."

Will smiled at her. *I was careful not to say she was sick, but if you drew that conclusion, who am I to argue? She is indisposed with a terrible temper. She is also certainly afflicted with pride, delusions of grandeur, and a total unawareness of anyone else's desires and needs except her own.*

Lydia stared at Catherine, her displeasure evident. "Why can you not hold your tongue?" She faced her mother and spoke in a whine. "But I want to see Miss Bingley. She is one of my dearest friends, and I know she must be bored to tears sitting with her brother. I know that I am tired to death of having nothing to do but sit here all day. I cannot believe that she is ill, either, for she was quite well last evening."

"Lydia." Mr. Bennet's voice was firm, brooking no opposition. "You will not see Miss Bingley today, no matter how dear she may be to you. You will not chance contracting her affliction yourself and spreading her contagion. There will be no further discussion on this matter. Do whatever you wish within reason, but you must remain in this room."

She opened her mouth to reply, but closed it quickly. Then she smiled. "But I must leave the parlour to visit the – er – necessary room."

Mrs. Bennet looked up at her, eyes opened wide. "Lydia!"

Elizabeth coloured to the roots of her hair but quickly crossed the space between herself and her sister and took her firmly by the arm. "I saw Miss Bingley this morning, and I can assure you that Mr. Darcy spoke truthfully. I shall go with her, Papa, so have no fear of her disobedience. Catherine, you may come as well, if you wish. We will return directly."

Jane stood gracefully, leaving her book on the settee. "I could use a bit of exercise myself; therefore, I shall come as well, Elizabeth."

Will smiled. *Again Jane surprises me. If the two girls go in different directions, she can go with one while Elizabeth goes with the other.*

In mid-afternoon, the interest of the party was stirred by the sound of a carriage approaching the house. Will, Elizabeth, Colonel Fitzwilliam, and Georgiana went to the front hall to receive Lady Matlock. The others were content to stay behind in the parlour and wait for their introduction to the new arrival, especially after Mr. Bennet prevented his younger daughters from joining the hosts as they left the room.

However, the lady who descended from the ornate carriage was most decidedly not Lady Matlock, much to the consternation of Will and the others assembled in the hallway, though they were too well-bred to voice their thoughts aloud.

Why in the world is she here? Whatever her motive is, it can't be good. Will stepped through the open door to welcome his least favourite relative – his Aunt Catherine. Her daughter Anne followed her, along with her companion, Mrs. Jenkinson.

Will helped Lady Catherine descend the carriage, greeting her formally. She nodded at both him and Colonel Fitzwilliam, and then frowned at Elizabeth before she turned imperiously to Georgiana. "We will take our usual rooms."

Will offered her his arm, leading her up the steps while Georgiana followed with Elizabeth.

The colonel assisted Anne and Mrs. Jenkinson from the carriage and escorted them to the front entry behind the others.

Georgiana was plainly distressed. She lowered her voice to a whisper. "Elizabeth, her rooms have been prepared for the Gardiners. Aunt Catherine has not visited Pemberley in several years, and we had no idea she was coming at this time. Lady Matlock will use the other chambers we refurbished, thinking they would be extra and unneeded."

Elizabeth leaned close to Georgiana's ear. "Do not upset yourself. My aunt and uncle will not arrive until tomorrow afternoon. Give Lady Catherine, Anne, and Mrs. Jenkinson the rooms. If Mrs. Reynolds cannot have other rooms in readiness before then, my relatives will stay at the inn in Lambton."

Anne spoke from behind them. "My mother has intruded again, I see. I tried to convince her to write before we left Rosings, but she refused. She also forbade me to write. I knew this foolhardy scheme would be an inconvenience to you, and I am sorry for her rudeness, but she was determined upon her course. Mrs. Jenkinson and I will gladly remove to the Rose and Crown in Lambton."

Colonel Fitzwilliam sighed audibly. "No one shall stay in Lambton. If we men must double up, we shall do so. The nurseries are in readiness for the Gardiner children, and Mr. and Mrs. Gardiner may have my chambers if necessary. Put a cot for me in Will's room. I have certainly lived in worse conditions."

Georgiana looked back and smiled at him. "Thank you,

Richard. I hope we can avoid such extreme measures, but I appreciate your willingness to make accommodations."

Elizabeth chuckled. "His idea is a good one. I shall move to Jane's chambers to free my room for my aunt and uncle. Several of us may need to adjust, but all will be well."

As they entered the hallway, Lady Catherine dropped her hand from Will's arm and turned to face Elizabeth, her voice commanding. "You will join me in the library."

Elizabeth raised an eyebrow. "I find that I am much occupied at present and unable to agree to your request. I must move out of my chambers to make room for your party."

The lady rapped her cane on the floor in agitation. "You will obey me at once. Obstinate, headstrong girl! You should know your place and the honour that I do you by attempting to dissuade you from making the worst misstep of your life."

Will moved quickly to stand beside Elizabeth and tucked her hand into the crook of his arm. "The only way you will talk to my betrothed is in my presence. I will not have her subjected to your fit of temper in my own home. She will, after all, soon be mistress here."

Everyone stood as if rooted to the floorboards, and Lady Catherine's harsh breathing was the only sound to be heard. After a few minutes, she smiled with malice. "Very well. Will the both of you condescend to join me in the library while Georgiana sees to Anne and Mrs. Jenkinson? I have come a very long way for this conversation, and I will have it before I rest this night."

Elizabeth nodded, and Will gestured towards the library door. "After you, Aunt Catherine."

Colonel Fitzwilliam stepped up beside his aunt. "Allow me to escort you."

She sniffed and took his arm, walking regally and with great pomp, head held high.

Georgiana rang the bell for Mrs. Reynolds and waited at the foot of the stairs with Anne and her companion, talking quietly.

When Will and the others were all in the room, Lady Catherine dropped the colonel's arm. "You may leave us now."

Will spoke with force, his displeasure evident. "You have no right to direct the movements of my relatives and guests. Whatever you have to say to Elizabeth, you can say in front of me and my cousin. We will not allow you to abuse her."

The lady seemed to grow taller, and her stance was rigid. "How dare you speak to me in such a manner! My sister must be turning in her grave to hear what a disrespectful son she reared."

"I highly doubt that." The voice emanating from the doorway was carefully modulated and cultured. "My sister-in-law would likely be very proud of her son for standing up to you. It is certainly time that someone did."

Lady Catherine turned. "Evaline. How very like you to appear at such a moment."

Lady Matlock smiled, stepped into the room, and closed the door behind her. "My moment was planned, Catherine, unlike yours, I would wager. I wrote to Georgiana and apprised her of my arrival. I am expected; obviously, you are not, from what I have seen of the bustling in the hallway and on the stairs. I daresay you have thrown the house into uproar, as it is already full of guests and relations. Were you invited? Did you even bother to tell them you were coming?"

Lady Catherine turned an unpleasant shade of red. "I do not need an invitation to my sister's house. Were it not already filled with upstarts and low-born, lowbred people, there would be plenty of room."

Will's voice thundered in the cavernous room. "Enough! Say your piece and leave my house. You have insulted my fiancée and her family, and I will not tolerate it."

She drew in her breath sharply as she pointed her cane towards Will. "Very well. I am here to warn Miss Elizabeth Bennet that a union with you, Nephew, would not be in her best interests. She should know better than to aspire to such a match. Her low connections and lack of fortune render her unsuitable to be a Darcy bride, and she would be shunned by the rest of the family. I am further trying to spare her the pain of a marriage to an unprincipled thief." She rapped her cane on the floor as her voice rose in anger. "You know that you stole large amounts of money from the Rosings coffers to keep Pemberley afloat. You admitted it to me in the presence of Colonel Fitzwilliam when you were in Kent. You also pledged to repay the money, but you have not done so. Your very character and reputation as a gentleman are called into question. I have no doubt that you have withheld this information from Miss Bennet. Now what have you to say for yourself?" Her expression was triumphant.

Will's smile was chilly as he narrowed his eyes at her. *You have no idea that Richard and I visited the bank and know that you took the money yourself. I'm so glad that I mentioned this to Elizabeth yesterday. If I hadn't, she might be inclined to doubt me.*

Elizabeth withdrew her hand from Will's arm and advanced to the older lady. "I do not know the particulars, but he did tell me and my father that you withdrew money from your own accounts and made it appear that he had done it."

Lady Catherine's "Humph!" was immediate. "That is foolishness, indeed! Why would I steal money from myself? And if I indeed took the money, why on earth would I want Fitzwilliam to think that he stole it from me?"

Elizabeth stood her ground with spirit, her colour rising. "I am not privy to the workings of a mind such as yours. Perhaps to blackmail him into marrying your daughter?"

Lady Catherine's face contorted into a sneer. "I would not have him for a son-in-law now. I know not how he has deceived you into believing these lies, but I will be glad to leave this house and never come back."

Lady Matlock moved from in front of the door and gestured towards it. "You always did love grand exits and entrances, Catherine."

Colonel Fitzwilliam held up his hand. "Not just yet, Mother. Aunt Catherine is unaware that Will and I have proof of her duplicity. When we were in London, we visited The Bank of England with our lawyer, Mr. Worth, and met with the bank president, Mr. Giles."

Will stepped behind his desk, opened a drawer, and withdrew a file filled with papers which he laid out on the desktop. "Did you know there is such a thing as a copying press? Amazing invention. The Bank of England prides itself on keeping up with all the modern conveniences, and they have just such a machine. I have here copies of the documents, signed by you and your former steward, Mr. Obadiah Stevens, proving that you set up that account yourself and authorized payments to Mr. Stevens for depositing money into it on a yearly basis from the Rosings accounts. Mr. Giles also provided us with paperwork outlining all the particulars. He expressed his willingness to swear to it in court, though he would prefer not to sully your name in such a way. I never took any money from Rosings; that is why I have never repaid it. I have no idea what you hoped to gain by such a scheme, but I am guilty of nothing in connection with the business."

Lady Catherine sat down abruptly, leaning back as if overcome, closing her eyes. Her voice was old and tired, but she refused to relent. Her eyes opened to slits. "How can you say such things to your elder? I have loved you all your life, and all I have ever wanted has been what is best for you. And now you would compound the injury by dismissing me from your house?"

Elizabeth hesitated, and her expression changed from angry to pitying. She looked at Will, pleading. "Could she not stay the night, Will? It is too late for her to travel, and I am truly concerned for Anne. She should not be subjected to such treatment when she has done no wrong. Your aunt is fatigued. Surely one night would not be too much to ask of us."

Lady Matlock smiled. "How does it make you feel to be defended by the person you most despise, Catherine? She would heal the breach between you. Would you?"

Lady Catherine's eyes were hooded, hiding them. "I should be grateful to stay at Pemberley for one night. Since I am your mother's sister, Fitzwilliam, I do not think it is too much to ask."

I don't trust her. His anger dissipated somewhat, and his tone was resigned. "Very well, Aunt Catherine. You may stay, though I may not be able to guarantee you your regular rooms."

Her eyes gleamed as she looked up at him. "Thank you, Fitzwilliam. I shall not be a problem. I need not stay in the family wing; a guest room will do very well."

Somehow, I know that I'm going to regret this. Will nodded and rang the bell. "Mrs. Reynolds will show you to your room and provide refreshment if you need it, Aunt."

He was weary to the bone, and he wanted to rest. *I can't wait for this day and night to end. At least Wickham will no longer be a problem.*

CHAPTER 21

Vanity and pride are different things, though the words are often used synonymously. A person may be proud without being vain. Pride relates more to our opinion of ourselves, vanity to what we would have others think of us.

Jane Austen, Pride and Prejudice

Fitzwilliam awakened slowly to feel the warmth of a softness snuggled against the length of his body, his arms wrapped around a curvy form, hugging her closely to him. *Am I still dreaming? If I am, I don't wish to wake up.*

Her hair tickled his nose, and he buried his face in it, inhaling deeply. She turned toward him, eyes still closed, and began to smile. *She is irresistible.* He kissed her gently.

When he drew back, she whispered. "Am I asleep, am I awake, or somewhere in between? I can't believe that you are here and lying next to me. Or did I dream that we were perfectly entwined? Like branches on a tree or twigs caught on a vine?"

He nuzzled his stubbled face against her cheek to kiss her ear. "It's not a dream, though I thought the same thing. I had no idea the woman I love is such a poet."

She opened her eyes. "I didn't make that up. It's from a song – 'Truly, Madly, Deeply' by One Direction." She laughed, her voice deep-tinged with sleep. "It's a couple of years old, but I used to sing it, and I thought that girl would never be me. I didn't think I could ever love anyone like I love you. I thought I would be alone forever, the crazy aunt to Jane's six children, teaching them to play the piano very badly." Elizabeth chuckled and shook her head. "This is a first for me, you know."

He pulled away a little to look at her, puzzled. "I don't understand. I've already told you that I love you, and you know that I won't ever leave you. I know you've been kissed and hugged, too. We've done that before."

She laughed again. "Oh, yes. I've been more than kissed, though it wasn't pleasant. I meant that I've never slept through the night with a man before. I've never woken up cuddling with anyone. No one has ever kissed me awake but my mother."

Fitzwilliam's smile was crooked. "I like your mother, but I don't want to remind you of her."

"I promise you, love, that I never think of my mother when you touch me." She sat up and stretched. "If I don't get up now, I may stay here all day." The clock on the nightstand caught her attention. "Good grief! It's ten o'clock. We've been asleep for hours. I need to go back to my room and take a shower. Too bad we don't have any fresh clothes to change into; what we're wearing now will have to do, I suppose."

She leaned over to kiss his cheek, and her phone vibrated. Shaking her head, she sat up and retrieved it from the bedside table. "Really? That's wonderful. Good news for a change... Have an agent bring you to my room and take him to Fitzwilliam's... Mom can stay with Dad... I'll tell Fitzwilliam so you don't have to call him. Mom can call Dad... I'll see you in a few minutes."

Elizabeth hopped out of bed and headed for the adjoining door. "I've got to go right now."

He got out of bed and followed her. "Was that Jane?"

"Yep. She, Lance, and Mom left a few hours after we did last night. They're in the hotel general manager's office, meeting with the FBI. They'll be up here in a few minutes, and I don't think we want to give them the wrong idea, do we?" She stood in the doorway, smiling at him.

I really wouldn't mind. Maybe Mr. Bennet would make me do the honorable thing. He smiled broadly. "Would they demand that I marry you since I've compromised your reputation?"

She grinned. "Nah. They might act disappointed in us, but I have a sneaking suspicion that Jane and Mom might actually be happy for me. They know me well enough to think that even if we slept in the same bed, we didn't do any more than just that. They would probably see it as an indication that I'm not going to let Greg ruin the rest of my life, and they would think that's a good thing. Lance and Dad would likely have other ideas. We're not kids any more, and adults don't usually have sleepovers without benefits. Even at that, no one would force us to marry. Don't worry about that."

His lips twitched as the corners turned upward. "Do I look worried?"

The smile left her face. "Actually, you don't."

Soft knocks sounded on both of their room doors, and she quickly turned to leave his room through the adjoining door. She looked back. "Don't forget to close your door, too."

Elizabeth blew him a kiss and shut her door.

I miss her already. Fitzwilliam closed the adjoining door just as his hotel room door opened and Lance walked in, followed by Agent Fry, dressed as a hotel employee and pushing a food cart.

Lance looked at Fitzwilliam speculatively. He dropped a couple of duffel bags on the floor and walked further into the room, arms crossed over his chest. "You just get up?"

Did he see me close the door? This would be a good time to have him thinking about something else. He walked across the room and picked up one of the bags. "Yes. Please tell me this bag is full of my clothes and toiletries. And is that breakfast? Thank you. I'm really hungry."

The agent nodded. "Mr. Darcy, you need to dress and eat as quickly as you can. Greg Whitman left his room about an hour ago, and Mary is alone right now. If she leaves their room, we'll direct her into Miss Bennet's room and contact you and Mr. Bingley."

Fitzwilliam picked up his bag. "I'll shower right away and eat afterward. Lance can let me know if you call before I get out of the bathroom. I'm going to hurry as much as I can."

He headed for the bathroom before Lance had a chance to speak, and the agent quietly left the room.

Fifteen minutes later, Fitzwilliam came out of the bathroom in clean clothes, freshly shaven, hair wet, carrying a towel.

Lance sat at the table, eating waffles and fruit. "It's a good thing you opted for the shorter haircut last week."

Rubbing his head with the towel, Fitzwilliam walked to the food cart. He threw the towel across the back of a chair, ran his fingers through his hair, and lifted the cover from his plate, placing it on the cart. "You were right about that. It's much easier to take care of. This smells good." He poured himself a cup of coffee, picked up his plate, and took them both with him as he joined Lance at the table.

Lance looked pointedly from the bed to Fitzwilliam. "So you slept on top of the covers, under a blanket?"

Fitzwilliam nodded as he chewed, swallowed, and took a sip of coffee. "I did. I was tired. Why is that so strange?"

Lance stared at him. "It isn't, except both pillows were used, and Jane texted me that Liz's bed hasn't been slept in." He frowned. "Liz is like my sister, you know, and she's been through a lot. Don't break her heart, or you'll answer to me – and don't lie to me."

Fitzwilliam slammed his fork down on the table. "I've never lied to you, so I have no idea why you think I would now. Elizabeth did sleep with me last night. She'd had a terrible day, and she didn't want to be alone. When I say we 'slept' together, I mean exactly that. We slept together. That's all – not that it's any of your concern."

Lance smiled. "So, do you love her? Is it serious?"

Fitzwilliam folded his arms across his chest and gave Lance his best Regency patrician glare. "I just flew across the country in an attempt to rescue Elizabeth's youngest sister, and, if I have my wish, Jane will be my sister one day. What do you think? More to the point, what are your intentions toward my future sister? Are you going to marry her, or will you toy with her affections and desert her again? I shall refrain from asking if you have compromised her, for I left my dueling pistols and swords back in 1795. If I find that you have, however, and you furthermore refuse to marry her, I shall purchase new ones and show you how 'tis done. Of course, I prefer a rapier, but I am also adept with the smallsword and the foil. I am quite masterful at using all three of those weapons, in addition to pistols. You will be given the choice."

Lance raised an eyebrow. "Just a little testy this morning, are we? Lapsing into Regency speak. Calm down and finish your breakfast, Fitz. It appears that we may end up being brothers-in-law, for I fully intend to marry Jane just as soon as she'll have me. And, for the record, I haven't 'compromised' her. I've learned a few lessons along the way. We're not high school kids anymore, and that's not the way we want our marriage to begin."

Fitzwilliam had the grace to look sheepish. His voice was gruff. "Sorry. I should thank you for bringing me fresh clothes. I was beginning to smell myself, and it wasn't pleasant."

"No problem. Your investigator called us last night and filled us in on all the details, so we decided to come here ourselves. We phoned Mrs. Thomas, and she brought your bag to us while we were waiting to leave for the airport. Jane brought fresh clothes for Liz." He took a drink from his cup. "I probably should have minded my own business instead of asking about you and Liz. I'm just very protective of her, and I don't want to see her hurt again." Lance forked another bite of fruit and chewed it. "Hurry and eat. We need to be ready if they call us."

They ate in silence for a few moments until they heard a knock on the adjoining door. Fitzwilliam hurried across the room to open it, Lance close on his heels.

They entered the room to see Mary sitting on the foot of the bed, obviously angry. "I don't have time to sit in here. Greg will be back soon, and he told me not to leave the room. He's going to be mad at me. I only left to get a diet soda."

Fitzwilliam looked at Elizabeth, eyebrows raised. *She's holding the camera remote.*

She pointed the remote at the camera and pushed the power button. "This won't take long, Mary. I want you to know that I'm videotaping everything we say in this room. Is that okay?"

Her younger sister made a face. "I don't care what you do. I'm going to be famous soon, so what's one more camera?"

Fitzwilliam walked to her and held out his hand. "I'm a friend to Elizabeth, Jane, and Lance. My name is Fitzwilliam Darcy. I wish we had met earlier, Mary. I should have made more of an effort to become acquainted with Elizabeth's family."

Mary looked him up and down. "So, you're Elizabeth's boyfriend? I feel sorry for you. Why are you here anyway?"

His voice was sincere. "I hope she thinks of me as more than a boyfriend. Everyone in my immediate family is dead, Mary, and I wanted to know why you would leave yours. I simply cannot understand that. If I had a family like yours, I would never run away."

She smirked. "You obviously don't know my family very well. They're always telling me what to do and treating me like I'm a five-year-old. Greg treats me like a woman. He understands me, and he's going to make me a star. I'm going to be famous," she said in a matter-of-face voice, glancing down at her painted nails. She looked up at him. "Red's a pretty color, don't you think?"

He treats her 'like a woman'? I hope that doesn't mean what I think it does. Fitzwilliam pulled the desk chair over and sat down in front of her. "A star … famous? If that's what you want, I have money, and I could help you get acting lessons and auditions. If you want to model, I know an agent who's looking for girls your age. How has Greg helped you?" *I wouldn't refer my worst enemy to Caroline Bingley, but she is the owner of a modeling agency, and I do know her. I'm certain I could find another agent easily if I needed to do so.*

She preened a little. "He's taken pictures of me and showed them to an agent. The guy said that he could get me parts in movies and commercials. He said I have the perfect looks for Hollywood."

Elizabeth drew in a deep breath. "What sorts of pictures, Mary?" she asked as she sat down beside her on the bed.

Mary looked down at her hands, clasping her fingers together nervously. "You wouldn't like them."

Jane sat on her other side, putting an arm around her shoulders. "Why not, Mary?"

Her voice was quiet, childlike. "He made me take off all my clothes." She put her hands over her face.

Lance made a noise of disgust, but Jane quieted him with a small shake of her head.

Fitzwilliam reached out and touched her knee lightly. "What did he tell you, Mary? Did he promise you anything?"

She raised her face to his. "Greg said that all the talent agents want to see the actresses and models nude. They want to be sure that you aren't wearing padding or anything to make you look better than you really do. He promised me that I'd be in movies, and he said that people who've looked at my shots already want me to be in print ads and modeling shots for them. I'll be in *Glamour, CoverGirl, Seventeen* – perhaps even *Vogue,* too. That's where he's gone now – to meet with an agent and get a contract for me." Her lip quivered. "Please don't tell Mom and Dad about the pictures. They won't understand."

Fitzwilliam's tone was calm and controlled, masking his anger. "Don't worry about that now. Has he given you money? Did he force you to do anything against your will?"

"He's given me some money, but he said there would be a lot more coming. He's kissed me, but that's all." She looked away. "I don't understand why he doesn't want me himself. I even asked him about it."

Elizabeth swallowed hard. "What did he say?"

"He said that we needed to keep our relationship all business since he's representing me. He also told me he used to be your boyfriend, and I could trust him. I was little then, but I remembered a few times when he came to our house. He's older than I am, but I really like him." She wiped a tear from her cheek.

"Mary." Elizabeth struggled to control her voice. "Why didn't you tell us you were seeing Greg?"

"He told me not to. He said that none of you liked him because he dumped you."

A bitter laugh broke from Elizabeth. "He didn't tell you the truth, Mary. Greg actually raped me twice – once when I was fifteen and again when I was seventeen. I'm just glad that he hasn't hurt you like he hurt me and we got here in time to stop him."

Mary stood, fists clenched by her sides. "I don't believe you. Greg would never do that! He was right. He said you all hated him and would lie about him. You're just jealous of me because Greg loves me and he never loved you. I'm going to be rich and famous, and you're all nobodies."

Jane got up and went to her suitcase. She came back with a manila envelope which she handed to Mary. "Open it." She looked at Elizabeth. "I'm sorry I never told you about this before, but we have to prove it to her. Please forgive me."

Mary undid the clasp on the envelope and reached inside. She pulled out a handful of pictures, gasping as she looked at the images.

Elizabeth saw the first picture and turned away, grabbing the trash can by the bed and retching into it, but Fitzwilliam looked at them, and his blood boiled. *I would love to choke him slowly. I want to make him bleed. He should be made to pay for what he did to you.* He glanced at Elizabeth. *My time period had it right. Jail is too good for that scum. At the very least, we would have transported him to a penal colony in an unsettled area.*

Elizabeth was apparently asleep in the photographs, but her beautiful face was badly beaten and bruised. One eye was swollen shut and bloody, and the other was blackened. Other pictures showed her battered body, close up and in detail. As the pictures became more graphic, he stood and turned his back, unable to bear anymore. He saw the images in his mind, and his fury grew. After a few minutes, he willed himself to calmness.

Fitzwilliam turned his head toward Jane. "You gave her sleeping pills and took those pictures?"

Jane nodded. "I suspected that he had abused her two years earlier from the way she had acted then, after Lance and I found Greg raping her the second time, I used the time Lizzy was asleep to look up information on the internet about what I should do. Under the statute of limitations in Georgia, Lizzy can still press charges if she has these photographs and DNA evidence. There is no time limit on filing charges under these circumstances. She wasn't yet eighteen."

Mary kept looking at the pictures, stunned into silence.

The sounds of Elizabeth's sobs filled the room, and Fitzwilliam went to her, pulling her into his arms. He looked across her shoulder at Jane.

"She said she never saw her clothing or the sheets and bedcoverings again. Is that your DNA source?"

Lance stepped up to put his hand on Jane's shoulder and nodded. "Jane had me contact my friend on the police force, and he told us what to do. He came to the house while Elizabeth slept and collected the evidence himself so there would be no break in the chain of custody, and he checked it all into the evidence room in case she ever wanted to press charges. She didn't want to at the time, but he made copies of these pictures to give Elizabeth later on in case she changed her mind. He wanted us to show them to her and try to convince her to have Greg arrested, but the time never seemed right until now. Greg can't be charged with the first rape, because there's no evidence. However, if Elizabeth wants to do it, she can file charges regarding the second rape up until fifteen years after it happened."

Elizabeth pulled away from Fitzwilliam, grabbed tissues from the nightstand to wipe her face, and looked at Jane and Lance. "I told Fitzwilliam on the plane coming here that I would tell Mary what he'd done, and I'd threaten him with pressing charges for both rapes unless he let her go. Fitzwilliam wanted to have some leverage over him to hold him while this deal with Mary is investigated, but I had no idea that I could make the charges stick." Her eyes were wide. "Thank you. Thank you for being stronger than I was. Thank you for giving me back the power to make him answer for what he did to me. Thank you for helping me stop him from doing this to anyone else."

Mary took a tissue from the box and wiped her own tears silently. Then she stood and faced the others. "He hasn't touched me, and I'm pretty sure he didn't bring me to California to rape me. He could have done that in Atlanta. I get that he's a scumbag, but why do you think he brought me here? Pictures of me naked are embarrassing, and I don't trust him anymore, but he hasn't committed any crime in bringing me here or taking pictures. He made me sign a paper giving my consent." She sighed and glanced around the room absently. After a moment, she returned her gaze to her sisters. "I think I've been stupid to believe he'd make me some kind of movie star, but I want to know if you have any idea what he has planned for me."

Fitzwilliam looked at her somberly. "You should sit down, Mary. This won't be easy for you to hear."

The girls sat on the bed, and Lance pulled up a chair beside Fitzwilliam.

Fitzwilliam sat, leaning toward her with his elbows on his knees and his hands clasped. "The FBI suspects Greg of deep involvement in human trafficking. They believe he has already sold many girls into sexual slavery in Middle Eastern countries. They hope that by following him, they can find some of those girls and return them to their families. I'm sure they'll want to talk to you about the details of your relationship with him."

When he was finished, Mary lay back, looking at the ceiling, tears running from the corners of her eyes into her hair. "I've heard about human trafficking at school. Girls and boys disappear, and they're never found. He's gone now to sell me, hasn't he?"

Fitzwilliam nodded. "We think so. The FBI is following him. My investigator told me on the way here that if they have enough to get a warrant, they'll probably put a video camera in your room, too. I suspect they've already done so. From what he said, I think they'll want you to go back into your room and wait for him. Try to get him to talk about where he's taking you without giving away what you know. Remember that we can see you on the camera, and we won't let him hurt you or take you anywhere. There are FBI agents and police detectives all over this hotel. If he tries to get you to go with him, you can leave the room with him, but don't leave the hotel property. Don't get into a car with him or anyone else, Mary."

There was a gentle rap on the door, and Lance went to open it. Agent Fry, still wearing his hotel uniform, stepped into the room and immediately closed the door.

He crossed the room and stopped in front of Mary. "What Mr. Darcy has told you is accurate, Miss Bennet. Greg Whitman met with a known associate of sex traffickers this morning. This man is known to procure young women for wealthy Arab men, and he handed Whitman a large, thick envelope. When he opened it, we saw that it was stuffed with money. We could probably arrest him now, but the case will be stronger if you can get him to admit what he has planned for you. If you push him enough, he'll brag about it."

Mary looked up at him, fear in her eyes. "What if he beats me like he did Elizabeth? He's really strong, and he's a lot bigger than I am."

"We had a warrant for the surveillance camera and wiretapping sitting in front of a judge, and he signed both of them based on what we saw and the evidence we presented. The camera is in your room now, and we have it turned on. We would never let him hurt you. Remember that we'll be right outside the door. Every hotel employee you'll see on this floor is a special agent. You don't have to do anything except go to your room and wait for him. He's on his way back to the hotel now. The man who gave him the money is following him, so he must plan to hand you over here, maybe in the parking lot. If it gets that far and you can't get him to admit that he's selling you, he'll probably say that the man is a modeling agent or a photographer. Under no circumstances are you to leave the hotel grounds with Whitman or anyone else. Do you understand?"

Mary nodded. She turned to hug each of her sisters, and then stood. "I'll go to the room and wait. It's my mess, and I need to try to fix it. Maybe I can help another girl. That would make all this worth it."

Elizabeth and Jane stood on either side of her. They each kissed her, whispering words of encouragement.

As Mary and Agent Fry walked to the door, everyone followed them.

Agent Fry turned to look at them. "Wait here. After Mary is safely in her room, I'll come back and take you to the surveillance room. Mr. and Mrs. Bennet are already there."

Mary looked back one last time. "I just want to say that, whatever happens, I'm sorry for all this, and I'm glad that I have people who love me enough to come after me. Thank you."

Fitzwilliam nodded. "Remember that while you're talking to Greg. Remember how much your family loves you and how much they're willing to do to protect you. Lance and I aren't family yet, but we both think of you as our little sister. We would do anything to keep you safe, Mary."

She was quiet for a moment. "I won't ever forget that."

She left the room, followed by Agent Fry, and the door closed behind them.

CHAPTER 22

It takes many good deeds to build a good reputation, and only one bad one to lose it.

Benjamin Franklin

After the eventful day and expecting an even more unsettling night, Will found the evening meal at Pemberley to be a trying affair.

Because there were so many new arrivals, and since the ballroom was already refurbished and cleaned in anticipation of the engagement ball, Georgiana and Elizabeth had decided to have tables moved into the ball room so as to ease any overcrowding. In order to avoid separating the company, the long tables had been placed together in the pattern of a rectangle opened on one end, and the effect was stunning. The arrangement of the tables also solved a problem. Because there was no "head" of the table, as there would have been in one single long line of tables, there was no more honour in being seated in one seat than there was in another.

The day had been unseasonably cool, so the fires were lit in the great fireplaces on either side of the room, creating a warm glow throughout, and the light from the fires and the candles danced on the chandeliers and table settings. Tablecloths of snowy white displayed the highly polished silver to perfection while huge vases of flowers from the gardens decorated the room. It was a banqueting hall fit for a king – simple, and yet very elegant.

At the appointed time, Will escorted Elizabeth into the room and seated her to his left at the center of the table which connected the two long rows. *From here, we can watch the entire room. If there is a problem, I will know immediately.*

The others in the party followed them in, selecting their own seats. Georgiana and Elizabeth had expressed the wish not to arrange the seating themselves, for they had no desire to offend anyone. Will had agreed that their reasoning was sound.

Georgiana sat to Will's right, and John Bennet took the seat beside her. Colonel Fitzwilliam sat between Elizabeth and Jane.

Earlier in the day, Charles Bingley had sent a note to Will and Elizabeth, asking if he and Caroline might attend the evening meal, vowing that she would be with him throughout the meal, and they would return to her rooms at its conclusion. The young couple felt sorry for Charles, and after discussing it with Colonel Fitzwilliam and Mr. Bennet, they had agreed to allow them to come, stipulating that they must not be seated near Lydia or Catherine Lucas.

Charles escorted Caroline into the room, walking directly to the table to take a seat by Phoebe Barlow. Wentworth placed himself between Caroline and Mary, and Mrs. Bennet sat to Mary's left.

Will was very nearly amused at how Mr. Bennet took charge of Lydia and Catherine, for he had a young lady on each arm and steered them across the room with determination, away from the Bingleys.

"But I want to sit by Caroline, Papa!" Lydia's exclamation was heard by the entire room, as was her father's answer, spoken into the strained silence.

"All the seats on that side are taken, my dear. You will sit with me."

She would not give way, shaking her curls in consternation. "Surely Mama would move so that I could sit by my dear friend. Would you not Mama?"

Mrs. Bennet fixed her gaze on her youngest daughter, a clear warning in her eyes. "Miss Bingley has just left the sick room, Lydia; therefore, I doubt she is ready for your high spirits. You will sit with your father, and there will be no further discussion of the matter." She smiled graciously as she turned towards Georgiana. "Such lovely arrangements, Miss Darcy. I compliment you on your ability to handle every situation with such grace and elegance."

Georgiana smiled. "You are too kind, Mrs. Bennet. Elizabeth and I do so enjoy a challenge. Your daughter has taught me not to take myself so seriously. Our courage rises with every event which could intimidate us."

Lydia watched the exchange with a pout before she stomped away to sit with her father.

Lady Matlock allowed the footman to seat her by John Bennet. "I think there is little the two of you together could not conquer, Georgiana. I begin to wonder whether or not I was needed here after all. Perhaps Phoebe and I shall walk the grounds while you two young ladies scheme away. We have much to talk about."

Elizabeth chuckled lightly. "For my part, I am very happy you have come, Lady Matlock. We have much to discuss concerning upcoming events, and I have heard so much about you from Georgiana and the colonel that I am most anxious to know you better."

Lady Matlock nodded at her. "And I you, my dear. Georgiana's letters have been full of your praises, and you have the approval of my son. You are a veritable paragon."

Lady Catherine, followed by Anne and Mrs. Jenkinson, advanced regally into the room, looking about her surroundings with a critical eye. Her eyes settled on the only available group of seats together – by Lydia, Mr. Bennet, and Catherine Lucas. She muttered as she walked to the seat being held for her by the footman. "I have sunk to this. I, who was born of such a noble lineage." She sat and waved the servant away.

Lady Matlock looked down the table with a sardonic eye. "Is everything not to your liking, Catherine?"

Lady Catherine turned her head slowly. "No, it is most emphatically *not* to my liking."

Her sister-in-law smiled. "There is a seat by me. You are most welcome to sit here."

The lady raised an eyebrow. "I will not leave Anne to fend for herself among such company. I shall stay where I am."

Lady Matlock's blue eyes sparkled. "Then allow me to exchange seats with you. I would enjoy some time with Anne, and you could converse with Georgiana."

Lady Catherine sniffed dismissively. "I think not. The young man beside you and next to Georgiana – I do not know him."

John Bennet blushed furiously, his handsome face displaying his extreme embarrassment. Elizabeth and Jane also reddened, to the displeasure of Will and Colonel Fitzwilliam.

Mr. Bennet turned to look at the lady, and his face was stone. "That is my son, John, Lady Catherine. He is both university educated and housebroken, and he is the heir to my estate. Does that raise him a bit in your estimation? Is he worthy enough to sit by you?"

Elizabeth spoke quickly. "Lady Catherine, Georgiana and I were unsure of whether or not you would come down, having so recently arrived from such a long and tiring journey. Had we known, we would have arranged the seating with more consideration to your rank."

The matron's voice was cold. "Yet you have more than enough seats. You merely neglected to place your guests properly. I expect no better than that from you, but Georgiana has certainly been taught proper etiquette. I instructed her myself after my sister passed from this life."

This is ridiculous. I will not allow her to insult Georgiana, Elizabeth, and her family in our house. I don't care who she thinks she is. I have more than enough to deal with. Under the table, Will clenched his fists with frustration, struggling to remain calm and keep his voice even. He could not hide the tension in his voice. "Lady Catherine, we have not stood on ceremony this summer. If you are unhappy with the arrangements made by my sister and my betrothed, you may eat in your rooms. Make your choice and have done with it."

He looked pointedly at his butler, standing at the door in stupefaction. "Please serve the first course immediately, Mr. Carlson, and make certain that those who are farthest from this table are served first, and that we are last."

Mr. Carlson nodded and gestured to the footmen. They hurried to serve the soup, beginning with Mrs. Jenkinson and Mrs. Bennet.

Anne stood and walked quickly to the seat by Lady Matlock. A footman stepped forward to pull out the chair for her, and she sat down, smiling at her aunt with firm resolve. "We have been apart for far too long, several years at least, and I was quite pleased to hear you express a wish to talk with me. We will leave for Rosings tomorrow, so I must take every opportunity which presents itself for us to be reacquainted."

Lady Catherine flushed and turned her attention to her soup with a vengeance.

The room began to hum with quiet conversation, but she retained her haughty demeanour and refrained from speaking again throughout the meal.

~~oo~~

As soon as the final course was finished, Lady Catherine stood and announced her intentions to retire to her rooms. "Anne, Mrs. Jenkinson, and I must bid you a good night as we will leave early in the morning."

Anne looked up at her. "Mother, I wish to stay a while longer. Aunt Matlock and I have much to discuss, and I have yet to spend any time with Elizabeth, Will, Georgiana, or Colonel Fitzwilliam. There will be plenty of time to rest in the carriage tomorrow."

Lady Catherine glared at her. "The overstimulation of such a large party will make you ill. You shall come with me."

Anne sighed with resignation and rose from her chair. The remainder of the guests stood with her and began to leave the room in groups.

After wishing those around them a good night, the Bingley siblings took their leave to return to Caroline's chambers. As they quit the room, Caroline looked back over her shoulder, directing a look of pure venom at Lady Catherine.

While the lady did not see it, Will and Elizabeth certainly did. They glanced at each other, eyebrows raised.

Elizabeth kept her voice at a whisper. "Do they know each other?"

Will shook his head. "Not to my knowledge. I doubt they have ever met. Lady Catherine would consider the Bingleys to be too far beneath her to garner her notice."

Meanwhile, Georgiana had gone to speak with Lady Catherine. "You are angry, and I am sorry for it, but Anne has done nothing wrong. Please, Aunt, allow her to stay an hour longer with me. I shall keep her by my side and make certain that she does not overexert herself."

Lady Catherine thought a moment as she looked around the room. "Perhaps I have been hasty. Another hour or two will not hurt any of us, and Anne would likely enjoy your company. We shall all remain for the evening's entertainment. There is little enough of that in Kent. Very few people play or sing well in that area of the country. I should have hired a master for Anne, but she was always too delicate." She paused. "Are there fires in all the rooms? I would not have her catch a chill."

Georgiana smiled as she took her aunt's arm and they began to walk from the ballroom. "We have had fires throughout the house all day, Aunt Catherine. The weather has been quite dreary and chilly today."

"Yes, my dear, as I well know. Travelling in such conditions is never pleasant."

Georgiana patted her arm. "It must have been trying."

They continued to converse in like manner as Georgiana skillfully led her from the ballroom to the large parlour and seated her in a chair that commanded a view of the entire room.

Anne smiled and nodded at Georgiana, placing her hand on the seat beside her on the sofa with an imploring look. Georgiana joined her, and they put their heads together and began to whisper.

Lady Matlock asked her goddaughter, Phoebe Barlow, to sit with her, and soon they were laughing together as longtime friends do.

Mary was the first to play and sing, and after she had acquitted herself creditably, she called to Elizabeth. "Will you sing, Elizabeth? I shall play for you if you like."

Mrs. Bennet looked up, a pleasant expression on her face. "I should like to hear Mr. Darcy play again. He and Elizabeth play so beautifully together."

Lady Catherine turned to her with a frown. "My nephew does not play."

Mr. Bennet chuckled. "Then he certainly does quite a good impression of it. I have heard him pronounced to be accomplished by many people who know a little of the instrument. Your niece, Georgiana, said so herself, and she is a true proficient."

The lady fixed him with a stubborn glare. "I have known him since he was born. He does not play."

Will stood and sighed, extending his hand to Elizabeth. "Shall we play a duet, or would you rather sing, my love?"

She took his hand and rose from the settee. "It appears you must amaze your family yet again, Will. Shall we play the same piece we played at my Aunt Gardiner's house?" She went to the piano and looked quickly through the music until she found Beethoven's "Sonata Four Hands in D Major, Op. 6." "You play the primo, and I shall take the secondo as we did before."

They finished to applause, but Lady Catherine narrowed her eyes. "What is this? I have never heard you play before, and suddenly, you play like a master?"

Will looked at her and smiled broadly, displaying his dimples. "There is much about me you do not know, Aunt. Mother and Grandmother Rose played extremely well, so they encouraged me, helping me when I needed it. I took lessons throughout my childhood, but I refrained from playing the instrument in public. I did not wish to make a display as I was extremely shy about performing. I played for my own enjoyment."

He glanced at Elizabeth, beside him on the bench. "Shall we sing 'Scarborough Fair'? Do you still have your paper with the words I wrote for you?"

She squeezed his hand, hidden by the instrument from the view of the rest in the room. "The paper is in a box in my chambers, but I have memorized the words."

She stood beside him, and he began to play, allowing the mystery of the song to be created by his hands and their voices. Elizabeth's high, clear soprano floated through the room, singing the haunting tune. Will joined her, weaving his deep baritone in and out of the melody, entwining their voices until they slowly ended the song as one.

As their voices faded on the final note, the room was quiet for a moment but soon erupted in applause.

Lady Catherine's mouth hung open until she closed it with a snap. "I confess I am all astonishment. Why have you never played or sung for me before now? You know how much I love music."

He smiled at her a second time. "I dislike performing by myself, and there was never anyone else in Kent who could play with me while I was there. When Elizabeth was at Rosings, we were not yet well acquainted. I had no confidence that she would consent to perform a duet with me." *None of that is false.*

Lady Matlock laughed and clapped her hands. "How wonderful! I knew that Georgiana played prodigiously well, but you are a surprise to us all, Will. Well done! Does anyone else have hidden talents?" She looked around the room. "Richard? Do you play or sing? No? Well since no one else is willing to surprise us, Georgiana, would you consent to amaze us with your skill?"

Georgiana nodded demurely. "I will exhibit, but after I finish, Elizabeth must play a duet with me."

And so the time passed, with first one and then another of the young people performing for the pleasure of the group.

Though the beginning of the evening was inauspicious, it improved as it continued. By the time everyone retired, even Lady Catherine had nearly smiled once or twice.

~~oo~~

As soon as everyone was in their chambers and quiet, Will, John, Colonel Fitzwilliam, and Mr. Bennet returned downstairs and met in the library.

Colonel Fitzwilliam stood at the fireplace. "Is everyone in place?"

Will nodded from behind his desk. "The property is covered with my men. Even the ones who just this evening returned from Copenhagen insisted on guarding the house. No one will get in or out without our knowledge."

Mr. Bennet sat on the settee, leaning forward with his elbows on his knees. "This could be an extremely long night, gentlemen. I considered having Lydia stay with Jane, but John was decidedly against it." He glanced at his son. "After some consideration, I agreed with him. We need to catch Wickham in the act, and he may not approach the house without seeing her at her window."

"Yes," John interjected. "We have no way of knowing his plans. I hate to think of using her as a lure, but she has done this to herself." He looked at Will. "I only pray that we can keep her safe."

Will turned towards them. "You may depend upon it. She cannot leave the house without assistance. Every entryway is guarded, and one of my men is watching her window." He opened a drawer and retrieved a pistol, which he placed on the top of his desk. "Are you all armed? Wickham may have a weapon. You may need to defend yourself."

The colonel pulled his jacket aside, displaying his firearm. "I also was able to procure several Springfield rifles. The men outside have been trained to use them."

Mr. Bennet shook his head. "I did not think to bring a gun. When we left Longbourn, I had no idea that I would need one. My coachman is armed, however, and so are my footmen."

John opened his tailcoat. "I always carry a pistol. One never knows what he may encounter while travelling."

Will smiled and turned his attention to the elder Bennet as he pulled another gun from the drawer and handed it to his future father-in-law. His voice was kind. "You should stay in the house, Mr. Bennet."

Mr. Bennet took the pistol and raised his chin. "I am not too old to defend my family."

Will nodded. "I know that; however, someone must stay inside to make certain Lydia and the others do not leave the house. If there is gunfire, it will be dangerous in the darkness."

John looked from Will to his father. "Will is correct, Father. It would be unwise for us all to go. Someone must remain behind. One of us must be here to look after the ladies – especially Lydia."

"Very well, Mr Darcy." Mr. Bennet sighed. "It looks as if I have no choice but to concede to the greater wisdom of you and John."

For several hours, the men occupied themselves with reading, talking quietly, or napping in turns.

In the middle of the night, the occupants of the library were surprised by a visitor.

Charles Bingley opened the door, looking almost wild. "I dozed off for a moment, and when I awoke, Caroline was gone. I searched the hallways, but I have not seen her. She may have gone to Lydia, but I cannot enter a young girl's room without a female or her father. Mr. Bennet, will you please come with me?"

Will stood immediately. "I shall come, too. Colonel, if you will, wait in the hallway while Mr. Bennet, John, and I go to Lydia's room with Charles."

The colonel nodded his assent, and the others left the room in haste, hurrying for the stairs, heading for Lydia's chambers. When they arrived, the door was locked. Will drew his skeleton key from his pocket and quickly unlocked the door.

Charles ran into the room and over to the open window. "Caroline what have you done?"

By the moonlight streaming through the panes and the candles lit on either side of the bed, Will could see the bed sheets – knotted together, tied to the bedpost, and disappearing out the window.

He could hear the sneer in Caroline's voice as she faced them. "I told you that Lydia lacked the cleverness needed to carry out a plan. Had I not been here, she would never have thought to do this once her way through the doors was blocked by your men."

Her brother grabbed her by her shoulders and shook her. "How long has she been gone?"

Caroline laughed with malice. "Long enough. She has probably met with Wickham by now."

Will stepped forward. "Where were they to meet?"

She turned on him. "Why should I tell you? There is no advantage to me in their being discovered. I have been turned out by my brother and will be shunned by society. I would wish a portion of that punishment to follow your precious Elizabeth. The Bennets will be ruined, and you and your sister shall share their disgrace."

John took a step towards her, fists clenched by his side. "How dare you, madam! To destroy my sister's life with such little concern."

Caroline laughed with a sneer. "Oh, but I do dare, sir! I dare very much to take my due." She shrugged. "If not me, then someone else. Your sister is simply following her own high, animal spirits. Your family should have checked her behaviour long before now. She is the object of gossip everywhere she goes."

John narrowed his eyes, but said nothing more.

Will looked at Charles, speaking roughly. "Take her to the library, and do not let her out of your sight. Bind her hands and feet if you need to do so."

Charles nodded with determination. "You may depend upon it." He grabbed her arm and nearly dragged her from the room. She protested with every step, but he would not give way.

Mr. Bennet and Will peered out the window, but could see very little as the clouds covered the full moon. As his eyes adjusted and the clouds parted, Will spotted a figure in white running across the lawn towards the front of the house. "Look – just there."

He turned and ran from the room, followed closely by John and Mr. Bennet.

Colonel Fitzwilliam stood at the foot of the stairs. "We have not a moment to lose, Will. I brought your weapon from the library. One of your men came to tell me that they have Lydia in their sights and they are following her. He awaits us just outside."

Will glanced at Mr. Bennet. "With all respect, sir, you should remain here. We must be quick, and the exertion may be too much for you. John will come with us. We dare not take the horses, as we may alert Lydia with the sounds of the hoof beats. Neither can we delay long enough to saddle them."

The elder man nodded, though he was plainly unhappy about staying behind, and the three younger men headed for the door. They left the house as quietly as they could before breaking into a dead run behind the man who waited to show them the way.

Before they had run a quarter mile, they spotted the white figure just ahead of them. She walked quickly to a creek which joined the natural lake in front of Pemberley. The men kept to the trees, careful to make no sound.

When she stopped at the edge of the water, Will pointed to a boat concealed in the plant growth along the bank of the creek. He could see the dark silhouette of a man. As the man reached out his hand to help Lydia into the small fishing vessel, Will and Colonel Fitzwilliam stepped from the trees. At least thirty men emerged from the darkness with them, surrounding the area, weapons raised.

A voice came through the moonlight. "Before you come any closer to us, you should know that I have a pistol pointed at Miss Lydia's head; I will happily shoot the chit."

CHAPTER 23

The acquisition of treasures by a lying tongue is a fleeting vapor and a snare of death.

Proverbs 21:6

After a few minutes, Fitzwilliam heard a soft tapping at the door and opened it to find Agent Fry still in his hotel uniform.

"Please follow me to the surveillance room. We have to hurry; Whitman is turning into the entrance of the hotel. After he parks his car, he'll come up here."

The agent turned, walked down the hall, and used his key card to open a door to a room not far from theirs. Elizabeth, Jane, Lance, and Fitzwilliam hurried after him.

As the door closed behind the group, Elizabeth and Jane were enfolded by the welcoming arms of Mr. and Mrs. Bennet.

Fitzwilliam glanced around the room. Agents sat in front of several monitors showing different locations around the hotel and grounds. He and Lance walked to the computer displaying Mary's room.

She was sitting on her bed, staring at the door. Fitzwilliam was surprised when she looked directly into the camera.

Agent Fry voiced his approval. "She's stopped crying, and she looks like she splashed her face with cold water like I told her to."

Fitzwilliam could see that her eyes were huge and filled with sadness. He was surprised when she spoke to the camera. "I suppose now we'll all see whether or not I can act. This can be my audition. Be sure to record it all."

The agent smiled. "Good girl."

I didn't expect to hear her so clearly. Fitzwilliam leaned down and looked at her on the screen. "Be brave, Mary. You can do this."

She nodded, and Fitzwilliam straightened up, looking at Agent Fry in surprise. "I didn't think she would answer me. She can hear us?"

"Yes, all of the cameras in your rooms have audio capability as long as we have the audio turned on in both directions." The agent spoke into the microphone. "Mary, we can hear everything that's said in that room. I'm going to turn off the audio from this room so Whitman can't hear us, but if you need us, we'll turn it back on and tell him that we're here. We're watching and listening, so you don't have to worry about anything. Try to look comfortable, but don't turn on the TV or play any music. The sound may mask what the two of you are saying. Okay?"

She nodded her head again, picked up a magazine and crawled up to lean on a pillow against the headboard, knees bent. She flipped through the pages as if she were a bored teenager tired of waiting.

Agent Fry muttered to himself. "Good job, Mary. Just hold it together."

The elder Bennets, Jane, and Elizabeth had crossed the room and were now watching the screen with Fitzwilliam and Agent Fry. Lance looked at Mrs. Bennet. "Did you hear what was said when we were in Elizabeth's room?"

She and Mr. Bennet both nodded, and it was evident that Mrs. Bennet had been crying. Mr. Bennet put his arm around her protectively, rubbing her upper arm with his hand.

Mrs. Bennet drew in her breath sharply and touched Elizabeth's face. "I'm so sorry, sweetheart. I had no idea what he had done to you. Why didn't you tell us? We would have protected you." Her voice hardened. "He should have gone to jail for what he did to you."

Elizabeth kissed her mother's cheek. "It was too late to protect me, so the only thing left to do was keep it from you. You hadn't done anything wrong, and there was no need to burden you with what had happened to me. It wasn't your fault, Mom, and I didn't want you to feel bad about it."

Agent Fry lifted his hand, and the room fell silent as they watched the door to Mary's room open. Fitzwilliam stiffened when Greg Whitman sauntered in, carrying a shopping bag and smiling from ear to ear. He crossed to Mary and leaned over to kiss her cheek, placing the bag on the bed beside her.

"Bored, love?"

Mary tossed the magazine aside, turning her face away from his. She managed to sound both irritated and whiny. "You've been gone a long time. There's nothing to do here since you won't let me leave this stupid room. I'm in LA. I should be having fun. You promised me we would have a good time, but all I've seen are these four walls." She sighed, tossing her long hair, flipping it back over her shoulder.

He looked at her closely. "Have you been crying?"

She looked away. "A little. I'm ready to go home now."

He sat beside her on the bed, twirling a lock of her hair between his fingers. "This is no time to be homesick. We're here on business; fun will come afterward. Big things are happening for you, babe. Go put on some makeup. There's somebody I want you to meet, and he won't be impressed by a blotchy face." He handed the shopping bag to her. "Change into this dress, too. Let the man see how beautiful your legs are. Don't cover yourself up so much. He wants to see what you look like in person before he puts you in movies or on magazine covers."

"I'm beginning to feel like a piece of meat." She reached into the bag, pulled out a skimpy dress, and then looked up at Greg, a scowl pulling down the corners of her mouth. "What is this? A joke? I can't wear this outside. I may as well put on a few Band Aids and strut around the hotel, offering myself out as a prostitute."

He laughed, stroking her cheek with his fingers. "That's what modeling and acting are all about, babe. You have to sell the goods. You already knew that."

Mary scooted to the end of the bed, looking at herself in the dresser mirror, holding the offensive dress in one hand. He was reflected behind her as he stood and walked to pull her to her feet. Greg turned her to face him. Bending to kiss her, he put his hands on her rear and drew her so close to him that there was no space between them.

When he released her from the kiss, she turned her head, and her profile was clear in the mirror; they saw what he could not. She was biting her lower lip, eyes squeezed closed. When she opened her eyes and moved away from him, everyone in the surveillance room saw her anger.

She took a deep breath, smiling up at his handsome face. "So, what's in this for you, Greg? I know you get an agent's fee, but what else do you want?"

He put his hands on either side of her face. "You, of course, Mary. We're going to be together. I want you."

"Then why have you waited? All you've ever done is kiss me. I've never discouraged you from going further."

Greg frowned, backing away a little. "You're only eighteen, Mary. I'm so much older than you are. I just wanted you to have your chance at fame and money before we took our relationship to the next level. You may not feel the same about me after you hit it big, and I don't want you to have any regrets. I was thinking only of what's best for you, babe. That's all I've ever wanted."

Elizabeth, hearing his words, quickly put her hand over her mouth to cover the sound of her derisive snort. Fitzwilliam took her other hand in his, stroking the top of it with his thumb.

Lance muttered under his breath. "Lying piece of crap. I should've ruined that pretty face when I had the chance."

Mary smiled at Greg archly, raising an eyebrow. "I let you take the pictures you wanted, but I can't wear this dress. I have some short-shorts that are sexy enough for anybody who wants to 'see the goods,' but I won't walk around in public looking like a hooker."

Agent Fry released a breath. "Smart girl."

Fitzwilliam looked at him. "Why do you say that?"

"Since I knew Whitman wouldn't try to sleep with Mary, I put a tiny mike on her bra before I left her room. It would have shown in that dress, if she could have worn a bra at all."

They watched as Mary went to her suitcase and pulled out the shorts, espadrilles, and a white, lacy top which was gathered in at the waist. She turned to look back at Greg. "The shoes will make my calves look great, and whoever we're meeting will see more leg in these shorts than he would in that dress. Any talent agent should be impressed enough. That's who I'm meeting – right? A talent agent? Not some sleaze-ball porn producer?"

He smiled, though it never reached his hard, angry eyes. "Sure, Mary. You know I wouldn't do anything like that to you. This guy is legit. He handles both models and actresses – some pretty big names, too. I wish you'd wear the dress, but I guess the shorts are okay. Hurry up, though. He's waiting in the lobby for us."

She walked toward the bathroom. When she got to the door, she looked back. "It'll take a few minutes if you want me to put on makeup. I'll be out as soon as I can."

As soon as she had closed the door, he picked up the hotel phone and punched in a number. His voice was low and urgent. "We'll be down soon... I want the rest of my money when I hand her over... I don't care what he says. If I don't get all of it now, you'll never see me again… That's right. I'll take the blonde and walk out the door, and there'll be no more pretty, young girls for your boss from me."

In the surveillance room, Agent Fry chuckled.

Fitzwilliam tapped his shoulder. "Why did you laugh?"

The agent glanced up at him. "He probably didn't use his cell phone because he thought we had tapped it. It didn't occur to him that we knew all about this set-up and were listening in on the hotel phone, too. Our net is closing around him nicely, and now we have the number of his contact, too. Kudos to Mary; she set him up really well. We have him on video perpetrating a fraud on her. Whitman told her that she's meeting a legitimate talent agent. He promised her modeling and acting jobs. Maybe the FBI should consider hiring her."

~~oo~~

Watching on the monitor, Mr. Bennet caught his breath when Mary walked out of the bathroom. "She certainly doesn't look like my little girl anymore. Where in the world did she get those shorts? I've never seen her wearing anything revealing anywhere near that much before."

Mrs. Bennet shook her head. Her voice was quiet. "I saw a charge on my credit card last month from a boutique in Atlanta for clothes, but I didn't ask her about it. I guess I paid for them. When this is over, we have to start paying more attention to where she's going, with whom, and what she's wearing. Maybe I should have gone shopping with her myself. I've been too busy, and it's got to stop. Mary is more important than my job."

Greg leered and whistled as Mary turned slowly before him. She winked. "You think this is sexy enough?"

"You're so hot I'm thinking about chucking the visit with the talent agent and staying in here with you." He looked around the room. "We can come back and get our things after this meeting so we can check out. I want to take you to my favorite restaurant tonight before I catch a plane back to Atlanta."

Mary stared at him, plainly astonished. "You're going back to Atlanta tonight? What about me?"

He smiled and pulled her into his arms. "You'll need to go with the agent today. He has rooms in a hotel close to his offices where his young talents stay until they get their big breaks. I can pick you up later today after I pack everything up. I'll bring you your suitcase when we go out."

Fitzwilliam looked at Lance. "I wondered how he was going to get her to go quietly with a strange guy she's never met before."

Lance nodded. "This is why the other girls never made a scene or put up a fight."

Mary shook her head, clearly distressed as she pushed him away. "What about my family? They're probably already worried sick. And I can't sign anything without discussing it with Mom and Dad."

Greg leaned back and looked into her eyes, his expression one of hurt. He lowered his voice, nearly to a whisper. "You don't trust me? After all I've done for you? I'm the only one who's believed in you, Mary. You know your parents and sisters won't want you to get into modeling and acting. Especially Elizabeth. She'd be so jealous of you for getting this opportunity she'd try to convince you to come back to Atlanta. They don't want you to be successful and rolling in money. You're eighteen, Mary. It's time for you to stop letting people treat you like a little girl. You're a grown woman now."

Elizabeth whispered so quietly only those closest to her heard what she said. "The master manipulator. Those are essentially the same words he spoke to me."

Mary chewed her lower lip and swallowed hard. "Of course you're right. I'm old enough to take care of myself. Let's go meet the man who's going to make me rich and famous."

He opened the door and held it for her as they left the room and continued down the hallway.

The surveillance room buzzed with activity as agents contacted their counterparts to tell them that the plan was in motion. Once Greg and Mary were on the elevator, Agent Fry stood up and stepped aside as another agent took his place, switching the monitor to the lobby camera.

The agent spoke briefly to the Bennets, Fitzwilliam, and Lance. "I'm going to the lobby. Stay here until I give the all clear."

They agreed, and he quickly left the room.

~~oo~~

Fitzwilliam, along with the Bennets and Lance, kept his eyes glued to the screen in front of them as they stood behind the agent in the surveillance room, waiting for Greg and Mary to meet Greg's trafficking contact.

Through Mary's wire, everyone in the room was able to hear what was said as the couple rode the elevator down and exited on the lobby floor. The elevator camera was for hotel security purposes only. It was equipped so that the hotel security detail could see into the elevators, but there was no sound.

Mary and Greg spoke very little. She was unusually quiet until he put an arm around her. "Really, Greg. Do you think it's wise to do that in public? The agent might get the wrong idea."

"What? That you're my girl? I don't care what he thinks." He tried to nuzzle her ear, but she turned her head to look at him.

"Greg, you're my agent. You've made it clear that our relationship is professional. You're flying back to Atlanta and leaving me here. I'm not your girl."

"Babe, it's not like that."

She laughed bitterly. "It's exactly like that, but don't worry about it. I'm a grown woman. Remember? I can handle it."

As the elevator doors opened, they stepped out. He held her elbow and guided her toward a man in a suit, leaning against a wall. Greg spoke into her ear. "All right then. If that's the way you feel, let's just get the job done."

She looked up at him, frowning. "So, I shouldn't expect you for dinner tonight?"

He smiled. "Let's just skip it. I'll leave your suitcase at your hotel, and you can settle in. I'll call you when I get back to Atlanta."

"Fine."

They stopped in front of the man, and he stood up straight, looking at Mary appraisingly. After nodding his approval, he handed Greg a thick envelope. "Here is the information you requested."

Mary raised an eyebrow, and Greg spoke quickly. "This is Khalid Asery, Mary. I wanted a copy of your contract for my files."

Lance muttered under his breath. "I suppose there's no need to try to pass him off as anything other than Middle Eastern, especially with his accent and dark good looks. He's obviously not Swedish."

Asery extended his hand to Mary. "Come with me. We can discuss the details of our agreement at my offices."

Mary hesitated. "I haven't eaten. Can we get something here in the restaurant?"

Asery looked at Greg, eyes hooded. "You have not fed her?"

Greg shook his head. "I've been out. Remember our meeting this morning? Now I need to go pack up and check out. I have a flight to catch. She can have lunch with you, wherever the two of you decide to go." He kissed Mary's cheek. "I'll see you later, babe."

He turned and walked back to the elevator.

As soon as the doors closed behind him, Agent Blackwell stepped out from behind a decorative screen. Agent Fry approached rapidly from the front desk.

Asery made a move to grab Mary's arm, but she was too quick.

She put her espadrille-clad foot squarely in Asery's groin before Agent Fry could move between them.

Fitzwilliam stopped himself from cheering only by remembering that Greg Whitman was on his way back up to his hotel room. *I wouldn't want to spoil the surprise.*

CHAPTER 24

Though the mills of God grind slowly;
Yet they grind exceeding small;
Though with patience he stands waiting,
With exactness grinds he all.

Henry Wadsworth Longfellow, "Retribution"

Upon hearing Wickham's threat to shoot Lydia, Will and the other men stopped well short of the water's edge, awaiting Wickham's next move. The standoff continued for a few moments, the only sounds coming from the bullfrogs and crickets.

A woman's scream suddenly pierced the night, followed by the sounds of a gunshot and someone thrashing about in the water.

Lydia's going to get herself killed, if she hasn't already. Maybe I should have let her leave with him. At least she would have lived through the night. Will and his men ran towards the commotion, stopping when they heard an enraged female voice raised to a pitch guaranteed to draw every dog in the county. Will had never before been so happy to hear his future sister-in-law's voice.

"You would shoot me? You filthy liar! My father will have you run out of the country unless I first kill you myself. If I had a gun I would shoot you, you coward! You said you loved me and promised to marry me. I hate you! I hate you! Go ahead and run away! You excel at that! Somebody help me!"

John and Will continued to the waterside; John reached out his hand towards his sister's voice, speaking gently. "Lydia, calm yourself and allow me help to you. Where are you? Are you injured?"

Her voice was small and frightened, like that of a little girl. "I am in the water, and nothing is hurt but my pride. I used my knee against him, the way you taught me to. When he fell out of the boat, it capsized, and now I am wet through and through. He can swim, but he left me here to drown." She began to wail loudly. "He knows I cannot swim, for I wrote and told him so when he thought up this scheme."

John waded into the water and helped her to her feet, speaking to her firmly. "Good girl to think so quickly. Come with me, little sister. All will be well."

"And what of Wickham? Will you go after him?" Lydia sobbed. "He would have shot me, John. He must be brought back, though I never wish to see him again."

John led her out of the water. "You may depend upon it. He shall not escape, and he will answer for what he has done."

Colonel Fitzwilliam and the other men moved closer to the shore.

As Will watched the shapes of Lydia and John emerge from the water, he removed his coat and hurried to them to put it around the girl's shoulders. He could hear her teeth chattering as she wrapped the garment around herself. *This is her own fault, but I can't help feeling sorry for her. She's young and foolish, but she isn't mean. And John continues to surprise me. I wonder if he taught all of his sisters self defense skills. Thank God he taught Lydia; it surely saved her life.*

Colonel Fitzwilliam looked back at the men, whispering. "Did anyone see where Wickham went?"

When they muttered rather than give a clear response, he held up his hand. "Quiet, everyone."

There was complete silence but for the sounds of Lydia's sniffles and the water as something broke the surface of the lake.

Will leaned closer to the colonel. "The brigand is swimming away, just as Lydia said." He turned to John. "Take your sister back to the house. She is cold and distraught. Tell Mr. Bennet what has happened, and awaken Elizabeth, Jane, and your mother to care for Lydia. We must be quick if we are to catch Wickham."

While John helped Lydia back to the house, Will pointed out to the men where he wanted them to go. He spoke in a low voice. "Surround the lake."

The men began to move at a rapid pace to do his bidding.

James Wright, Will's investigator, stepped to his master's side. "There are armed men stationed on the other side per my earlier instructions. We saw him when he rowed the boat across, and I thought he might try to use the water to escape."

Will smiled in the darkness. "Excellent. He will not get away this time without answering for his actions as he has done previously."

As Mr. Wright hurried away, Colonel Fitzwilliam turned to Will. "I have thought a great deal about this. Exactly what shall we do with Wickham when we get him? I would happily shoot him and rid the earth of the scum, but you prefer to do things by the book. What charges shall you level?"

Will was quiet for a moment while he scanned the surface of the water. *I don't know the laws as well in this time period as I do in my own.* "Kidnapping?"

The colonel shook his head. "Lydia would have to testify to that in open court, and the papers would use the information to sully your name as well as the Bennets'. Everyone would know that she went willingly – that it was, in fact, a failed elopement. She and her family would be disgraced."

I wouldn't care about it, but I won't have the Bennet family distressed and embarrassed. "Trespassing?"

Colonel Fitzwilliam nodded. "That is certainly a possibility, for I know that Fitzwilliam told Wickham he would have him arrested if he ever again came back on this property. However, Wickham would serve a few years in jail and be out again, preying on the people of this country who are too easily fooled by a smooth tongue and a handsome face."

Will thought a moment longer. "He has run up debts everywhere, and while Fitzwilliam bought many of them which I now hold, I have no doubt that he has amassed more debt in the years since he attempted to elope with Georgiana."

"I agree with you, but again, he will go to debtor's prison. Unless he happens to meet with a vicious criminal while there, he shall survive. If I know Wickham – and I do – he will even find a way to prosper."

"Attempted murder with attempted kidnapping and trespassing should hold him for a while. We all heard him threaten to kill Lydia, and the gun went off. Obviously, he was shooting at her. Add the unpaid debts, and I may be able to have him transported to Australia." Will spoke with a grim note of satisfaction.

They both turned around at a sound a little distance behind them. A familiar voice chuckled. "So the two of you are deciding my fate, it would seem."

Will grimaced. *It must be Wickham. Though I've never met him, there's no mistaking that oily voice. It's the same one that threatened to shoot Lydia. He always manages to be one step ahead of us.*

Colonel Fitzwilliam swore an oath. "Wickham! How did you evade the men?" He started to raise his weapon.

Wickham laughed. "I would rethink that if I were you, Colonel, for I have a gun trained at your cousin's head. As to your question, I waited until a group of your men passed me; then I quietly came ashore and crawled into the woods to hide. I doubted that anyone would expect me to leave the water so close to the place where I went into it. They are more likely waiting a little distance from here."

Will narrowed his eyes. "Your gun is wet. The gunpowder will not fire."

He could almost feel Wickham's smile. It made his skin crawl.

"You are correct. *My* gun is wet, for it sits at the bottom of the lake. However, this is not my gun. I caught one of your men coming through the woods, hurrying after the others. After I hit him in the head with a rock, he was most obliging and gave me his gun. Shall we test it? It certainly seems dry to me, and it is a superior weapon to the gun I originally possessed."

Colonel Fitzwilliam drew in his breath. "He has one of the Springfield rifles. The moonlight gleams along the long barrel." The colonel threw his weapon towards Wickham and raised his hands high. "I am unarmed. What do you want?"

Wickham took a step closer to them, out into the open. "I wish to see Darcy's gun beside yours on the shore. Posthaste, sir, or I shall shoot you where you stand."

Will leaned forward to toss his gun beside the colonel's and straightened up. "May I ask a question before you shoot us?"

Wickham tilted his head. "You amuse me to no end. Certainly. Ask what you will, but be quick about it."

Will cleared his throat. "I know that Caroline Bingley helped you, and Charles has told me her motives for doing so. What I cannot understand is why you chose to attempt an elopement with Lydia. In all likelihood, I would have paid you to quit the area and leave the Bennets alone."

Quiet laughter floated on the damp air. "You still will, Darcy; that is, if you survive. In truth, I would never have chosen Lydia on my own. She is singularly stupid and boring, whiny and unattractive. Ten minutes in her company is enough to drive any man mad. I much preferred Elizabeth; however, you were able to steal her away. Quite the shame, too; I know how to please such a woman, but I doubt that a prig such as you would have any idea of how to satisfy both yourself and her at the same time. When she chose you over me, I was fully ready to leave this place, but Lady Catherine made it well worth my while to remain."

Will's anger threatened to override his good sense. *How dare he speak of Elizabeth in that way!* He remembered all the martial arts classes he had taken and briefly thought of different ways to disable Wickham and cause him considerable pain, but he was brought back to reality when he heard the colonel swear again. "So Lady Catherine is the member of our family who Caroline Bingley referenced. She is the traitor to us."

Will's mind whirled. *The money Lady Catherine accused me of stealing went to Wickham! I knew she was untrustworthy, but this is low, even for her.* "How were you able to contact my aunt? She insulates herself from the world."

Wickham's voice took on an edge. "Her former steward, Stevens, was our liaison until you ruined our arrangement by having him dismissed. I have done her bidding for several years, including the incident involving your sister. Stevens carried messages between us and brought me my money regularly. Lady Catherine wanted you to marry her insipid daughter and forget the beautiful Elizabeth. Since I could not interest Elizabeth in a romance with me once you had told her of our dealings, Lady Catherine chose to have me pursue Lydia. She had heard much of the girl's shenanigans from her parson, and she insisted that Lydia was the most likely of all the Bennet girls to agree to an elopement. She thought you would turn to her and Anne once the Bennets were ruined."

Lady Catherine wanted Wickham to elope with Georgiana? Why? She will answer for that later. For now, if I can hold him here long enough, perhaps the men will circle back around. He controlled his anger with great effort. "How do you expect to be paid now that Stevens is no longer at your disposal?"

"I know that you are attempting to keep me here until the others return, but I shall answer that last question and be on my way.

Caroline Bingley has been very useful. She has used my situation with Lydia to ruin the Bennets, break up your engagement, and ingratiate herself to Lady Catherine, thus earning herself a small fortune and an entry into society in the process. I could almost admire her were her tongue not so sharp. After she wrote Lady Catherine of your infatuation with Elizabeth while you were at Netherfield, your aunt made her the go-between, sending her money and instructions which were forwarded to me. Now I really must leave before your men return. You will both live if you let me go." He began to back away.

Quickly, the colonel pushed Will aside and dove for his gun which lay a few feet in front of him. Two shots were fired simultaneously, and both Will and Wickham dropped to the ground.

Colonel Fitzwilliam rolled to cover Will with his body, watching Wickham to make certain he was truly down and unable to do further damage.

Will groaned. *He weighs a ton. If he doesn't get off me, I may pass out.* "Richard, I know you wish to protect me, but you must move. Your hand is on my shoulder, and the pain is terrible."

The colonel looked at his hand. "You are bleeding like a stuck pig. I must get you back to the house."

Clenching his teeth through the pain, Will pushed him. "Make certain that Wickham is disabled before you take me to Pemberley."

The soldier grunted his assent, retrieved his pistol, and rose to his feet. He walked toward Wickham and knelt down, using his hands to find the man's wound. "He will bother no one else, and there will be no need for a trial, for Wickham is dead."

The other men had run towards the sound of the gun shots and now began to gather around the fallen men, murmuring. Several of them saw their master was wounded and went to him immediately, removing their shirts to stanch the bleeding.

The colonel pointed to John Hill, the head groomsman. "You

there! Send someone to fetch the doctor and take him to Pemberley. We shall meet him at the house with Mr. Darcy."

As Hill dispatched a boy to do his bidding, Colonel Fitzwilliam stood, facing the woods, and shouted, "Come out from the trees and show yourself! You have nothing to fear from us. You have saved our lives and will be amply rewarded."

Will raised his head slightly and turned it to see a man walk from the cover of darkness into the moonlight. He heard the whispers of amazement from the men as they recognized the hero. "That be Sam, the innkeeper!"

Sam walked slowly to the colonel and Wickham, standing over the fallen man, still pointing his gun at the corpse. "I dinna need no coin. Seein' t' bastard dead is all I wanted." He looked down at Wickham and spat upon him.

The colonel went to the man and put his hand on his shoulder. "We are grateful that you saved our lives. Now let us show you our gratitude."

Sam looked up at him, tears streaming down his face. "'e was in 'is cups one day and came upon me poor Meg carryin' water from the well. 'e forced her, and now she's poisoned. I saw 'er gettin' bigger day by day, so I made 'er tell me 'is name, for she was in a fair way t' do away 'erself. She were that 'shamed – she wanted naught but to die. Meg's a good 'un, a church-goin' girl, so I went to 'im and told 'im what 'ed done." Sam kicked the body viciously. "'e laughed, t' scum!" He raised his tortured face again to Colonel Fitzwilliam. "'e said me Meg dinna mind it none, and she'd spread her legs for all uh Lambton an' liked it. 'e lied! 'e called 'er a whore. My Meg 'ad ne'er been wi' any man. But 'e wouldna do right by 'er. 'e earned that bullet through 'is 'ead. I ain't sorry neither. They can 'ang me, an' I dinna care. 'e'll rot in 'ell!" His grief howled through him as he fell to his knees.

Will's heart was touched by Sam's pain, and he could feel no remorse concerning the death of Wickham. *How can I be relieved, even glad, about his death? And even more, I don't feel guilty about my lack of sorrow for a soul sent to Hell. May God forgive me, but I'm not sorry that he died. He caused pain and destruction wherever he went.*

He spoke in a voice that was weak but firm. "You shot him to save my life, and Colonel Fitzwilliam is a witness to it. He would have killed me, and maybe both of us, had you not taken him down. There will be no further discussion of the matter." He looked at his steward, Justice Miller, who knelt beside him, trying to stop the bleeding. "Send for the constable. I want this handled tonight. And look in the woods for one of the men. Wickham struck him with a rock, and he may be badly injured." His voice became weaker. Now get me back to Pemberley before the doctor arrives there and tells Elizabeth I am wounded." *I will not have her worried or upset when it may be only a minor injury.*

When Will tried to sit up, he felt the darkness enveloping him, and he fell back. He welcomed oblivion, for it was a relief from the searing pain.

CHAPTER 25

At his best, man is the noblest of all animals; separated from law and justice he is the worst.

Aristotle

Everyone in the surveillance room watched as Greg exited the elevator and, after striding with purpose to his hotel room, stopped to open the door with his key card. He stepped into the room, took the envelope from the inside of his jacket, and opened it. Fitzwilliam and the others could see that it was stuffed with money.

Fitzwilliam could hardly contain his anger. *His smile is nauseating. He just sold a young girl into sexual slavery, and all he cares about is the money he made. He wears the face of Evil, and in my time period, someone would have killed him. That man is truly amoral. There is no right or wrong for him.* Then he reflected on his own past life and his dealings with a man who was very similar to Greg Whitman. *Wickham lived a scandalous life, and he survived. I wonder whatever became of him. Perhaps Will shall address the matter in one of his letters.*

Agent Fry, still in a hotel uniform, opened the door to the

surveillance room quietly. "Mr. Darcy, Mr. Bingley, Elizabeth Bennet, and Jane Bennet, please come with me."

Mr. and Mrs. Bennet looked toward him expectantly but, when no further instruction was given, soon returned their attention to the monitors.

Fitzwilliam and the others followed the agent from the room and down the hall, waiting behind him as he opened the door to Elizabeth's room. Once the door was standing open, he turned to face them, looking at Elizabeth and Jane pointedly. "Do you have the pictures you showed Mary?" Jane nodded, and he smiled. "We have to hurry. He'll leave the hotel as soon as he can pack his things. Mary is safe now, but this is the best chance we have to help the other girls."

Jane quickly retrieved the manila envelope from her luggage and rejoined the group at the door.

Agent Fry looked at each one of them. "Don't say anything unless I ask you a direct question. Don't volunteer any information or reply to Whitman in any way. Understand?"

They all nodded before they walked the few steps to Greg's room, then waited in the hallway while Agent Fry knocked on the door. "Housekeeping."

After a moment, Greg opened the door. "Come back in a couple of –"

He took one look at the group and tried to push the door closed, but Agent Fry jammed his foot between the door and the frame, stopping him. The agent pulled his identification from his pocket and held it up to Greg's face. "FBI. We're coming in now, Mr. Whitman. Step back."

Greg hesitated before he moved and opened the door. "I have to let *you* in, but I don't want them in my room."

Agent Fry smiled. "I think you might want to hear what they have to say, Mr. Whitman. We can do this out in the public hallway or at headquarters if you prefer, but I thought you would rather talk in the privacy of your room."

"Really? This is all for my comfort? How considerate of you." Greg smiled. "Did Lance tell you he assaulted me?"

Lance opened his mouth, but the agent held up his hand to stop him, never looking away from Greg. "That's a serious charge. Do you have any proof of that allegation, Mr. Whitman?"

Greg drew his brows together, frowning. "My mom took a couple of pictures, but I don't know if she kept them or not."

Agent Fry nodded. "So, she took pictures of Mr. Bingley beating you? She was present at the altercation?"

Greg shook his head. "Of course not. He knocked on our door and left me in my own front yard, but she didn't see him. He was gone by the time she came to the door. She took pictures of my face, though."

"Did you tell her that Mr. Bingley beat you? Did you call the police and report it?"

Greg raked his hand through his hair. "I was a kid. I didn't tell her anything, but she has the pictures. I wouldn't let her call the cops. They never liked me in Atlanta."

Agent Fry smiled. "So, let me make sure I have this right. Your mother took some pictures of you after you had been beaten. You didn't tell her who beat you, and she didn't file a complaint with the police. Did you keep any sort of proof – fingerprints, DNA evidence – anything like that? Do you have pictures of Mr. Bingley's bloody knuckles in a time-stamped photograph perhaps? Were there eyewitnesses who would testify to the beating?"

Greg looked past the agent at Lance, Elizabeth, and Jane. They stared at him in contempt.

"No, I suppose I don't."

"Are you afraid of Mr. Bingley now?"

Lance glared at Greg, who shook his head. "Definitely not."

"Then shall we continue this conversation in your room?"

Greg shrugged nonchalantly, gestured with his hand for them to come in, and then turned and walked to the windows. "Let's get on with it. I have a plane to catch."

The agent smiled. "This won't take long, Mr. Whitman. Before we begin, I want you to understand that you have the right to remain silent. If you give up the right to remain silent, what you say can and will be used against you in a court of law. You have the right to an attorney. If you cannot afford an attorney, one will be appointed to you. Do you understand these rights as they have been read to you?"

Greg's eyes were wide, his face shocked. "You're reading me my rights? What for? I haven't done anything illegal, so I don't need a lawyer, and I don't need to 'remain silent'."

"I'll take that as a 'yes.' We have special agents all over this hotel, and you have been under constant surveillance since you brought Mary Bennet here. In fact, she cooperated with us today and is willing to file charges and testify against you."

Whitman laughed. "What charges? She's eighteen years old, and she came here willingly. Now she's decided not to stay with me. Instead, she wants to go with some guy who's promised her fame and fortune. Those are her choices, not mine. I haven't broken any laws."

Agent Fry pointed to the camera. "You should know that we've had eyes and ears in here since shortly after Mary left Atlanta with you. Mr. Darcy's security chief, Steve Walker, contacted our office and alerted us to the circumstances. It was no accident that you got this room. Once the Bennets confirmed that they had no knowledge of their daughter's whereabouts, we went to a judge for a warrant to tap the phone and put you in here. He agreed to let us use the camera as soon as we confirmed your first meeting with a known trafficker."

The color drained from Greg's face. "I had no idea he was a trafficker. I thought he was a talent agent."

"Mr. Whitman, when I said we tapped the phone, I didn't mean only your cell phone, though we've been listening in on that, too. You confirmed the sale of Mary Bennet less than half an hour ago with a known trafficker, Khalid Asery. He procures young, blonde women for his employer, a Saudi sheik. We have pictures of you with him and several other girls who have mysteriously vanished. You perpetrated a fraud on Mary Bennet when you promised her a career in modeling and acting, and that's the only reason she came here with you. You knew the man was not a talent agent when you handed her over to him. That's the definition of human trafficking, and you will be arrested and tried in Mary's case. Unfortunately, we have a long list of missing girls, and we'd like your help in finding out where they are so that we can determine whether or not they're still alive. Their families want to know. They need closure if their daughters are dead."

Greg sneered. "And why would I implicate myself in other cases? Maybe I do need a lawyer after all."

Agent Fry nodded. "One can certainly be provided for you, but if you call in a lawyer right now, you'll never know why these four people are in here with me – until you meet them in court. Also, any chance of a better deal for you will be off the table."

Whitman turned his back for a few moments and then turned to face them again. "I assumed they were here because of Mary, but I guess I was wrong. Whatever they told you, it happened a long time ago, and they have no proof of anything – like I can't prove that Lance committed assault and battery on me."

Fitzwilliam glanced away for a moment, his hands clutched together behind him. *He is a waste of air and food.*

The agent looked at Elizabeth and Jane, nodding his permission for them to speak.

Elizabeth held her chin up. "You're wrong about that, Greg. You raped me twice, and though I have no proof of the first rape, I can certainly prove the second, thanks to my sister and Lance."

He laughed. "Their eyewitness testimony won't mean much if that's all you have."

Jane looked at him without pity, though she spoke softly. "Greg, we have much more than that." She pulled the pictures from the envelope and showed them to him.

Greg folded his arms across his chest. "So what? I have pictures of my beating, too. The good agent here just told us all that pictures don't mean squat."

Fitzwilliam clenched his fists by his side. *If only I could wipe that smirk from his face. Her pain is nothing to him. I should love to have him back in 1795. There are so many ways to die accidentally – drowning, a riding accident, an overturned carriage, a gun misfiring during hunting. The possibilities are nearly endless. I could likely arrange something in this era, too, but Elizabeth would not condone it. She would rather defer to the authorities, and I must respect her wishes in this.*

Lance stepped up beside Jane and put his arm around her. "I have a lifelong friend who's in the Atlanta Police Department. I called him that day, Greg, and he came over to the Bennet home. Jane did everything he told her to do, so we have the sheets and Elizabeth's clothing checked into the evidence locker at the police station. My buddy sealed up everything himself. We have a clear chain of evidence, and I wonder whose DNA will be found all over those things."

Greg was quiet, looking at the floor. His eyes lifted to meet Elizabeth's, and his expression was evil. "There's nothing you can do about it. It was more than seven years ago."

She squared her shoulders and faced him. "But I was not yet eighteen, Greg, and, regardless of how much time has passed, with DNA evidence, there is no statute of limitations. I'm sure your lawyer can bring you up to speed on the changes in the law since the arrival of the more high tech methods now used in law enforcement."

"That still doesn't prove I raped you. DNA doesn't mean that you weren't willing. You know you liked it."

Fitzwilliam glared at him and stepped up behind Elizabeth to wrap his arms around her. He could feel her tension in her shoulders. *Perhaps she will feel differently about going through proper channels of justice if he continues to mock her. Maybe fatal accidents can still be arranged.*

Jane bristled and leaned forward toward Greg, her voice strident. "She *liked* it?! She was screaming 'no' when Lance and I came through the front door. We ran up the stairs and saw you raping her while she fought you. I think our testimonies combined with the pictures and the DNA evidence will prove beyond any shadow of a doubt that she was neither willing nor enjoying it. You raped her, and now you'll pay for it!"

Greg's eyes blazed. "Don't threaten me, Jane. I know people who would love to have your address."

Agent Fry's eyes were hard. "By the time you get through with your trial and serve your sentence for trafficking here in California, and probably in Georgia, Texas, and Florida as well, along with the jail time and trial for rape in Georgia, you won't see daylight again. You'll spend the rest of your life in prison. The rape alone carries a minimum sentence of ten years up to imprisonment for life. In some cases, the death penalty is handed down when the victim is young or badly beaten. We're talking about Georgia, not a liberal state. You can get capital punishment for rape there, and they still use the electric chair. They have over one hundred people on death row now. We'll also be sure the jury knows that after you raped Elizabeth, you tried to sell her sister as a sex slave to a sheik in the Middle East. That's going to look like you're trying to get revenge because of the rape charges, Greg.

"You may also be interested to know that new laws have increased the penalties for human trafficking. A conviction in California can get you a prison sentence of twelve years and a fine up to one and a half million dollars *per offense*. Think about all those twelve year sentences strung end to end. You'll die an old man in prison. That money will go to victim services and law enforcement. You'll have to register as a sex offender and provide information regarding your internet access and any identities you use online. Many of the girls you've sold were minors, and you'll be ranked right there with the child molesters in the inmate population. The pictures you took of those girls will be used to convict you of child pornography in addition to the trafficking. There will be years added to your prison time for each count. Even murderers will view you as the lowest form of life, and they'll make your life a living hell. You're going to be popular in prison with that pretty boy face." He smiled knowingly. "Um … yes, Pretty Boy. That's what they'll call you. You'll be Bubba's – well, you know."

Fitzwilliam's eyes brightened considerably. *According to the television shows, there are inmates who will do nearly anything for money. He may not survive prison after all.*

Greg sat on the bed, his face drained of color. "What are you offering?"

The agent walked to stand in front of him. "The FBI, the Department of Health and Human Services, and the Department of Homeland Security are working with state law enforcement on your case. We can have the sentences run concurrently in California and take the death penalty off the table in Georgia, if you cooperate fully. I've personally talked to the District Attorneys in those states. If you're charged in Texas, Florida, or other states, we'll try to get your sentences reduced, but each state will want their piece of you. In exchange, we want the names of all the young women and all of your contacts. We want any information you have as to the whereabouts of the missing girls."

Greg shook his head. "The people I know don't mess around. They'll kill me. I'll never make it to court."

Fitzwilliam smiled. *Sounds good to me.*

Agent Fry shook his head. "We can protect you. You may spend your life in prison, but you'll be alive. We'll keep you out of the general population, unless you refuse to help us. If that happens, you'll be on your own with the rest of the inmates. If you don't take the offer, we'll push for the death penalty in Georgia and full prison time everywhere else."

"And if I ever get out?"

"If you cooperate, serve your sentences, and are released, we'll put you in the witness protection program. They'll relocate you – give you a new identity and a new face. No one will know who you are, though we'll always keep a close eye on you for the protection of those around you. This offer is good for about five minutes, so think quickly." The agent looked at his watch.

Greg stood, reached in his pocket, pulled out a card, and handed it to Agent Fry. "I don't need to think about it. Call my lawyer and tell him to meet us. If he signs off on this, I'll cooperate."

As Agent Fry nodded and took his cell phone from his pocket, the door opened and Agent Blackwell stepped into the room, holding a pair of handcuffs. "Hands behind your back, Whitman. We're going downtown."

Agent Blackwell put the handcuffs on Greg, and everyone in the room heard the satisfying "click" as the agent spoke. "Greg Whitman, you are under arrest for human trafficking in the case of Mary Bennet and for the rape of Elizabeth Bennet ..." The agent continued to speak to Greg as Elizabeth turned to face Fitzwilliam. He wrapped his arms around her as she cried softly.

"It's over. It's finally over."

He kissed her hair. "There's still the trial, but I'll be with you through it."

"I never thought he would have to answer for what he did to me. I thought he would prey on others because I let him get away with it. Now he can't do that anymore. It's over for me."

Fitzwilliam pulled away to kiss her tears. "One ending and a new beginning."

CHAPTER 26

Nothing makes us so lonely as our secrets.

Paul Tournier

Will returned to full consciousness in his own bed but kept his eyes closed. He could hear the voices of the people in his room and chose to use their distraction with their conversation to test his toes and hands, careful to draw no notice to himself and thankful to find that he was not paralyzed. *Someone removed my boots and pants, but I am covered by a sheet and blanket. I'm glad it was done while I was unconscious so I didn't have to feel the pain of being moved around. It's bad enough while I'm still.* After assuring himself that his injuries were confined to his shoulder, he turned his full attention to the conversation taking place a few feet from him.

Colonel Fitzwilliam confronted Lady Catherine. "Leave the room, madam, for you are no longer any relation to me or the Darcys."

She sniffled. "How can you say such a thing to me? I have ever watched after you and your cousins as if you were my own. Why would you take the word of that odious man over mine? I have told you I had no part in this business. I have met George Wickham only a few times, and those few times were here at Pemberley, years ago."

"Desist from telling your falsehoods, especially as we stand by my cousin's bed where he lies injured because of you. We shall continue this conversation when we are assured of his recovery." The colonel's voice held a note of finality and no hint of deference.

After a moment of silence, Will heard the door open followed by the sounds of soft footsteps and the closing of the door. Elizabeth spoke quietly as she crossed the room, her voice trembling with her love and concern. "Colonel, is his condition very bad? Please tell me he will be all right."

Will's overwhelming urge to see her caused him to open his eyes.

As she bent to hold her face near to his, he attempted to comfort her. "Do not distress yourself, my love." He heard the weakness in his voice and attempted to sound stronger, for her sake. "It does cause me pain, but I think all will be well."

A man leaned over him on the other side of the bed. *The doctor, I presume.* Will turned his head towards the man, watching him begin to remove the makeshift bandages from his shoulder. *I'm thankful that the men donated their shirts to stop the bleeding, but they must be filthy, and who knows whether or not the doctor is any cleaner?* "Thank you for coming. Please forgive my directness, but have you washed your hands?"

The man opened his eyes wide and took a step back. "I was awakened from a sound sleep and brought here in the middle of the night. My hands are not in need of washing."

Colonel Fitzwilliam cleared his throat. "Will, Mr. Jenner has been taking care of you and your family for many years. I am certain that he knows what he is doing."

Lady Catherine snorted in a most unladylike fashion, and the doctor glared at her.

Will barely stopped himself from rolling his eyes. *And I know that he doesn't have an inkling of how to treat a gunshot wound without doing me more harm than good. I don't want to hurt his feelings, but I refuse to die from an infection to keep from insulting him.* "Mr. Jenner, I appreciate all the trouble caused to you by bringing you here at this ungodly hour, but I ask that you go to my dressing room and wash your hands with soap and hot water before you examine me further. Austen, my valet, will assist you with whatever you need. Austen, please have hot water delivered to the dressing room."

Austen stepped from the shadows and gestured to the doctor. They both disappeared into the adjoining room.

Will turned his attention to Colonel Fitzwilliam. "How long was I unconscious?"

The colonel seemed surprised by the question. "Not long. Perhaps an hour or a little longer. You came to and muttered a few times."

I don't remember anything. I probably passed out from the bleeding. I must have lost a pint or two. If I can avoid infection, the wound will be painful and inconvenient but not life-threatening. "Please have someone fetch some whisky immediately. I also need water to drink, along with the juice of a few oranges. And tell Mr. Carlson to have another basin of hot water with some clean cloths sent up as well. Tell him that the water is to boil for twenty minutes before it is taken off the fire and delivered to this chamber."

The colonel nodded, stepped to the door, and spoke to Mr. Carlson who waited just outside. He then returned to his cousin's side.

Elizabeth choked back a sob, and Will turned his head towards the noise. "Truly, love, I think I may have lost a good bit of blood, but the wound appears to be at the very top of my shoulder. The bullet may not be lodged in my body at all. However, the removal of the bandages and cleaning of the wound may be too much for you to bear. I believe that the blood has clotted now, and it may be difficult to remove the cloth without causing the spot to bleed again. It will cause me pain, and that will distress you. Perhaps you should wait outside."

She stood up straight, tension in every line of her form. "I will not leave you, and I am done with my tears. Why did you not tell me what you were going to do? Foolish man! Will you keep such things from me when we are wed?"

He managed a small smile. "You must think I will survive, or else you would not berate me in such a fashion."

She leaned over him, brushing his hair back with her hand, and kissed him on his forehead. "Do not dare to go to heaven without me, Will Darcy." Her voice caught. "Do not take such risks again, my love, for I could not bear the loss of you."

Lady Catherine's voice was acid. "Desist from your familiarity with my nephew, Miss Bennet, and return to your chamber. This is most improper."

Will lifted his head to look at her, his anger showing in his eyes. "How dare you order my fiancée about as though she were a servant. You address the future mistress of Pemberley, madam. Leave my bedside immediately and go to your own rooms. As soon as I am able, I will send for you, and we shall have an enlightening conversation. Colonel, please place a guard by her door to make certain that she does not leave Pemberley. Instruct Hill not to ready her coach should she send for it. She is to have no communication with anyone other than Mrs. Reynolds."

The lady stared at him in astonishment. "Am I to be a prisoner in my sister's house then? Who will protect you from that quack who calls himself a physician?"

Will's head fell back upon his pillow. "I am exhausted and in pain, largely because of your meddling, Lady Catherine. One man is dead, and another may be dying as we speak. Do as I have ordered, or I shall have the constable summoned here to take you into custody. He is already on the grounds, I believe. Surely there is some sort of law against conspiracy."

She rapped her cane upon the floor. "I will not be threatened. I have done nothing wrong, and I shall not be treated in this rude manner."

Colonel Fitzwilliam took the lady's arm. "Enough! For once you will do as you are told." He forcefully guided her from the room, even as she struggled against him.

Mr. Jenner came back into the bedchamber, followed by Mr. Austen. "Now, Mr. Darcy, I have scrubbed my hands thoroughly." He held up his hands in front of Will's face. "Shall we get to the business?"

"Have you heard of John Hunter or John Pringle, Mr. Jenner?"

The doctor sighed. "Has your mind been affected, Mr. Darcy? I have been your physician in London these many years. I only recently moved to Lambton with my wife to leave the busy life of Town and be closer to your family. I may be a country doctor now, but it was not always so. In answer to your question, yes, I have heard of the gentlemen. I was saddened to hear of Hunter's death a couple of years ago, but I am quite familiar with his work, and Mr. Pringle and I were colleagues."

Will sighed with relief. "So you know of Mr. Hunter's work with war wounds and Mr. Pringle's work with mineral acids?"

"I do. I also followed the French surgeons' discussion of antiseptics, and I found it to be quite intriguing, though I am not convinced."

Oh, no. I'll have to be careful. It will be many years before this is accepted procedure.

A knock sounded upon the door, and Austen hurried to answer it. He returned to the bedside bearing a tray which held a bottle of whisky and glass containers of orange juice and water. A crystal goblet was beside the items. Mr. Carlson followed Austen with a pitcher. He crossed to the washstand and poured the hot water into the basin. He then bowed and left the room.

Mr. Jenner raised a brow. "Do you intend to drink yourself into oblivion to be spared the pain, Mr. Darcy?"

"No, Mr. Jenner. I want to be fully awake during the entire procedure. I would like for you to use the hot water to clean the wound, and then thoroughly douse a fresh cloth with the whisky and clean it again. Use the whisky as an antiseptic for your instruments as well."

The doctor shook his head. "Applying whisky to your injury would be quite painful and unnecessary, Mr. Darcy."

Elizabeth spoke gently. "Mr. Jenner, please do as my betrothed requests. I know that what he asks is unusual, but he truly does know what is best in this situation. You must trust him."

Mr. Jenner's mouth set in a hard line before he replied to her. "I have forty years of medical education and experience which he does not have. How is it that he can know better than I? What if he should die of this wound? How would I live with myself? I brought him into this world, and I should not like to be the means of his leaving it."

Her eyes filled with tears. "Please, Mr. Jenner."

The man shook his head. "And how is it that he does not know me? I have cared for his family since before he was born. How can it be that he has changed so drastically from the last time I saw him, only a few months ago? Mr. Darcy has never questioned my methods before, and suddenly he has acquired a prodigious knowledge of medicine?"

Will closed his eyes tightly and gritted his teeth against the pain. *While we are talking, the situation with my shoulder could be getting worse.* He opened them again and sighed. "Mr. Jenner, I was in a riding accident this past spring at Rosings. I was thrown head first into a tree, and my memory was severely affected. I have never regained it in its entirety. Please forgive me for not knowing you, for I cannot help it. Nearly everyone who knew me before that time has remarked to me that I have changed greatly, but most agree that it is for the better."

The doctor was unconvinced. "And why was I not informed of your injury?"

Will struggled to keep his composure as his shoulder throbbed. "Simply because I did not remember you. I suppose no one else thought of it, either. Lady Catherine sent for Mr. Perry, the local apothecary, and he took charge of my illness."

Mr. Jenner made a sound very like "Humph!" and frowned. "Of course she didn't send to London for me, though she knows very well that I am your physician. She has always blamed me for your mother's death, and she dislikes my modern ways. It is a wonder you survived at the hands of a true country doctor. I confess I had heard rumours in Lambton concerning what you have told me, but I put no stock in them. I thought you would have spoken with me yourself if it were so. I did not realize you would have no memories of me. Regardless, you require treatment. We have talked long enough."

Elizabeth nodded. "I fully agree. I am willing to help you if needed."

The colonel returned to the room and stood by her. "I, too, can assist."

The doctor's smile was small as he turned to Fitzwilliam. "Excellent. Then I have no need of the lady. She should not be subjected to the appearance of the wound, nor should she have to bear the pain of her betrothed. It is not proper."

She squared her shoulders and shook her head. "I shall not leave unless Will requests it of me. I do not intend to be parted from him again, especially under these circumstances. Now I must insist that you proceed as he requested."

Mr. Jenner looked at Will, one eyebrow raised.

She's very determined and a little bossy. Dear God, I love her. "She stays as long as she so desires." *I hope she stays this way forever.*

Mr. Jenner frowned. "Then she and the colonel must submit to the hand washing. I will not be blamed if you develop some sort of infection after I have done all that you demanded."

Elizabeth and Colonel Fitzwilliam left the bedside immediately, ushered one at a time into the dressing room by Mr. Austen who carried the pitcher of hot water.

By the time they returned, Mr. Jenner was carefully removing the cloth covering Will's shoulder as Will closed his eyes tightly against the pain.

~~oo~~

An hour later, the doctor straightened up, satisfied with his work. "I suggest you all get some sleep. Mr. Darcy should fully recover, though he must rest in bed for the remainder of the week. If he attempts to use that arm, it could cause the wound to bleed again." He patted Will's arm. "You are a fortunate man. The shot was not embedded, and it hit rather close to your neck without severing the major arteries. You escaped with no broken bones and only one wound, for it skimmed the top of your shoulder – not through and through, which could have been serious indeed. There should be no permanent damage, only a rather large scar, for I did not sew it closed since I preferred to allow it to drain."

Will opened his eyes, glad that the most painful part was over. "I would have been less fortunate had not Richard pushed me out of the way. That shot may have been between my eyes or through my neck rather than at the top of my shoulder. Wickham meant to kill me."

Mr. Jenner nodded solemnly as he wiped his hands on a clean cloth. "I do not doubt it. Wickham always had a mean streak, though he hid it well from those in authority over him. Even when you were boys, he was no real friend to you. Most of your childhood injuries came at his hand. I always knew he would come to a bad end. I wondered why he was allowed to live at Pemberley, for he never favoured the steward or his wife. It seemed strange that he was brought up beside you, practically as another son, though I would never suspect your father of any underhanded dealings. He was an honourable man, even paying for the boy's education. I thought it very odd at the time, but it was not my place to question. Now, I shall leave you with a vial of laudanum to help you sleep."

Colonel Fitzwilliam chuckled tiredly. "I can tell you that he will not take it. He also eschews the usage of leeches or mercury. Do you have any tincture of willow bark?"

The doctor reached into his bag at the foot of the bed. "I have not used leeches for years, and I am not surprised about his objection to laudanum. It is common knowledge that the stuff is addictive. However, willow bark does not work nearly as well, and laudanum is not harmful in small doses for a short period of time. That being said, arguing with Mr. Darcy is a useless endeavour; therefore, here is the tincture." He looked sternly at his patient. "Try to sleep. I shall come again tomorrow."

Mr. Jenner placed the medicine on the nightstand and left the room.

Colonel Fitzwilliam helped Will to sit up while Elizabeth administered the tincture. He drank the full glass of water she offered, and then pointed to the juice. When she held it to his lips, he swallowed it in gulps. *I need to replace the fluids I lost. If I can sleep, perhaps the pain will be less severe when I wake up.*

After they settled him back against the pillows, seeing to his comfort as best they could, Will touched Elizabeth's hand. "You should go to your chambers and get some rest while I try to sleep. You look exhausted, love. Richard and Mr. Austen are here should I need assistance."

Her eyes were sad. "Do you truly wish for me to go?"

"No. I would wish for you never to be away from me, but I try to think of what is best for you."

"Then I will go tonight, but tomorrow we shall talk." She kissed his cheek, nodded to the colonel and Mr. Austen, and left the room.

The colonel turned to Mr. Austen. "Shall we take turns sleeping on the couch? I will keep the first watch and awaken you in an hour or two."

The valet nodded. "Your plan is a sound one. I will gather the bloody cloths and leave them outside the door for the maids to clear away in the morning."

Will had never been so fatigued in all his life. Even the aching in his shoulder could not keep him awake. He drifted to sleep, thinking of Elizabeth and their coming marriage, when he would always keep her by his side. *I don't care what the servants or anyone else says or thinks. We will always share a bedroom.* He smiled at the thought. *If she wants a room of her own, she can choose any parlour in the house, but we will not sleep apart.*

~~oo~~

After a restless night, Will was ready to face Lady Catherine and have done with the business entirely. By ten o'clock the following morning, Colonel Fitzwilliam and Mr. Austen had helped him to bathe and don a dressing gown, and breakfast had been delivered to his room. Will sat propped on several pillows, his lower body covered by the fresh sheets on his bed while he ate his morning meal from a tray.

When he was finished, he indicated to Mr. Austen to remove the food and called his cousin to his bedside. "Please have someone fetch Lady Catherine and Elizabeth. A frank discussion is long overdue."

The colonel rang the bell, and when Mr. Carlson appeared, he relayed Will's wishes.

Within half an hour, the ladies stood on either side of his bed. The colonel positioned himself by Elizabeth.

Lady Catherine scowled at the younger woman. "Why is she to be a part of this? She is not family."

Will clenched his jaws. "She is more family to me than you will ever be, and I will keep no secrets from her. She and Colonel Fitzwilliam shall be witnesses to this exchange."

The lady smiled unpleasantly. "I have no secrets to tell."

"Then you will listen to my recitation of them. You have been in league with Caroline Bingley, Obadiah Stevens, and George Wickham. Your plan was to ruin the Bennet family by having Wickham elope with Lydia so that I would turn from Elizabeth and marry your daughter. In this, I understand the motives of all involved."

Elizabeth looked at her in shock.

Lady Catherine sniffed. "You have no proof of any of that."

Will looked at her with disgust. "Caroline alluded to a member of our family who was betraying all of us, and Wickham confirmed that you were paying both him and her. Caroline was your means of communicating with Wickham and delivering your payments to him after I had your steward, Stevens, dismissed. The bank has records of large withdrawals from a private account you set up with money siphoned off from Rosings. You used my memory loss from the accident to try to convince me that I stole that money when, in fact, Stevens was taking the funds by your authority and paying Wickham to work for you. You attempted to use that leverage against me to force me to marry Anne. Those are the facts, and there is no disputing them."

The lady lifted her chin. "I have made no secret of my desire for you to marry Anne and unite our families. You were formed for each other, and it was the favourite wish of both your mother and me. I have done nothing wrong."

Will met her stubborn gaze with one of his own. "If trickery and deceit are not wrong, you are innocent. If planning to ruin a young girl and a respectable family's reputation is acceptable, you can stand before God blameless.

"However, that is not the only charge Wickham levelled at you, madam. According to him, you paid him to elope with Georgiana, your own niece. That is beyond my comprehension. Why would you do such an abominable thing?"

Elizabeth covered her mouth with her hand, her amazement reflected in her eyes, but she remained silent.

Lady Catherine shook her head. "I did no such thing."

Colonel Fitzwilliam's face reddened, and he looked at her with revulsion. "You, madam, are a liar. Wickham had no reason to implicate you if you did not do it. According to him, you paid him for years to do your dirty work. Why? Why have you been giving the scoundrel money?"

She stepped back and sat down in a chair. "I swore that I would never tell. It is a secret, but it is not mine."

Will attempted to sit up, but Elizabeth put a hand on his arm to restrain him and watched him while she spoke softly. "Lady Catherine, you have materially damaged your relationship with your nephews already. I would never have suspected you capable of such wickedness. Perhaps if you tell your nephews the truth, it will not be necessary to involve Anne or Georgiana in this discussion. In that way, you could preserve the good opinion of your daughter and your niece. If you refuse, I would suggest to Will that he summon both young women immediately."

Lady Catherine's horror was evident as she looked at the two men. "Surely you would not do such a thing! Darcy? Fitzwilliam?"

Colonel Fitzwilliam nodded. "I certainly would. I shall fetch them directly."

Will inclined his head. "If there is no other way to get at the truth, I agree. Furthermore, we shall include Richard's mother in the conversation. You will be cut off from all good society."

The lady leaned forward on her cane with one hand and held up the other, suddenly seeming very aged. "Enough! You have won." She breathed deeply. "Wickham was the illegitimate son of my husband's younger sister. No one outside of the de Bourgh family ever knew of her unfortunate affair, for she was sent away while she carried the child. My husband had a kind heart, and he could not bear for the child, his own nephew, to be abandoned in another country, so he went to your father for help."

She looked at Will. "George's piety and Christian charity were well-known, and Louis knew that he would not refuse the request.

Your father took the baby in and placed him with his steward, old Wickham, and the man's wife. They were childless and overjoyed to have the care of him. George treated him well, giving his nephew everything he could without raising too much suspicion. When the Wickhams, George, and Louis died, I began to send the boy money on the pretext of doing errands for me. It was the only way to support him without telling the secret. Eventually, he was old enough to be more useful in what he did. Since I could not tell him who he really was, I took the opportunity to give him money by employing him. Otherwise, he would have questioned why I financed him. It began innocently enough. He was my nephew, after all."

The room was so quiet Will was sure he could hear the old woman's heart beating against her ribs. Finally, he spoke. "But why pay him to elope with Georgiana?"

She began to cry, and the tears dripped from her cheeks to her dress. "I thought that if I ruined the Darcy name, you would marry Anne and change your name to de Bourgh. I had no son. I would have made you my heir. I would have appealed to the House of Lords and the king to pass the title to you rather than have it die out. You would also have retained control of Pemberley and your other lands and properties."

Colonel Fitzwilliam tilted his head as he watched her. "But what of Wickham, your favourite nephew? Had he married Georgiana, what would he have received?"

Lady Catherine's voice was low. "He would have had my niece's fortune of £30,000 as well as a substantial settlement from me. I planned to give them our estate in Scotland. She would have wanted for nothing."

Will's voice was deadly quiet. "She would have wanted for her family. She would have wanted for love and kindness from her husband. She would have wanted for money eventually, for he would have gone through every farthing in a matter of a few years. What you attempted to do to Anne and me was despicable, but what you would have done to Georgiana is nearly unforgiveable. I would have taken care of Anne had I married her, though I would never have loved her as a husband, but Wickham would have been cruel to Georgiana. He was worthless and corrupt. You knew that, and you helped to make him that way. You even took advantage of his low character. You would have sentenced my sister, as well as Elizabeth's sister, to miserable lives to please yourself. I ask that you leave my house today. Anne may stay as long as she desires, but you are not to return until my future wife and I come to terms with this knowledge. If we ever do, Elizabeth and I shall visit you. Do not expect it to be soon."

Lady Catherine stood. "So you cannot forgive me?"

Will shook his head. "Not yet. Perhaps in time."

She looked at each of them in turn. "But you will keep the secret?"

Elizabeth glanced from Will to Colonel Fitzwilliam. "I see no good that can come of telling it. Wickham is dead, as are most of the others involved, but for you, Lady Catherine."

Colonel Fitzwilliam walked to the window, gazing at the beauty of the landscape. "I agree with Elizabeth. Making everything public would serve only to humiliate Georgiana and Anne. It would cause a great scandal, and that is needless." He walked to stand beside his aunt. "However, be assured that I agree with Will. I will not see you again until I can put this to rest in my mind. I cannot know whether or not that will be possible."

She bowed her head. "Very well." She straightened her back and walked to the door, leaving the room without a glance back at them.

Colonel Fitzwilliam crossed to the window again. "I think I shall go for a ride to clear my head, if you have no objection, Will."

"I have none, Cousin. In fact, I would appreciate a moment alone with Elizabeth. Before you say it, I know that it is not proper. Please give us five minutes before asking her father and mother to join us."

The colonel smiled at him. "Only take care not to reopen that wound. The doctor would not be pleased to see blood flowing again this afternoon."

Elizabeth bent to kiss Will's forehead. "I shall take good care of him, Colonel. Have no fear."

The colonel strode from the room, and Elizabeth stroked Will's hand. "What do you wish, my love?"

"I want to marry you."

She laughed. "And so you shall."

He gripped her hand. "I want to marry you now."

Her eyes sparkled. "As I do you, but there are arrangements to be made."

He used his good arm to pull her down to him for a passionate, thorough kiss. When he let her go, she remained over him, looking into his eyes, dazed and breathless. "What of the ball?"

"It shall be a wedding reception rather than an engagement party."

"What of my mother's wishes for a wedding and breakfast at Longbourn?"

He smiled. "I love your mother, but I am wounded and very pitiful. I think I have the stronger argument in this case. You cannot leave me to return to Longbourn. I would suffer."

She pushed him lightly. "Have you no shame? What of the guests?"

He shook his head. "No shame at all. The guests who are here will suffice for our wedding. Your aunt and uncle will arrive this week with their children, and everyone we love will be here. We can wed in Pemberley Chapel, and everyone else can come for the ball. We need not change the date of it."

She chuckled. "What of the license?"

He raised one eyebrow. "I have a special license in the drawer of my desk in my study. I obtained it when we were in London, in the event you agreed to marry me earlier than we had originally planned."

"Did you actually plot this to get your way?"

Will smiled. "I learned in modern times that one should never let a good crisis go to waste. The opportunity has presented itself, and I am seizing it. I would not have us live apart any longer than is absolutely necessary."

She stroked his cheek. "So you will agree to wait until your wound is healed? I think that necessary."

His eyes were hooded. "A week will be sufficient. Trust me on this matter."

She arched one brow herself. "Since it is my fondest wish as well, I trust you absolutely."

He smiled broadly. "Then it is settled."

"There is yet one thing to be done."

"Yes?"

Elizabeth laughed aloud. "You must tell my mother."

CHAPTER 27

Happy is the man who finds a true friend, and far happier is he
who finds that true friend in his wife.

Franz Schubert

The flight back to Atlanta on the Darcy jet was a quiet one. The Bennets and Lance joined Fitzwilliam and Steve Walker for the return trip, but the high emotions and stress of the past two days had left everyone exhausted.

Fitzwilliam immediately claimed one of the large recliners, and he motioned to Elizabeth to join him. She went to him willingly and started to squeeze in beside him, but he pulled her to himself, legs across his lap. He wrapped his arms around her and, sensing no resistance, guided her head to his shoulder. She melted into him, snuggled closer to his neck, and sighed. He tilted the recliner back. *She fits as if she were made for me. My Elizabeth.*

He was acutely aware of her parents and Mary, seated across from them on the couch, talking quietly. *They appear to think there is nothing improper in our embrace, and they are our chaperones.* In the face of their acceptance, he rested his cheek on her head, enjoying the strawberry smell of her shampoo and the silky feeling of her hair.

Fitzwilliam knew she was asleep when she relaxed against his chest. He could hear her steady breathing. *She feels safe with me, or she would not sleep in my arms, especially in the company of her family. I can't recall a time when I've been happier.*

The attendant walked into the cabin, offering drinks, blankets, and pillows. When she turned to him with a smile, he lifted his head and whispered, "Just a blanket and two pillows, please."

Before long, he had a pillow tucked under each of his elbows where they rested on the arms of the chair and a blanket draped over the two of them. He tried unsuccessfully to stifle a yawn, careful not to move and awaken Elizabeth. *The warmth of her is wonderful, and she feels so right in my arms. I haven't been this contented in a long time, and I've never been this comfortable with any other woman. I wish that it could last forever.*

His eyes were so heavy that, despite his best efforts, he could not keep them open, and his mind drifted into sleep and lovely dreams of the woman who slept in his arms.

Feeling movement against his body, Fitzwilliam awakened, and he lifted his head to a smiling Elizabeth. *I could definitely get used to this.*

She kissed his cheek and lingered a moment, breathing deeply. Her voice was a whisper in his ear. "I love the way you smell." She nuzzled his neck with her nose and kissed him again. Then she stretched her arms, moving his in the process.

She poked him in the chest, but still spoke quietly. "Wake up, sleepyhead. We're about to land in Atlanta."

Fitzwilliam had been fully alert since the moment she first breathed into his ear. He looked around her at Mr. and Mrs. Bennet. He was pleased to see they were still stretched out asleep while Mary slept further down the long couch. He turned his head to see Jane and Lance in the other recliner, too wrapped up in each other to pay any attention to him and Elizabeth. Steve Walker was nowhere to be seen. *He's probably making arrangements for a car and driver for us.*

He pulled her back down to him and used his fingers, tangled in her hair, to lower her face to his. His kiss was firm but gentle until she deepened it into something more, and his response to her was immediate. He let himself be lost in her for a few precious moments and then broke the kiss, tilting his forehead so that his was touching hers.

His voice was husky and low. "Elizabeth, your parents ..."

"Are awake now." Mr. Bennet sat up. "Time to put your seats into an upright position, folks; we're approaching the Atlanta airport."

Fitzwilliam quickly raised the back of their chair, and he saw Lance was doing the same. Mrs. Bennet and Mary swung their feet to the floor, rubbing their eyes and straightening their clothes.

Before long, Fitzwilliam felt the plane begin its descent. He moved to the side of the recliner, and Elizabeth slid into the space close beside him. He kept his arm behind her neck, around her shoulders; he disliked the thought of breaking all physical contact with her.

As soon as the plane came to a stop, Steve Walker walked into the cabin and looked at Fitzwilliam. "A car is waiting to take everyone wherever they need to go. I asked for a larger vehicle to accommodate eight people. The driver will drop me off at Darcy Enterprises last."

Fitzwilliam stood and nodded. "Thanks, Steve. I'm not going into the office today, and you don't have to either. Whatever you want to do is fine."

Steve chuckled. "I do have a few things to check on. I'll probably see you tomorrow then." He exited the plane, and the others followed.

Fitzwilliam was the last off the plane. He lagged behind to make a private phone call. "Hello, Mrs. T. I have a favor to ask of you."

~~oo~~

Since Fitzwilliam's car was still at Mr. and Mrs. Bennet's house, he directed the driver to take them there. "Lance and I will drive Elizabeth and Jane home if that's all right with everyone. Lance's car is still at their townhouse."

The elder Bennets expressed their wishes to rest for the remainder of the day, and Fitzwilliam's idea was gratefully accepted.

Soon, the company car with Steve Walker was headed to Darcy Enterprises; the elder Bennets and Mary were resting in their home; and Fitzwilliam, Elizabeth, Lance, and Jane were on their way to the ladies' residence.

Fitzwilliam held Elizabeth's hand as they sat in the back seat. He leaned over to whisper to her. "Are you hungry? We can stop and eat if you'd like."

She put her head on his shoulder. "I'm not dressed for a restaurant. Do you want take-out? We can eat at the apartment."

He nodded and leaned forward to tell Lance. After they all agreed on Chinese, Elizabeth used her phone to call in an order. Before long, they were in the townhouse enjoying their meal, watching a movie the girls had rented from the box outside the restaurant.

Fitzwilliam found that he was far too restless to watch the film. He got up and walked to the window facing the street, parting the curtains with his hand. *She should be here soon.* He turned back to face Elizabeth. "Would you like to go for a walk?"

She glanced up at him from the couch. "What did you have in mind?"

"I wanted to walk in a park this afternoon, and I've heard The

Atlanta Botanical Gardens are interesting. The weather is perfect for being outdoors. Do you enjoy looking at flowers and plants?"

Elizabeth smiled. "I've been there before, and I love all of it, especially the orchid house, the rose garden, and the sculptures. The fountains are beautiful, too." She quickly looked down at herself. "Do I have time to change clothes before we leave? I look like I slept in these ... I guess I did." She laughed.

Excellent idea. Maybe the timing will work out after all. "Of course. We're not in a hurry. I'm a bit rumpled myself, so I may do the same. I still haven't worn all the clothes Mrs. Thomas sent by Lance."

She picked up their empty take out boxes from the coffee table and threw them away in the kitchen before heading up the stairs to her bedroom.

Fitzwilliam remained at the window, peeking out while he held the curtains aside.

Elizabeth had barely left the room when he spotted Mrs. T.'s familiar van pulling into a parking spot near his car. He dropped the curtains back into place and went outside to meet her before she could ring the bell.

She stepped from the van and came to him, arms opened wide for a hug. "My dear boy. I'm so happy for you."

Fitzwilliam hugged her, laughing. "She hasn't accepted me yet, Mrs. T."

Mrs. Thomas stepped back, smiling and handing him a gift bag. "She will. I have no doubt about it. That girl loves you. I can tell, and I'm always right when it comes to those things."

"I sincerely hope you're right."

She chuckled. "Oh, I am. Trust me."

Fitzwilliam grinned broadly and then looked into the bag, drawing out an elaborate antique box. "What's this?"

Her face crinkled into a smile. "What you asked for is in the smaller box. The box that you hold contains something even more precious – your Nana Rose's pearls. She made sure in her will that

I received them, along with a letter directing me. I was to give them to you only when you had found your own Elizabeth and become engaged. They've been in the Darcy family for generations. Darcy brides wear them on their wedding days."

He opened the box and shook his head slightly. "I don't remember them, so they must not be from my era. I never saw my mother wear these, and I'm sure I would have noticed such a beautiful strand." He examined them more closely. "They are quite exquisite and unusual. Elizabeth will love them."

"Mrs. Rose wore them often." Mrs. Thomas reached for the box and carefully removed the necklace. "The strand is sixty inches long and has several hidden clasps so that they can be worn in different ways. Quite ingenious, if you ask me." She returned the box to him and demonstrated what she was saying. "See – she can wear them as two or three strands, or she can make a choker of four strands."

"Very clever. The pearls are perfectly matched, and the luster is wonderful."

The lady returned the necklace to its box and handed it back to him. He opened it and touched the pearls.

He smirked a little. "She may agree to marry me just to have this beautiful necklace."

Mrs. Thomas chuckled. "If that ring doesn't do it, the necklace will certainly give her a push in the right direction." She hugged him again. "You know that I'm only joking. Elizabeth would never accept you because of what you have or what you can give her. She will marry you because she loves you and wants to spend her life with you."

Fitzwilliam's broad smile displayed his dimples. "That's precisely why I love her." He looked toward the townhouse. "Thanks for bringing these to me and for sending my clothes with Lance and Jane." He glanced at the townhouse and then back at his housekeeper. "I hate to say this, but you'd better go now, Mrs. T. She'll be downstairs soon. I want to surprise her, and she'll know this isn't a normal walk in the park if she sees you here. I'll call you and let you know what she says."

She smiled broadly, took an envelope from her purse, and handed it to him. "Here are your passes for parking and admission, dear boy. You probably know that The Darcy Foundation contributes to the Gardens, so you have unlimited access. I didn't think you'd had a chance to visit there yet, so I have a few suggestions. Be sure to look at the private Trustee's Garden. If you don't want to be watched, that's the perfect spot for a proposal. As soon as you told me your plans, I took the liberty of phoning ahead to let them know you were coming. Fortunately, the Trustee's Garden had not been booked for today, so they're expecting you. You two lovebirds have a wonderful afternoon and evening." She kissed him on the cheek, then went to her van, waving as she drove away.

She's such a dear lady, and for all practical purposes, she's my family. I think she truly loves me, even though I took the place of her beloved Will.

After Fitzwilliam had put the ring box and passes in his pants pocket and stowed the pearls under the front seat of his car, he retrieved his and Lance's bags from the trunk and went back inside. He was humming as he crossed the room. He paused to drop Lance's bag at his feet and turned to Jane. "Do you mind if I use the downstairs bathroom?"

She raised an eyebrow. "Be my guest. There are clean towels in the cabinet."

Fitzwilliam could hear Lance and Jane whispering as he strode toward the bathroom door, and his eyes twinkled in excitement.

He took a quick shower and shaved, leaving the ring box on the counter. When he looked in his bag, he was less than thrilled. *I really should wear a suit when I ask her to marry me, but I have nothing clean in here except a black T shirt and black jeans. I'll look like a harbinger of doom.* He noticed something neatly folded at the bottom of the bag. *I guess if I wear this khaki blazer I won't look too much like the bad guys in those action films Elizabeth loves.* He dressed, putting the ring and passes into the inside pocket of his jacket, and looked down at himself. *I suppose it will have to do. Besides, if I wore a suit to walk in the gardens, I'd look rather odd. She would think I was behaving strangely, and she'd figure it out.*

He smiled as he combed his hair, picked up his bag, and walked out of the bathroom.

Jane and Elizabeth were at the foot of the stairs. *Are they waiting for me?*

Elizabeth looked at him, a stunned look on her face, and held her hand out to Jane. She kept her eyes on him as she said, "Pay up. Definitely more like a blue-eyed Chris Evans now that he has that haircut."

I wonder if she means Captain America or the Human Torch. The Torch is a jerk. Besides, I thought she liked Henry Cavill. Should I let my hair grow back out?

Jane slapped five dollars into her sister's hand and went back to the couch to sit beside Lance. "Why don't you ever dress up like that for me?"

Lance grinned. "Do you like that look?" He stood up and pulled her from the couch into his arms. "Let's go shopping then. I'll let you pick out my clothes today. I want to take you somewhere special tonight."

Her eyes lit up. "Great! Let me go change, and you're on."

Lance looked at Fitzwilliam. "Thanks a lot, buddy. Now instead of snuggling up and watching chick flicks all afternoon, I get to go shopping." Lance picked up his bag and headed for the bathroom. He glanced at Fitzwilliam before he closed the door. "Don't wait up on us."

Elizabeth and Fitzwilliam were alone in the room, and his eyes drank in her softly curled hair, hanging in layers midway down her back. Her light blue sundress was short and fit her perfectly, accentuating her soft curves, showing her toned legs. Her simple sandals were chosen for a day of walking, yet they gave him an unbroken view from her lower thighs to her toes. *She is so beautiful. She takes my breath away.*

"Do you like it?" She spun around for him, and the dress swirled around her legs.

I can't tell her what I'm really thinking. "Do I like what?"

She went to him and put her arms around his neck. "My dress, silly. Do you like it? I had you in mind when I bought it."

"Oh … the dress." He blushed a little, hoping she didn't realize his thoughts weren't entirely chaste. "Yes, I like it very much. I like everything you wear." *I'll show you how much I like it after we're married.*

He bent his head to kiss her, and she opened herself to him, standing on her toes to meet him. Everything about her attracted him – her intelligence, her kindness, her fragrance, her form – and he wanted her bound to him in every possible way. Knowing what he planned to do later that evening gave him the strength to end the kiss before it became something more.

He pulled back a little. "Are you ready to go?"

She blinked. "I think we should."

Maybe she can read my mind.

~~oo~~

Fitzwilliam insisted on driving the car himself. "I have my license, I'm over eighteen, and I'm with an adult, licensed driver. I need the driving experience, so buckle up, love."

"When did you get a license?"

"I've always had one as Will Darcy. The Department of Motor Vehicles has no way of knowing I'm not actually Will, so they never revoked the license. I just didn't realize it until I asked my driving instructor about taking the test. He thought I was taking lessons because I had forgotten so much in my accident. When he checked on it, he said that I was already licensed and it had not expired."

She finally gave in gracefully. "You have a point, I suppose, so I'll be the navigator."

Their drive to the Garden was uneventful, and he parked without any problem. "See. My driving instructor says I'm doing quite well. I'm doing all the testing privately, so that I can be a safe driver. I don't actually have to do any of it, you know."

Elizabeth laughed. "Yes, Mr. Darcy, you do. I'm sure you don't want to injure yourself or anyone else in a driving accident. I will say, though, that you're doing very well. In my opinion, most people driving in Atlanta should take lessons from your instructor."

He went around to open her door, helping her from the car, and they walked hand-in-hand to the entrance. He retrieved his passes and a guide greeted him by name. "If you need anything at all, Mr. Darcy, please tell any employee of the gardens. They have instructions to contact me."

"Thank you. Could you direct us to the Trustee's Garden, please?"

"Of course" The young woman handed them maps of the Gardens, gestured for them to follow her, and walked briskly in front of them, pointing out attractions along the way.

Elizabeth turned her face up to his. "More philanthropic work by The Darcy Foundation?"

He nodded. "Yes, we support the conservation efforts of the programs here. They propagate endangered plants and have recovery plans to nurture them. It's a global effort using a tissue culture laboratory. They are also involved in amphibian conservation because of their declining populations. Their International Intern Program is renowned. It facilitates the exchange of ideas, expertise, and plant collections around the world between botanical gardens and institutions."

The guide smiled as they arrived at their destination. "This is the entrance to the Trustee's Garden. Just take the Flower Bridge, and you'll see it through the columns of the first pavilion. Do you need me for anything else right now?"

Fitzwilliam shook his head. "Thank you, no. I'm sure we can find our way with these maps. This is a beautiful spot, and Elizabeth and I want to explore."

After the young lady walked away, Fitzwilliam and Elizabeth ambled across the bridge, taking time to enjoy the beautiful flowers and greenery. As they stopped to view the Cascade Garden, Elizabeth faced him and reached for both of his hands. "I'm so proud of the work you do, Fitzwilliam. Places like the Gardens and the Aquarium need donors like The Darcy Foundation to continue to operate. Without people like you and your family, they would close. So much beauty would be lost. Who knows? The cure for some terrible disease might be found in the research done on the plants."

Now or never. He grasped her hands more firmly. "For some time now, I've hoped you would join me in that work. As you said, it's important and worthy."

She withdrew her hands and began to walk again. "I've struggled for so long to get myself to the point where I could realize my dream of opening a physical rehabilitation center. I'm nearly there, Fitzwilliam. Should I give up my dream for yours?" She stopped to lean against a column in one of the formal pavilions. "I love you, but I'm not sure we could work together. Sometimes too much togetherness kills a relationship."

He put his hand on her cheek and stroked it. "I would never ask you to give up your dream, Elizabeth. All I want is for you to be by my side. You have wonderful ideas and training in finance that I lack. I need you. We could work together and accomplish much more than we're doing now, and you could still open your own business. You could spend as much time as you needed to there until it's running as it should. When you feel confident enough to leave it for a day or two a week or a few hours a day, hire someone to manage it for you."

She was silent for a few moments, her eyes searching his. "It would still be my business?"

"Entirely yours. You know that if you would allow me, I would help you financially so that you could have it more quickly, but I would never tell you how to run it."

"A partnership then?"

He shook his head. "Only if that's what you really want. Though I would happily fund the center, I doubt that you would accept my money. However, I can loan you financial support, which you could repay, or I could own a percentage of the business. Have it drawn up in whatever way suits you best."

She tilted her head. "Hmmmm ... I'll think about it. So this is why you brought me here. To talk me into working for you?"

He kissed her lightly on the lips. "No, but I wanted to ask you that question before I asked you a different one." *Please don't let her say no. I couldn't bear it.*

Fitzwilliam dropped to one knee and pulled the ring box from his pocket. "You will never work *for* me, Elizabeth. I asked you to work *with* me. More importantly, I want you to marry me. I love you with all of my heart, and I want to be with you for the rest of my life."

He opened the box to display a beautiful, rose gold ring with a pear shaped champagne diamond. The band was studded with tiny, matching stones.

Her brown eyes grew wide. "With all you know about me, you still want to marry me? You know you won't be my first. I'm fairly sure that was a big deal in your time period."

He gazed at her, understanding her hesitation. "You won't be the first woman I've ever slept with either, but you will be the first and last woman I'll make love to. Isn't that what's important?

Elizabeth's eyes were shining. "Yes."

What does she mean? He stood, still holding the box open. "Yes, that's what's important, or yes, you'll marry me?"

"Both!" She held out her hand, and he slid the ring on her

finger. It fit perfectly, just as her lips did against his.

When she finally broke the kiss, she asked, "How did you know my ring size?"

His eyes twinkled. "Jane was happy to give me that information last week. This ring was made especially for you. It's one of a kind, love, just as you are."

"I'll have to watch the two of you. So sneaky."

He held her closer to him. "You should know that I don't want a long engagement. In my era, people made their declarations and married quickly."

She swallowed hard. "How quickly?"

"As quickly as we can tell your parents and arrange a simple ceremony. I've been reading about a thing called a 'destination wedding.' How would you feel about that? Surely there's some place you've always wanted to go. If we take your parents, Mrs. T., Jane, Lance, and Mary, I'll be happy anywhere you choose."

She kissed him again. "A cruise to Alaska?"

He kissed her lightly. *Too many people.* "If that's what you want."

She kissed his nose. "A week in Tahiti?"

He nibbled her ear. *Must have air conditioning installed in our hut.* "Just don't make me wear a grass skirt."

"That tickles." She giggled a little.

He smiled against her cheek. "Not what I was going for, but I'll take it as long as you're happy."

She smiled and kissed him again. "Oh, I'm happy. Let's go make my parents happy, too."

He looked astonished. "You don't want to tour the Garden?"

"Later. We can do anything we want to later."

"I love the sound of that, future Mrs. Darcy."

"I plan to make you happy regularly, future husband."

He grabbed her hand and began to pull her across the Flowered Bridge and through the Gardens. "Let's go see your parents now."

"But what about the Garden?"

He grinned. "Put it on our list of things to do after we're married."

"You have a one-track mind. I like that."

"Don't distract me now. I have several goals in mind, and I'm prioritizing."

She chuckled. "I bet I could change your mind."

He stopped and turned to her, eyes glittering. "I'm fine with that."

She bit her lower lip and began to pull him toward the car. "Let's go see my parents."

CHAPTER 28

My most brilliant achievement was my ability to be able to persuade my wife to marry me.

Sir Winston Churchill

Will and Elizabeth received her parents with all the dignity they could muster, considering that they were convening in Will's private bedchamber and he lay injured upon his bed. Elizabeth stood at his bedside, holding his large hand and stroking the top of it.

His inner CEO came to the surface. *This is too important to talk about lying down. It puts me in a weak position, and I want to see their faces while I negotiate.* He grimaced as he struggled to sit up.

Mrs. Bennet made a little sound of distress and put her hands out before her. "Oh, no, Will! You must not exert yourself for us. We would not have you in further pain on our behalf."

Maybe this position is the best after all. Mrs. Bennet's mothering instincts are taking over, and she feels a great deal of sympathy for me. Will settled back into his pillows and looked up at Elizabeth. "Please fetch Mr. Carlson for me, dearest. I believe he is hovering just outside the door, making certain that we want for nothing."

She went to the door and returned with the butler.

Mr. Carlson bowed to those in the room. "What do you require, Mr. Darcy?"

"There is a package secured in my study, Mr. Carlson. Colonel Fitzwilliam can open the safe for you. The colonel knows all about it, so he can show you the correct one. Tell him you need the box that was delivered from London a few days ago."

"Immediately, sir." Mr. Carlson turned quickly, intent upon his mission. Will heard the door close behind him.

Mr. Bennet raised a brow. "You sent for us, Will? Are you sure you are fit for company just now? I cannot help but feel that you should rest."

Mrs. Bennet nodded and dabbed at her eyes with a handkerchief. "Had it not been for our family, you would never have been shot. Words cannot express how sorry I am for Lydia's behaviour and how grateful we all are for your protection of her. John told us how she acted. Appalling! What must you think of us!" She sobbed into the bit of lace. "And now you are injured because of it. I do not blame you at all for calling off the wedding or asking us to leave."

"Mama –" Elizabeth began to speak, but Will caught her eye and shook his head slightly to quieten her while he thought through the situation.

Mr. Bennet put his arm around his wife, whispering comforting words into her ear.

Will was astounded. *She thinks I summoned them here to break off my engagement with Elizabeth and send them away? I suppose she would jump to that conclusion. It's probably what Fitzwilliam would have done. Obviously, Mr. Bennet has kept his own counsel about all that happened before tonight.*

Will's voice was gentle. "Mrs. Bennet, there shall be no talk of your leaving Pemberley. I assure you that I have no greater desire than to marry your daughter. I have absolutely no intentions of disengaging myself from her. In fact, I have a great favour to request of you regarding our wedding."

She lifted her red eyes to his. "Anything! We will do anything you ask. You have done so much for us – more than we can ever repay."

This is much easier than I ever anticipated it would be, though I hate to see her so upset. I feel almost guilty taking advantage of the situation, though not guilty enough to stop. Maybe having us marry sooner than planned will rest her mind. I'll keep telling myself that.

He cleared his throat. "Mr. and Mrs. Bennet, I want to marry Elizabeth as soon as possible, here at Pemberley in the chapel. I cannot abide the thought of her leaving me."

Mrs. Bennet's eyes were wide. "But you are in no condition to marry right now. And what of the ball? And the wedding breakfast at Longbourn? What of her wedding clothes?"

Elizabeth smiled at her mother. "Mama, Will is quite adamant that we marry in a week's time. The wedding will be very simple; we shall marry in Pemberley Chapel with the guests who are already here, along with the Gardiners. The ball will still be held as planned, but it will celebrate our wedding rather than our engagement."

The poor lady was shocked. "What of our friends in Meryton? None of them are here. And Will shall not have recovered sufficiently in a week's time."

Will nodded solemnly, allowing a hint of the pain he truly felt to show briefly in his eyes. "I fear I shall not be able to travel so far as Meryton for two months at least, Mrs. Bennet. As I do not wish to postpone the wedding, I thought we could marry here and come to Longbourn when I have fully recovered. You may host any sort of event you wish while we are there, and you are at liberty to invite all of Hertfordshire should you choose to do so. I am perfectly content to celebrate our marriage in both locations."

Mr. Bennet chuckled. "Well done. I must remember never to

play you in chess."

Mrs. Bennet was speechless, and Elizabeth touched her arm. "Mama, is it not a good plan? You may set the date, and we shall come a few days early to assist you."

"But your clothes, Elizabeth!"

"The seamstresses are working on my wedding gown now, you know, and Aunt Gardiner is bringing new gowns with her. Those will do for the present. As for any other clothing, I can purchase whatever I might need in London when we pass through on our way to Longbourn. Georgiana will travel with us, and we can visit her modiste together. There truly is no impediment to moving the date of our marriage forward."

The lady was deep in thought. Suddenly, she looked at Will in distress. "You cannot marry until the banns are read in church. That will be three weeks at least."

Will smiled. *Gotcha!* "I bought a special license when we were in London. We can marry whenever and wherever we choose."

"Checkmate," Mr. Bennet muttered while casting an amused glance in Will's direction.

Mrs. Bennet put her hand over her mouth. "You think of everything! A special license! You must love my Lizzy very much to go to so much trouble for her."

"There is nothing I would not do for her."

There was a knock on the door before it opened and Mr. Carlson entered, bearing a long box covered in brown paper. He laid it on the bed by Will, bowed to everyone, and then left the room.

The Bennets turned to Will expectantly, and he gestured to Elizabeth. "Open the box, my dear, for I think it will take two hands. I ordered this to be specially made when we were last in London. I even drew sketches for the jeweller, but I have had yet to find the time to look at his work. I hope you like it."

She tore off the paper and removed the lid from the box, drawing out an ornate jewellery case. When she lifted the lid, she gasped. "Oh, how lovely!"

As she held up the necklace, her parents exclaimed at the beauty of the pearls.

Mr. Bennet reached out to touch it. "I have never seen anything like this."

I have, and I can hardly believe my eyes. Nana Rose, you are with me still. His eyes misted and he swallowed hard, forgetting that Mrs. Bennet did not know his secret. "Those pearls belonged to my grandmother. I saw her wear them many, many times. She let me hold the necklace and showed me how it was made. I drew the pictures for the jeweller from memory. It is sixty inches long with clasps that enable the wearer to use it as two, three, or four strands. Elizabeth, I want you to wear the pearls on our wedding day."

The room was quiet for a few moments until Mrs. Bennet tilted her head. "If they belonged to your grandmother, why was it necessary for you to have them made?"

Elizabeth looked from Will to her mother. "You must excuse Will, Mama. He has been somewhat confused at times this morning. I think the shooting, in conjunction with his horse riding accident at Rosings, might have affected his memory a bit. He designed the necklace based on his grandmother's pearls. Is that not so, Will?"

What Elizabeth said is true. I had forgotten that she doesn't know about the time switch. I'll have to be more careful. He nodded. "It is. I thought I would never see anything like her necklace again, for I had no idea what had happened to it. I sketched it for the jeweller, and he made it for me. They are so much alike, I was sure for a moment that they must be the same."

Mrs. Bennet looked puzzled. "But surely they could not be identical."

Mr. Bennet bent his head and kissed her cheek. "Exactly so, my dear. You are so observant. I have been thinking … Perhaps you should help Georgiana and Mrs. Reynolds plan a wedding breakfast here as well, my dear, for we must eat after all."

He knows her so well. Diverting her attention with the promise of an event to plan is sheer genius.

"An excellent idea, Papa!" Elizabeth turned to Will. "Do you not think so?"

Thank you. "I do indeed. You shall have a breakfast here, Mrs. Bennet, and host another at Longbourn if you like."

Mrs. Bennet clasped her hands together, her face wreathed in happiness. "Oh, my! You must all excuse me. There is so much to be done. I must go and speak with Georgiana posthaste. This shall be such a happy occasion. Happy indeed! To think that I shall help in the planning of a wedding breakfast at Pemberley!"

She bustled happily from the room, chattering quietly to herself.

Will reached for the necklace.

Mr. Bennet watched him. "Did they truly belong to your grandmother?"

He nodded. "Yes, my Nana Rose wore them on every special occasion and to church. She must have known they came from Elizabeth and me, so I shall have to write her a letter to tell her about today, though I shall not have that letter delivered on her wedding day. On that day, she will simply receive the pearls with a note telling her that other Darcy brides have worn them. After all, her own child, my father, was not born for several years after her marriage. I would not spoil her wedding for her by telling her that her grandson will switch time periods. She must not know that her husband and my parents will die before her, either. Later, some years after her marriage, I shall send a second letter telling her everything about the pearls. She will be greatly amused by the knowledge that I actually designed her necklace – or perhaps she knew that I would design it, so she took care to show it to me. I even remember seeing pictures of my own mother wearing the pearls on her wedding day. I am certain Nana Rose was responsible for that.

His voice held wonder as he turned the pearls over in his hands.

"All of my life, up until the day she died, she was there, guiding me, equipping me to know what I needed to survive and prosper in this time period. She was an extraordinary woman, and she would have loved Elizabeth. I only regret that they shall not meet until the afterlife."

Elizabeth smiled, wiping a tear from her eye. "I think I shall write to her as well. I want her to know me, even though I can be acquainted with her only through your memories, my love."

Will allowed the pearls to slip through his fingers. "She told me that people can be like those pearls. Pearls are formed when a grain of sand or a bit of food slips in between the shells of an oyster. Layer by layer, mother-of-pearl coats the irritant so that it will no longer hurt the mollusk. Out of the pain comes something beautiful and costly. I loved the thought of you, Elizabeth, before I ever knew you. I suffered because I could never find you, but because of that, I know better how to appreciate you. I protected myself against hurt by building walls, layers if you will, between me and other people outside of my family until I came here. The pain I suffered after the horse riding accident was nothing when compared to the joy of having you by my side, and the walls have come down. Perhaps it will be the same with Fitzwilliam. It is possible that the hurt of your refusal and the shock of living in a modern world have changed him – I hope so. I hope he has found his own Elizabeth."

Mr. Bennet had been quiet throughout the exchange, but when Will was finished, he spoke into the silence. "You have written letters to those in the future? How is that possible?"

Will smiled. "I arranged for your brother Philips to be my attorney, and I leave the letters with him, along with detailed instructions. The exchange greatly favours him financially. He, and his descendants, will keep the letters safe and deliver them on the appointed days. I have settled an amount on his family to fund an education for at least one lawyer in every generation. I now can be certain that the letters will be received because of this necklace and the way Nana Rose directed my attention to history and finances."

Mr. Bennet shook his head in obvious admiration. "Absolutely brilliant."

Will turned the necklace in his hands and held it up to Elizabeth and her father. "Look at this largest clasp."

Mr. Bennet and Elizabeth leaned over to see it better.

Will pointed to the design. "I told the jeweler to use a gold filigree ornament, but I did not specify a design. That "D" entwined through the limbs of the tree is his own design. It is exactly the same as the one on Nana Rose's pearls. Elizabeth and I will make sure that she receives this necklace after we are gone."

Mr. Bennet straightened up. "Fascinating. Would it not be wonderful if Fitzwilliam gave this very necklace to his own bride one day?"

Will smiled broadly. "There cannot be two women like my Elizabeth, but I fervently hope that Fitzwilliam finds his own Elizabeth, the woman best suited to him."

Elizabeth nodded. "I wish him all joy, though I hope, for her sake, he has changed."

Two weeks later instead of one – for Mr. Jenner was absolutely immovable on that point – Will was dressed in his best black coat and trousers, and after allowing Mr. Austen to fuss over his master's attire to his heart's content, he stood patiently awaiting Elizabeth at the altar of Pemberley Chapel. The small, stone church, decorated with white flowers and greenery of various sorts, was filled with their friends and relatives, both those who were summering at Pemberley and those who resided near enough to travel to the event.

Caroline Bingley and Lady Catherine de Bourgh were absent, having left the day following the final altercation with Wickham, and the Gardiners had arrived two days later. The absence of the two ladies in no way dampened the cheerful spirits of anyone in attendance, and the company was much enlivened by the addition of the Gardiner family.

Anne de Bourgh had insisted on staying at Pemberley for the remainder of the summer, and as she was of age, there had been no way for her mother to force her to leave, though she had made one concession to her mother. She allowed Mrs. Jenkinson to stay in order to care for her and make regular reports concerning her health to Lady Catherine. Her companion was not at all displeased with her assignment, regardless of the fact that it would remove her from the splendours of Rosings Park for at least two additional months. She had sighed and said, "I will bear it as best I can," though the sparkle in her eyes belied her words.

Since Will had hardly been allowed to stir from his chambers, he put his time to good use. He was unwilling to have Elizabeth's beautiful face hidden from him under a wide bonnet during the ceremony, so Will had sketched a veil and amused himself with showing the seamstress how it should look. He had seen a pearl and diamond tiara in the Darcy jewels, and he had instructed the lady to attach the simple lace veil to it so that the thin fabric would fall gracefully and trail several feet behind his bride. Will was quite pleased to hear Mrs. Bennet remark only once on the abundance and finery of the lace, and even then her response was quite subdued.

To Will and Elizabeth, the veil symbolized purity, and Will wanted to lift the short front of her veil in remembrance of a passage in the Bible, likening Christ to the Bridegroom and the veil to faith. As he remarked to Elizabeth, "One day He will lift that veil, and we shall see Him face to face."

So it was that she came down the aisle in the old church wearing her lovely gown, carrying a bouquet of white roses, with her face covered and the veil flowing in a train behind her. She had chosen to wear the pearls in four strands, close around her neck, and she wore the ring he had given her upon their engagement on her right hand as her left was reserved for her wedding ring.

Will was entranced. *She looks like an angel. I have never seen anything or anyone more beautiful in my entire life.*

As there was to be no modern "You may kiss your bride," Will lifted the front of Elizabeth's veil just after Mr. Bennet gave her away. From that point forward, he was oblivious to anything but her beautiful face.

Jane, Mary, Colonel Fitzwilliam, and Charles Bingley stood up with the happy couple. Lydia, Catherine, and Phoebe sat with Georgiana. Lydia and Catherine had been exceedingly subdued since the affair at the lake, and the general opinion was that it was a great improvement.

In addition to the traditional service, Will and Elizabeth quoted parts of I Corinthians chapter 13 together, substituting the word "love" for "charity."

They faced each other and held hands as they spoke. "Though I speak with the tongues of men and of angels, and have not love, I am become as sounding brass, or a tinkling cymbal. And though I have the gift of prophecy, and understand all mysteries, and all knowledge; and though I have all faith, so that I could remove mountains, and have not love, I am nothing. And though I bestow all my goods to feed the poor, and though I give my body to be burned, and have not love, it profiteth me nothing. Love suffereth long, and is kind; love envieth not; love vaunteth not itself, is not puffed up, doth not behave itself unseemly, seeketh not her own, is not easily provoked, thinketh no evil; rejoiceth not in iniquity, but rejoiceth in the truth; beareth all things, believeth all things, hopeth all things, endureth all things. Love never faileth: but whether there be prophecies, they shall fail; whether there be tongues, they shall cease; whether there be knowledge, it shall vanish away. And now abideth faith, hope, love, these three; but the greatest of these is love."

Once they had duly exchanged vows, the vicar pronounced them man and wife. The happy couple signed the church registry, adding their names to those of the generations of Darcys who had come before them.

After Will and Elizabeth received the heartfelt congratulations of everyone in attendance, the entire party set out on the short walk back to the great house. Elizabeth's mother had shortened her veil by means of a hook cunningly concealed just behind the tiara so that the length now hung midway down her back.

Just to Will's left, under an oak tree, he noticed three familiar people standing partially hidden among the low branches. He took Elizabeth's hand and led her to them, motioning everyone else to continue to the wedding breakfast.

When they were alone with the trio, Will and Elizabeth smiled at them. "Sam, I am glad to see you and Meg. Robert Hawkins, how came you to be here with Sam and his daughter?"

Robert, the son of Will's coach driver Adam Hawkins, blushed to the roots of his hair. "We all wanted you to know, Mr. Darcy, and this is the first time you have come outdoors since that night. My father agreed that I could offer for Meg's hand in marriage. He and Ma said we could live with them, as I have a room to meself there. Sam, here, has agreed. He knows I always loved Meg; there has never been anyone else for me, and I could be a father to the child."

Meg looked down at her feet, clearly mortified.

Elizabeth reached for the girl to embrace her as Will shook the young man's hand. "This is wonderful news, Robert, but there is no need for you to live with your parents. A young family should have their own house. There is a vacant one on the estate which is being repaired at this time. You and Meg shall have it; I shall speak to your father directly. You are to have a promotion, second to your father in driving my coaches. With a new wife, I may need two experienced drivers. There may be times when we need to go in separate directions, and one day we will have children to drive about. What say you? Would you like the job?"

Robert inclined his head. "You are too good to us, Mr. Darcy."

Will smiled. "Not a bit of it. You have earned it, Robert."

He turned to look at the innkeeper. "And you, Sam? Are you well? I have not yet repaid you. Had you not stepped in when you did, there would have been no marriage today. Elizabeth and I will always be grateful to you."

Sam wrung his hands and bowed. "I dinna spend e'en one night in jail, all thanks t' you, sir, and I coulda swung for killin' that scum. Ya set up me girl in 'er own house. No other gent has ever been so decent t' us. Thank ye."

Elizabeth took Will's arm, smiling brightly as she looked at them. "You all must come to the servants' quarters after the breakfast. "There shall be a celebration for everyone associated with Pemberley in the dining hall there. Will and I shall look for you there."

They nodded in assent.

"And, Meg," continued Elizabeth, "my sisters and I, along with the other ladies here this summer, will enjoy making clothes and blankets for the little one. I look forward to seeing you in your new home soon. When is the wedding to be?"

Meg swallowed. "Just as quick as the banns are read, Mrs. Darcy. We want to be settled afore I get too heavy and the bairn comes."

Elizabeth's eyes were sympathetic. "Of course you do. Mr. Darcy can likely speed up the repair of your cottage. Please let us know if you lack anything. We have great quantities of furniture in the Pemberley attics that will never be used again. Some of it could be used to furnish your home. I shall see to it myself."

Meg bowed her head. "You are too kind – just like an angel."

Elizabeth laughed. "I am practical. When I have a child one day, I shall need a good nursemaid. You will be an experienced mother by then. If you like, you can help in the nursery at Pemberley when that time comes."

The young woman nodded, keeping her eyes lowered. "I will do my best for you, ma'am."

"I know you will, Meg."

Will took his bride's arm. "We must rejoin our party, but be sure to come to the house later. Robert knows his way around Pemberley."

As they walked away, Will leaned over to whisper to his wife. "We have a custom in the future that I sorely missed today."

Elizabeth looked at him, brow arched in a question. "Whatever have we neglected, husband?"

"When a couple is pronounced to be man and wife, the minister says, 'You may now kiss the bride.' I was quite disappointed, my love, for I have always looked forward to that moment."

She glanced around, and seeing no one loitering about, she pulled him behind a tree. "Then we must honour the customs of your era, for I would not have you unhappy on your wedding day."

And there, behind the cover of an English oak tree, Will took his bride into his arms and kissed her thoroughly, more than once.

If they were a little later than expected arriving at their wedding breakfast, no one remarked upon it, though Will thought he saw a twinkle in Colonel Fitzwilliam's eye as he smiled at them.

~~oo~~

The highly anticipated ball held two weeks after the wedding was deemed by all to be a great success. Just before dinner was served, the colonel had surprised everyone by announcing that Miss Jane Bennet had agreed to become his wife. The new Mr. and Mrs. Darcy were overjoyed to have their wedding celebration become what it was originally intended to be – an engagement ball.

And so it was that two months after their own marriage, Elizabeth and Will, along with Georgiana, made the long trip to Longbourn for another ceremony. Mrs. Bennet presided over the wedding breakfast admirably, making certain that both couples were honoured. She was quite in her element.

It was whispered by all the neighbourhood that John Bennet and

Miss Georgiana Darcy seemed to be conversing amiably and often, and that Charles Bingley was constantly by the side of Miss Phoebe Barlowe, but one can never be certain about affairs of the heart.

As Will sagely remarked to Elizabeth, "Only time will tell."

EPILOGUE

'For I know the plans I have for you,' declares the Lord. 'Plans to prosper you and not to harm you, plans to give you hope and a future.'

Jeremiah 29:11

Fitzwilliam was edgy with anticipation and a little pique. He and Elizabeth were to be married in the morning, and he had yet to spend a moment alone with her since they had boarded their rented yacht with their wedding guests that morning.

Finally, he could bear it no longer. As soon as they finished their dinner, he stood and reached for Elizabeth's hand, and then cast a glance over their assembled guests. "As much as I love all of you, I would like some time alone with my fiancée."

Fitzwilliam's words were met with smiles and chuckles, but he did not spare them a backward glance. He led her to his cabin, aware with great satisfaction that it was his last night as a bachelor. *After the ceremony in a few short hours, I'll move my belongings to her room. She will live with me, and I will see her every day. I will hold her in my arms every night, and she will be my wife in every way. She will be mine.*

His joy shone in his breathtaking smile, and Elizabeth stared at him as he paused before the door and turned to her. "I have a surprise for you, my love. I've been waiting all day for a chance to give you a special gift, and I can't wait any longer."

She chuckled and stood on her tiptoes to kiss him on the cheek. "Some gifts will have to wait, Fitzwilliam. Just a few more hours."

He shook his head. "This gift can't wait. It's for tomorrow." He opened the door and stood aside for her to enter, pointing to an ornate, antique jewelry box on the table in his sitting area. There was a sealed envelope beside the box with an inscription written in flowing script.

She crossed the room and picked up the envelope, reading aloud. "For Fitzwilliam Darcy and his bride, to be presented to her on the day before their wedding."

Elizabeth looked up at him, and he strode across the short space. "Open it, Elizabeth."

"It looks so old. I don't want to destroy it."

Fitzwilliam turned the letter over in her hand. "Just break the seal, and you can unfold the letter."

"Is this what I think it is?"

He smiled. "I believe so. I think Will has written to us. I recognize his handwriting."

Hands trembling with excitement, she carefully broke the seal and began to read aloud.

Dear Fitzwilliam and soon-to-be Mrs. Darcy,

Elizabeth and I wish to congratulate you on your marriage and extend our best wishes to you. We sincerely hope that you will be as happy and blessed in your life as a couple as we have been in ours. Elizabeth is with me now, giving her input as I write.

God has given us four beautiful children, all of whom are now married with children of their own. There can be no greater joy than holding your grandchildren. Embrace every stage of your lives as it comes. Each one will be better than the last.

We will soon celebrate thirty wonderful years together, though they have not been without sorrow. Many of our friends and relations have passed from this life, but we shall see most of them again in due time.

Fitzwilliam, Elizabeth wants you to know that Georgiana is well and happy. She married John Bennet, and they inherited Longbourn. John is very astute, and he did quite well for his family. You are an uncle to two darling girls, both now married themselves.

I should tell you that Miss Austen published Pride and Prejudice just after the deaths of several persons who would have objected to the book. Suffice it to say that they could not have prevented its publication in any way. I had legal documents drawn up long ago to prevent her from enduring any action on the part of those mentioned in the book. At any rate, once you and I switched places in time, what actually happened veered wildly from the plot of the book. Even before we assumed each others' lives, there were great differences, as you know if you've read the novel or watched the miniseries. I was always firm that the novel had to be published, even to the point that I paid the publisher myself to take it, once I had spoken to the people mentioned in the book and secured their written permission. After all, that book led each of us to our respective paths in life. I would never have sought my Elizabeth without it. Since you are reading this letter, I assume you have found your "Elizabeth" as well. I wish that I could know what happened to you, Fitzwilliam, but I somehow feel that all is well with you. Mrs. Thomas and those who were my friends and colleagues would make certain of that.

Pemberley was struck by lightning multiple times and burned to the ground several years ago, as did a great number of other English country houses. As I knew the history of the time period and had warned Elizabeth, it was not such a shock to us. We chose not to rebuild at that location, knowing that there would be no Pemberley in the future.

Instead, Elizabeth and I designed and built a beautiful, fairly modern home nearer to the city with plenty of room to accommodate the visits of our growing family. Society, recognition, and wealth were never of much importance to us, so we have kept what we loved and released the rest. Wise investments have allowed me to retire from business and enjoy the final years of my life to the fullest.

You will find no mention of us in the history books, for we were always careful to avoid joining our names to any of our philanthropic endeavours. The Darcy fortune has been carefully secured to ensure that future generations of Darcys may also follow this path. My children have already assumed control of the assets, and they are well-trained in how to best manage them. You would be quite surprised to know what they have accomplished. Ah! There is my pride. It is well that I have Elizabeth to help me regulate it, or I would be quite the boor, bragging of my children.

And now, future-Mrs.-Darcy, Elizabeth and I would like for you to open your gift from us. Oddly enough, I designed it myself, and Nana Rose wore it quite often. Don't give yourself a headache trying to figure that out. Because I wrote her, asking her to make certain that you received it, I am certain that it was done.

My Elizabeth wore it on her wedding day, as did the brides of our sons, and eventually, my own beautiful mother, and my darling Nana Rose. I hope that you will love it as much as they did. Mrs. Thomas can show you how to use the clasps to make it into several lengths.

I feel certain you already know that pearls retain their luster, brightness, and colour by absorbing the oils from the skin of the person who wears them. Your bride and Elizabeth, as well as the other Darcy brides, are joined by this phenomenon.

May God bless both of you richly as He has blessed us.

Our accidents were not accidents at all, you know. It was all part of His design.

Affectionately yours,
Will and Elizabeth Darcy

Fitzwilliam picked up the box from the table and opened it, displaying the pearl necklace to his Elizabeth.

"Oh, my! It is truly beautiful." She looked up at him. "Can I wear it tonight?"

He smiled. "I've wanted to see it around your beautiful neck since the first moment Mrs. Thomas gave it to me."

She turned, lifting her long hair, and he looped it into four strands, securing it with the clasp in the back. As she released her hair, he took her shoulders, turning her to face him again.

He sighed in contentment. "Lovely. Quite stunning."

She smiled, looking in the mirror behind him as she touched the pearls. "It really is."

He caught her chin in his hand and lifted her face to his. "Yes, the necklace is nice, too."

He kissed her fervently, knowing that all was now as it should be in his world. *Will was right. It is no accident that she is mine. It was planned all along.*

The End

Books by Robin M. Helm

Guardian, SoulFire, and Legacy
The Guardian Trilogy

Accidentally Yours, Sincerely Yours, and Forever Yours
Yours by Design Trilogy

ABOUT THE AUTHOR

Robin M. Helm is the author of a modern Christian fantasy fiction series, The Guardian Trilogy, which includes *Guardian, SoulFire,* and *Legacy*. She has just concluded her Yours by Design series (*Accidentally Yours, Sincerely Yours,* and *Forever Yours*), a Regency/Modern Romance with a time switch of two characters.

Mrs. Helm shares a blog, *Jane Started It,* with the other writers of the Crown Hill Writers' Guild, and is one of the founders and administrators of *BeyondAusten.com,* a website for readers with common interests. She has also published three Regency short stories, *First Kiss, The Prize,* and *Treasure Chest,* which can be read on *Jane Started It* on her author's page, or at *BeyondAusten.com*.

She has one husband, one grandchild, two daughters, four family dogs, five part-time jobs, and six published books.

Robin Helm thinks you might enjoy these books by Wendi Sotis.

Made in the USA
Columbia, SC
16 November 2018